The Plouffe Family

Roger Lemelin

Translated from the French
by
Mary Finch

Introduction by John Moss
General Editor: Malcolm Ross

New Canadian Library No. 119

McClelland and Stewart Limited

This book was originally published by
McClelland and Stewart Limited in 1952.

0-7710-9219-9

The Canadian Publishers
McClelland and Stewart Limited
25 Hollinger Road, Toronto

Printed and bound in Canada

Contents

Introduction

Roger Lemelin set the revolution of modern Quebec literature in motion and gave it its founding principles. Since his three novels about the Lower Town of Quebec City, the grotesqueries of social realism have become commonplace; an ironic vision and the satiric mode are endemic; the language of French Canada has assumed literary stature; the despotism of institutions, both secular and religious, and the tyranny of their traditions have been explored over and over. The lot of the average man in a rigidly homogeneous society has now been depicted by writers as different as Marie-Claire Blais and Hubert Aquin through delineation of the misfit, the outsider, the isolato. The pastoral romance has all but faded from the scene: the countryside of Quebec is now haunted by the ancestral past, a gothic refuge from depraved modernity or its ironic inversion. Lemelin alone did not effect the changes but he rang them in. A number of novels, chief of them being *Thirty Acres*, anticipated his contribution. Gabrielle Roy, his contemporary, shared in the achievement that, in any case, may have been historically inevitable.

Gabrielle Roy is the more disciplined stylist of the two, and more comprehensive in her reportage of the social scene. Where Lemelin excells is in describing peculiarities of his society and in the very lack of narrative objectivity and control that mark Roy's finest writing in *The Tin Flute* and *The Cashier*. Lemelin's fiction surges with personality. The narrative voice is intimately concerned with its subject and uses detachment as a rhetorical device to cast ironic judgments on what it purports merely to describe. Lemelin is an ironist, whether being broadly satirical or eloquently romantic. But he is also a realist, rendering experiences of the urban poor in

Quebec into a medium for social criticism. He is a recorder but he is also a crusader and his art consists of both in equal measure.

The Plouffe Family is the middle section of what Robert Kroetsch, borrowing a term from the visual arts to describe his three Alberta novels, calls a triptych. Unlike the trilogy, in which three works are related by a developing story or theme, the triptych holds the three in juxtaposition, the vision of each a complement to that of the others. Lemelin's *Les Plouffe* originally appeared in 1948, preceded by *Au Pied de la Pente Douce (The Town Below)* in 1944 and followed by *Pierre le Magnifique (In Quest of Splendour)* in 1952. These novels may have been intended as entirely separate works but, together, they depict a world that is no less unified for its being somewhat distorted in each of the three perspectives from which it is viewed. The focal planes upon which the story and themes of each are resolved sit at angles from reality which best reflect one particular aspect of experience or another.

Lemelin's novels, like Kroetsch's and, even more, like Roch Carrier's *La Guerre, Yes Sir!, Floralie, Where Are You?* and *Is It the Sun, Philibert?*, differ immensely, one from the other – not only in plot, but in point of view and, to some extent, literary technique – despite the recurrent presence of an occasional character, of a setting or a scene. Yet each author has created a triptych illuminating separate dimensions of his own time and place. Carrier exploits the possibilities of the folk tale to reveal the effects on a bucolic Quebecois sensibility of impinging reality. Kroetsch uses myth to reconcile the Alberta of imagination, history and dream with that of contemporary experience. Lemelin's novels bear the strong impress of an ironic conception of life, with the first tending towards social realism while the second is considerably more satiric and the third carries a strong element of romance. Together they define the anomalies, the indignities and the emerging splendour at the heart of the French Catholic nation in Canada, in historic metamorphosis. That is not to say that they are not also about more universal themes, nor concerned with more parochial events.

The first of Lemelin's novels, *The Town Below*, radiates outwards from the story of Denis Boucher and his family and friends to encompass the whole community, a working class parish in the Lower Town. Society is portrayed with an ironic detachment that is both devastating and essentially humane. The most recent of the three, *In Quest of Splendour*, tells of a Lower Town youth in pursuit of his own innate genuis – literally, it is the story of a soul in quest of its most appropriate self, told with vigour and compassion. Again, Denis Boucher figures large, although he is not the central character. Between fictions focussed on a community and on an individual, Lemelin offers the splendidly engaging story of a family. The incomparable Plouffes are atypical in so many ways, yet strangely representative. Their idiosyncrasies obviously set them apart from the norm. However, the precarious conditions of their existence and the forces of ossification and decay working upon them from inside and outside their parish are common to a good portion of their society. They are, in effect, a whole world in grotesque miniature, rather than a curiosity taken from within it.

In *The Plouffe Family*, as in the other two novels, Denis Boucher is present as a sardonic persona of Lemelin himself or, at least, that is how he seems. A misfit and a dreamer, his meddling in the affairs of others takes on the caste of ironic inevitability. It is he more than any other in whom the irony of actual coincidence and the irony of narrative voice converge. He is the cynic with a conscience who embodies the paradox of Lemelin's caustic rendering of a world he clearly loves.

Lemelin's triptych, if such it is, holds together by virtue of more than a common setting and a shared character or a refulgent style and ironic tone. Each novel tells the story of a young man who struggles against the society which shapes him. Denis Boucher in *The Town Below* ultimately prevails in a modest way by writing about the very world he wants to rise above. In the other two novels, however, while remaining in character he is reduced to cynical meddler and then embittered layabout. Ovide Plouffe emerges early as the pivotal character of *The Plouffe Family*. Intelligent and sensitive, he disdains common experience in favour of the esoteric. Yet his ardour for Rita Toulouse and the weaknesses of his own personality eventually draw him into the world he scorns. Deflated, he endures. Pierre Boisjoly, the protagonist of *In Quest of Splendour*, is of more heroic proportions. Destined for the priesthood as the best possible route out of a mean and ugly life in the Lower Town, he rejects his vocation – and takes it up again only when it has become a sacrifice for him, and a form of atonement. Each young man discovers eventually that he cannot escape his mundane origins.

Denis tries to exploit them and fails. Ovide submits. Pierre commits himself to an alternative. There is a progression here, certainly, but the modern Quebecois sensibility, in Lemelin's triptych, is a blend of all three.

In the story of the Plouffes, family relationships take narrative precedence over individual characterization or the delineation of social milieu. Not that *The Plouffe Family* is without psychological insight: nor that Lemelin is not often at his most penetrating when describing the contemporary scene, whether at the parish level or on an international scale. His accounts of motivation ring true, while seeming surreal in their oversimplification. Ovide, for example, is said to have realized at twenty that his meagre body would develop no further and therefore to have turned with fanatic zeal to the appreciation of fine music – plausible as a process, but somewhat foreshortened in the telling. Ovide's behavior is, on the whole, more fully detailed than that of any of the others, although he is closely rivalled by Napoleon. The latter's honest and simple devotion to his beloved Jeanne is in marked contrast to the indulgences of Ovide's passion for Rita. Significantly, Ovide is reduced from lord of his parents' household at the beginning to uncertain cohabitant of his own with Rita, while the humble Napoleon cheerfully shoulders the burdens of both master and drudge for his own family at the novel's close. Ovide simmers and Napoleon smiles. Psychologically, they have changed little, although their lives have dramatically altered course. Lemelin's concern with them is not primarily behavioral but sociological and symbolic, revealing more about their environment than about their separate selves.

Still, his depiction of Ovide's anguish and ecstasy in relation to both Rita and God is graphically convincing. Lemelin is able to describe emotion without feeling called upon to analyse. For example, Ovide, with mid-passion repugnance at his own lust for Rita near the wall of the monastery, suddenly

...began to tremble all over. His misty eyes conjured up ghouls with rotted teeth who laughed mockingly through the chinks of the wall, preparing to seize him and carry him off to hell and plunge him into a sea of boiling oil filled with the bodies of the lustful. He was powerless to rise; his legs gave way under him, just as when he was being pursued in a dream. Languorously, pleadingly, Rita renewed her request....

He does manage to summon the presence of mind to send Rita packing, then torments himself with thoughts that even the Pope "would be compromised, in giving him absolution." Lemelin has effectively shifted the direction of his character's passion without allowing it to dissipate, shown the conflicts within him and yet left the inner workings of his mind relatively obscured.

The world of church and state comes under the same sort of glancing scrutiny which nevertheless yields a great scattering of profound insights and searing judgments. As well, there are a number of episodes which act as hallmarks of reality amidst the almost fantasy quality of his characters' lives. Two of the most significant describe processions, panoramas, as it were, of the larger world unrolled before their eyes. The first is profane; the second, holy. The first is the Royal visit of 1939 when King and Consort visited this corner of the realm possibly, cynics such as Théophile say, to stir up support for the impending war with Germany. History is brought into the lives of Montmagny Street as the entourage passes directly beneath the Plouffes' balcony, an act with leads capriciously to the loss of Théophile's job and a great shift in the direction of the family's lives. The other procession, an annual event in homage to the Sacred Heart, is turned in 1940 into a massive protest against possible conscription which is deemed a form of genocide. Lemelin describes the moving scene as thousands of marchers, in a column extending from the Church of St. Roch to the City Hall, raise supplications, not to the "God of ordinary Sundays," but to "the God of 1837, of 1917, and of 1940, the God of nationalism, the God of the people of Laurentia, the God of those great historic moments when the fatherland is threatened." A mass of humanity gathers in mysterious rapture, only to hear the Cardinal, speaking bilingually, betray them to the war effort. As the other procession indicated the effect on even the most ordinary people of great events, this one reveals the sacrificial inseparability of the secular and the religious in French Canada at the time.

Between the two processions, like an ominous set-piece, is Lemelin's searing description of a most immovable affront to the spirit of a subjected people:

> The English having taken Canada from France in 1760, and the Quebeckers having obstinately remained French in their customs, language and architecture, the conquerors seem to

have thought it well to challenge such resistance by erecting an edifice, on a strategic spot, to mark their victory: the Chateau Frontenac. This enormous and luxurious Canadian Pacific Hotel, whose most important shareholders, so they say, are Anglo-Saxons, crowns Cape Diamond with its massive brick turrets, admires its own reflection in the St. Lawrence and looks coldly down at the ships that come and go. Placed on the top of a mountain, facing east, above the shoulders of a town that runs down the slope behind it, the structure turns to the sunrise a rigid mask, completely disguising the turbulent face of Quebec. This pacific fortress is perched so high that it exceeds the most audacious steeples by a hundred cubits and casts a shadow over the schools, the Archbishop's palace, the monasteries and the convents.

The voice is inseparable from the vision – and both are clear.

The lives of the Plouffe family seem determined in good part by remote control. The Catholic Church and the French nation within Canada possess them beyond their comprehension. They are representative of a populace which Lemelin describes as "Roman at heart, Norman in mind . . . a complete mystery to foreigners [a term he would surely mean to include the rest of Canada] who try to understand them. They are, at one and the same time French and American, simple and complicated; are happy to be so, and wittingly let themselves be drawn into vicious circles with a knowing smile." Caught up in the cavalier machinations of secular and religious politics, victims of their own convictions and unprepared by their limited experience of the world to adapt easily to the shifting loyalties forced upon them by a World War, the Plouffe family, nevertheless, endures.

They are conceived ironically to provide anomalous commentary on the French Canadian world they represent, a world stultified by the same traditions and allegiances that have made it unique. Josephine Plouffe maintains an emotional tyranny over her spouse and offspring who at first seem little more than absurd cut-out figures for whom she is the servile retainer. Gradually, the effect of her obeisance to the principles embodied by curé Folbèche is revealed. Her children, in 1939, range in age from twenty to forty-three, yet none has been allowed to mature. Josephine's pliant demeanour, her devotion to family and her obvious piety have undermined the possibility of their self-reliance. Guillaume, the champion, is mindlessly irresponsible; Ovide is melodramatically self-indulgent; Napoleon is childishly obsessive; Cécile is petulantly unpleasant except to her beloved Onésime, whom she lacked the resolution to marry when he was still available. Even Josephine's rabidly Anglophobic old husband, Théophile, rests on laurels earned as a cyclist years before and sputters political vehemence from the safety of her kitchen. Eventually, paralysis reduces him to being little more than an inconvenience.

On the positive side, too, these Plouffes combine the separate characteristics of a whole people: single-minded, sensitive, diligent, faithful and passionate. Yet under the dispensation of Josephine and Folbèche, they have become literally impotent. Not until the disruptions brought about by events in Europe does the life-blood begin to surge. With the War, the old way gives over, if not to the new, at least to a period of transition. In 1945, Ovide and Napoleon have both married the women they desired and have children. Cécile has adopted Onésime's son and Guillaume writes from the front that he is engaged in mortal combat. Old Théophile is dead, having passed with the dawning of a new age as Guillaume entered their home in the uniform of his enemies, six years before. Josephine, who has always seen herself and her kin as the victims of tragedy, is incredulous that her youngest could kill. Her world of ignorance taken for innocence, of fear and guilt for piety, is expiring at the novel's close.

Family life is not the object of Lemelin's satire, although it is the primary substance of his story. The Plouffes are used to embody aspects of a people at a particular time in their history. As well, they are individuals who gradually emerge from caricature to give a greater depth and dimension to their context. As feelings are attached to each member of the family, the typifying trait by which he is known becomes simply a convenient label evoking a much more complex person than it originally suggested. Thus, Napoleon is introduced as "the collector" for his scrapbooks full of clippings and statistics. This seems far and away the most significant thing about him, a child-like innocent in his early thirties. But his enthusiasm shifts from sports to the tubercular Jeanne and he collects her health-statistics instead of batting averages, and doggedly devotes himself to prayer for her recovery with as much energy as had previously gone into the acquisition of trivia. His simplicity becomes a virtue and the name "collector" assumes ironic significance. Similarly, Cécile gives the title "the old maid" extra dimension as she resolves her unrequited devotion to Onésime by becoming his surrogate widow, even to the point, eventually, of adopting one of his children. Likewise, the familiar expressions of endearment or derision which are used to identify the others are a form of ironic shorthand, allowing them to have both a two-dimensional satiric role and a more fully rounded personality within the developing narrative.

The Plouffes are unique creations; occasionally grotesque, sometimes quite astounding and often charming. In presenting them, Lemelin avoids being subject to the accusation he levels at Denis Boucher of exploiting "the quaintness of Quebeckers." Boucher, in his efforts to ingratiate himself with the American pastor, Tom Brown, gleefully introduced him to the Plouffe family – being confident of the outsider's amusement at such curiosities. Lemelin, however, invariably identifies the foibles of his characters with their human nature rather than their culture, nationality or beliefs. On the level of personality, it is humanity that is subjected to his ironic wit. Only in what they represent, through a display of the forces working on them, is French Canada brought under critical scrutiny.

This version of *The Plouffe Family* is a translation which, like all translations, is something akin to the photographic reproduction of an oil painting. The imitation cannot provide an equivalent of the original, even with brush strokes embossed on the cardboard. When the medium of art is language, it is inevitable that the characteristics peculiar to the language will in part determine the vision it transcribes. Gabrielle Roy noted this phenomenon in an interview with Donald Cameron when she admitted that she would possibly have been a much different writer, had she written in the English language. Unfortunately, we cannot all see Botticelli's "Venus" at first hand and many cannot read Stendhal or Tolstoy in the original. Thus, translations, like reproductions, serve an important function. On occasion, a translation itself will rise to the level of art, but then it is a new work, based on the old, and is original in its own right. A novel such as *The Plouffe Family*, in which the language of a particular people is a crucial aspect of the subject-matter, is particularly problematic. In the popular television series Lemelin developed from the novel, the English version benefited from the accents and Gallic demeanour of the actors which communicated many of the subtleties lost in print. Yet an honest and direct translation such as this one has the effect of being almost transparent. It allows Lemelin's world to emerge nearly intact.

The awkwardnesses that do exist in *The Plouffe Family* are due as much to the contrivance of plot and character as to linguistic difficulties. The complete candour with which Lemelin confronts an event or an emotion can be disarming, however – usually with a thoroughly positive effect. By risking such directness, Lemelin has been able to strip bare to the soul French Canada at the time of his writing which, perhaps due in part to the efficacious impact of his vision, is not the French Canada of the present, only a quarter of a century later. Yet the very authenticity of his writing makes it remain universally contemporary.

John Moss
Concordia University

TO MY WIFE

PART I

SUMMER 1938

CHAPTER ONE

SEE you at the championship tonight, Monsieur Ovide. Cheerio!

Rita Toulouse waved her hand to him and rejoined the group of girls who were hurrying towards the bus.

The workers were pouring out of the shoe factory, making their escape from a now silent building. Ovide Plouffe, a leather-cutter, took no part in their noisy dispersal. He stood alone on the pavement, assuming the haughty attitude of an operatic tenor. His stunted and puny body and the neatness of his dress gave him the appearance of a clerk rather than a manual worker, yet in his passion for opera he was beginning to achieve some resemblance to the heroes of his imagination.

He stood there, thinking over his unexpected good luck. 'See you tonight, Monsieur Ovide!' Incredible. Rita Toulouse was a pretty blonde, with a pleasing figure; she made inventories of the shoes that were cut out in Ovide's department. The serious-minded Ovide, now twenty-eight years old, had never felt such an imperious desire to know women, with whom he had always been desperately awkward. But Rita Toulouse! To persuade her to go out with him for an evening he had used all his oratorical resources, and had told her the names of the famous singers of whom he owned recordings. It was no use; she invariably made polite excuses. And then, finally, to enhance the prestige of his family, or to make his own career as an opera-lover seem even more lofty by comparison, he had told her about his young brother Guillaume, a local prodigy in sport. To his surprise, the subject of sport brought to Rita's face, which had remained blank at the mention of such names as Thill and Caruso, an expression of lively interest.

More delighted at having caught her attention than mortified by her indifference to opera, Ovide had told her all about the forthcoming 'rings' tournament in which Guillaume was taking part and which would decide the city championship. 'What! Is he your brother? Take me to the match, will you?' she had exclaimed. 'I know the referee—Stan Labrie, the famous baseball pitcher!'

What did rings or baseball matter as long as she would be walking beside him? Such good fortune at first overflows a man's nature; but as its halo of joy evaporates, it subsides within the limits of self-love, soon finding its level there. Ovide's face twisted suddenly with annoyance, and he set off towards home, muttering:

—Nothing but sport. Athletes and champions! It's all you hear. Ah, music!

What a life! Sport was a menace which might keep Ovide forever imprisoned in mediocrity. At home his strange tastes were respected, but the talk was only of championships. His family! His mother, Josephine; Napoleon, the eldest son; Cécile, an old maid of forty; and Guillaume! It was hard for Ovide to believe that he was of the same blood. At the factory the men thought him a sissy and the women disappointed him by their love of jazz and sport. Their lack of appreciation for beautiful things filled Ovide with such profound disgust for modern life that, for some months, he had been thinking of entering the monastery of the African White Fathers. Not without pleasure he pictured himself, clothed in a spotless robe, converting, baptizing, and absolving the Negroes, enjoying the respect and consideration due to the noble calling of the priesthood. With his knowledge of *bel canto* he felt himself sufficiently prepared to assume the musical duties of the monastery. It never occurred to Ovide that opera had not given him the intellectual background necessary to a priest and that he would, in all probability, become an obscure lay brother.

But suddenly Rita Toulouse had come into his life. Good-bye to the monastery, the priesthood, and sanctity. The opera was preparing to do battle with sport; and the music-lover hurried home, his legs chopping the distance like a pair of avenging scissors.

On reaching the edge of the parish playground he saw his brother Guillaume on the pitcher's mound, idly tossing a ball while a few people looked on.

—Guillaume! Ovide called to him, with an air of authority.

The prodigy walked over gawkily to join Ovide, whom he topped by a whole head.

—Yes, Vide. What's up?

—It's six o'clock! Are you forgetting tonight is the championship?

Guillaume adjusted his peaked cap, serenely.

—Phooey! Rings! A game for old men. Give me baseball. Now, now . . . don't get so het up!

He strolled along beside his brother, humming a cowboy song:

Aye, aye, aye, aye,
Beautiful girl of the prairie.

—Do you know a chap called Stan Labrie? asked Ovide.

—Sure. Pitcher for the *Canadiens*. I could beat him. Well, look at this, here's Napoleon. He's all het up too.

A bicycle, its rider almost lying on the handlebars, came to a sudden stop with its brakes squealing.

—About time you came home, the cyclist panted. Mother's got supper waiting. You'd better hurry, Guillaume. The game's at eight o'clock.

Without further comment Napoleon Plouffe rode off, pedalling at full speed. Employed, like Ovide, in a shoe factory, he was now thirty-two years old, and his little round head seemed merely a continuation of his strong neck. He stood only five feet one inch; was a virgin; went to bed early, curled up and slept soundly. His brown hair, short and fine, grew in an unbroken line like a little cap around his head. He had small, round eyes and a reedy voice which made his words crackle between his false teeth with the same jerky rhythm that characterized his gait, for Napoleon took many brisk steps to cover a few yards. This sportsman-cyclist was a Napoleon such as Bonaparte, with all his genius, could never have imagined.

On the way back, Napoleon passed an old man who was cycling slowly.

—Don't fall, Papa!

From his perch on an old-fashioned racing model, Papa Théophile glared at his eldest son. His pipe jumped about in his mouth, emphasizing his indignation.

—In my time, I should have lost sight of you, my boy.

But Napoleon was already far ahead. As he neared home, he waved triumphantly to his mother, who was looking out from the end of the balcony.

—They're coming, he said.

Napoleon did not notice two men standing on the pavement across the street, talking to each other and pointing at the Plouffe house. Napoleon lived each moment too feverishly to watch curious idlers. He stood on the pedals and, crossing the pavement at a bound, entered the yard and propped up his bicycle. His small feet pattered up the steps like a round of shots, and he rushed into the kitchen only to reappear immediately on the balcony with a paste-pot, scissors, and an enormous wallpaper sample-book of cuttings which hid him almost completely. He spread the book on the floor, knelt down, and respectfully opened it at the page on which he had pasted his latest pictures; then he pulled from his hip pocket a bundle of old newspapers through which he began to search avidly for the illustrations on the sports pages. Napoleon had been collecting, since he was fifteen, the

14

photographs of a whole generation of famous athletes on the American continent. His happiness was to paste, paste, paste incessantly.

—Goodness! Pasting cuttings again? What a time to begin! Get out of the way.

It was Cécile, just come in from her work, which was stitching shoe vamps. She stamped about impatiently and Napoleon, embarrassed, closed his album. Cécile spoke to her mother, who was still at her post at the end of the balcony.

—Has Onésime gone by?

—I haven't noticed. I've been too busy watching for the men. They're late tonight, the rascals.

Cécile shrugged her shoulders and went into the house. Onésime Ménard, a streetcar conductor, never missed coming to say a few words to her every evening. He had been her sweetheart ten years before, but not finding her lively enough had married someone else. A slave to habit, Onésime continued to visit Cécile. In talking to him about his wife and children she was as unmoved as she had been when, in earlier years, boys tried to kiss her and she used to ask, in a bored tone, 'What do you get out of that? You must have time to waste.'

Indeed, nothing excited Cécile. She thought that, in this world, too much time and money were spent on useless things. As for her, time spent itself in turning her hair grey. Cécile saw neither her ageing complexion nor her greying hair; yet she often said, almost anxiously:

—It's queer, Mother, there don't seem to be so many boys now.

She went to bed every night at ten o'clock, after a final sneer at her brothers.

—There's your father, exclaimed stout Josephine, her head turned towards the street. I'm always afraid he'll have an accident.

Napoleon's wounding admonition, 'Don't fall, Papa,' was still ringing in the ears of the old cyclist. How dare that insignificant dabbler in sports speak like that to the celebrated Théophile Plouffe, who had won the bicycle race thirty years before! A feeling of disappointment came over Théophile. Not one of his sons had followed in his footsteps. Yet Guillaume had good legs. Baseball! Rings! Faugh! As for Napoleon and Ovide, he refused even to think of them. His disappointment was all the more painful because his arthritis made pedalling difficult, and the brilliant July sun was burning the nape of his neck. When he caught sight of his wife and saw that she was watching him he straightened up. Ah! She was afraid he would fall! He gave a sudden push on the pedals and the bicycle shot forward while the old man grimaced defiantly.

—Look out, Father! What are you up to?

Napoleon almost dropped his paste-pot, and Madame Plouffe thought she would faint. His short pipe bobbing this way and that between his loose teeth, Théophile rode straight into the yard, his bicycle jolting over the wooden kerb just as in his youth. Why didn't he lean against it, so that he could dismount without danger? In his feverish efforts he imagined himself at the finishing line which he had once been the first to cross. Théophile's final spurt, before the eyes of a naïve collector of pictures and a wife who thought him fit for the wheelchair, was his way of protesting against the ignorance of youth and the laurels of second-rate sportsmen. Were they forgetting he was once a champion? A triumphant smile spread over his wrinkled face. He had succeeded! He tried to swing his left leg over elegantly, as he had done in the old days, while the bicycle was still moving and while his right foot firmly pressed the rubber tread of the pedal. But oh! catastrophe! His left leg trembled too much and his hip muscles were too stiff to lift it up sufficiently. His powerless thigh hit the seat, which he had not thought so high, and his old hands clutched the handlebars so that the front wheel staggered, sending his bike into the wall of the shed. His pipe fell to the ground; but the ex-champion, with a superhuman effort, finally succeeded in heaving his slothful leg over the saddle.

He picked up his pipe with a trembling hand and went gloomily up the steps. Napoleon, not yet recovered from his fright, watched him pass and said nothing.

—Do you want to kill yourself? said Josephine, quite pale.

He looked askance at her.

—Oh, that's nothing.

Théophile, followed into the kitchen by his wife, proceeded to hook his bicycle clips over the nail in the wall where he hung his watch, his knife, and his razor strop. Then he took a fistful of matches, holding them for a moment in a steady hand while waiting for the usual scolding from his wife, who reprimanded him daily for the number he used. Josephine did not speak.

With his arthritic gait, he walked out on to the balcony and sat down heavily on the bottle-green bench, obtained through Onésime Ménard's influence when the old streetcars were scrapped. Théophile succeeded in lighting his pipe at the fifth try and blew into the air thick blue puffs of smoke which soon dispersed because, humiliated by his unfortunate arrival, he was breathing heavily. Ordinarily, when he was calm, and recollecting the great deeds of other years, he took pleasure in blowing rings and pretty patterns which would float up and disappear in the sparrows' nests under the eaves of the rotting roof.

The old man's eyes roamed around the neighbourhood. The two idlers had gone. To the right, the fields stretched as far as the eye could see, for the Plouffes lived on the edge of town. The horizon was bathed in early evening light. Opposite, there was the parish steeple, then the cliffs of Cape Diamond. Théophile turned his head and said mockingly to Napoleon:

—Your rings don't interest your Guillaume much.

Napoleon did not notice the irony.

—You know, Guillaume's always steady, Father. Nothing upsets *him*. He'll win because of that.

Guillaume had been born on the 8th of January 1919, during a cold spell when the mercury fell far below freezing point. This unexpected infant had fallen into the household ten years after Ovide, who had long been regarded as the last and had, until then, been shown off to all the relations as definitely the Benjamin. However, one never knows just what one can do; and Théophile, who could not forget that he had won his championship in an open sprint in the last hundred yards, had been right to shake his head when, in 1918, there was talk of selling the baby clothes. Was Guillaume's composure due to the Siberian temperature when he was born, or did he owe his phlegmatic temperament to his mother, made placid by too many unsuccessful pregnancies?

—There they are now, said Napoleon.

The two Plouffe brothers strode on to the balcony. Ovide, slight and fidgety, stood in the doorway of the kitchen.

—Have you ironed my collars, Mother?

His curt voice, emphasized by the convulsive stiffening of his bony fingers, his angular knees which made his legs look like broken sticks when he walked, and the servile haste with which his mother submitted to his whims about his shirt collars, proclaimed that Ovide was the chief power in the household. Having felt the collars, he remarked coldly:

—A bit stiff, Mother. They scratch me.

Unconcerned by Josephine's consternation, for she had taken some time to prepare the starch, adding to or reducing the amount, Ovide removed his jacket carefully, exposing a lean torso which, even when covered, seemed thin enough. His shirt was not damp like Napoleon's, for Ovide never sweated; and if his face was shiny, it was merely pallor. His hair, combed in pompadour style, was shiny too.

He put his hands on the bones which served him as buttocks and paced up and down the kitchen with an anxious air.

—I've observed, he said, that nobody talks about anything

18

but sport in this house. My brothers don't notice half of what goes on. Why Napoleon, who is thirty-two years old, hasn't realized yet that there are women in the world.

Josephine, relieved to see that Ovide was forgetting her failure with the collars, exclaimed:

—Thank God! They're better off with their mother. As for you, Ovide, I feel that you'll leave us one of these days for the religious life, and since you have the call, I'm not the one to stop you.

—Is supper ready? Ovide interrupted.

Everyone sat down at the table in the place assigned as though by rule. On one occasion the family had almost come to blows. That was when Ovide, feeling bilious, and annoyed by the sun in his eyes, had chosen to sit in Napoleon's place which, as the eldest, he held tenaciously at the end of the table. Usually, however, the meals were quiet. Only the sound of chewing accompanied the heavy step of Madame Plouffe going to and fro from table to stove.

Why talk? What could the Plouffes talk about? Too many sports pictures passed before Napoleon's fixed gaze; too many cavatinas resounded in Ovide's ears while his jaws crunched the mouthfuls with more than their usual vigour and at the same time formed replies which would incline Rita Toulouse towards opera. As for Cécile, she was busy enough cutting the fat off her ham. Théophile concentrated on keeping his hand steady as he spooned his soup with fingers half-paralysed by arthritis; but he was telling himself, over and over, how he could still swing his leg elegantly while dismounting from his bicycle. Guillaume was worrying about his yellow cat; he liked to stroke him after supper and could not see him in the kitchen. He was not worrying about the rings tournament. Madame Plouffe was going over her calculations: decrease the starch by two pinches and Ovide's collars would be perfect.

CHAPTER TWO

THE Plouffe family possessed very active jaws. In less than a quarter of an hour the meal was finished. While Madame Plouffe and Cécile moved between table and sink, clearing and washing up the dishes, the men took their ease. Théophile sought refuge on his streetcar bench, the only seat which afforded him complete relaxation because the brick wall against which he rested assured absolute security to his vulnerable spot: the nape of his neck. Guillaume liked to tease him by planting sly kisses on it.

While Ovide was shaving, Napoleon fussed about, changing into his new suit. He had not been in his room five minutes when Madame Plouffe stopped her work to exclaim:

—It's taking him a long time tonight. Is he dead?

Napoleon, out of breath and ashamed of his tardiness, rushed into the kitchen.

—Here I am, Mother. Blast these braces! They're twisted. See to them, will you?

Napoleon had no equal in changing his clothes in record time. When they were praising him to others the family never failed to mention the speed with which he put on his pants. Smart Alecs would ask for his recipe: did he climb on a chair and leap into his trousers like Beau Brummel? But Napoleon would say nothing, thinking in a confused way that these little secrets contributed to the interest of his personality. Madame Plouffe murmured her astonishment while her hands, whitened from the dishwater, untwisted the braces and attached the leather thongs to the buttons. Josephine felt very queer helping Napoleon to dress himself in this way. She made a gesture used when he was a child, and since forgotten, to tell him he was ready. But Napoleon, with a rush of self-respect, pulled free at the last button.

—I'll be back in five minutes.

He was just going out when Cécile, who was drying the last spoon, broke her long silence.

—Ovide was right before supper. The men in this house are very odd. Not one of them takes a girl out.

In front of the mirror Ovide hid his nervousness with a generous lather from his shaving-brush. Napoleon made a defensive gesture.

—Women? Bad for athletes. Like drink and cigarettes. Look at Max Baer.

He went out. Everyone knew where he was going. Guillaume, seated on the floor near the stove, was caressing his cat. He smiled mischievously:

—Women cost too much. No money, so . . . no women.

—Just listen to that, said Josephine indignantly. Only nineteen and he talks about women.

The old maid went her one better:

—Yes, a great, big softy who wastes his time playing and doesn't pay a cent for his board.

—Better look out, he said. There's a lot of dough in your money-box.

—Just you lay your hands on it.

While Josephine was trying to settle this quarrel before it went further, Ovide, his face puffed out with thick lather, prepared to make a sensation. His ferret-like glances stole sideways under his thick eyebrows. When he was quite sure that the atmosphere in the house had reached that calm propitious to a difficult announcement he laid his razor prudently on the table.

—Mother?

Madame Plouffe folded her hands. Was Ovide going to begin remonstrating about the starched collars?

—Your shirts, Vide?

21

Ovide's impatient twitches detached a blob of lather which fell on the toe of his right shoe, the one that this amateur opera singer turned up when performing.

—No! No! I was going to say, make it tidy here this evening.

—But my house is always tidy!

Ovide took a deep breath, picked up his razor, drew nearer to the mirror and opened his right eye very wide as if he were about to shear off a whole stretch of fleece with one stroke.

—Rita Toulouse, a girl from the factory, is coming here for me tonight.

Only the ticking of the clock could be heard. Ovide, his razor motionless in his fingers, watched his mother's reactions in the mirror. She sat down, hands on knees, and stared at her son.

—What! You have a girl?

She let fall these words in such a tone that Ovide did not wish to hear the irritating remarks that would follow. He cut in:

—Yes, I know. The monastery, religious vocation, and all that. I don't want my actions discussed; and I mean it.

Subdued, Josephine feverishly seized hold of the broom, straightened a picture, then smoothed the oilcloth table cover. Cécile ran to re-do her hair and to powder. What an event! Ovide with a girl!

—Heavens! How do I look? You should have told me. What time is she coming, Vide?

—At eight. You've time. Finish your job.

Cécile was delighted. At last another woman would enter this den and become her ally. The great dream that Cécile had always cherished for her brothers assailed her at this moment. She would have liked to see their hair curl naturally. Approaching Ovide, she boldly ran her fingers through a lock of hair falling over his ear. Ovide knew that his straight hair could not be changed, for he had often tried every possible dodge to make it curl after everyone had gone to bed. One evening Napoleon had found him, unexpectedly, with his head crowned with makeshift curlers cut out of old handkerchiefs. For a long time Ovide had trembled every time his brother opened his mouth, but Napoleon minded his own business. That was why, ever since, opera had not openly declared war on sport in the Plouffe home.

Ovide pushed Cécile away sharply.

—Do you think I'm a sissy? It isn't my hair that attracts the women.

Cécile was not rebuffed.

—Does she like you very much?

—It looks like it, said Ovide, bridling. She's been making up to me for some time. Tonight I felt like taking her out.

—And they had many children, concluded Guillaume, who was stroking his cat as usual.

Ovide looked threateningly at him.

—Stop joking, youngster. And I warn you: don't start hugging her. She's no relation of yours.

Guillaume picked his nose.

—O.K., Vide, I'm busy enough with my own gang. I'll let you look after her. You should try it. Do you good. You never hug anybody. I have the kitten.

He rubbed his head lovingly against the cat's fur.

—You yellow beauty, you. Do you know any girls who have beautiful soft skins like yours to stroke? It's just like silk.

Ovide, offended, took refuge in the silence of a superior man. But Cécile loved to pick a quarrel.

—Watch what you're saying! Listen, Mama, you've let him have his own way too much.

Josephine was unperturbed.

—That's a proof he isn't bad. He's a good boy.

Cécile was the only one in the family whom Guillaume dared to jeer at openly, first of all because she did not like strawberries, which he adored, and then because she always removed the fat from her ham as carefully as he did.

He raised his guileless eyes.

—Don't be an old maid. Go out on the balcony and watch for Onésime.

—You little brat!

—That's enough! Ovide called, making a face as his bay-rum lotion stung him.

Guillaume hung his head, hesitated, and asked:

—Vide, are you going to bring that girl to see me play?

—Yes. Don't you want me to?

—It's all the same to me. But you know it's got to be quiet when we play. Women always talk. If she starts to chatter, the guys will put her out, I'm telling you.

Ovide turned slowly towards his brother and two sharp ominous points, which passed for shoulders, jutted under his white shirt. He seemed to be pinned up in the air.

—I'd like to see them do it!

—If you think she can keep quiet, then O.K., the champion concluded calmly.

Ovide could scarcely contain himself. He was feeling in good enough voice to succeed in singing the famous A, in the prologue of *Pagliacci*, which he had been trying to reach for two years. But it was no use pretending any longer that music allowed him to despise sport; nothing had come of it. He owed it to sport that he would be walking beside Rita Toulouse that evening.

At this moment, a heavy tread shook the steps. Théophile, his pipe trembling in his old fingers, rushed into the house.

—Denis Boucher, with a caller!

The points which had threatened to pierce Ovide's shirt became blunt, then disappeared. The Plouffes assumed a defensive attitude. Two long shadows travelled past the kitchen windows. No sooner had sharp knocks shaken the door than Denis Boucher's ringing voice announced:

—An important caller for you people, Madame Plouffe.

Ovide, who knew that Denis Boucher, his young neighbour, only brought home highbrows, handed his shaving kit to Cécile who fled to the store-room. Having donned his jacket hastily, he ordered:

—Come in!

Denis Boucher, hair tousled, shirt open, a big smile lighting up his round face, came into the kitchen with a stride which his twenty years and his height made almost a graceful leap. His merry impudence gave his off-hand manner a good-natured sauciness which made it acceptable. In any case, every eye was fixed with so much curiosity on his companion that no one paid any attention to his mocking air.

—I'd like to introduce Mr. Tom Brown!

Old Théophile had retreated a step and was looking at the stranger arrogantly.

—An Englishman!

Denis Boucher sensed the antagonism, and hastened to add:

—No, American!

Théophile's stiffness slackened. He sighed with relief.

—An American? All right. No English for me!

Denis Boucher glanced quickly at his companion.

—I forgot to tell you that Monsieur Plouffe doesn't like the English. On the other hand he has a great admiration for the Germans, and it was precisely to honour the Kaiser that he named his youngest son Guillaume.

—Yes, monsieur, he was a great soldier, Théolphile said.

—Mr. Brown is a Baptist pastor in Cincinnati. Reverend Brown, let me introduce the Plouffes. Ovide, a great lover of opera (a big smile spread across Ovide's face, which had become gloomy on hearing the pastor's status), Cécile Plouffe, and Guillaume Plouffe, your champion.

The tall pastor bowed to each one with a severity which was immediately compensated for by his childlike smile. But when one's glance encountered his long nose, this severity, which his lips allowed one to forget momentarily, seemed to be fixed and settled there. Madame Plouffe was less moved by those searching

eyes and that childlike mouth than by the black clothes of the
Reverend Tom Brown. She inspected him from shoulder to
waist, and then began at the top again, having been abashed to
see that his waistcoat degenerated into trousers instead of showing an ample cassock. Cécile, who had aged unconcerned by
men's glances, was caught by that of this thirty-nine-year-old
pastor who smiled like a girl and examined you like a sphinx.
She whispered to Ovide:

— He has a funny collar.

Ovide, disconcerted, spread his arms and spoke loudly to
indicate to the stranger that he was the worldly man of the family.

— But he's a pastor, Sister!

At Ovide's reproof Cécile, Josephine, and Guillaume nodded
their heads knowingly as if to show that, after all, they understood the status of Tom Brown. To tell the truth, the word
'pastor' stirred up in them such a saraband of varied terms stored
vaguely in their memory, that they dared not show their uncertainty for fear of seeming ignorant. Either mental laziness or
timidity prevented them from inquiring whether it was the title
'pastor' which was given now and then to the priest, or a figure
of speech which they recalled having observed in their very
occasional reading. But as the Plouffes had always lived in the
hothouse atmosphere of a country in which priesthood and
rhetoric flourish, each time they nodded their heads the word
'pastor', like a drop of mercury in a tube, shuttled back and forth
between the brain cell that inclined towards the church and that
which was attracted by legend and honorary titles. However,
their stronger leanings were to the side of the priesthood, and
slowly in their minds Tom Brown was installed as an incomplete
priest who wore the title pastor instead of a cassock.

So Josephine Plouffe, seeing Ovide's woebegone face, felt that
Cécile had made a blunder. She was the first to emerge from the
torpor into which they had been plunged by the stranger's
arrival. Rushing over to Théophile's rocking-chair, she pushed it

near the pastor. Denis Boucher sat down on the table. Ovide broke the silence:

—Are you a pastor in Cincinnati itself?

Tom Brown's first words were spoken through his nose with a strong American accent.

—Yes, I'm in the east end of the town. I have about two thousand parishioners.

—We met at the University where he is taking a summer course, Denis Boucher cut in.

Ovide straightened his tie, satisfied. So the University was looking him up. Happily, everybody is not a rings champion! Denis Boucher, without doubt, had breathed a word in the pastor's ear about his musical knowledge. So Ovide nodded encouragingly to the American, who was searching for his words with obvious difficulty.

—I was very happy to meet Denis. He has been more than very good company. He has been a perfect guide for my fiancée and me. Your town is certainly picturesque!

—Fiancée? The query flashed from the eyes of Josephine and Cécile. Théophile shrugged his shoulders. Ovide, congratulating himself on his broader outlook, lowered his eyelids and smiled imperceptibly with the air of one who understands a mistake and excuses it with complacency. Denis Boucher was enjoying the entertainment he had hoped for and said:

—Yes, Madame Plouffe, Protestant ministers are allowed to marry.

At the word 'Protestant', pronounced for the first time, the Plouffes unconsciously made a frightened movement. Even Ovide made it. Cécile was thinking:

—I was right when I said to myself he hadn't got Catholic eyes!

Such a distinguished man a Protestant! Josephine threw a glance at the bronze crucifix removed from Grandfather Plouffe's coffin. Wouldn't Ovide decide to chase this heretic out of the house? But Ovide was struggling against the recollections of his childhood, when, with gangs of urchins from the neighbourhood, he used to throw stones through the windows of non-Catholic churches. For years at home, hadn't they called 'Protestants' all those who acted in a reprehensible manner, or were supposed to have criticized certain actions, even civil, of the Church authorities? And at a time when it was not yet the custom to wave the scarecrow of Communism, hadn't the priest accused of Protestantism all who seemed lukewarm towards Christ and the rectory? This sheaf of prejudices, that Ovide had thought forever buried deep in his past, cropped up again, bringing with them the shades of Henry VIII and his six murdered wives. Ovide heaved a sigh. Tom Brown was certainly not like other Protestants. Didn't he want to learn French, and wasn't he calling on the Plouffes? All these thoughts went by in a flash. The University and Ovide's vanity won the victory. He calmed down.

—You know, Mama, the Baptist church is very much like ours.

—You can't tell me that, Josephine retorted. At least, our priests don't marry.

Cécile was talking more than usual. Religion, if it sometimes strikes dumb those who are elevated by it, makes talkative those who have nothing to say. The minister's garb impressed her so much that she could speak of nothing but vestments.

—Monsieur le pasteur, do you ever wear a cassock?

The Reverend Tom Brown, flabbergasted by this reception, shook his head and twisted his fingers with embarrassment. Denis Boucher was enjoying himself, and Ovide was thinking only of proposing to play some records. Théophile, out of patience with all these secondary matters, spread out his arms.

—Now, now, you women. Religion is a personal affair. Isn't that true?

—Yes, indeed, Monsieur Plouffe, Tom Brown agreed, cheering up.

Théophile opened the cupboard and came back with a bottle

of beer. The doctor had forbidden him to drink it and Madame Plouffe allowed him but one glass daily. This would be his second today. Josephine folded her arms and said nothing. She knew very well that Théophile's tolerance had only one object, to take a glass with the pastor, and she owed it to herself not to call her husband a tippler before a Protestant.

—To the health of the United States, my dear pastor. Between ourselves, don't you think we'd be better off with them than with England?

Having sipped a quarter of his glass and thrown a victorious glance at Josephine, Théophile rolled his tongue over his upper lip as if preparing to make an important announcement.

—We were speaking of religion a few minutes ago. You know, Father, I earn my living through priests.

—Oh? Tom Brown said, interested.

Denis Boucher's eyes shone with mischievous enthusiasm and, catching Ovide's eye, he traced a circle in the air with his index finger.

—Don't be surprised, Tom. Vicious circles are not rare *here*.

Ovide's thin fingers met sharply in a decisive gesture as he buttoned his jacket. It seemed the moment to make himself felt.

—Denis, if you want a discussion, you're going to have it, even in theology.

The pastor was replying politely to Théophile:

—Do you happen to be a sacristan?

Théophile drew himself up.

—Excuse me, I'm a compositor at *Christian Action*.

—Him, a sacristan, Monsieur le pasteur! Josephine said, laughing. He doesn't even fold his pants before he goes to bed. He leaves everything all over the place.

Théophile, who did not carry his beer well, was developing a persecution complex at the second glass.

—That's right, make your little joke in front of the visitor. You always try to make me feel small.

Tom Brown, who was not following the dialect very clearly, thought that the interchange was about printing.

—Indeed, it's a splendid occupation.

—That it is, Théophile said, bridling. We print one hundred thousand copies; *Christian Action* is a fine paper, let me tell you!

—I bet it is, the American said. Hasn't your admiration for the Germans put you in wrong with the paper?

—On the contrary, the publishers have a good deal of sympathy for Fascism, Denis Boucher hastened to reply. This is the very newspaper for which I'm trying to become a reporter. All I need now is a letter of recommendation from Father Folbèche, our parish priest.

Ovide was becoming impatient. The pastor was being slow to ask for a recording of Gigli or Pinza.

—Of course you're interested in music and opera, he broke in with a knowing look.

—Very much. But you must be wondering why I am calling on you. I've come to talk to you about this young man, the pastor said, pointing at Guillaume.

Ovide turned pale. Sport again! Guillaume did not look round. His mother drew near her youngest as though to defend him. Josephine, who too long had believed Ovide her masterpiece and had never succeeded in understanding Guillaume's astonishing birth, was watching over this supplementary Benjamin uneasily, as if to prevent him from disintegrating suddenly and disappearing into the limbo from which he had come so unexpectedly.

—I was watching him pitch this afternoon. His accuracy is extraordinary, the pastor continued.

—I forgot to tell you that Mr. Brown is a great sportsman, Denis explained. He's organized a lot of baseball teams in Cincinnati and he knows the manager of the Reds quite well.

—And I can assure you, the American went on, that I have never met in an adolescent such accurate, speedy, or, above all, such well-controlled pitching. In the United States he'd have a fine future. He could become a splendid recruit for the major leagues.

Guillaume went over to the pastor and began to scrutinize him.

—Oh, I know you. You were on the playground this afternoon. Where do you come from?

—From Cincinnati, Guillaume.

—Yes, over there, Ovide cut in dryly, pointing to the south.

Ovide's bad temper was growing. For the second time that day it was being forced on his notice that, in the eyes of women and highbrow strangers, his brother's ability constituted the most interesting element in his family. Théophile finished his glass with a chortle of pity.

—When I hear them talk of baseball and rings! You should see his calves! How they could pedal! He could be a Torchie Peden.

—You ought to feel satisfied, Cécile said to Guillaume, who was eyeing her mischievously. All this praise should please you.

The Reverend Tom Brown raised his index finger sententiously towards Théophile.

—I'm against bicycle-racing myself. It causes heart ailments. But I think Guillaume's talent for pitching should be developed. If you'll let me, I can coach him during the few days I'm here.

Josephine, overwhelmed, placed herself between her son and the American in an attitude which signified: 'You can have him only over my dead body.'

—I think Guillaume's too young to go in for such things, she said shortly.

A succession of explosions ascended the steps, and Napoleon appeared. Denis Boucher, on seeing him, sprang to his feet as if Napoleon had been the principal person to whom he had promised to introduce Tom Brown. Napoleon was impassively sucking an ice-cream cone.

—I'd like to introduce Pastor Tom Brown. He's a Baptist priest in Cincinnati.

Nothing, it seemed, could distract Napoleon from curling his tongue over his ice-cream. Only his eyes looked up.

—Good day, Monsieur l'abbé.

And he crossed the kitchen and went to his room. This ice-cream, bought each evening, had become a rite in Napoleon's life. He would set to work on it in his room and, listening from the kitchen, they could tell from the crunching of the biscuit when the ceremony of the cone was entering its critical stage. When the dome had been completely licked off, Napoleon's tongue, which had acquired a wonderful elasticity from this exercise, would push the rest of the cream to the bottom of the container. Then, holding the cone to his eye like a telescope, he would make sure that he had collected all the cream and forced it as deep down as it would go. Fateful moment! It was then that his teeth, like voracious vandals, broke into the biscuit, which disappeared quickly under the savage attack. After that there was another pause, while Napoleon held the end of the cone between his finger and thumb. After long hesitation, did he use all his skill to suck the last mouthful? No! He balanced the end of the cone on his thumb, curved his first finger, raised his hand shoulder-high, thumb pointing backwards, and, closing his eyes, released the sacrificial flick. The treasured object rose, skimmed the electric light bulb, and fell behind the large valise his mother had used on her honeymoon. In this way Napoleon sustained a taste for living; every day he could look forward to the mouthful at the top of a new cone that would make up for the mouthful sacrificed at the end of the old.

Guillaume, hearing the faint sound produced by the fall of the projectile, broke his silence.

—Well, here comes Napoleon again.

Wiping the corners of his lips the eldest son returned to the kitchen and went over to the watch hanging on the wall.

—Hurry, Guillaume! Dress. Quarter to eight!

This rough reminder brought Ovide back to his sentimental preoccupations. He leapt out on the balcony to see whether Rita Toulouse was in sight. He was frowning; why hadn't she wanted him to call for her, as the etiquette books directed?

—Is the championship match tonight? Denis Boucher asked, in the kitchen.

Napoleon, who was standing guard over Guillaume and urging him to dress, replied:

—Yes, tonight it's the Quebec championship. That won't get him down.

—Could I come to this match? the pastor asked.

—Yes, of course you must come! Denis exclaimed.

Napoleon regarded the Reverend Tom Brown more attentively.

—Do priests go in for sport over in your country?

—Oh yes; you weren't here when I was saying how much I admired your brother's ability at sport.

—Yes, except for bicycle racing, which affects the heart, Théophile said bitterly.

Napoleon seemed not to have heard his father. The dull face of this paste-pot sportsman brightened with serene pride. Tom Brown had pronounced the magic formula that opened wide the doors of the Napoleonic Olympics. He raised his finger.

—In that case, just a minute.

He ran over to the cabinet, and bending his short legs he pulled out his most recent album and said:

—You must know Babe Ruth. Were you there when he made his 475-foot home-run? I have the picture here.

Ovide, irritated beyond measure, threw his arms out indignantly:

—I ask you! Shut that up. There isn't time.

At the same moment, Cécile crossed the kitchen at a run. Her eyes were on the door, and through the screen they spied

Onésime Ménard, tall and lanky, dressed in his streetcar-conductor's uniform. Hands in pockets, he jingled the numerous coins his occupation obliged him to keep on his person, the sound of which served as a signal to Cécile when there were visitors.

—There's a knock at the front! Guillaume exclaimed.

All the Plouffes looked at one another in dismay. What an evening! It must be a stranger, because all their friends and even the priest always came in by the kitchen door. The door 'at the front' opened into the parlour where the piano, the armchairs, and the phonograph were; objects so precious that it did not seem as though one should have access to them without first paying one's respects in the kitchen. Louder knocks were heard. Ovide, struck by a sudden thought, burst out:

—That's her! She's probably been knocking there for five minutes!

Wildly excited he crossed the kitchen twice, looking for his tie.

—It's round your neck, Vide, his mother said.

He ran to the phonograph and set it going. The battle of opera against sport was beginning, with Georges Thill as first gunner.

> *What is it that charms me?*
> *And with passion true and tender warms me!*
> *O Margarita! Thy unworthy slave am I!*
> *All hail, Thou dwelling pure and lowly! . . .*

Ovide opened the door.

Fifteen minutes later, Théophile Plouffe, watching from the balcony, saw Tom Brown, Denis Boucher, Guillaume, Napoleon, and many fans of the aspiring champion disappear. The group were climbing towards the Upper Town. Denis Boucher and Tom Brown seemed to be discussing some important matter, for they were conversing without gestures, as if their whole attention were engaged. As for Ovide, he had pretended he knew a shorter way to the scene of the contest.

When Théophile was sure that they were finally out of sight, he went down the steps in his turn and mounted his bicycle.

Cécile was sitting with Onésime Ménard on the streetcar bench and their conversation revolved around the difficulties of summer traffic.

Finally, Madame Plouffe, dressed in her Sunday best, came out of the house, pulling on her black gloves. She was hurrying to the rectory, to confess to having received a Protestant in her home and to warn the priest of the danger threatening Ovide's religious vocation.

CHAPTER THREE

RITA TOULOUSE gave a short peal of astonished laughter, then in a boyish, offhand manner she pushed away Ovide's arm which he was hesitantly sliding under her own.

—Oh, Monsieur Plouffe, that's old-fashioned.

And her firm, vigorous ankle, which was the pivot for an agile calf and thigh, rose higher as she walked, as if to emphasize her remark. At this moment, Ovide knew less than ever what to do with his right hand. His quivering fingers, which in his embarrassment were clutching at the air, plunged into his pocket and brought out a match which he broke between his teeth.

—You know, chaps like me, Mademoiselle Rita . . . Oh! Will you let me call you 'Mademoiselle Rita'?

The girl peered into her pocket mirror, inspecting her lipstick.

—Why sure! Of course. Let's make it short, Ovide. You were saying: chaps like you . . .

Ovide Plouffe, who wished nothing to be short that evening, especially the walk that led to the sports meeting, frowned, trying to remember what it was he had been going to say.

—Oh, yes! Chaps like me, Mademoiselle Toulouse, we're too much taken up with intellectual and artistic things like music and literature, to drop, all at once, the French manners that go with them.

Ovide almost stopped walking in astonishment; a gaping mouth was all he could present to the uneasy glance he now received from the first woman in his life. Was his memory, so faithful to cavatinas, playing tricks on him? That was a journalist's sentence! But no; that thought, that turn of the sentence was

36

his own. Seized with sudden pride, he promptly threw out his chest. Woman's presence was freeing his spirit from the lair into which it had been driven by men's gibes. Friendship, confidences, love, were liberating Ovide from his bonds—those of the opera enthusiast imprisoned in the desiccated skin of a too meagre body.

With a sure hand he hung a cigarette from his lips and, carefully putting away his cigarette-case, prepared to go on with his speech.

—I can take a drag too, you know.

Ovide looked at her in surprise. Then he hastily offered her a cigarette. It wasn't necessary to rush things; it was better to satisfy Rita so that she wouldn't be frightened off. Once conquered by the glamour of opera, she would fall under his sway.

—As a matter of fact, he said, for our musical evening at my place next Thursday, I think I'll sing you some parts from *Pagliacci*. I don't do so badly with it. François Thibodeau will be at the piano and his sister, Bérangère, will sing a duet with me. We aren't beginners, I can assure you.

—I'm just crazy to hear you sing opera, Monsieur Plouffe. You'd never know you could sing by looking at you.

Ovide threw back his head.

—Mademoiselle Rita, opera is the most beautiful thing in the world. It's because I know you have a fine mind that I thought of offering you this treat. And then you'll understand how contemptible sport is compared with great music.

The music-lover was rejoicing prematurely over the crashing victory that opera would gain over sport during this musical evening designed to dazzle Rita and convert her.

Lost in thought, the girl suppressed a smile and kept silent. Ovide was happy. Their eyes half-closed, their lips pursed, the two puffed out their first curls of smoke into the sweet air of this July evening. Rita's finger, with its long varnished nail, shook the ash from her cigarette.

37

—I'm listening to you, Monsieur Ovide. You talk so well!
How is it you're a leather-cutter when you can make sentences
like that?

Ovide's thin body stiffened with satisfaction and his big toe,
which gave Madame Plouffe so much darning, stuck out so far
that it threatened to pierce his shoe.

—It's not the job that makes the man, mademoiselle, it's the
man that makes the job. For instance, if I knew how to write
everything I know, correctly, and I'm not telling you this out
of boastfulness, you understand, why, I'd be a journalist, a
magistrate, a member of parliament, or even a cabinet minister!

A laugh swelled in Rita's chest and, proving irresistible,
escaped in an ascending scale from between her pretty teeth.

—Oh . . . boy! Don't kid yourself. I have a cousin who
worked for the government under the Conservatives. Believe it
or not, she had to correct the letters the minister dictated to her,
and his secretary even wrote his speeches, and all that.

Ovide looked down with an air of disappointment, while the
dream of social success faded from his eyes.

—Yes, yes. But I haven't any intention of becoming a cabinet
minister. I'm too musy with music.

There was a long silence. The couple had entered Arago
Street at the foot of the Cape, that steep rise which divides the
city of Quebec in two and serves as a ladder in the social scale.
Ovide's glance, now lost in his thoughts, now on the look-out
for people he knew, was suddenly clouded by the misgivings of
a lowly breadwinner, unworthy of a pretty woman like Rita;
then, as suddenly, lighted up at the sight of a neighbour's wife
who, hands on hips, feet apart, endeavoured to suppress her
start of astonishment.

—Well! Good heavens! Ovide with a woman! I should have
thought he'd become a priest. Ovide Plouffe with a woman!
There's trouble ahead.

And Ovide, waving and bowing extravagantly, greeted people

to whom he customarily allowed only the bored glance of a great artist.

They were nearing a small restaurant. The syncopated tune from a juke-box reached them; then the smell of fried potatoes; the ring of the cash register; the stamping and humming of boys and girls. Ovide made a grimace. Rita seemed piqued by sudden curiosity.

—As you like music so much, Monsieur Plouffe, what do you think of Bing Crosby? I'm crazy about him!

Clucking from a chicken-run they were passing prevented Rita from hearing his abusive remark:

—Crooners are cheap, third-raters . . .

—What?

Ovide checked himself in time:

—It's an easy style, and a lot of people like it.

—Easy? That's what you think? Anyone who wants to imitate him on amateur nights has a job. They're not worth Bing's little finger.

—Lots of people would like to sing like Georges Thill, too.

Ovide bit his lips, humiliated by permitting the comparison between Georges Thill and Bing Crosby. But Rita was becoming excited.

—There are plenty of great singers like Thill, but try and find any great crooners like Bing.

Ovide opened his mouth, then closed it again, shrugging his shoulders. He heaved a sigh. Had he ever thought that such a conversation could take place between him and the first woman who would go out with him? During the ten years he had dreamed of her, the sweet holding of hands he had first desired had expanded into a vast embrace, which now encircled all the feminine sex and brought it to him, concentrated in Rita. How many illusions have taken flight because a woman did not say the words put into her mouth! While Ovide was repairing the chinks in his patience and postponing the fruition of his hopes,

39

Rita was humming, *Lazy bones, lying in the shade*. The tune was lost in her sighs of admiration.

—Bing Crosby has a voice that could land him in opera if he wanted.

—Let him try! Ovide cut in, threateningly.

His blazing eyes pictured the famous American crooner tumbling down an interminable staircase, while at the top, the tall figure of Ezio Pinza, with a head like that of a Shakespearian Ovide, surveyed the downfall as he brought his avenging toe back to the ground. Satisfied, Ovide pointed with his finger:

—There are the steps of the Côte Victoria. We can go that way to the Upper Town.

Rita Toulouse concealed her annoyance.

—We're moving to the Upper Town next year. I shan't have to climb up any more. My father has been promoted manager of the store.

Ovide was worried.

—Do you want to leave the factory?

—No!

—Oh! Then you'll have to go up and down very often.

Rita eyed him and shrugged.

—Work's not the only thing in life! There's the evening. Dancing and movies. And then sometimes the supervisors come around to take us home. I'm not keen on having a manager or an American take me through the Lower Town.

Ovide clapped his hand to his forehead.

—So that's why you didn't want me to call for you this evening? That wouldn't have made any difference to me, you know.

They were climbing the first steps of the Cape stairway. Rita pretended to be out of breath to hide her embarrassment. She could not tell Ovide that the parlour chairs were getting old and that the numerous kids of which she was the eldest would swarm around him the whole time he was in the house. They stopped at the first landing, and turned towards the Lower Town, gazing over a jumble of chimneys. Rita shook off her drab recollections of torn chairs and nosy children.

— Tell me, where is this match?

— On St. Olivier Street.

— But it's not a short cut to go up here. What are you doing it for?

Her glance, that of a cunning adolescent, both mocking and vulgar, slid over Ovide. He looked dignified and bored.

— No, that's right, it isn't any shorter. But I thought it was rather awkward for you to be the only woman in that bunch of men.

— Not at all! It's lots more fun!

Ovide stared at her and knitted his thick brows. His left eye, which he closed like a marksman while trying to guess the meaning hidden in a sentence, flickered several times. He gazed at the girl's lips. Rita was smiling mockingly. It did not cross Ovide's mind for an instant that his presence interested Rita very little, since she preferred a bunch of men to him.

— Oh! I understand! It's Guillaume.

He turned round and began to climb the steps again with a jerky stride. Rita caught up with him and the effort made her smile all the more tantalizing.

— Not only him. There's the older chap, Denis. He's odd, but he's nice all the same. And the American! Doesn't he look *cute* for a pastor?

Rita's mention of the pastor soothed Ovide's budding jealousy. But while his imagination was boiling actively, a recollection which bore no relation to his present state of feelings arose from his subconscious thoughts, clearing a way straight into his mind.

In the space between two steps, through which the shrubs of the Cape were visible, the attitude of the pastor and of Denis on their arrival at the house came before him and held his eyes fixed and absent. Why was Denis trying to ridicule the Plouffes before strangers, to present them as curiosities? Especially as Denis had been his friend since childhood.

—Yes, you're a queer guy, Rita Toulouse concluded, not understanding why Ovide was slowing up. All at once, you set off nobody knows where. You don't like people, that's obvious.

Ovide was just about to confess his former resolution to enter the monastery, but he refrained. The big street lamp, which made a bright circle in the middle of the steps, reddened the girl's face while it whitened Ovide's. He breathed deeply and, with a long stride, reached the third landing, from which he gazed fondly over the misty sea of roofs that broke beneath their feet. There, below him, was the suburb of St. Sauveur in the dusk, and the dream he had cherished so long was blossoming at last. This was all his boyhood recaptured at a glance—a glance from the third landing, with a woman beside him. His feelings were ready to overflow and flood the whole scene. Rita was asking why he had chosen this way. Ovide turned towards her, tender confidences on his lips; but she was looking at the distant floodlights of Victoria Park, which seemed to repulse the nightfall. A wave of shouts reached them on the warm breeze that caressed their hair. Rita spoke as though she were trying to shake off a doubt.

—The *Canadiens* won last night. Stan Labrie was pitching. Do you know him? He's the one who's going to referee the match tonight. A nice boy. He's got his eye on me, too.

The tone in which Rita began these remarks became less assured as she went on speaking. Rita had not enough imagination to lie properly. It was not true; Stan Labrie had never even looked at her and, if she had asked Ovide to take her to the tournament, it was to see his champion.

She bit her lip, while Ovide, in whom she had killed a confession tinged with the poetry of a theme in *Tosca*, shrugged his shoulders sadly and began climbing again. Strange, all the projects and hopes which he had conjured up in recalling a great aria were turning into big balloons that could find no anchor. Some day or other they would shrivel, or burst and disappear.

So Rita had never seen the lovers loitering on the landings of the long stairway, when radios were stopped and parks were closed? If she had, she would not have asked him why he had chosen this way. Could she not guess that for ten years Ovide had dreamed of that stairway, making the five landings into magic carpets of the Arabian Nights, bronzed by the soft light of the electric lamp? What long summer evenings he had spent, sitting on the streetcar bench, on the balcony, dreaming, watching the distant shadowy figures linger on the landings, while beside him, Papa Théophile Plouffe patiently sucked at his extinguished pipe. Ovide had appropriated for himself the centre landing, so that if he should ever be lucky enough to have a pretty woman beside him he could count on two other landings to complete his happiness. He had prepared his plans carefully: one hundred steps to create the atmosphere and another hundred to enjoy it.

Sadness made Ovide aware of his aching legs. Stan Labrie had lost him the centre landing. Soon they would reach the top, and he could not count on a chance of returning. Rita would certainly want to come back with the others after the game. Suddenly, in the depth of his chagrin, he felt Rita's arm slide under his, and the pulsations of her flesh penetrated him to the bone.

—Monsieur Ovide, won't you help me?

Her voice was plaintive and caressing. Ovide didn't realize that he owed this burst of affection to the indifference of a certain pitcher. Complacently, he scolded himself:

—Fool! It's when you're nearing the goal that you think all is lost!

He reached the fourth landing, and paused, triumphantly. It is good to look down from a height on the houses one lives in; their light and smoke seem to make friendly signals. Ovide, still clasping Rita's arm, looked at his district with tender pride.

From here the odours of St. Sauveur perfumed the evening breezes and the dilapidated houses blossomed into coloured pictures. Ovide was dreaming. He was perched just high enough for his imagination, born of this district and stimulated now by his conquest, to see in this conglomeration of houses, jumbled together, a fleet of old French ships abandoned in America and forming a village in a dried-up port.

—You hold yourself very stiff, Monsieur Plouffe. You'd think you were posing for a wedding picture for the paper.

Ovide felt his exaltation detach itself from him and go tumbling lifelessly down the steps, Rita's staccato laughter hastening its fall to where the dreams of the poor lie buried.

—Oh! I've hurt your feelings, Rita said, surprised and apologetic.

Ovide's eyes glittered with rage. Did she think she could console him like this? She opened her arms suddenly.

—Don't you know how to kiss, you old musician?

His back supported by the guard-rail, he was almost on the defensive. Caressingly, she bit his chin.

—You musician, you!

Petrified, Ovide offered his lips. He stretched out his head cautiously, as though at the supreme moment he might lose his footing. No, Rita's chin rubbed easily against his own, which he had never shaved so smoothly. And his two hands which, in awkward haste, he had clasped around the girl, went sliding towards the small of her back as she yielded to his hug. She was a real woman whose flesh, plump at the waist, burned under his fingers. And it was with closed eyes that Ovide consummated his first kiss, imagined, polished, and turned over from all angles for many years.

But what was wrong? Surely he wasn't getting old! Was it that he could not attain the supreme joy he had hoped for because all his listening to the greatest opera singers had failed to teach him what it was? He opened his eyes and studied the lines of

44

Rita's narrow forehead. He began to grow conscious of his own powers, felt himself master of the situation and at once started elaborating plans to smooth out the unattractive aspects of this woman's character and make her feel his authority. The task would be easy after the musical evening the following Thursday.

—It's easy to see you haven't kissed very often, Rita was saying, as she repaired her make-up.

Ovide, staring at the stadium lights, did not reply. He did not hear the distant cries of the crowd. It was as though he were paralysed by his dead dream. His reason for living, Woman, that lamp he had kept lighted secretly for so long, ever since the pride of his twenty years had been submerged in jibes, was fading into the dullness of the daily grind. He braced himself against this disappointment.

—I think this place lacks atmosphere, he sniffed. Imagine a gipsy orchestra and palm trees around us.

—Wipe your lips, you're all smeared, Rita said, shrugging her shoulders.

Ovide took out his handkerchief and stared down at the third landing. His eyes shone. He could explain the failure of the kiss. It hadn't been done on the right landing. Everything had been spoiled. And the talk about the singers had been far from helping matters. He hummed with exaggerated enthusiasm:

> *Oh, Love is a Bohemian lad*
> *who snaps his fingers in the face of law.*

Poor Ovide! He was unaware that love adapts itself to all settings, to all arguments. He did not know the ineffable gifts of a woman in the transports of voluptuousness and her infatuated heart, and then in the languor of her weary eyes and her exhausted arms. He was ignorant of the tenderness of the woman who is loved, a tenderness which refreshes one for action, sweetens one's hours of triumph, and shields one in times of adversity.

But this opera-lover, hemmed in on every side since his childhood by lack of understanding, his ambitions laughed at, his mannerisms ridiculed, had so lost, while growing up, the faculty of discrimination that the first woman he desired was the one least suited to him.

Rita Toulouse was a typical nineteen-year-old adolescent, plump, just tall enough not to appear fat, short-waisted, and with firm breasts. She had blue eyes which lighted up too often; thick, fair hair; a slightly turned-up nose, which kept her face from being commonplace; these, and the succession of curves springing from calf to shoulder at a turn of her lively heel, promised to make of Rita a desirable woman as soon as she knew how to use her resources. She was pleasing enough to the owner of the factory for him to have accepted her as office girl, although she could not type, spell or do shorthand, and shouted American slang along the aisles of machines and men.

Rita Toulouse! The eldest of nine children who engulfed her in their childishness; greedy for movie magazines, her nose eagerly turned to the Jerichos of the South, ready to extol the kings of entertainment and sport; Bing Crosby, Joe DiMaggio, and, within easier reach, the popular singers of the Quebec radio and the stars of the local baseball diamonds. Rita Toulouse, who mistook pleasure for happiness.

She was infatuated with Stan Labrie, the pitcher. She talked about him too much. Rita knew nothing of moderation. Labrie was unaware of her existence.

And this was the first woman in Ovide's life; the first woman he had dared wish to possess. He was a shackled dreamer, pulled this way and that by the predilections of others; different from others, yet unable to be himself.

Ovide cast a last look at the third landing. With shining eyes and confident expression, he took Rita's arm and attacked the last steps of the stairway.

—Rita.

—What?

—It takes you by surprise when you're not expecting it. You can't really enjoy it. Next time we'll know how. Perhaps after our party on Thursday, eh?

—Isn't Stan going to be surprised when he sees me come in, she replied, dreamily.

She hurried up, anxious to arrive at the match, and Ovide began to think seriously about Stan Labrie.

CHAPTER FOUR

F ROM groups of men enjoying some spectacle there arises a murmur that walls and doors seem unable to restrain. Like a vapour, it seeps through, eddies and escapes, its muted tone enriching the chorus of sound.

The sound of cheers, coming from a block of tenements thrust haphazardly against the cliff in an age of generous and careless romanticism, wound through alleys and flowed out to increase the cacophony of the main street.

Ten o'clock. Pedestrians on St. Olivier Street would all of a sudden turn their heads towards a large shed in the shadow of a courtyard. Their ears would strain to hear more clearly the muffled clanging of the rings, then catch a sudden wave of boisterous exclamations. Most of them shrugged and continued on their way.

An old man, perched on a racing bicycle, was hanging about, pedalling slowly as he went interminably to and fro, the pipe between his teeth tracing cabbalistic signs on the air every time he mumbled his indignation.

—They let women go in, but not bicycles! That's the first time I've seen that.

It was Papa Théophile Plouffe, whose bicycle the proprietor of the place had refused to allow on the premises, advising him to leave it in the yard. But the old compositor, who feared and abhorred bicycle thieves as he would great criminals, had preferred to remain on guard beside his celebrated bike, and to wait outside for the results of the contest.

Monsieur Plouffe had just passed in front of the courtyard entrance when, all at once, a bright rectangle opened abruptly in

48

the shed to let out, amidst a hubbub of shouts, the figures of two men. The patch of light disappeared, sealed by the bang of a door. The Reverend Tom Brown drew a deep breath and exclaimed:

—That boy Guillaume is tremendous!

—Nothing bothers him, Denis Boucher rejoiced. Did you notice the referee, Stan Labrie? The one that Rita Toulouse couldn't take her eyes off?

—Yes?

—He's the pitcher-manager of the *Canadien* Baseball Club. The best club in Quebec.

—I'm only interested in Guillaume. Do you think he's going to win?

—Certainly. Doesn't the name Stan Labrie mean anything to you? Why, this would be just the time to organize a game against the *Canadiens*. Labrie won't refuse. You could see what Guillaume can do.

The pastor snapped his fingers energetically.

—Right! Splendid! I'm leaving Quebec on Saturday, so the game should be arranged for Friday night. Let's go and see Stan Labrie right now.

A wave of lusty shouting made them hurry in to see what was going on. It was stiflingly hot. At the back of the long, narrow hall with its low ceiling, the late-comers stood about, first on one leg and then on the other, observing stoically the ups and downs of the sports drama which was unfolding in the smoke at the other end. Through this haze loomed the silhouettes of the principal players, suggesting a purgatorial scene in which sinful souls had been condemned by the tribunal of God to play at rings until the supreme throw was made: 84. And Napoleon Plouffe, charged by St. Peter to oversee the penitential performance, stood on guard, unyielding, near the prizes. There were five trophies of varying sizes placed on a little table in a corner, at the front of the hall, and Napoleon never left them except to go over and encourage his protégé.

D

The other spectators were divided into two camps: those for Guillaume Plouffe, or the 'Lower Town', and those for Charles Métivier, who were known as the 'Upper Town'.

The stifling heat, the shouts revolving about the arena, rose in waves against the fly-bedecked ceiling. Instinctively, the spectators, in an effort to draw themselves out of this furnace, crouched along the wall in Indian fashion, particularly Guillaume's supporters who were lining the benches on the left side of the hall. These earnest fans of St. Sauveur, more accustomed to working in the open, digging sewer conduits or mixing cement, were sweating profusely and discreetly wringing their shirts under their Sunday suits, which they had thought appropriate for this match in the Upper Town.

The temperature of the place had an entirely opposite effect on Guillaume's opponents, ranged along the opposite wall. Civil servants for the most part, accustomed to wear shirt, tie, and suit, they gave way to the need, too often suppressed, to take off their coats, undo their collars, and roll up their sleeves. It did not matter before these boys of Lower Town, and this was the time, if ever, to take their ease. Despite the humid atmosphere, trousers stuck less to the wooden bench than to the leather office cushion, and it was in comparative comfort that the office clerks applauded their champion. The game of rings is as good as communism for smoothing out social distinctions and making the workman don the coat that the bureaucrat takes off.

—You're catching up! Come on, Guillaume!

Guillaume, unperturbed by the volley of applause, returned to his place on the bench of honour, also occupied by Ovide and Rita. The latter, her eyes on Stan Labrie, seized hold of the champion's hands.

—Atta boy, Guillaume! You're going to win!

Napoleon, alarmed, came bustling up, and gently pushed aside the only woman in the place.

—Pardon me! Mustn't excite him. This is the championship.

Rita sat down hastily. Stan Labrie had scarcely looked at her. Ovide, who, all the evening, had assumed the detached and condescending air of an opera-lover, while jealously watching the exchange of glances between his companion and Stan Labrie, bent towards the girl with a satisfied look:

—I thought you were more intimate with Monsieur Labrie. It looks as though he scarcely knows you.

She bit her lips and assumed a knowing attitude.

—He's like that. He's a gentleman. He doesn't like to compromise women.

Ovide was not taken in. He whistled a bar or two of the *William Tell* Overture.

—You're made for someone better than Stan Labrie, he said. You don't know your own worth. Foolish child!

The noise died down for a moment. Stan Labrie, a sheet of paper in his hand, called for silence. The pastor and Denis hurried to take their places beside Rita and Ovide. Stan Labrie walked to the centre of the room. He was a tall, stoutish fellow, brown-haired, whose fat face appeared to be beardless, the side-whiskers terminating at ear level. From his face one would have taken him for twenty, but the lines under his eyes showed him to be at least thirty. He raised his thin, almost feminine voice:

—Score after the twenty-second round: Charles Métivier, 1,050; Guillaume Plouffe, 1,041. Each player still has three rounds to play.

—What a pansy! Look at his behind, scoffed Denis under cover of the shouts.

—Play up! Stan Labrie concluded.

The tenseness of motionless waiting seized the spectators again as they fixed their eyes on the five iron stakes, fascinated by the encircling steel rings as they glinted under the electric light.

Guillaume's opponent, Charles Métivier, picked up the rings and trotted towards the platform, which was about fourteen feet from the stakes. He looked doltish. He smiled in a superior way and, with the gesture known to all the Quebec ring-fans when he was preparing for a great throw, he tightened his belt one notch and slapped himself on the belly. He was about forty, and was a night watchman at the Parliament Buildings. The rings encircled his left arm; he showed all the signs of physical oddity with which those who give themselves up long enough to a sport are marked. The snowshoer takes long strides; the skater drags his feet; the cowboy is bowlegged and the dumb-bell enthusiast waves his arms in and out of season. Rings had marked Charles Métivier with even more obvious stigmata.

All adepts of this sport acquire a manner of throwing the ring peculiar to their temperament. The style is the man; the 'bearing' is the player. Guillaume's bearing was nonchalant, but he had a 'beautiful ring'. However, the most eccentric bearing ever seen in Quebec was Charles Métivier's. He grasped his ring and raised it to eye-level as though looking at the five iron stakes through a telescope. He held himself rigid like this for a few seconds; then he bent, touched his right knee with the steel disk, and stood upright again while the ring, which had caught at his stomach in passing, grazed his forehead, and the circle would float through the air towards its goal unwaveringly as though carried by an invisible hand. The steel had touched his knee, caught at his stomach, and grazed his forehead so many times that all his pants were patched at the waist and on the leg, and the front of his skull shone bald although his temples were covered with thick hair.

Charles Métivier now began his celebrated flourish. Smoke and anxiety stifled the clamour. Every head turned eagerly. There was a 13. Then a 12. Napoleon scarcely breathed. Guillaume could never make up the lost ground. Good-bye cups! The enthusiasm of the clerks rang out, dashing the sporting pride that sleeps in the hearts of all lads born in the Lower Town. A total of 68! Charles Métivier went slowly back to his chair, with a mocking glance at his opponent. A kid like that presuming to face him!

Guillaume observed the position of the rings, then withdrew his finger from his nostril. Sixty-eight! He seemed the calmest person there. Unconcernedly, he was about to stoop. But Napoleon, who was quicker, had picked up the rings and was holding them out to him.

—Take it easy. Don't tire yourself. You'll do it.

The collector's stubby hands kept opening and stiffening in his absorption. Guillaume replied with an ironic growl and took up his position. He kept his eyes on his feet and placed his right heel in a manner which he alone knew. Pastor Brown, in his anxiety, clutched the case of his camera. Would Guillaume justify his admiration? Guillaume threw his first ring as though he wished to get rid of it. Napoleon closed his eyes. A rich, heavy clang filled his ears and then his heart. It was a 14. He knew this rare and exquisite sound that the ring makes when it encircles the centre shaft and the one on the right. His features relaxed and then set in a kind of ecstatic fulfilment. Another 14; then two more! And a 13. Then suddenly it seemed as though a dagger had pierced Napoleon's breast. The sixth and last ring, hurled a little too far, had caught the single rear stake, the one that counts only three points. What a miserable, sickly sound; it tore through the skins of Guillaume's supporters. All the same, it was a total of 72. Four points gained!

The cheers broke out. From that moment, Guillaume's supporters seemed electrified with sudden hope. In a hotly contested sporting event it is as though waves of encouragement flow in the direction of the winners, whilst a strange pessimism filters slowly through the hearts of those who are to lose, penetrating them with a vague defeatism at the moment when they have every reason for thinking that victory will be theirs.

—Beat him, Guillaume! You're right on his tail! shouted the Lower Town lads exultantly.

While Rita Toulouse was hanging on to Guillaume's arm with her plump hands, while Napoleon used his handkerchief alternately for the cups and for his brow, and the spectators once more concentrated their attention, Métivier mounted the platform, moving with dignity as though affected by the magic atmosphere that now surrounded his opponent. He looked at the position of his feet, then traced a flourish in the air more finished than ever, as if he were trying to inscribe in the smoke his wish to excel. Were the iron stakes coming alive and defending themselves? The first ring rebounded on the ground. A rumble of ill-concealed satisfaction escaped from the Lower Town clan, and a hitherto unseen fear froze the faces of their adversaries. The second ring suffered the same fate. Anxiety was general. Métivier succeeded in placing the four remaining rings, and scored 49.

A hubbub of mingled chagrin and triumph arose. Napoleon slavered with joy. In his imagination he was already arranging the cups on the piano at home. Rita applauded, and Ovide still wore his superior smile.

—Métivier's all over you! He can eat up ten like you, a courageous voice called from among the clerks.

—You're a liar then! a young tough from the Lower Town retorted.

Napoleon jumped up from his corner and pointed angrily at the interrupter.

—Against the rules to speak to the players. Against the rules.

The Upper Town supporter, a lift man, stood up, fists clenched—an odd gesture, in view of Napoleon's size. Almost all the 'Guillaume Plouffe' clan were on their feet. The clerks were not all warlike, and they made gestures of appeasement towards the Lower Town boys who were already showing signs of battle. Charles Métivier who, back turned, was ostentatiously rubbing his famous arm, ordered:

—Pipe down, you, I don't need that to beat him.

Guillaume looked about him.

—Row over? Good!

He mounted the platform. Cigarettes, which nervous fingers had mechanically begun to roll, were held with their edges still unlicked while tongues, half-out, grew dry with excitement. Would Guillaume profit by his opponent's weakness? Guillaume threw. The ring soared, but in its fall passed over the centre stake and the one behind. The gleam of satisfaction shining already in the eyes riveted on its flight died mournfully as the ring, instead of encircling them both, rebounded and fell again zigzagging around the single centre peg. Five points. The clerks hardly dared to shout their joy and Guillaume's supporters were hanging on to the edge of the bench with both hands. The young prodigy's eyes scarcely hardened. He wet his lips, then threw the second ring. Once more the playing-square quivered throughout, then shook off the iron lasso which only caught its tail—the rear stake. Three points. Napoleon muttered a prayer. Guillaume gathered saliva and spat, his eyes fixed attentively on the five upright, scintillating stakes. He did not look around for sympathy. He seemed to consider, then let his left arm fall beside his thigh, the rings swinging in his half-closed hand. He raised his eyes to the ceiling as though waiting for the cloud of bad luck to move away. His supporters, for whom this game represented an epic battle between the Upper Town and the Lower Town, were bent almost double, clutching their stomachs to subdue the pains of discouragement. Guillaume seemed to come out of his reverie and set his feet in position again. He threw two 13's, a 12, and a 2, making a total of 48.

With bent head, Guillaume went back to his seat while his supporters pulled wry faces, and moaned.

—You had your chance to regain the lost ground, youngster, said Ovide severely.

Rita's encouragement to Guillaume was interrupted by Stan Labrie's treble voice.

—Twenty-fifth and last round. Charles Métivier, 1,167;

Guillaume Plouffe, 1,161. Charles Métivier is six points ahead. Play!

Charles Métivier picked up the rings with a sinewy hand, determined to show his superiority by a magnificent throw. He was irritated by the optimism of Guillaume's supporters and by the uneasiness of his own. But an aureole floats around sports champions which intoxicates crowds and makes them believe in invincibility at the moment when all hope seems lost.

—Yah! Shine up the old mugs while you've got them. Two more minutes and you won't have them, a clerk called out to Napoleon.

Denis stood up threateningly, but the pastor restrained him. Nobody paid attention to the abuse because Métivier was waiting for silence. The air became more and more suffocating. The spectacle of purgatory was turning into a scene from the Inferno. The fans were completely absorbed in the drama of the moment. They were not thinking of the day that had preceded this contest, nor of the-morrow. They were not fathers, brothers, and sons; they were neither poor nor rich; they no longer had country, wife or religion. They were oblivious to everything else as they fashioned a golden calf: a champion. Their tongues still had not yet licked the cigarettes that hung at their fingers' tips when Charles Métivier, tracing his famous flourish, began to throw again. The rings encircled the stakes in an indescribable tangle which put death in the hearts of Napoleon and his friends. Métivier had made 74.

The triumphant cries of the clerks were met by a gloomy, dejected silence on the part of Guillaume's followers. Guillaume would have to make a total of 81 to beat Métivier; in other words, perform a miracle. Métivier haughtily asked for his hat, and some of the crowd were putting on their coats and moving towards the door. Napoleon's anger burst out. Protecting the cups with his body he cried out, his voice vibrant with an apostolic faith in his brother:

—Sit down! Sit down! It's not finished!

The pastor nodded vigorously to show his approval. Now he would see if Guillaume possessed the self-control of a great pitcher. As Guillaume headed for the platform in a silence thick with the pity of his followers and the contempt of his adversaries, something new in the history of the game was taking place.

—Rita, come here! Ovide's scandalized voice protested.

But Rita Toulouse was picking up the rings and putting them like a sword into the hands of her knight, at the same time smiling at Stan Labrie who was watching her. Guillaume did not thank her and, with nonchalant step, walked to the platform. There was not a sound. The spectators breathed in rhythm with his slightest motions. Guillaume did not seem aware of them. He was looking at the ground, staring at a fly. He tried to stamp on it, but the tiny insect escaped. He looked around the walls, then up at the ceiling.

—Go on, throw! We want to get out of here! a voice called impatiently.

Guillaume pointed at the ceiling:

—The fly!

Napoleon leapt up, pursued the insect, and crushed it with his cap. Nobody laughed. A champion's whims are sacred. Guillaume's eyes were now fixed upon the stakes. Suddenly a man's deep voice burst out at the back of the room, near the half-open door. Papa Théophile Plouffe stood there, grasping with one hand the handlebars of his bicycle, which was half-way into the shed.

—Hey! Guillaume, my boy!

Everybody turned round with Guillaume, who winked slyly at his father:

—Yes, Papa?

—Beat him to it. O.K. Give him the works.

Coming just then, old Plouffe's order took on the aspect of a prophecy. The spectators, electrified or dismayed, awaited the miracle.

Guillaume smiled, closed one eye and threw. It was a 14. Not one vein quivered in his hand, steady as a robot's. Nobody breathed. Another 14! The miracle began to unfold in all its majesty. Four more 14's.

—*Eighty-four!*

The roar of admiration and joy had sprung from every throat. Clannish animosity disappeared before the tremendous total. Eighty-four!—the prodigious feat, said to have been performed once, long ago. And Guillaume Plouffe had just repeated it, in front of the men of his generation, on a July evening, in a little shed, henceforth historical, on St. Olivier Street. The uproar had scarcely burst out when Guillaume, flabbergasted, Rita's lips printed on his cheeks, found himself hoisted on the shoulders of the fanatics. Hysterical singing rose above the cheers. Stan Labrie shouted in his high-pitched voice:

—I now proclaim Guillaume Plouffe champion of Quebec. The score: Plouffe, 1,245, Métivier, 1,241. He has defeated a great champion.

—Whoopee!

Charles Métivier, scarlet, approached Guillaume:

—Congratulations, my boy. But you were lucky.

Napoleon, his mouth open and his hands on his brother's shoulders, was looking at him ecstatically. Then he went down the line of fans, stopping before each one, spreading out his arms with delight and smiling affectionately. Unable to speak, he gave a shrug of emotion, turned from the equally happy person opposite, and began his pantomime all over again with the next. Then he began to mutter:

—Guillaume, you damn' old Guillaume, you!

His happy expression faltered. His face grew long with astonishment. He was dying to use his father's favourite oath; that oath which horrified him and at which he crossed himself when Théophile lost his temper at home. But Napoleon got around the difficulty.

—Viourge! Viourge! The beautiful cups! Thanks, Holy Virgin, he murmured by way of amends. Then: We'll go back in a taxi, he announced.

Stan Labrie was preparing to leave when Denis Boucher accosted him.

—Monsieur Labrie, the famous baseball player? This is the Reverend Tom Brown, of Cincinnati. We have a proposition to make you . . .

Rita Toulouse tried to sidle up, but Ovide steered her to the door.

CHAPTER FIVE

T HE next evening, about six o'clock, Denis Boucher went briskly out of his house. Life was wonderful. All his plans were succeeding. Last night Stan Labrie had accepted the pastor's offer, and already the parish club was fully organized. Tom Brown never ceased praising the quaintness of the Plouffes and the fine sporting spirit of the people of Quebec. Denis smiled. All that remained was for him to secure his position as a reporter on *Christian Action*.

He had scarcely reached the wooden pavement that led to the Plouffe house when he stopped dead and paled under his tan, as if the jolt of his abrupt halt had caused some of the uncertainty that fills an adolescent's head to spread to his face.

Father Folbèche at the Plouffes!

The priest, one foot outside, the other still on the step, one hand holding the door open as though he were ready to leave, seemed to be giving important instructions to Madame Plouffe which she was acknowledging with violent nods. Denis thought at once of the Reverend Tom Brown. He began to retreat. But Madame Plouffe had seen him and pointed him out to her visitor. The priest turned and raised his arm animatedly as a signal for Denis to wait for him.

—Be guided by me, Madame Plouffe. We're in grave danger.

—Never fear, Father, I'll see to it. You know me. I'm religious. Take care you don't slip, the steps are steep.

When Father Folbèche had made sure that Denis was waiting for him on the pavement, he bent his head, picked up his cassock a little at the front and tackled the descent of the steps, his expression one of dual concern in which anxiety over not missing a step was superimposed on the more important concern which had led to his warning visit to the Plouffes.

Finally Father Folbèche set foot in the yard, around which he threw the perfunctory glance of a noble landowner who seems through force of habit to be taking inventory in the most remote corners of his domain. Then he reached the street. Perhaps another priest, realizing that Denis Boucher, instead of coming to meet him, had remained stationary thirty feet away, would have intimidated the whole street with a dominating look. But the virtue of humility seemed, in this worthy priest, to have killed all the reflexes that self-conceit keeps in reserve in ordinary men. Even the faults which one corrects at last by honouring God are sometimes like deep boils which have to find some way of release, whereas Father Folbèche's indignation never brought fire to his eye, nor pinched a nose swollen with taking snuff, nor contracted his thick lips. On the contrary, when he was astonished or when he was aroused, he closed his eyes, blew out his cheeks like a trombone-player, and exhaled a puff which thickened his lips still more.

So, with cheeks puffed out and lips heavily pouting, Father Folbèche moved towards Denis Boucher. Monsieur Folbèche was not pleased. He was concerned and looked almost unhappy. He advanced towards Denis, his right hand on his breast where his fingers kept turning round and round the little silver cross that hung about his neck. He lacked the traditional large paunch with which anti-clericals like to reproach the clergy. His shoulders were rather drooping, as though pulled down by his sober, neat cassock, which seemed to have become too heavy for him. Fortunately the pedestal was reassuring in its solidity. Monsieur Folbèche's boots aroused the envy of lovers of thick soles, and even the most obsequious churchwardens had never been able to persuade the shoemaker to give them soles similar to those of Monsieur Folbèche. Those who had attempted this had made, in the presence of their priest, a discreet comparison of feet. Invariably, the priest's soles exceeded theirs by a quarter of an inch, at least.

Denis Boucher anxiously watched the priest approach. He was ten steps from Denis and his imposing head, thrown back, serious and pale above the black garment, had never seemed so preoccupied by the importance of the priesthood, or so tormented by uncertainty—the uncertainty that is felt before some foe who seems immeasurable because he waits, his size still undiscernible in haze.

For some time Father Folbèche had been worrying over his parish. Had the epidemic which had been spreading through Christendom for twenty years contaminated the united family of his flock with the much dreaded microbe of communism?

His parish! It was a family of several thousand children, in keeping with the priest's dream, of which he had taken charge twenty-five years before. It seemed to him that he had adopted them and held them all in a cradle, even the old people. And he had reared them with the firm hand of a real father, sternly castigating them from the pulpit and, if necessary, telling them stories of bogymen either to put an end to their childish pranks, or to punish them for disobedience to their mother, Holy Church. Slowly the family had become united. The infancy of his parish, if it had brought him sleepless nights, had also been very sweet to his paternal love. That strict upbringing had not, in his opinion, prevented his family from prospering, from building a beautiful church, a handsome rectory, fine schools. But the dangerous and ungrateful period of adolescence and youth is always to be feared. How could he keep it in check? Today, didn't the family want to kick over the traces when the father wished for quiet? They considered him old-fashioned, and claimed the right to adapt catholic ideas and ideals to their own needs. They had read the newspapers, interpreted the Spanish War in their own way, discussed his sermons, criticized the contributions, based on their incomes, that the Father demanded. Even the churchwardens wanted to make decisions.

And now a Protestant pastor had just formed a baseball team in his parish. That was the last straw! Monsieur Folbèche, his shoulders sagging under the weight of these problems, stopped short in front of Denis. He came so near that Denis drew back a little. Not wanting to appear guilty, he fell into step with the priest, walking along heavily, stamping on the wooden boards of the pavement to lessen the embarrassing silence.

—Warm, isn't it, Father Folbèche? Don't you think so?

The old priest cast a doleful glance at the young man's bare arms and open collar. Denis was watching the thick mouth of this priest who had been responsible for his education, both religious and secular. His question had been thrown out like bait, and he waited for the reply, friendly or dictatorial, to lighten or contract his heart.

—I think you mistake your parish for a beach! Dress yourself properly and you'll be protected better from temptation.

Denis Boucher set his lips, checking the ironical reply that had risen to them. All the respect, all the fear, with which religious authority had saturated his childhood, were dispelled by that first sentence of Monsieur Folbèche. He was ready now to fight on even terms, to feign innocence, to fool this old moralizer in order to serve his purpose. He burst into guileless laughter.

—It's just youth, Monsieur le curé. Just youth. We feel lighter, like this. The sun burns our arms, our necks, and our faces. Then we seem to be better people. Today I feel as though I could give away everything I have.

The priest froze him once more with an almost contemptuous look.

—You haven't much.

For a moment, his blue eyes lit up. He was thinking of his fine, consecrated church which took up a whole block, of his spacious rectory, of his schools, of his whole parish. Then he looked gloomy again; he always did when he was tracking down the devil which dared to tempt him or threaten the unity of his family, but Monsieur Folbèche pursued him implacably into every corner. This time the Imp had taken shelter in the University.

—Are you still taking the summer courses? he inquired mildly.

The sigh of relief which Denis began to breathe out was interrupted by a counter-current of uneasiness. He glanced furtively at his companion's profile. Oh! no, he wasn't going to let himself be taken unawares by this enemy who wished to seem fatherly. He would remain on guard, cautiously continuing to fence, keeping a sharp watch. To cover up his slowness in replying he carelessly smoothed back a lock of hair which tickled his lids.

—The courses? I haven't missed one of them, Monsieur le curé. I work away steadily. And frankly, I rank with the best.

He gazed at the priest, then opened up with a burst of the enthusiasm of which his heart was so full that he could squander it, even in fun. His face was beaming and his eyes blazed with artless confidence.

—You know I'm in a hurry for you to give me my letter. I'm ready for newspaper work. Give it to me, and you'll see how my pen will slash the face of our enemies the English.

The youth raised an avenging arm. Monsieur Folbèche blew out his cheeks and the usual sound came from his puffed lips. The sound increased, then shaped itself into words:

—Tut, tut, my boy. You don't become a journalist like that. You have to be a reporter first. And then, even to be a reporter, it takes more than just commercial studies and a course in literature.

The features of the ambitious youth set with amazement and despair.

—But, Monsieur le curé, you told me . . .

The priest's voice cut him short:

—Above all, I told you not to degrade yourself with Protestant pastors by bringing them into my parish to sow the seed of schism. That's what I want to speak about, my boy.

Denis closed his eyes in order to see his way more clearly and muster up all his strength to meet the attack. What could he reply? How could he excuse himself? The idea that he was trapped scarcely crossed his mind. With his lids thus lowered he could almost see the feverish search for an answer going on inside his head. The priest was vibrating with too much righteous anger to be pacified by a poor excuse.

—Everything gets known, my boy, everything gets known. Fortunately, I've attended to it in time. Madame Plouffe has orders not to let that man into her house again. (His mouth drew down in a contemptuous pout.) Reverend Tom Brown! And English into the bargain! That kind slips into good Catholic families in a seemingly innocent way and puts doubt into their hearts. Then confusion follows. And it's you, a boy who wishes to be a reporter on *Christian Action*, who makes friends with a Protestant pastor and brings him into my parish to organize a baseball team. And you come to ask me for a letter of recommendation! Either you're a hypocrite who has deceived me or else you're a fool!

All the muscles of the youth stiffened under the insult. He ground his teeth together as though he were crushing sand. His pride boiled up into a storm of abuse which he held back between his clenched teeth. The priest's word 'fool' had pierced the blister of petty humiliations which had accumulated since his mind's awakening to the power of ecclesiastical rank and the injustices that proceed from it.

—I wonder what the Cardinal is thinking of, letting people who aren't Catholics go to the University!

Frightened to think he had made this remark in front of the youth, the priest glanced covertly at him to make sure he had not understood it. But the torrent of rage to which Denis was prey had, with the aid of the priest's remark, just uncovered the much-needed excuse. Denis beamed with sudden good humour. He was one of those lucky persons whom the discovery of a good joke fills with so much merriment that they forget all their anger. He turned towards Monsieur Folbèche a respectful face in which the eyes alone triumphed.

—Monsieur le curé, tell me all you think I've done wrong. Perhaps I deserve your reproaches but, I assure you, I think I've behaved well.

He gave the priest time to show surprise, then continued:

—Suppose I told you that I'm not the only one at the University to associate with the Reverend Tom Brown?

The priest shrugged and looked at him with pity.

—Of course. The Cardinal has certainly met Mackenzie King, but he hasn't brought him into my parish to start a club.

Because he controlled his smile, Denis Boucher felt himself the stronger, although he understood quite well that, for the moment, Monsieur Folbèche did not think he had sufficient judgment to be a reporter. Slyly, he watched for the priest's reaction:

—And suppose I added that these friends are priests, and some of the cleverest people in the University!

Monsieur Folbèche did not succeed very well in hiding his astonishment. Then he examined Denis's face as if he suspected a snare. The youth's gaze was still frank. Monsieur Folbèche rubbed his chin anxiously.

—What priests? What do they . . .

He broke off in time to avoid making another remark like the one about the Cardinal and the Prime Minister. He preferred to add it to those arguments that he used when he censured young priests for their too free and modern conduct. Meanwhile, he glossed over the fault of which he thought his fellow-priests at the University guilty.

—A priest, very well, he won't allow himself to be influenced, but humble workmen and baseball players . . .

Denis Boucher interrupted him with the same timorous finger which he had raised ten years before to ask a meaning in the catechism.

—But here's something you don't know. The Reverend Tom Brown is on the way to being converted.

—A conversion?

—Yes. It's going slowly. But it will soon come, I believe. He gave me to understand that the Catholic religion attracts him more and more. So, of course, I'm doing all I can. That's why I thought I acted rightly.

The priest's whole body stiffened defensively while the folds of his cassock seemed to turn to stone. The pastor's sudden appearance in the parish having taken on the proportions of a catastrophe in the eyes of the priest, all that that Protestant could say and do to minimize the consequences of his visits, even to letting people believe in his coming conversion, seemed to the cautious priest a Machiavellian ruse to outwit his vigilance.

Moreover, he did not think much of these conversions of educated men, warped as he was by the practice of preaching about, and collecting for, the evangelization of distant, ignorant, and miserable heathens. When one reaches the position of priest or pastor in a religious hierarchy, one isn't converted again without good reason, Monsieur Folbèche was thinking. He laughed, the little, mocking laugh of the man of experience.

—You really believed that he wants to be converted? I know the brand. (Interrupting himself, he pulled out his snuffbox and placed a pinch of snuff at the wing of each nostril where it was gathered up by a sniff.) Yes, we know those fellows. You young, inexperienced people are ready to believe anything. Take my word, he said, tapping Denis on the shoulder, they are up to all the dodges. They pat you on the back, tell you they are going to change their religion. They only mix with us so that they may be in a better position to study us and make fun of us in the United States afterwards. Undoubtedly it's like that with his visit. He's all sugar and honey in order to be on a good footing in your house.

Denis was listening attentively, now frowning, now shaking his head in denial.

—I tell you, he's sincere. He isn't satisfied only to refer to this idea before his close friends. If that's all he did, I should be on my guard. But he spends long evenings studying and meditating on our dogmas and he has important conferences with our best theologians at the Grand Séminaire.

Monsieur Folbèche took part so rarely in long arguments that whenever he saw himself about to be led into such an adventure without preparation he seemed suddenly to hear the urgent call of one of his numerous duties, and hurried away. He was a good priest, a true celibate, who needed forty-eight hours to prepare for a half-day's journey. At the time when he was sure of his authority over the members of his great parish family, it would have been child's play to reduce Denis to humiliating silence. But since the appearance of certain symptoms of disobedience, he was less sure of his infallibility. He pulled an enormous watch from the bottom of a deep pocket and nervously disentangled its chain from his rosary.

—Six o'clock! I must hurry. Anyway, as for your pastor, I don't want to see him here again, converted or not.

Denis Boucher was losing ground.

—Do tell me that I haven't done wrong. Tell me.

—I told you I didn't wish to see him in my parish.

The priest was moving off, rocking on his enormous soles. Denis opened his mouth two or three times, then almost shouted:

—Anyway, the pastor leaves Quebec next Saturday. All the same, I can't stop him from coming if he wants to.

The priest scarcely turned.

—Then all the worse for you.

The youth clenched his fists, then bent his head thoughtfully. The priest's threat of not giving him his letter of recommendation placed a difficult choice before him, to become a reporter or to continue to interest the Reverend Tom Brown. His tormented mind stopped at this last point of the difficulty.

Why was he so desirous of holding this American pastor's interest? Denis was too ambitious not to be surprised at himself for having aimed at a target that would bring him no benefit. Was this a luxury demanded by his pride, an unnecessary venture with which he was gratuitously overloading his powers already strained to the utmost by his frantic wish to succeed? Not at all. Nor was philanthropic sentiment his strong point. He frowned, refusing to accuse himself of a folly that could only waste his time. Entirely absorbed in his reflections, he walked slowly. Then his face clouded over with disillusionment. The search for an excuse with which he could satisfy himself led him to recall his argument with Monsieur Folbèche from the point at which he had pleaded Brown's pending conversion in order to justify his friendship with the pastor. Now that the priest was no longer there, the idea about conversion, which had become a truth for Denis by the end of his conversation, shed the short-lived foliage with which his imagination had garnished it, and withered; even the roots which had permitted the lie to blossom were dead. These roots were, precisely, a jumble of observations that Denis had made unconsciously in regard to the pastor. Engrossed by a constant wish to arouse Brown's interest, he had accumulated those observations without considering them. Now they were dancing before his eyes, as the dull glimmer of humiliation replaced the clear light of self-approval.

There were, to begin with, the circumstances which had made him acquainted with Tom Brown. As the pastor, on leaving the University, loitered to look at the old architecture of the houses, the winding streets, Denis, urged by an inexplicable wish to appear to be *somebody* to this stranger, had offered to show him even more picturesque places.

Perhaps this ironist wished to show strangers that his province, although separated from Europe by the ocean and isolated from the rest of America by speech and customs, offers such interesting sights that visitors are dumbfounded? Indeed, there was in him, as in all the Plouffes of his neighbourhood, a kind of wish to re-establish his province, so universally disparaged. But he was ashamed of this sentiment which he saw shared by those of his countrymen who found a refuge for their mediocrity in a fanatic provincialism.

Moreover, he was not a youth on whom institutions had heaped kindness, or one who, having an assured future because of influential friends and a well-to-do family, looks to the reputation of his countrymen as to an inheritance.

No, Denis Boucher, having finished his higher elementary studies, nurtured himself on the world of Maurice Barrès to console himself for seeing his fine talents refused by the secondary colleges because he had no money to spend on the studies required for a layman's career. Denis harboured no rancour against the social system which treated him as a person of no importance, good enough to become a skilled worker, at the very most. But he aimed higher. He saw in the position of reporter a springboard capable of bouncing him to success. Besides, in order to justify himself for expecting so much of the future, he needed esteem now. Since his own people did not appreciate him, he turned to strangers, and to interest them be brandished the weapon within his grasp: the quaintness of the Quebeckers. On a rash impulse he had taken the pastor to the Plouffe home, his heart throbbing with childish glee at the idea of showing Tom Brown some genuine specimens.

Denis Boucher, now at the foot of the Plouffe steps, bit his lip angrily. He hesitated to climb the first step because he was recalling the customary reaction of the pastor when Denis pointed out to him the ludicrous aspects of his town. The American would smile gently, as if amused, like a man who has seen a vaudeville show and admits that it was worth the money.

And the pastor carefully kept the distance that the white traveller from the southern United States maintains between himself and his negro guide on an expedition among the Zulus. What! Was it possible that Denis had used the role of guide in vain to prove that he was a man apart in this city of Quebec populated with such amusing characters? Momentarily he hated the pastor in order not to have to detest the real culprit: himself.

Then his face became serene. His decision was made. The letter of recommendation first. He was thinking of a way of persuading the pastor not to come back to the parish, when a hand was laid on his shoulder. It was Ovide.

—How are you, old chap?

His whole face beamed with happiness and triumph.

—Pretty well, Denis replied absent-mindedly.

—What! No women in your life yet, slowcoach?

He spoke with the satisfaction of a man who has just won a lottery. Hadn't Rita Toulouse, whom he had just left, put a drop of perfume on his coat, and hadn't she told him she could scarcely wait for the evening of operatic music next Thursday? Above all, hadn't she let him understand that she wished to make up for the bungled kiss?

Denis, shaking off his thoughts, looked at Ovide more closely.

—That makes me think of last night. You're right! She's very pretty. It's serious, her and you? What about the religious vocation?

Ovide smiled rakishly.

—Oh, love is a Bohemian lad. . . . Look here, Denis, you fathead, what would you do in my place?

—Probably the same thing, Denis admitted, smiling.

Ovide slapped him gaily on the shoulder.

—Come up then, for five minutes, I must tell you about it!

*　　*　　*　　*　　*　　*

71

—Life is good, eh, Denis old man! Especially tonight! Ovide exclaimed, a gleam of delight on his face. As they neared the kitchen, his thoughts went from it to the parlour in which, next Thursday, Rita Toulouse would be dazzled by his talent as a singer! He took off his coat hastily and walked towards the screen door, rolling up his sleeves, his hands ready to attack the water from the tap as if, by advancing the time usually given to his ritual of washing, he could earn a reduction in the number of hours separating him from the great occasion.

Denis followed him, smiling. By the time Ovide began rolling up his sleeves, Denis had already forgotten everything: the priest's threat; his fleeting hatred towards Tom Brown. Only curiosity filled his thoughts. Ovide in love! In a daze, he entered the house after the music-lover and stared at the half-obliterated pattern on the linoleum. How could Ovide, with his temperament, be in love with that hot little blonde! He had scarcely passed through the doorway when, suddenly, a sharp, angry voice startled him out of his reverie.

—Stop, you!

At first he saw two, large, motionless feet. Then his gaze anxiously travelled up Madame Plouffe's large person. Her back to the table, holding a handful of knives, head high, shoulders pulled back in the manner of round-shouldered persons who are trying to stand straight, she fixed the young man with such a cold, dignified look that he did not even notice her spectacles. He felt again the fright which had disabled him at the moment he had seen the priest coming out of the Plouffe house. How could he have forgotten! Then he felt annoyed. What right had this old woman to dictate to him? He pointed his finger at her, and spoke in a chiding tone:

—Now, now, Madame Plouffe, are you going to quarrel with me?

He turned towards Ovide and took a step in the direction of the living-room.

—Don't budge, I tell you! Stay near the door.

He drew back, cautiously, yielding, to avoid offence. She continued to stare at him. Ovide, bent over the sink, turned round in surprise. The soapy water dropped off his hands on to the floor.

—What's the matter, Mother?

Josephine made no reply. Silence is sometimes like a falling stone that becomes heavier as it descends. Guillaume, in the middle of the kitchen, was practising his gym exercises. He was carrying out the most difficult contortions without effort, with the coolness of a fish in water.

Madame Plouffe took off her spectacles and wiped them with her apron. Denis Boucher, at the mercy of this threatening silence, was wondering what attitude to take. He no longer recognized the Madame Plouffe of every day, slave of her children, unconscious tyrant to her husband, kind Madame Plouffe. She said:

—Monsieur Denis Boucher, the priest has ordered you not to bring the Protestant pastor into the parish again. If you do, I can't receive you in my house any more.

She breathed as if she had just finished a long race. Denis was uncertain whether to suppress his smile or his astonishment.

—But, Madame Plouffe, why do you speak so formally to me?

—Don't try any tricks. Look me straight in the eye and tell me you're going to stop this Protestant from coming back. If it's yes, stay; this is your home, as before; if it's no, I don't know you, and go away!

She put her hands behind her and, her neck distended, waited with dignity. Denis's first impulse was to laugh loudly at this pompous injunction from Josephine. But Ovide, the head of the house, instead of intervening, seemed surprised and dismayed.

—What, Mother! Does the priest know already that the pastor has been here?

—Yes, I've done my duty. I've confessed. I'll tell you all about it later.

Glancing briefly at Madame Plouffe, Denis saw that she was in earnest and decided to put a damper on his impatience. The old woman, plump, flabby, and wrinkled, yellow from liver trouble and worn out from prolonged motherhood, swelled up all at once under the influence of an imperious will, like a leather bottle empty for years that is suddenly filled with fresh water. With a blind fatalism which was not even resignation, Madame Plouffe had submitted without a murmur, with scarcely a look of annoyance, to her trials: her miscarriages, her drunken husband, her wayward children. For forty years she had been going to and fro in her kitchen preparing the meals, washing the dishes, eating whatever the children did not want. And this domain, which she had scrubbed and cleaned so often, which ought to have been hers by every right, was removed piece by piece as the children grew older. Ovide said: 'My gramophone, my records, my piano, my singing, my quiet.' He filled the whole house with elaborate songs that Madame Plouffe did not understand, and before which her own ballads had to yield. Fearful of displeasing Ovide, she always sang her lullabies and unintelligible chants under her breath. The large cabinet was given over to Napoleon's albums. She only went into the boys' bedrooms to make the beds and to dust. Each of them had a locked chest in which to keep his treasures. The big rocking-chair in the kitchen was reserved for Théophile, who had also annexed the commode in the nuptial bedroom for his half-filled pipes. And Cécile, on pretext of being younger than her mother, had appropriated the dressing-table and the large oval mirror. Finally, yesterday evening, Napoleon, loaded with trophies, had entered the parlour with a triumphal step, and had come out with two beautiful ferns, cherished by Madame Plouffe, which he placed on the kitchen floor. His trophies had taken the place of the ferns on the piano and in the window.

It was as normal for Josephine Plouffe to submit to this thankless life as to pull out a loose tooth with a piece of string. Her sole pastime was to read serial stories with insatiable voracity, pitying the least misfortunes of the aristocratic heroines and going into raptures over their nobility of character. She had reread certain of the serials five or six times, at intervals of a few months or years, solemnly deriving new pleasure every time. She could remember neither persons nor books—nothing, except her knives and forks. She had once had a quarrel with her sister over a butter-knife which she identified as hers. The only heroine that Madame Plouffe could call to mind was Joan of Arc, whom she admired humbly.

And now, all of a sudden, here was an opportunity for heroism. She was bowled over by it, and she quivered with the fervour of a brave man preparing to face the battlefield for the first time. The Lord, through the voice of Father Folbèche, had commanded her to drive the Protestant Tom Brown out of her house and out of the parish, even as he had charged Joan of Arc to drive the English out of France.

Denis, ill at ease before this obstinate intolerance, preferred to get round it.

—Madame Plouffe, said he gently, you don't know me very well. You're judging me too quickly. I'll obey the priest. I'll fix things up so that the pastor doesn't come back. Will that satisfy you?

Josephine's whole body relaxed, and a smile that made her almost pretty revealed her two loose teeth, expressly saved to stretch and tease her chewing-gum.

—Well then, sit down at the table, Denis. You're eating with us.

She went back to the stove. Guillaume stopped his exercises and said placidly:

—Oh well, no Pastor Brown, no club. Our game on Friday evening against the *Canadiens* is all washed up. You always put a spoke in the wheel, Mama.

The sound of the door interrupted the lofty reply that Josephine was preparing to make. It was Napoleon. His features ready to beam with good humour, he glanced, birdlike, at the furniture to see which piece might be holding the precious package he had thought about all day long. Disappointed, he went towards his mother.

—Ma! Hasn't he brought the photographs?

—Who do you mean? Josephine asked, carefully preparing Ovide's beefsteak.

—Abbé Brown, of course. Supposed to come early this evening. Sure to be here any moment, though.

He shook his head importantly.

—A long job, pictures like those.

He sat down, a smile hovering on his lips, his eyes blinking with his passionate pleasure in photography. Ovide's beefsteak had fallen back into the frying-pan, spattering the hot butter over Josephine's apron. A duty stronger than Ovide's steak was calling her. Denis followed Madame Plouffe's pantomime eagerly. She glanced cautiously at Ovide as she took the frying-pan off the fire.

—What did you say just now, boy? Say it again. I want to hear it.

Still influenced by maternal reprimands of long ago, Napoleon shrank.

—The pictures, Ma, he mumbled. Monsieur Brown took our championship photographs last night. He's going to bring them.

—There's no question of bringing pictures. The Protestant won't ever come into my house again, or even into my parish. The priest and I have chased him away.

Napoleon's dismayed glance shuttled from his mother to Denis, who said nothing. The photo collector was fighting despair which already showed in his face and made his lips tremble. Satisfied with her action, Josephine took out her gum and struck the final blow:

—And I hope we've heard the last of that.

—My pictures! My pictures! Napoleon wailed. And our game

on Friday with the *Canadiens*. Guillaume would have beaten Stan Labrie, I'm sure.

Whenever he was overcome by grief, Napoleon Plouffe blew his nose, for he never managed to cry. He took out his chequered handkerchief. He was just going to bury his face in it when all at once something extraordinary happened. With a curt gesture, Napoleon stuffed his handkerchief back in his pocket. Every bit of authority that was rightfully his as the eldest son, and which he had not exercised since the day he had defended his place at the end of the table, filled his voice, his eyes, his movements, his whole body. He was discovering his privileges, just as his mother had discovered her duty. He leapt up with surprising ferocity:

—I'm sick of being bossed! Abbé Brown is going to bring me my pictures, I tell you. The priest has nothing to do with my pictures. He sure has his own put up in people's houses! Viourge de Viourge! (Since the rings championship Napoleon used this swear-word exclusively.)

Before a petrified Madame Plouffe, an astounded Ovide, a flabbergasted and delighted Denis, a quiet, calm Guillaume, a father who, nose glued to the screen door, was smiling with satisfaction to see himself avenged for his wife's domestic tyranny by his eldest son, the Napoleon of the lightning decision hurried across the room with jerky steps. Passing near the stove he spat into the fire and looked at the clock.

—It won't be long until he comes. And besides that, we are going to play the *Canadiens*!

He shot a glance at everybody which meant: 'That's that!' He took his mother's silence for consent. His face lost its glaring mask as quickly as it had been covered by it. His low forehead cleared again, his small eyes regained their vague expression, and his mouth prepared to smile pleasantly as he walked to the parlour to look at his cups before supper.

A sob made him turn around. When he saw his mother hiding her face in her apron, he stopped, dismayed, his eyes wildly searching for the culprit responsible for this grief, so little accustomed was he to giving pain to others. When he saw all eyes turned on him he smiled in confusion, failing to realize his responsibility and to take the proper attitude. Then he paled. Like a villain suddenly unmasked, Napoleon stepped back, his arms wide, his fingers clutching at the wall. Between sobs, Madame Plouffe was saying:

—Heartless child! Heartless child!

Her assumed heroism had been unable to resist the commanding tones of her son, this man of thirty-two who out of his childhood of obedience and diffidence loomed up suddenly to impose his authority in the paternal household. And Ovide, the younger, disagreeably surprised by this new aspect of his elder brother, supported his mother, whom he alone had ordered about till now, against this tramp of a Napoleon who had grown up with the tenderness of a Jacob and unexpectedly shown the sternness of an Esau claiming his mess of pottage. Ovide ranted with the emphasis of an honest man who reprimands a captured bandit:

—The rings championship seems to have turned your head, brother. Aren't you ashamed to make your mother cry? It's disgusting!

But Napoleon was too overcome to listen to this reproach. He had sprung towards his mother. Not daring, from modesty, to put his arm around her, he patted her on the back, held her shoulders to stop them from heaving, and tried to lift her hands and her apron from her face; he put his fingers over her eyes, attempting to dress the wound that he had given her. So excitable people treat a child that chokes while eating: they try to close his mouth. Napoleon spoke quickly as if he wished, by consoling her, to outstrip his mother's pain and leave it behind.

—Now! Now! Don't cry, Mama. Look at me. You know it's the pictures that got me all worked up. Listen, I'm speaking more quietly now. But for goodness' sake stop that!

—No, let me alone, heartless creature! Josephine sobbed

78

harder than ever, trying to ward off the feverish attentions of Napoleon.

Sweat appeared on the collector's forehead. In his nervousness he shook his mother roughly.

—Stop, I tell you. If you like, I'll give you the little cup to put your sugar in. But don't cry any more. It's all right. The pastor won't come into the house again. I'll meet him outside.

Josephine began to be appeased.

—You're going to tell him not to come back again?

Ovide, who had shrugged his shoulders at this whole scene, intervened:

—Listen, Mother. This Protestant is leaving next Saturday. So let him organize his baseball team. It's just about time that Stan Labrie was beaten by a youngster like Guillaume.

—Oh, you! Since you were wicked enough to give up your vocation, I'm not surprised you favour the Protestant.

She had grumbled feebly because her heroine's role was beginning to tire her. Muttering, she returned to her kitchen tasks, leaving to the others the duty of safeguarding Catholicism. Théophile, seeing that the storm was over, came in. As the balance of power was momentarily upset he took advantage of the general confusion to assume the mantle of authority he had worn on his wedding day, and ordered in a rough tone:

—That's enough, that's enough, all of you! Sit down at the table! Then we can eat.

—That's right, start eating, and I'll join you in a few minutes, Ovide called, straightening his tie. Mother, take my steak off the fire.

Ovide and Denis went into the parlour and closed the door behind them. The six o'clock sun filtered into the room through the cracks in the blinds, spreading fan-like in the gloom. One of the bright beams made the silver of the trophies on the piano sparkle and, now and again, glinted on a handle, a pedestal, or the curve of a cup. Ovide sank on to the big covered sofa, above which there hung a large picture of Théophile perched on his racing bicycle. He spread his hands over his eyes, and a beam of sunlight X-rayed the skeleton of his thin fingers.

— You shouldn't have brought that Protestant here, he said. You see how much trouble it's made. If only he'd been a musician!

— Never mind! Denis said impatiently. It's complicated enough already. Tell me about Rita.

Ovide jumped up and gaily struck C sharp on the piano with his forefinger.

— To begin with, I had noticed that she often smiled at me . . .

CHAPTER SIX

THE Thursday evening which was to be the turning-point in Ovide's life arrived.

—Eight o'clock! he murmured.

He was arranging the chairs, humming the opera airs which presently he would be singing. At last Rita Toulouse should discover her road to Damascus: beauty would be revealed and true greatness discovered.

The enthusiastic shouts of a crowd were reaching the house in gusts. Madame Plouffe, standing behind the curtains and stepping back from time to time, seemed to be on the look-out for someone.

—If only Father Folbèche doesn't come, she said. I'd sooner be in Montreal than that! It's all Napoleon's fault.

The truth was that neither the priest nor Madame Plouffe nor Denis had been able to stop the craze. As soon as the news had got round, the parish had been seized with baseball fever. An American promoter was organizing a team to see how good Guillaume was, and this team was going to challenge the famous *Canadien* Club. In no time at all the Reverend Tom Brown had become an idol, for people are prouder of the legends they create than of those which are forced upon them, and for this reason admire their champions more than their great men. And now, at last, the whole parish hoped to have a parish champion to worship.

—There's one thing I wanted to ask you, Mama, Ovide said anxiously. When you went to confession, did you mention Rita Toulouse?

—I may have. Yes, I think I did, she stammered.

Ovide raised his arms in a sudden fit of temper.

—You can warn Guillaume, Napoleon, and Cécile to keep quiet during the party tonight. They're lucky to be asked into the parlour at all. Ten past eight! And they're still fooling around on the field. They needn't think they're going to insult *me* by coming in after the concert's begun, like the snobs at the Palais Montcalm. I'll go and get them.

He dashed down the steps and caught sight of the priest who, stationed at the edge of the field, hands behind him and rocking back and forth on the soles of his shoes, was surveying the distant crowd of his parishioners in the act of betraying him.

Ovide tried to retreat, but the priest had seen him.

—Ovide!

The music-lover turned pale. Without a doubt, the priest intended to reproach him for giving up his idea of a religious vocation.

—I'll be back presently, Father. It's something very urgent.

Ovide started to run towards the playing field. The priest smiled pityingly. Even Ovide was forsaking him. All at once the smile froze on his lips. Denis Boucher was approaching.

—I couldn't stop that, Father Folbèche.

Denis pointed apologetically to the field. The priest eyed him up and down scornfully.

—So! It's you! You still have the impudence to face me!

—I want to explain to you.

—There's nothing to explain. The mischief is done, and it's your fault.

The young man was obviously most distressed.

—I know very well that you will never write the letter for me now.

—How do you even dare think of it? You're doing harm to the Church. And besides, I haven't seen anything in the papers to say that your pastor was becoming a convert!

Denis wiped imaginary sweat from his forehead and stared at

the priest's enormous boots without seeing the cars that whizzed past them.

—You're mistaken, Father, I tell you, I've done all I can to keep him from coming back here. Ask Madame Plouffe if I haven't. It's Napoleon who has made a mess of everything. You know what he's like. Crazy about sport. It was Napoleon who took on the job of organizing the team. He even goes to call for the pastor at his hotel.

—Of course, you're a poor, innocent lamb! the priest replied, shrugging his shoulders.

The youth clutched at his arm pleadingly.

—I admit I am the most responsible. But I'm young and ought to be forgiven. One of the reasons I brought the pastor here, for that matter, was to show him one of the finest parishes in the diocese.

He had touched the right chord. Father Folbèche gazed at Denis with an intensity which he tried to mask under a stern and aloof countenance. Young Denis couldn't be trying to flatter him. He, an experienced priest, was too practised in foiling the craftiest tricks of the devil; he ought to know, by this time, how to guard against professional deformation. Denis Boucher was right. Father Folbèche was head of one of the finest parishes in the world. No Protestant pastor could boast of having one as good. He coughed slightly to repress his satisfaction.

—Well, I've other fish to fry. The mischief is done. We'll talk no more about it.

—But what if I made up for it? Suppose I make you as popular as the Reverend Tom Brown?

The priest pulled at a hair in his nose and his long, scrutinizing gaze rested on Denis.

—Are you hinting that I'm not popular with my parishioners?

The youth hesitated, bit his lips, then looked straight at the priest.

—No, you are, but it's up to you to continue to be.

—What do you mean?

—I think this craze for a Protestant pastor in the heart of your parish is a real break for you. Surely you must see what it means: the preference your parishioners show for American sports is as great as the distance that separates them, more and more, from our priests.

—Tut, tut, tut, my boy! It's time you learned that the Church is in a better condition than ever, the priest retorted in a haughty manner.

Denis took a long breath and launched the final blow:

—Perhaps, but our priests don't join in our games. They should lead and encourage them instead of ignoring them. Then you'd see your parishioners carry *you* in triumph, and not bother about pastors any more.

The priest's eyelashes fluttered. A roar of shouts reached them from the playing field as though to emphasize Denis's words. Father Folbèche remained silent. Was the young puppy right?

—I know that religious matters occupy all your thoughts, Denis continued, encouraged by the priest's worried air. But remember the Jews in the wilderness. While Moses was conversing with Jehovah they were building a golden calf. Today your parishioners' golden calf is baseball. Don't leave them to their own devices.

Father Folbèche set his jaws to suppress the emotion stirred up in his heart by Denis's words. The puppy had just laid bare the cancer that was tormenting his old age. The parishioners were deserting their Father and raising up strange, Protestant gods.

A weary, painful sadness seemed to benumb the old man. He had watched over a multitude of souls, step by step, for thirty years, only to have himself advised to play baseball in order to bring them back to his side. A complaint escaped him:

—I'm too old to play baseball!

Denis, his muscles tense and his fists clenched, scarcely

breathed. Was he going to succeed with an almost impossible scheme?

—It's very sad to see a superior mind like yours obliged to lower itself to that of the crowd in order to hold their affection. But you have to face the facts. It's this childish American mania for sports. It's caught up with us!

—I'll *never* take up baseball.

—That's not the point, Father Folbèche. You have to humour children. You stand by me, and I'll make you so popular your parishioners won't give another thought to the pastor.

A responsive note was again touched. Father Folbèche felt a sudden affection for this boy whose precocious wisdom he had underestimated. Indeed, why shouldn't he do better than Moses? He looked severely over his spectacles.

—Come to the rectory, then, if you wish to talk seriously. But see that you're not up to any nonsense or you'll pay for it.

—Oh no! I'm too fond of you for that, Father.

Denis was jubilant. Now his future was assured.

They walked along together rapidly and soon arrived at the iron fence surrounding the flower.beds of the parsonage, in which the flowers were planted, here in a rectangle, there in a circle, and yonder in a star. A fine spray from the automatic sprinkler threw up rainbows and danced in the evening light. Behind the pollarded poplars whose damp leaves twirled gently, beyond patterned flower-beds bathed in the continual shower, the trellis encircling the veranda of the presbytery caught the rays of the setting sun. Three silhouettes rocked to and fro behind the lattice, through which filtered blue pipe-smoke. Cassocks threw green shadows, and the creaking of chairs answered the idle cheeping of sparrows.

*   *   *   *   *   *

Half an hour later the sky grew overcast. Heavy clouds rolled up, slowly massing into a stormy backdrop. The hasty banging of windows could be heard, and the anxious voices of women who were calling their children in. The crowd was deserting the playing field. Cars whirled along, pursued by growls of distant thunder. The dusk thickened into darkness, and a silence filled with expectation spread over the district. The town seemed to be waiting for the curtain to rise on the performance of *Pagliacci*.

Guillaume opened the door for his yellow cat, which had crouched under the streetcar bench. Madame Plouffe nervously turned on the switch. A blinding light flooded the kitchen; the electric bulbs were shining more brightly than usual. Ovide, who was in the parlour with his guests, poked his head into the kitchen.

—We're ready, you can come in! And once more, *keep quiet*!

The Plouffe family leapt up, startled. The fateful moment for going into the parlour was at hand, and they were seized with a fear like that of falling into a suddenly yawning pit. But it was too late to retreat now. Théophile shook out his pipe and Josephine straightened Guillaume's tie, while he clasped his cat close to his chest.

—Try to behave like a man, Guillaume. Show Mademoiselle Toulouse she has come into a family of 'gentlemen'. Be a credit to Ovide, you know.

—O.K., Ma, Guillaume promised. I've already seen this dame. Don't worry. I'm not going to kiss her.

He jerked from Josephine's hands and, with a light bound, sprang at Théophile, whose back was turned, and planted a resounding kiss on the nape of his neck. Josephine, with dignity, seized the arm of her angry husband.

—Come on in.

Thèophile cautiously refused to proceed until Guillaume was in front of him. Cècile, her head crowned with a wreath of pansies, and dressed in purple, took the hand of Onésime Ménard, who was wearing a streetcar-conductor's uniform from which the brass buttons had been removed. Napoleon, in his nervousness, executed a few steps characteristic of a boxer in training and placed himself at the tail-end of the procession. The company began to walk towards the parlour. On the kitchen table two enormous bottles of soda water remained as though on guard.

Ovide closed the door carefully behind his family. His hair, combed into a pompadour, shone under the dim light, for he had drawn the blinds and lit a single lamp as though this were a musical conspiracy. He planted himself in the middle of the parlour and opened his thin arms, indicating the family group, standing petrified in the doorway, to three silhouettes who sprang up from the sofa on which they had been ensconced.

—Mama, Papa, I don't have to introduce Bérangère and François Thibodeau. You're old acquaintances.

The brother and sister responded almost simultaneously.

—We come here often enough to deafen you with our music!

—Don't say that, François. You play better than a player-piano. And you sing like an angel, Bérangère. And more than that, you're an actress! Josephine added, crossing her hands under her chin ecstatically.

Rita Toulouse, during these civilities, had emerged from the shadow and come forward slowly, conscious of the heroine's role which was hers for this evening. She blushed with a charming shyness as Guillaume persisted in staring at her. The high heels of her red shoes made her look taller; she wore a white dress and a celluloid belt which accentuated her hips and bosom. Above the low, triangular neckline her plump neck looked more slender, giving her head a saucily pretty carriage.

—And Mademoiselle Rita Toulouse, whom I've told you so much about, Ovide articulated, with closed eyes, his voice almost toneless from the painful thudding of his heart.

—Pleased to meet you, Madame Plouffe. You must be real proud to be Guillaume's mother.

Josephine stammered, for she had caught her tongue between her loosened teeth while pursing her lips in order to speak in a refined way.

87

—It's a pleasure to know a ladylike girl like you. Ovide has good taste, eh what, Mademoiselle Rita? (Ovide made a grimace). As for Guillaume, we're so used to him being good at sports, we think nothing of it. He's our baby, you know. We're very fond of him, she added, glancing affectionately at Guillaume.

—Their father was a champion before *them*, Mademoiselle, Théophile interrupted, running his trembling hand through his few hairs.

—Monsieur Plouffe! Guillaume looks so much like you!

Rita touched the old fingers lightly and turned gracefully towards Onésime Ménard, standing very straight at attention, his eyes staring ahead as though driving his streetcar through heavy traffic.

—Monsieur Onésime Ménard and my sister Cécile, Ovide recited rapidly.

—Your husband? the girl inquired.

—Why no, it's Onésime! Me, I work! Cécile stammered, bowled over by this question which fell into her life like a stone into a pond.

Astonishment filled her at the thought of man and wife. She examined Onésime from head to foot, then blushed and tilted her head, crowned with its garland of pansies. She gazed at Rita Toulouse and, for lack of something to say, bit her lower lip and gave little nods of her head.

Napoleon had been trying to attract the attention of the guests to his trophies. Were they going to speak about them? But he saw that something more serious required his vigilance. It would never do to let Rita go too near the champion Guillaume.

Ovide assigned a place to each person: to Monsieur and Madame Plouffe and Napoleon, the chesterfield (from which Madame Plouffe had removed the slip-cover and which she had been mechanically examining for cleanliness ever since she entered the room), two chairs to Cécile and Onésime, and the small armchair to Rita Toulouse.

—Go and get a chair, Guillaume, Ovide commanded.

Josephine made a move towards the kitchen, but Rita exclaimed:

—Please don't bother! Guillaume can sit on the arm of my chair.

Watching with a tense expression, Madame Plouffe seemed to be trying to ease the strain of Guillaume's weight as he smilingly took the seat to which he was invited, glancing sideways as he did so at the pointed 'V' of Rita's low-cut dress. Napoleon stood up abruptly.

—Come and sit on my knee, Guillaume. That arm isn't strong enough.

—That's what you think! I paid one hundred and fifty dollars for that suite, Théophile said good-naturedly, still glowing from Rita's remark that Guillaume resembled him.

Ovide exchanged a look with Rita and, happy in his approval of her, smiled the indulgent smile of the opera-lover.

—All right, you can stay there.

—Good. Can we begin now? demanded Bérangère, whose sharp face appeared tormented when the least thing went wrong.

For some years she had belonged to an amateur theatrical group which entrusted the sad, emotional or serious roles to her. But since her brother had discovered her tiny thread of a voice she dreamed only of operas—those high-class melodramas for tragic temperaments.

Ovide, standing in the middle of the room, rubbed his hands. With eyes half-closed he was trying to gauge just how much his audience wanted to hear him.

—I've been thinking it over, he said. Perhaps you'd rather hear recordings of *Pagliacci* sung by great artists. I'm not in very good voice.

—Why, Ovide! François Thibodeau protested, his face falling with disappointment.

Bérangère had turned around with a suppressed vehemence

that tossed her mass of black hair from one shoulder to the other.

—I've missed a rehearsal to come here this evening. Try any how; you'll see, your voice will soon be just as good as usual.

—Come, come, Vide, his mother scolded. You're always the same, too modest to live. Come on now, sing!

Rita joined in the persuasion. She did not want to return to the factory the following day with an empty bag. She had promised her pals a tasty report on Ovide as a singer.

—You're sure? You're really interested? All right, I'll sing.

They applauded him loudly. Bérangère shrugged with vexation because Ovide attached more importance to the whims of the blonde hussy than to those of a well-known actress. François Thibodeau's pleasure was the most sincere. He shook hands fervently with the beaming Ovide.

—You're always the same, you old Richard Wagner. Don't worry, you'll be magnificent, as usual. And I'm with you, you know.

—Thanks, old Franz.

Franz sat down on the piano bench and hastily opened the instrument. François was a commercial traveller for chewing-gum and, like Ovide, for whom he cherished a friendship which he often compared to that of Liszt for Wagner, he spent all his money on records and on the best concert seats. His ear was extraordinary, for although he had never learnt the theory of music, or piano technique, he could play the most difficult compositions with an astonishing verve after hearing them only once. Puny, timid, and lacking self-confidence, he represented the type to whom life has not afforded the opportunity of development through work and study. The working class swarms with these latent talents. You see people like this, here and there, tied to mediocre jobs, which they fill mechanically, lost in a dream that never comes true. They pursue it in all directions, and are destroyed in the end by a reason for living that was beyond their grasp.

François opened the score of *Pagliacci* and his long hands pressed back the rebellious sheets as carefully as though his life depended on it. The five black lines sown with quavers and semi-quavers fascinated him, and he knew them so well by ear that he could imagine he was reading them. Moreover, these pages of music made his listeners more attentive. His nimble fingers rippled over the keys in a vague and sentimental improvisation which soon resolved itself into the *Valse Brillante* of Chopin.

Ovide dropped the pile of librettos and faced his audience, holding a hand-written sheet. When the murmur of conversation stopped he opened his mouth solemnly:

—Mademoiselle Toulouse, and everybody. First of all I ask you to observe the most religious silence during the prologue to *Pagliacci* which I am going to try to sing to you. You all know this opera in two acts by Ruggiero Leoncavallo, performed for the first time in Milan on 21 May 1892, and in the United States on 15 June 1893, at the Metropolitan. (He glanced at Rita with the look of a superior being who reveals himself.) The first scene of the opera . . .

While he was explaining the chief incidents of this popular drama, Rita's hand was idly stroking the cat which purred as Guillaume caressed it. The girl's face, turned towards Ovide, feigned an ardent interest. She even went so far as to protest

—A man doesn't kill his wife because she loves another man!

Ovide shook his head mysteriously as if to say: 'Wait till you're older, mademoiselle, and then you'll see that great love can lead to murder.' Monsieur Plouffe, who had known all about this story long before Ovide was born and was no longer touched by the tragedy, looked at Rita with satisfaction. After hesitating for a long time, he pointed to the picture on the wall and cut in:

—Mademoiselle Toulouse! Do you see the cyclist on the wall? Do you recognize him? That's me!

Ovide had more attentive listeners. Napoleon, who had never been allowed to attend Ovide's musical evenings, was sitting on the extreme edge of the chesterfield, his hands flat on his bent knees, his body rigid, and his eyes round with incredulous fear.

—He doesn't kill her really?

—Pagliacci stabs Columbine till she's dead, Ovide snapped impatiently.

—That's frightful! Cécile stammered, very pale, moving nearer to Onésime Ménard who was shrugging and muttering to himself:

—That's an old-country story. It happened long ago. People killed each other a lot in those days. Here in the city, there's an average of two people killed every year by streetcars.

And he leaned back in his chair so that its two front legs were lifted from the floor. Madame Plouffe looked pityingly at these poor children who hadn't seen much.

—That's nothing! St. Joan killed so many Englishmen you couldn't count 'em.

—If you take war, it's not the same thing, Théophile interrupted, proud of his discrimination. Don't think that the Kaiser's soldiers didn't kill plenty in 1914.

—We're talking about opera now, Ovide said irritably. Can't we have silence?

Standing squarely in the middle of the room, his arms crossed like a miniature Mephistopheles, he shut with a look all the mouths that seemed about to open.

—I had thought of singing in Italian. But you don't understand it. Bérangère will sing Columbine's role. I'm the clown, Canio. We'll begin in a moment.

He ran to the green drapery folded back along each wall and pulled it, cutting the room in two and concealing Bérangère. Then he leaned over the pianist and whispered in his ear:

—That will be all right for the G in the prologue. But play the 'Sobs' a tone lower. If I can't get it easily, help me.

François agreed with an understanding nod. He often had to sing contralto parts because he was a lyric tenor. Ovide, having tried to determine just how much his stage-setting had impressed Rita, tiptoed behind the curtain.

While waiting for the traditional three knocks the audience were staring at the curtain ready to see it slide along its rod with a jingling of copper rings. Only François had his back turned. Facing the piano, he quivered with anticipation. There was a loud clap of thunder, very near. With a frightened movement Rita Toulouse cowered against Guillaume's hip. This gesture released a current of family solidarity by which all were carried away, because they saw in Rita's impulsive move towards Guillaume the first sign of tender confidence shown by a future sister-in-law to her future brother-in-law. Madame Plouffe, her eyes moist with approval, her face filled with delight at rediscovering a sentiment she had forgotten, seized the arm of a gently grumbling Théophile and pressed it against her. To Onésime Ménard, whose right hand was fiddling with pennies in the bottom of his pocket, Cécile repeated with ever-increasing astonishment:

— She thought you were my husband! She thought you were my husband!

Napoleon's troubled little eyes, like drops ready to fall, tried to catch up with all that was happening. He looked at Onésime, whose thigh was brushing Cécile's; calmly he took note of Rita's shoulder which was touching Guillaume's elbow; he looked very carefully at the entwined hands of his father and mother, to convince himself he was not dreaming. He forgot his trophies, and thought no longer of the possible danger presented by the coming of a woman into the life of a champion like Guillaume. In the grip of profound reflection, he wedged himself back into the sofa, and, his head between his hands, began to think laboriously about women.

Then three sharp blows on the floor from Ovide's foot cut through the stifling heat. The figures silhouetted in the diffused light stiffened again, abandoning their sentimental unconstraint. The piano resounded under the signal to begin, given vigorously by François Thibodeau. The trophies trembled, tinkled, and wavered under Napoleon's anxious eyes. The curtains rippled as first the nose, then the whole simpering face of Ovide pushed through:

Good day! It's I!

—Good day, Vide, Guillaume said softly.

Ovide did not hear this witticism, being too occupied in successfully making a dramatic entrance. Arms extended, hair ruffled by the curtain, the veins in his neck a little swollen, he burst out in a rich, strong baritone, astonishing in such a puny man:

> *Ladies and gentlemen.*
> *I pray you, hear, why alone I appear,*
> *I am the Prologue!*
> *Our author loves the custom of a prologue to his story,*
> *And as he would revive for you the ancient glory,*
> *He sends me before you to speak the prologue!*

The singer, exhausted by his effort, crossed his hands over his diaphragm and with pinched lips and closed eyes drew a long breath. Napoleon, thinking he had finished, applauded madly. Ovide interrupted his breathing and looked angrily at him. Ah! How he regretted inviting his family! These Philistines were ruining his concert and making his task of converting Rita Toulouse to the beauty of opera cruelly difficult. An attack of stage fright, mixed with despair, suddenly seized him. What an atmosphere! The cups wobbled on the piano, enormous bunches of roses bloomed on the wallpaper, from the kitchen came the odour of fresh strawberry jam. His father was playing with his shirt buttons, his mother was looking at him ecstatically, Napoleon was staring at him with round, foolish eyes, Cécile was casting a fond look at the sleepy Onésime, Guillaume was watching his toes wriggling in his shoes, and Rita, he felt, was listening with cold curiosity.

The music drawn forth by François Thibodeau's fingers gathered Ovide's pain and, like a prism, broke it up; his face cracked into a grimace which showed that tears were not far away. His voice broke, as it burst forth again:

> *But not to prate, as once of old,*
> *That the tears of the actor are false, unreal,*
> *That his sighs and cries, and the pain that is told,*
> *—He has no heart to feel!*
> *No! No! Our author tonight a chapter will borrow,*
> *From life with its laughter and sorrow.*
> *Is not the actor a man with a heart like you?*
> *So 'tis for men that our author has written,*
> *And the story he tells you is—true!*

Madame Plouffe wiped away a tear. She was used to a look of authority on Ovide's face, and this very different expression affected her profoundly. Théophile, who for a long time had accepted a passive role in family matters, and knew little of his children's interests, observed Ovide's features furtively from beneath his bushy eyebrows. He was trying to understand. The singer brought his lines to a close with a generous display of dramatic tremolo:

> *Come then! Ring up the curtain!*

Bent and breathless, Ovide disappeared through the curtain. Papa Théophile started the applause, which continued for a long time. Rita, her cheeks swollen with an irresistible desire to laugh, clapped her hands frenziedly in order to repress it. What a story she would have to tell at the factory! But if the prospect of a savoury account of Ovide's quaintness aroused her vanity, her strategic designs on Guillaume now made greater claims on the energy that she had been using to remain serious in face of

Ovide's affectations. It had just occurred to her that the champion Guillaume could serve as bait to attract the interest of the phlegmatic Stan Labrie towards herself. So, when Ovide timidly reopened the curtain to thank the audience, the girl half-rose from her chair, applauding vigorously. Delight took the place of the weary sadness in the singer's face.

—Did you like it as much as that? he asked, confused and enraptured.

—Oh! Yes! It's beautiful! Sing some more!

Rita sprang in front of Ovide and entreated him, before the eyes of a Madame Plouffe now bursting with pride. The girl's enthusiasm was all it took for the whole audience to clamour for him in chorus. But Ovide saw and listened only to Rita Toulouse. He'd been able to do it, after all! She was dazzled by the beauty of opera! What lofty soul wouldn't be?

—Didn't I tell you how beautiful it was?

The fever of success took hold of Ovide with the same intensity as the discouragement which had crushed him a few minutes before. Ovide, so sensitive to ridicule except where opera was concerned, forgot the atmosphere of the parlour and imagined himself a great singer on a famous stage. He loved this art with so much fervour that he believed himself to be one of its most worthy servants; so much so, that his actions appeared to him to be pulsating with beauty when others saw only comic gestures and grimaces. Ovide had no more doubts. Rita Toulouse was conquered, and opera reigned supreme.

What a great day in his life! Ovide walked from the kitchen to the piano three times, looking for something he could not see. Then, before disappearing into the kitchen for the last time, he bent over Rita, who had sat down beside Guillaume again, and whispered in her ear:

—Now, Rita dear, I'm going to dress like a clown for the rest of it.

His enthusiasm blinded him. Everything must serve the turn

of opera. The most comical trappings looked to him like the garb of tragedy.

During Ovide's brief absence a burst of thunder gave the whole district a resounding slap. The electric light bulbs blinked. Everyone clenched their fists and breathed unevenly. Cécile quickly made the sign of the cross, and Rita, with exaggerated fear, frankly threw her arm around Guillaume.

—Guillaume, Théophile called. Come and sit here.

The youthful champion half-turned his head towards his father without taking his eyes from Rita's bodice. He had shifted his cat to the floor so that the girl need not move to avoid its tail, which was beating time to the music. Guillaume was living through a disturbing experience, but he remained calm. He replied, with absent-minded impertinence:

—Presently, Pa, presently. The chair won't break. You paid a hundred and fifty dollars for it.

—*Per bacco*, silence! Ovide cried joyfully, behind the curtain.

His warning seemed to split the storm clouds, already torn by flashes and disturbed by thunder. The rain beat down, plashing on the roof, the windows and the pavements. The whole town was hidden under the deluge. The heavy atmosphere of the Plouffe parlour seemed quite refreshed. Then, suddenly, in a moment's time, the downpour stopped. Ovide, who had been waiting for the din to end, raised his voice:

—The action takes place in a village. Canio the clown has just caught his wife with her lover, who manages to get away. Canio pursues him in vain, returns, furious with his faithless wife, and orders her to tell him the name of her accomplice, threatening to kill her. Curtain!

The two pieces of drapery, pushed apart by an invisible Ovide, slid towards each wall. Bérangère's angular silhouette appeared in profile. Head thrown back, her dishevelled jet-black hair down her back, her face pale and racked with fear, she held out clasped hands trembling with entreaty, love, and defiance. Suddenly,

G 97

Ovide, covered by a strange, particoloured cloak, shot from the corner of the room, his hair disarranged, his mouth distorted in an angry grin.

—My table-cloth! said Josephine stupefied.

It was true. Ovide was enveloped in a cloth with an Oriental pattern which his mother used on Sundays to cover the oilcloth on the kitchen table. Ovide acknowledged Rita's astonished smile with a knowing look. François Thibodeau's fingers crashed down and Ovide began to sing, his legs spread apart, his head thrust back between his shoulders:

> *So again, he's fooled me. Baffled again!*
> *He knows the path too well.*
> *But no matter. This moment thou shalt tell me*
> *Thy lover's name.*

With a vengeful motion Ovide pulled the bread-knife from his belt and brandished it about. Napoleon, his nostrils wide with fright, half-raised himself, his eyes round and his short hands clutching his knees. Cécile hid her face in the hollow of Onésime's shoulder.

—Careful, Vide, Josephine begged.

Ovide was carried away by the drama. He proudly threatened the defiant Bérangère Thibodeau, whose eyes were burning with passion, and declaimed:

> *If here now this moment, I have not cut thy throat,*
> *'Tis because before I kill thee, and thy blood stains my*
> *   dagger,*
> *Thou shameless woman, thou shalt tell me*
> *Who is thy lover. Tell me!*

Bérangère Thibodeau's acting was so perfect, her impassioned tones so well rendered, that the inequalities of her slightly guttural soprano voice were forgotten. She placed her hand on her breast:

> *Vain are thy insults.*
> *My lips are sealed forever.*

Ovide lowered his weapon as he roared:

His name, I tell thee. This moment, thou shalt tell me.

Before a raging Ovide, Bérangère with heaving breast, her head shaken by spasmodic signs of denial, her mass of hair flowing over her shoulders, drew back against the wall whence she defied Canio Plouffe in impassioned tones:

No! No! Never will I tell thee!

Ovide then grabbed his partner by the hair and, gnashing his teeth, lowered the bread-knife slowly. The rumbling of the piano turned into fury:

Die then, serpent!

The point of the knife grazed Bérangère's palpitating skin. Madame Plouffe cried out and hid her eyes. Onésime shuffled his foot nervously, feeling for the bell on his streetcar. Napoleon could not stand it. He sprang at Ovide and seized him:

—Don't be a fool, Vide!

Napoleon gazed stupidly at the table-cloth which remained in his hands. The pianist struck some murderous chords which shook the floor and half-deafened the audience. Napoleon dropped the cloth and made a dash for the piano to put his arms protectively round his wobbling trophies. Ovide, smiling, happy over the effect produced, took Bérangère's hand and bowed. The applause was warm and prolonged, but it was not for the performers. Everyone was rejoicing in his relief that the knife thrust had finished in so happy a way, except François Thibodeau, who dashed forward and shook Ovide's hand with fervour.

—Tremendous, my dear Richard Wagner!

—It's easy when your voice obeys you, my dear Franz, Ovide said humbly, looking at Rita who was still applauding him with sparkling eyes while she tickled Guillaume's ribs. Then she said:

—Monsieur Ovide, as well as having a beautiful voice you're a fine actor, do you know that?

Ovide closed his eyes and, in his embarassment, ran his finger around his stiff collar. Madame Plouffe, who felt the need to celebrate this exciting tragedy, raised herself by leaning on Théophile's knee.

—We must have some drinks now.

—No, not yet! Ovide cut in impatiently. I still have 'On with the Motley' to finish the first act.

Onésime Mènard, with a disappointed pout, drew in the tongue that was already licking his parched lips. Ovide violently drew the curtains together in order to preserve the dramatic fever which was consuming him. Guillaume was the only one who had observed the threat of Ovide's dagger calmly. He jumped to his feet, stretched himself, and announced:

—I'm going to play my record of Gene Autry. This opera bores me stiff.

Napoleon was all smiles. This would leave the cups safe on the piano. Ovide, charged with the electricity of success, said furiously:

—You can play that imbecile of a Gene Autry tomorrow! Music, Franz!

Once more he draped himself in the table-cloth and pulled the curtain behind him. As it stopped swaying a frightful crash seemed to split the house in two. The thunder had gathered up its scattered bursts and at one blow ended the electric storm which had lasted quite long enough. In the Plouffe parlour, when the commotion was over, they felt their bodies fill their clothes once more.

—The lightning struck very near, Josephine said, her face pale.

—I'll go and see, Guillaume decided, making a discreet gesture with his head to Rita.

—Don't get your feet wet, Josephine called, alarmed.

Madame Plouffe had scarcely given Guillaume her consent when Rita, her eyes alight with childish curiosity, exclaimed:

—I want to see too. I'll be back in a minute.

Before anyone could protest she had slipped out behind Guillaume.

—Silence! 'On with the Motley'! Ovide called from behind the curtain.

* * * * * *

In the street Guillaume looked right and left. No yawning gap had been left by the lightning. Storm clouds, leaving the sky to the stars, were rolling along the horizon. Ten o'clock. It was a beautiful evening, serene, freshly washed. From the wet asphalt of the gleaming streets an indefinable murmur arose; the sigh of drops that hang and fall; shreds of moisture torn by the tyres of cars and bicycles from the squeaking macadam. From the eaves fell a few last drops of rain. From the fields nearby came first the sharp complaint of the frogs, then the gentle cantilena of plants refreshing themselves tranquilly in the darkness.

Guillaume took off his coat and tie and threw them on the lower porch. He rolled up his shirt-sleeves and strolled along the pavement carelessly, humming; for, out of the corner of his eye, he had seen a white silhouette running down the steps. The irregular tattoo of high heels awkwardly descending made him smile and murmur to himself:

—I knew it!

There was a liveliness in his gawky gait. With a white shirt, hair well combed, in all his glory as champion, alone on the pavement at ten o'clock at night after a storm, and followed like this by a woman, Guillaume suddenly felt himself the real he-man of the family. A subdued call reached him with the sound of quickened footsteps.

—Guillaume! Guillaume! Wait for me!

He pretended not to hear, and looked up at the Bouchers' poplars which were still dripping. His ears alert, he kept on humming:

Aye, aye, aye, aye,
Beautiful girl of the prairie.

—Won't you wait for me, please, Guillaume? asked Rita, breathless but laughing, hanging on to his arm which she pressed firmly against her breast.

—Look, that's the arm of a champion, he said, drawing it away, his face serious. —Look at it!

His hand clenched, he flexed his muscles under the light of the street lamp. The girl felt them respectfully, uttering little clucks of admiration. These goings-on could hardly fail to attract the attention of a young man who was propped against the telephone pole, day-dreaming, fidgeting from one foot to the other. It was Denis Boucher. His head was still full of his astonishing interview with Father Folbèche. He'd actually pulled it off! He smiled: Denis Boucher, *Christian Action* reporter.

The flexed muscles and the white dress drew his gaze. Then his eyes widened with amazement. By the time his lips had finally formed a stupefied 'Well, I'm damned!' Guillaume and Rita had already passed, giving him a wink that left him wondering.

—Where did the lightning strike, Guillaume? Rita simpered, her eyes riveted on the pavement in order to miss the puddles.

—The lightning? That's all bunk! It never strikes in this parish because the church has lightning-rods. I was fed up. I wanted to come out.

—Well then, be quick. What did you want to tell me? I have to get back.

He laughed.

—Nothing. I thought you were bored stiff too. No need to go back. Ovide won't notice anything. When he's lost in singing he doesn't see anybody, and he keeps that up till midnight.

Rita hesitated. In following Guillaume she had yielded to a childish impulse. Now she realized her mistake. All at once, Guillaume pulled her into the shadow of a porch.

—Let's hide!

—Guillaume! Guillaume! Madame Plouffe yoo-hooed into the night.

Guillaume did not seem to hear, and peered into the dark porch with sharp eyes.

— That's funny, there's always a bunch of cats hanging around here. Nobody home!

Rita began to enjoy the adventure. At the word 'cat' she pretended to shiver and cowered against Guillaume. A blonde hair tickled the champion's nose and he scratched himself briskly. He took a step towards the street, but Rita, frightened, held him back.

— Your mother will see us!

— I don't think so. She can't see well. Come on out. I'll tell her we went to pick raspberries.

He said this between gusts of laughter that shook his shoulders. Rita looked hard at him, wrinkling up her forehead. Then her face lit up with pleased astonishment. She seized Guillaume by both arms: her little, turned-up nose almost touched the chin of the youngest Plouffe.

— Guillaume, we really like each other, don't we? And you aren't such a kid after all!

He held up his head proudly.

— I know. At home they think I'm only a kid. But that's bunk. I'm nineteen, you know. But when I go into the house and hear my mother's voice, and see Ovide with his boring songs and his long words, and Cécile with her umbrella and Papa with his big red neck, I feel as though I was back in my cradle. But I know a thing or two, and I know something about women, too!

— I'll say! Rita replied, gently caressing his biceps.

— Yes, women. And I know how they're made!

Guillaume stopped talking to enjoy his own importance. Rita laughed and rumpled his hair mischievously.

— Dirty little beast! But you're very nice. Say, butter wouldn't have melted in Cécile's mouth when she snuggled up against the boy friend, would it? That big booby tapping his foot! What did you say his name was?

—Onésime. He's married and has a family. He was Cécile's boy friend when I was a kid. I get her goat about that every time she waits around for him at night.

He was picking up pebbles while speaking and aiming them at the cracks in the paving stones. Rita, frowning, thought of the jealousy she had felt when she saw Stan Labrie speak to another girl.

—Married? But doesn't Onésime's wife say anything?

—No, my sister gets along quite well with her. Sometimes Cécile minds the children, or helps her with the work. Everything's O.K., Guillaume explained unconcernedly, for he found the conversation quite uninteresting.

Rita Toulouse threw back her shoulders proudly, swelled her chest, and raised her head to breathe in the evening freshness.

—When did you learn how a woman was made?

—Oh, that! I'm not telling!

Rita was suddenly aware of Guillaume's glance which rested on her swelling bosom. Ill at ease, she stopped looking at the stars. She wondered how to change the conversation and saw that Guillaume was turning into the Pente Douce which sloped away, despite the guard-duty of a few lights, to lose itself in darkness.

—Hold on! Just where are you taking me? It isn't sensible. I must get back to the house. People will take me for a hussy. Ovide will be furious.

—So what! Come on. Ovide's singing. Come on, I'll show you one of my raspberry patches, he said, ingenuously, his arm outstretched.

Guillaume was being carried away by a current he did not try to resist. Ovide's opinion on Rita's departure left him superbly indifferent. He was living this adventure without anxiety, with unconcern. He felt no astonishment. His whole body swam in a new pleasure, as tranquil as the smoke from an abandoned cigarette. Words came from his mouth like the bubbles he had blown, not so long ago, from his father's clay pipe and had followed blissfully with his eyes until they burst. All at once, he crouched down, dragging Rita with him in his alarm.

—Napoleon's looking for me!

The elder brother, standing in front of the Plouffes' house, was peering through the darkness in all directions. Then his attention turned to a street that led into the town. Relieved, Guillaume stood up.

—Aren't you coming, Rita? It's a fine patch. I wouldn't fool you.

Rita didn't move. Suddenly Guillaume seemed like a dangerous enigma to her. The darkness of the Pente Douce, cut in the side of the Cape, was changing this adolescent, who in the light had seemed like a lamb, into an animated sphinx with shady intentions. She bitterly regretted her two-facedness and scolded herself for having thoughtlessly lured this Casanova, disguised as a sports champion, with the charms of her young body.

—Listen, let's be sensible. Let's go back. What will your parents say?

—What are they to you? he replied. Come on.

Feverishly, for Guillaume was getting the upper hand, she searched for an excuse: her shoes would be spoiled, the ground was soaking; her dress was only thin tricolette, and it was chilly. She conjured up the image of Stan Labrie to defend her, but the sole result was a new rush of desire to make an impression on that indifferent creature. He'd begin to wake up, when he saw her going out with someone else.

—O.K., then.

Head high, hips swaying, she boldly joined Guillaume in the darkness of the Pente Douce. They walked along for a few minutes without saying anything. Guillaume was thinking.

—Have you had any boy friends? he asked carelessly.

—I'll have you know a man more or less doesn't matter to me!

—What do you mean?

—I've had several, and good-lookers too.

—Oh! guys that can't do anything, I'll bet!

—You've got a nerve! I've had radio announcers, singers, baseball players, and Americans!

He smiled sceptically and looked with satisfaction at his tanned muscles quivering in obedience to his thought. He felt in a class by himself. There wasn't a Gene Autry in Quebec, or a Bob Feller.

—Have you had a rings champion of the Province yet? he asked slyly.

—No, but I will! she replied, pushing him coquettishly with her shoulder.

He pretended he had received a vigorous push and stumbled, holding his sides, then, in his turn, poked the girl with his elbow. They laughed. They were already half-way up the hill. On their right, nocturnal murmurs reached them from the fields below. Near the long streetcar shed lying at the foot of the slope, a large lozenge of beaten earth surrounded by white lines made a grey spot in the stretch of long grass. Guillaume pointed to it.

—That's where we play the *Canadiens*, tomorrow night.

—Tomorrow night? Is it tomorrow night? Rita stopped.

—Sure. I'm pitching. We'll win.

—You've got to beat Stan Labrie. I hate him! (She was quivering with excitement.) I'll be there, and I'll cheer for you. But you've got to beat him. Go on, say you'll do it for me.

—Sure. That's easy. Pastor Brown said he'd take me to the States next year, to play for the big leagues.

She took his arm lovingly and leaned against him.

—Oh, you're nice! I like walking with you, Guillaume.

—You do, eh?

His head high, he waved with his free arm to the distant fields with their clumps of bushes dotted here and there.

—That's my patch, down that way.

—Have you had a girl already, Guillaume?

—More or less, he replied proudly. Mama doesn't know it,

but when I go to pick raspberries by myself a little kid from St. Malo comes and meets me.

—Is she prettier than me?

—Just about the same.

—You're not nice.

All at once she felt protective, like an older sister.

—How're you getting along at school?

Guillaume started like a man whose virility has been insulted.

—What the . . . Hey, I'm nineteen! I don't go to school any more. The Brother had his little pets, he never gave me a chance to finish my arithmetic. He was jealous because I was good at rings. But I like baseball better.

The word baseball revived Rita's affection. She hung on his arm.

—Say, Guillaume, you're just kidding. You're not taking me into that raspberry patch. The fields are all wet. That would be crazy. Look at my thin dress and my high heels.

She ran her hand lightly down from shoulder to hip, and put her small, arched feet together, tilting her head as she showed them to him.

Guillaume roared with laughter; his shoulders heaved.

—That was only a joke. We can't go for raspberries; I haven't even got a basket.

—Where are you taking me, then?

—Over there, where the slope turns at the edge of the Cape. There's a small gravel path and a big flat stone at the end. I go and sit there in the spring to watch the rooks coming back. We can spread out our handkerchiefs and talk.

Rita, as if relieved at the idea that she would not get wet or have to cross the fields in the dark (although she had not for a moment believed it would come to that), laughed with childish glee.

—Guillaume, the more I know you, the smarter I think you are.

He nodded approvingly. They were reaching the top of the

slope. At their left, a wall of reinforced concrete shielded the road from the debris of the cliff. Now and then there was the dull slithering sound of clods of wet gravel falling to pieces as they tumbled down. Above the wall, on the Cape, the put-put of a motor-cycle came from the level ground which was Battlefields Park. It was a policeman making his rounds, flashing his search-light at the lovers on the benches. Guillaume calmly waited for this noise to die away, then shrugged his shoulders.

—They don't know the best places. Come on, ours is over there.

He took her hand and walked along in front of her on the short gravel path that led to the edge of the cliff.

—That's my stone.

—What a lovely, quiet spot! Rita exclaimed joyously, as she took note of the solitude of the place and felt the surface of the flat stone.

—It's dry already! All the same, lend me your handkerchief. Mine's all over lipstick.

Guillaume absent-mindedly spread out his handkerchief. Rita sat down, modestly pulling her dress over her knees. The champion remained standing, in a proprietary attitude, his sharp eyes scrutinizing the low bushes some distance away. Then he looked towards the dark mass of the town. A chain of lights seemed to encircle it and prevent it from going beyond Montmagny Street. At the opening of the long shed a few streetcars were waiting their turn to enter. The mechanics were manipulating the pole-lines, trying to connect them to the right wires in the copper maze. At each contact of the poles with the electric current a blue light split the darkness. Guillaume strained his ears. Only the plashing of the springs that gushed out of the cliff-side made the silence less intense.

—Rita! Look!

He made his arm into a ring and, slowly sitting down, en-circled Rita's head with it.

—Eighty-four!

—Don't. Guillaume! Stop it!

And they gave themselves up to all the amorous little tricks and caresses, short of a serious embrace, that can be indulged in without too much remorse by a shrewd young woman who intends herself for another man.

*   *   *   *   *   *

> *Aye, aye, aye, aye,*
> *Beautiful girl of the prairie.*

Guillaume was singing softly. He had just taken Rita home, and was reviewing with pleasure the various stages of his escapade. All at once he put out his right arm to encircle an imaginary waist then, laughing, eluded a kiss from some invisible sylph.

It was half-past eleven. Seeing a light in his kitchen and a dark shape on the streetcar bench, he stood still. But he quickly escaped from his uneasiness by a psychological retreat, converting the satisfaction he had felt as a lover into that of a spoilt child who has had a good time. Protected thus by his innocent, baby-like view of the situation, he walked confidently into the yard.

—Here you are, at last!

Ovide, at the foot of the steps, stood like a judge. Such ferocity hardened his glance and his pale features that Guillaume felt apprehensive.

—It was only in fun, Vide. Don't thrash me.

—Thrash you, stupid! It wouldn't be worth the trouble. But you're going to take this letter to your Rita Toulouse at once. And you can tell her I'm not a bit upset. Go on! Faster than that!

Guillaume turned and ran back to Rita's house. He gave her the letter, which read:

Mademoiselle:

I was too kind. I thought you were intelligent. Alas! The beauties of opera being inaccessible to you, you interest me no longer. Furthermore, I despise you and send you back without regret to imbeciles of your own sort—to Stan Labrie, if you choose, for I don't give a damn.

OVIDE PLOUFFE

Guillaume lost no time in coming back. Mounting the steps, he heard Napoleon's loud snores, for he slept with the window open. The snores stopped suddenly, and Napoleon began to dream out loud in a firm tone:

—I'm the oldest here. I'm going to have my blonde, too.

Guillaume was too busy establishing his innocence to smile. He tiptoed towards the screen door, and then his eyes fell on Cécile and Onésime, sitting side by side on the streetcar bench. He caught a scrap of their whispered conversation. Onésime appeared to be defending himself:

—If you hadn't been so slow yourself, that time. How could I know how you felt?

A heavy, quick step shook the kitchen floor. Madame Plouffe ran out, and cried:

—Bless me! there you are at last, child! I'll get you a nice glass of hot milk. Oh! your face is all over blood!

—Just raspberries, Guillaume murmured modestly.

—I'll raspberry you, my boy!

It was Théophile, barefoot. He advanced threateningly, holding a leather strap he used for stropping his razor. The most practical result that he hoped to gain from this first punishment was an end to a reign of terror: the kisses on his neck.

—Don't touch him! Josephine shouted.

It was useless. The leather belt made on Guillaume an indelible mark: he had become a man.

CHAPTER SEVEN

THE following day, Friday, the Plouffes were overtaken by disaster. Ovide had disappeared.

At ten o'clock that morning, according to Cécile, he had suddenly left the factory, exasperated by the gibes of his fellow workers who had heard, from Rita Toulouse, all about the antics during the evening of *Pagliacci*.

It was now seven o'clock in the evening and desolation reigned in the Plouffe kitchen where all were prostrate with silent dejection. The table was set, but as yet no one had eaten. A clamour reached them from the playground, for in a few minutes the game with the *Canadiens* was due to begin. Napoleon was pacing nervously up and down the kitchen, and every time he passed Guillaume he gave him a dig with his elbow, which meant:

— Come on there, they're waiting for us!

But Guillaume, sitting at the table with his head between his hands, seemed crushed by grief and remorse. Cécile began to complain again:

— I was so ashamed today. Heavens above! Everybody was laughing at Ovide, calling him a sissy and singing 'Laugh then, Pagliacci!'

Mother Josephine suddenly burst into tears, her head turned towards Napoleon.

— I knew we'd be punished some day, because of that there Protestant. Poor child. He's such a good soul. It's easy to see that God wants him to be a priest. And now something tells me my Vide had gone and drowned himself.

— Now! Now! Théophile scolded.

—Don't say that, Mama! shouted Guillaume, who seemed to have lost his usual composure.

He went to the window, his nose glued to the pane, and stared at the playground, in bewilderment. A light breeze was blowing. The sun, on its way down, bathed everybody and everything with its slanting rays of transparent light, making the bricks of the houses glow, giving to the playground an unsubstantial look, an exciting beauty to the women, and to the men the appearance of big children. Merry groups of brightly dressed people kept emerging from the streets, and settled along the edges of the diamond where players in red or yellow sweaters were strolling about. Bats twirled, balls were struck and caught, and disputes which ended in bets rang out here and there among the impatient onlookers.

—S'pose we had it announced over the radio, Napoleon said; then we could go and play our game.

At his post, Guillaume stiffened suddenly and looked as though he wanted to break the window with his head. Was that really Rita Toulouse arriving beside Stan Labrie? She was laughing and pointing to the house with a piece of paper in her hand. The letter! Ovide's letter, which was allowing Rita to speak to Stan Labrie at last. Guillaume fell back a step and clenched his fists.

—Damn that girl! Just wait!

With Napoleon at his heels, he tore down the steps and ran to the diamond. The colourful scene and the noisy crowd were transformed into an indistinct and shifting mass before his misty eyes. Everywhere he looked, he saw the family parlour, and in it a very narrow coffin: Ovide's. Guillaume was blaming himself for this death. He paid no attention to the shouts that greeted his arrival. His threatening glance searched for Rita Toulouse. But the pastor Tom Brown, with Denis Boucher and the boys of his team, were already crowding around him.

—Quick, Guillaume, warm up a bit; you're late, said the pastor, handing him a ball and a mitt.

He pushed them aside and tried to force his way through the fans. He saw Rita Toulouse sitting on the enemy's bench, laughing loudly, and pointing him out to Stan Labrie who was beside her.

—What's the matter with you? asked Denis, seizing his arm.

—Let go of me! It's that Rita Toulouse. Look at her! She's making fun of me to Stan Labrie. Let me go and push her face in!

—Hold on! You can't do that!

Denis was straining to hold him back. He was nonplussed. His forehead was damp with sweat. His future as a reporter depended on the success of this baseball game. The priest hadn't arrived; the crowd was impatient; and here was Guillaume threatening to attack Rita Toulouse. He didn't understand Rita's change of front, nor what had happened at the Plouffes', and he hadn't time to think about it. All he could see at the moment was a fit of jealousy which he must appease at any price. Guillaume was behaving like a madman.

—Listen, he said, are you crazy, attacking a woman? Act like a man!

—Let me go, I tell you!

Tom Brown, the club supporters, and a distracted Napoleon surrounded them.

—Listen to me, said Denis, breathing hard. Don't get upset over Stan Labrie. He's a queer. He can't have any children, or love a woman. Don't give him another thought! Rita's barking up the wrong tree!

—Well! exclaimed Guillaume, calming down and looking in a puzzled way at Denis.

The latter, relieved, slackened his grip. Guillaume still looked angry as he stood there motionless, thinking. Suddenly he said:

—If that's the way it is, I'll go and tell her mother. She's going to find out what kind of a girl she's got. Be back in a minute.

There was no time to stop him. He was already off, running

madly. The pastor raised his arms in dismay, and Denis swore. The players were grumbling and the crowd, with cat-calls and applause, was clamouring for the match to begin. In anguish, Denis looked in the direction of the rectory. Had the priest changed his mind? Had he feared ridicule at the last minute? All at once the youth gave a joyful cry. A group in cassocks was crossing the field. Denis ran to the mound, lifted his arms, and called for silence.

—Ladies and gentlemen! he exclaimed. We have a great surprise for you. Monsieur le curé Folbèche has agreed to pitch the first ball of this game. Here he comes now. Three cheers for Monsieur Folbèche.

The parishioners, at first dumb with surprise, began to shout their approval. Monsieur Folbèche was accompanied by his three curates, the school principal, and three churchwardens, brought by him as a measure of prudence, so that if there were any humiliation to suffer, it would be shared among eight. Hearing the cheers directed at him, Monsieur le curé, eyes staring and heart pounding, walked more quickly. His escorts were mopping their brows and, between breaths, discovering a new Monsieur Folbèche. The group filed past the first lines of onlookers scattered about the field.

—Thanks for coming! The crowd is waiting impatiently for you, Monsieur Folbèche, Denis exclaimed, as he joined him.

—All right, all right! I'm here, he said gaily.

Monsieur Folbèche's eyes shone with unusual friendliness. He walked as though his soles were made of chamois. The old priest, habitually so reserved, distributed more bows than a cardinal on a mission to a foreign diocese. He crossed the diamond, elated by the shouts and applause which greeted him. The group was now surrounded. Denis warded off undesirables.

—This is the Reverend Tom Brown. I told you how much he admired your magnificent garden and your beautiful parsonage.

The pastor, who wore a white cap and was in his shirt-sleeves and without a collar, his neck protected by a handkerchief, wiped the sweat off his forehead. For an hour, he had not spared himself in giving professional advice and knocking grounders and high-fliers to the players.

He shook hands vigorously with Monsieur Folbèche, who returned his greeting uneasily.

— Glad to know you, Monsieur le curé. I admire you. At your age, playing baseball to please your parishioners!

Monsieur Folbèche attempted a timid smile. He was relieved of a great weight. Because of numerous sermons in which he had recounted imaginary and always victorious arguments in English with Protestants, he had feared that the Reverend Tom Brown, when he met him, would begin to argue the superiority of his religion in the language of Shakespeare.

The pastor moved towards the big bench reserved for guests of honour, to the right of the home plate.

— Come and sit here, gentlemen! Just a moment. Let's turn the seat a little to the left so that you won't have the sun in your eyes.

The two already seated stood up: the pastor's fiancée, a tall girl whose eyes were hidden behind dark glasses, and Napoleon, who was watching the horizon anxiously to see if his brother were coming. Denis Boucher went back to the mound again and announced:

— The game will be opened by Monsieur le curé Folbèche, pitcher; the Reverend Tom Brown of Cincinnati, batter; and the Reverend Brother Principal, catcher. Play!

Monsieur Folbèche went slowly to the mound. He had been given a new ball which he now examined, turning it round and round in his fingers. Mechanically, he asked the price of it and, to cover his embarrassment, made an impish face at the Principal who was pounding the mitt with his large fist, doubtless because he was delighted at the chance of returning a ball on equal terms;

for Monsieur Folbèche usually looked down upon him from the height of his priesthood, and now and then allowed himself to make ironical remarks. As the pastor grasped his bat and walked over to the plate, Denis Boucher appealed to him once more:

—For goodness' sake, do as I asked you. My future depends on it.

The pastor smiled, struck the plate with the bat, and turned towards the priest who, in his agitation, had put the ball in his pocket. The curious crowd was reduced to silence by the importance of the event. Monsieur Folbèche, who had never even consented to play cards, was opening a baseball game! Was a new era beginning? He raised his arms:

—My children. I am not used to playing. So, you must excuse my awkwardness. Laugh if you like; it's a holiday. I came because I'm very fond of you and I want our parish club to begin this game under happy auspices. I should also like to thank the Reverend Tom Brown, who returns to the United States tomorrow, for the fine sporting spirit he has shown. I also wish to welcome the *Canadiens* who, in spite of their superiority, were kind enough to meet our club in an exhibition match.

The umpire gave the signal. Monsieur Folbèche squeezed the ball with all his strength and stared at the batter. The missile rose feebly, about as high as a man's head, and moved out past the plate. Tom Brown sprang, made a great swing, and missed. At first the crowd gave an astonished murmur which quickly swelled and burst into frenzied shouts.

—Strike him out, Monsieur le curé! Strike him out! You can do it!

The three men left the diamond, Monsieur le curé rubbing his hands with satisfaction and bowing to his wardens with a great flourish of his hat. But from all sides, although it was not the custom, there was a demand for them to return to the diamond until a definite result had been obtained; either the pastor should withdraw after three balls, or make a hit. Monsieur Folbèche was the first to accept, eagerly seizing the ball as someone brought it to him.

They cheered, and Monsieur Folbèche, as happy as a child, threw a high ball which the pastor, having taken a too vigorous swing, missed again. This time, even the *Canadiens* applauded. The crowd was jumping, whistling, and thrilling with a new pride: that of being Catholic baseball fans. Delighted, Denis smiled and made gestures of encouragement and congratulation to the priest who, overwhelmed by success, stood with his legs apart and his arms dangling. Father Folbèche was regaining his children's affection by joining in their sports. He was jubilant. His face alight with the spirit of the game, he wished these moments might last forever. As for the pastor, who had agreed to play the role of loser out of friendship for Denis, he felt rising up within him, before this crowd who seemed to be taking the priest's success seriously, the religious self-respect that slumbers in the heart of every Protestant minister. His unhappiness ripened into a decision when he saw the tense attitude of his fiancée, to whom he had not explained his generous deception. He grasped his bat resolutely: the comedy was over. Monsieur Folbèche, who was looking into the distance, seeming to listen to the heartbeats of the breathless crowd, turned round briskly and threw a perfect ball which smacked into the Principal's mitt while the pastor, taken by surprise, turned completely around, carried away by his tardy spring.

There was a long shout. Hats were thrown into the air. A band of men left the crowd and rushed at the bewildered priest. They hoisted him on their shoulders, singing:

He has won his epaulettes, maluron, malurette!

Tears of happiness appeared in Monsieur Folbèche's eyes as he cast a triumphant glance over his enraptured flock. The victory of truth shone forth: Protestantism had been struck out by Catholicism. Denis Boucher forced his way through.

—Bravo! Bravo, Monsieur le curé! What did I tell you?

Monsieur Folbèche was deposited on the ground. Feverish and breathless, he took Denis by the arm and answered:

—You can come to the office presently. Your letter is ready.

Dumb with joy, Denis did not even say thank you. The priest looked furtively towards the pastor and whispered to a paralysed Denis:

—We can beat these Americans without even practising! That's the first time I've played. Not bad, eh? And my cassock was a nuisance. Oh! if I only had more time!

The pastor, annoyed and silent, looked at his wrist-watch. Where was Guillaume? Napoleon burst into a joyous shout:

—There he is, coming now. Viourge! Just in time!

Guillaume was led quickly to the mound. He had regained his composure and was smiling defiantly. Ovide was avenged.

The match began.

*   *   *   *   *   *

Darkness had now settled into night. The playground was deserted, but the waves of Guillaume's triumph still floated through the air. He had been extraordinary, winning the game almost single-handed. Without staying for the congratulations of his admirers he had slipped away to wait with his family for Ovide's return.

Madame Plouffe went out on the veranda for about the hundredth time and leaned down towards the street, her mournful face contracted with lines of anguish that crossed the lines of age.

Behind the screen door, the three shadows of Théophile, Napoleon, and Guillaume stalked her, imitating her gestures like a back-stage chorus. Josephine shook her head and went back into the kitchen. Like three urchins caught misbehaving, the father and two sons scattered about the room, their faces screwed up with worries apparently other than those of Madame Plouffe.

—Oh dear! Oh dear! she complained as she replenished the stove. Here I was thinking that after sixty years the worst thing that could happen to me was to grow old!

The fall of a log that the fire was consuming answered her complaint. The table was still set. To chase away her fear that Ovide had met with some misfortune, and to persuade herself that he would come back home safe and sound, Mother Plouffe had brought out her best table-cloth with the flowered pattern; and she had placed the dishes with the unusual care that is warranted only by the return of the prodigal son whom one had thought lost. Cécile was beginning to feel hungry, and her grief was seasoned with bad temper.

—If he hadn't been in such a rush to get a girl friend! Everybody knows what the girls of today are like. In my time, I wouldn't have done that to Onésime. I've had enough humiliation for one day!

Josephine's grief burst into indignation.

—You hadn't any business to be humiliated! Oh, that Rita Toulouse! I knew what she was the moment I saw her. Ovide's too good. When I think that she made us look like a family of fools! We're a happy family, we like to be together, we practise our religion, the priest often visits us, and we don't give anybody any trouble. As for Ovide, he's a wonderful singer. Only it's classical, so ordinary folks can't understand it. He's a genius; everybody said so when he was little. And to call him a sissy into the bargain! A man like him that holds himself as straight as a rod, and never kisses me, dresses and talks like a gentleman. When I think of it! I hope you stood up for your brother against the fibs of that little pest. It's you who ought to be ashamed, always being with a married man!

At this sentence, which she had said without thinking, Josephine stopped, astonished, as though examining the trace that the words had left on her tongue. Cécile stammered:

—You can't trust boys, nowadays!

Napoleon, who was hanging about the parlour door, not daring to visit his trophies during this time of general gloom, stuck up his nose and swelled out his chest:

—You husband-snatcher! Don't say that. There's good enough boys around, only you're not smart enough to take them. Married women—not for me! Oh! If I only had a girl friend! I wouldn't sing songs to her and I wouldn't come out with words that long. No! Every evening we'd go for a little walk along the highway. At nine o'clock we'd come back, buy a cone each, and sit on the balcony and look at pictures. Then we'd go to bed. It's easy.

Irritated by these discussions, Guillaume slipped out on to the balcony. Théophile interrupted a long train of thought to follow his son with his eyes.

—You may well hide yourself, after what you did last night.

Though he was as troubled as his wife, he did his utmost to hide his anxiety by the lightness of his tone. He shrugged his shoulders:

—Women! Women! I know something that's far better than a girl friend. It lasts longer, and you can steer it: a good racing bicycle. A girl friend lasts two years at the outside. Then you get married. The funniest thing about it is, you never think your wife could have been your girl friend. Eh, Phine? No more sport. She keeps you from going out and having a good time, and orders you about, he concluded, glancing longingly at the cupboard where Josephine kept the beer locked up; sadness was making Théophile thirsty.

Madame Plouffe did not hear him. She was sourly emerging from a disagreeable thought.

—Cécile! About Onésime! In my opinion, you're too sweet on each other, the two of you.

At that moment Guillaume burst into the kitchen, shouting happily:

—Here comes Vide! He's drunk!

—No! It can't be, Josephine stammered, her hand over her heart. He belongs to the Temperance Society!

—Yes, he's drunk. He's walking like Pa. Come and see, Guillaume rejoiced. He isn't drowned, after all. Gosh, I'm glad.

Josephine sank into the rocking-chair, sobbing:

—Like his father! Like his father!

—No drama, now. Give me the cupboard key, Théophile cut in peremptorily.

Josephine groped in her apron pocket and held it out to him. Théophile, suddenly filled with the authority peculiar to a sober drunkard in the presence of an intoxicated man, took charge of the situation and seized the family helm. He planted two bottles of beer among the dishes on the table and opened them without a tremor. Madame Plouffe struggled to her feet.

—Poor child! How he must have suffered! Cécile, get his bed ready. I'll help him up the steps.

Cécile hurried, to offset the anxiety her mother had caused by her reference to Onésime. Napoleon, holding a bowl, waited for his father to finish rinsing the glasses, so that he could take the water needed to refresh Ovide's face; it had always been his job to wash Théophile when he came home drunk.

The door opened, and Ovide appeared. His tie was undone, and a stupid smile was fixed on his shining face. He clasped his mother around the neck and from time to time gave her little pats on the cheek.

—You beautiful little mother, I love you. Are we going out together tonight?

Guillaume tried to attract his attention:

—I beat Stan Labrie, you know. Six to three. I struck him out three times, and I made a home run.

—Poor Stan, Ovide hiccoughed.

He pulled free and stretched his arm out solemnly.

—Good day, Plouffes!

Napoleon approached, conscientiously carrying a towel which

he wiped over his brother's face. Ovide's neck arched like a cat's under a caress.

—Your bed's ready, Vide, Cécile announced.

—Let him be. He's a man. He can stand up, Théophile protested, holding two brimming glasses. Here, Vide, take this to pull yourself together!

And he glanced significantly at Josephine who was feverishly brushing Ovide's soiled suit, a glance which meant: 'Let that be a lesson to you for the future, when I come home in that state.'

Ovide emptied his glass and shouted:

—Let's eat: I'm hungry!

Josephine poked hurriedly at the fire and worked veritable wonders to start the fat sizzling. Ovide took off his coat, slapped his chest with his fists, and began to laugh uproariously.

—I'm the man everybody was talking most about in Quebec today, isn't that right, Cécile?

—Oh no, Vide! Not as much as that, she stammered.

—On the contrary, a whole lot! he yelled, his mouth distorted, and staring goggle-eyed. Moreover, I'm going to sit here, he decided, grabbing the chair at the end of the table.

—I'll lend it to you. I'll lend it to you, Napoleon blurted out, sitting down on another chair.

Pensively, Ovide examined the cloth and the dishes, and cast a brief look at his open-mouthed family. He hiccoughed. Then a grave pallor hardened his weary face.

—Mother, come away from the stove. Sit down with us. I want to make a little speech.

Josephine came timidly, for it seemed to her unnatural that she should sit down while her children were eating. Ovide threw out his arms emphatically.

—Mother, I love you. I don't often kiss you; that's because I feel embarrassed! And I don't want to be taken for a sissy when I'm not, you understand! I love you very much, Mama, and I'm going to prove it.

He walked around the table and kissed Josephine lingeringly on the cheek. A tear ran down Madame Plouffe's nose. Motionless, she was moaning softly, like an animal that has always been beaten but one morning is caressed because it is to be killed.

—Another glass, Vide? Théophile suggested, dreading a possible kiss from Ovide and preferring to exchange it for permission to take a glass himself.

—No thanks, that's over. I'm really very happy. I think it's stupid for happy people to get drunk. Don't ever drink, Napoleon. Nor you, Guillaume.

—No, Vide, the two sportsmen chorused obediently.

The opera singer coughed.

—Mother, you've set the table as though it were a holiday to welcome a prodigal son; a son who, instead of coming home for dinner and supper, crawled into miserable taverns to drown his shame and grief; but Pagliacci had the courage to laugh at his sorrow.

—I'm going to give it up too, Théophile said, pushing his glass away guiltily.

For a few seconds Ovide closed his eyes and seemed to be collecting his thoughts.

—Alas, instead of welcoming the return of an ungrateful child, God wishes this magnificent table to celebrate the departure of an apostle. Yes, I've left my job, and I'm going to enter the monastery of the African White Fathers as a lay brother tomorrow.

Feeling immaterial, so drawn was he to the sublime, Ovide awaited his family's reactions. Madame Plouffe had not raised her head, and was still crying, but more quietly. Théophile, who was accustomed to making a host of resolutions when he was drunk, did not believe Ovide, but pretended to do so. Furthermore, Ovide's religious plans had always pleased him because Théophile was used to having priests for his employers and he imagined that ecclesiastics must swim in cloudless bliss because of the importance attached to them. The old printer, horror-stricken at heart by the moral sufferings that Ovide must have endured, nevertheless kept up a jocular tone.

—The monastery is about ten miles from here. With the bike, that'll take me a little less than an hour to go to see you. Twenty years ago I could have done it in fifteen minutes.

—With the wind behind you, it would take you less than that, Father, Napoleon added judiciously.

Cécile, who was the miser of the family, seemed more overwhelmed than the others by Ovide's decision. In order to make both ends meet, Madame Plouffe took four dollars each week from the children's wages, and Cécile feared that her mother would increase her share and Napoleon's to six dollars to make good the loss of Ovide's contribution. On her guard, she stared at the cupboard, where that implacable enemy, the family budget, was kept. To forestall the blow, she said:

—I've decided to have my teeth out next week and get a good-looking denture. All the girls at the factory are doing it. It's going to cost me around forty dollars. So as I don't want to touch my little savings, I'll take it out of my wages. You can't increase my board.

Ovide looked around contemptuously:

—Is that all the emotion you feel about this? My Plouffes, you're all children. You, at least, Mother, shouldn't cry because I'm courageous enough to be a man.

—But you've been drinking, my Vide, Madame Plouffe said at last, through her groans.

Ovide held his head with both hands and yelled:

—I tell you, tomorrow I leave for the monastery! Me, drunk? My mind's never been clearer. I've millions of words that want to come out.

He stammered, as if tortured by his inability to prove the exceptional good health of his brain.

—Look, I see all of you as though you were on a cinema screen, he said, holding out his hands protectively. I see you all as little children. Only your outward appearance is older.

—That's what you think, said Théophile sadly, doing his best to sound detached, so that Ovide would understand that he didn't take his sorrow seriously. You're not experienced, Vide, you don't carry your beer very well.

Ovide grabbed the edge of the table because the kitchen was beginning to revolve, carrying in its gyrations the strained faces of his family who had become preposterous stars in a stormy sky; his head grew lighter, emptied of its miraculous clarity by the whirling of his dazed heart. He tried to prevent the ebbing of waves of ideas, which might never reach him again, concerning the crisis of infantilism that seemed to him to be gripping America. By dint of fixing his gaze, he succeeded in making everything stand still. His world was now in an oblique position. The ceiling was leaning; the electric bulb had found another centre of gravity; and the furniture failed to slide, though the floor sloped.

—Yes, we're forced to be children all our lives. That's why those of us who want to become men are unhappy. Do you want to sing opera? You're laughed at. Do you want to succeed with the ladies? They call you a sissy if you're not a champion with muscles that big. Do you want a good position in an office? It's always somebody else who can do the job.

—Could we eat? Napoleon suggested timidly.

Madame Plouffe brightened up. On the whole, she was happy because Ovide was drunk, for in that state it was impossible for her son to make a final decision. This religious vocation of Ovide's, which she had always desired, frightened her now that it threatened to be imminent. All at once Ovide opened his eyes, which were growing big with terror. The fumes of intoxication had dissipated during his speech, leaving his mind exhausted by the suffering from which he had fled. He stammered:

—Cécile, have you told them what everyone's saying about me?

—We know it isn't true, she said soothingly.

He slumped down in his chair, his elbows on the table and his head in his hands, his back bowed with timorous sobs.

—Oh God, I'm so unhappy!

He raised his head, staring at his mother through tears as opaque as oil, and said softly to her:

—It's true. I'm leaving tomorrow for the monastery. Empty your wedding suitcase. I'll need it.

PART II

SPRING 1939

CHAPTER ONE

MAY 1939! Hitler was challenging Europe. The papers were flooded with important news. For the first time in the history of the British Crown, the King and Queen had disembarked at Quebec and were to tour Canada. What was happening? The peaceful Quebeckers began to be anxious about the feverish wind blowing from the east. Another war? Unemployment preoccupied them less; they watched the horizon now as if the sun might not shine again. Another epoch was beginning and, gropingly, everyone was trying to adjust himself to it.

The Plouffes, on their rung of the social ladder, did not escape the vicissitudes of the time. With them, one year usually passed into the next with nothing changed except the calendars. But since the arrival of the Baptist minister, Tom Brown, their own new era had been unfolding, and within it was the mysterious seed of unforeseeable events.

Napoleon nervously hitched up his trousers as he walked along beside a pensive Guillaume. They were returning from the playground. The collector's face had lost the calm expression of other years. It was lengthening with the weight of serious matters, and the eyes, usually prominent, seemed withdrawn and veiled by melancholy.

— Guillaume! Must tell you. I've got a girl friend.

Guillaume looked at him sideways.

— That's something new! You know it's dangerous for athletes.

— Jeanne isn't like other girls, Napoleon said sharply.

Then a little laugh of delight gurgled in his throat and he began to roll a cigarette, for he had taken up smoking in order to appear manly. Suddenly his brow puckered:

—I promised Jeanne a seat on the balcony to see the King and his wife go by. Do you think Mother will be against it?

Guillaume spat, then began to whistle his favourite tune. Napoleon waited patiently.

—Gosh, you know Mother can't stand girls since Ovide's affair. Me neither! I'm off dames. I've other things to bother about.

—It struck me all of a heap. I'd never have believed it!

—That's your business, you Viourge, you! Give the dame my chair. I won't be on the balcony when the King passes.

—You won't!

In his joy, Napoleon failed to notice Guillaume's mysterious look.

—I can't wait till you see Jeanne. Viourge! but she's pretty!

This lover's rapture left Guillaume unmoved:

—Napoleon!

—Yes? his brother said eagerly.

—About the King. They don't go in for baseball over there in England, is that so?

—I think so. I haven't a picture of any English baseball player. But that's not surprising! Those English, as Father says.

Guillaume licked his lips and his eyes sparkled.

—In that case, I have a scheme for making him jump.

Napoleon, occupied with his emotional upheaval, didn't think of questioning his brother. He smiled tolerantly, his thoughts elsewhere.

—You're always full of ideas!

At this moment the long, raucous shout of an old woman was heard. Madame Plouffe was calling them. They hurried home.

Montmagny Street was decked in its holiday finery. Festoons of multicoloured ribbons were looped across the fronts of the houses. Streamers inscribed with the most varied slogans formed an archway above the road. In great red, blue or gilt letters one could read: 'St. John the Baptist, protect the nation', 'St. Joseph,

130

give us large families', 'Sacred Heart, enlighten us', 'God of Armies, grant us a good death', 'Saint Joan of Arc, save France', and so forth.

All kinds of flags, from the Blue, White and Red to the Fleur-de-lis and the Union Jack guided the eye through the riot of tawdriness and served as rallying-points for the various groups of colours which without them would have been an offensive hotch-potch. This multi-coloured decoration flapping in the wind made a rather pretty sight; it was indicative of an artistic temperament, if one remembered that it was planned by a people without a flag, obliged to use the flags of others to achieve a festive air.

Alas, an enormous blot spoiled the show. The Plouffe house, stubborn and squat, had hoisted no banner. In its dingy nakedness, among neighbours decked out with the gayest of trimmings, it was preparing to defy the King of England, despite the fact that in a recent pastoral letter the Cardinal had asked the diocese to adorn itself in all its finery to receive the sovereigns, had ordered all the sextons to ring the bells, and had requested the priests to sing the *Domine, Salvum Fac Regem* with the verses of the prayer *Pro Rege*.

The two Plouffe brothers ate their supper quickly under the impatient eye of a displeased Josephine.

—Lazy bones! If Ovide hadn't been in the monastery he would have made me clear the table and you wouldn't have eaten. Things have come to a pretty pass in this house since he went away. Everybody wants to be boss.

She looked spitefully at Théophile who was rocking vigorously, his hands clutching the arms of the chair. With his long beard, his stern expression, and his grunts of indignation he was, like his house, the picture of intransigence. He caught Josephine's glance.

—Complain if you like, it's not going to make me change my ideas, wife. I told you we're not going to put out any flags. That's final. Pooh! The King! He comes to see us when things are in a bad way. He's afraid of Hitler; he comes and speaks to us in French so we'll accept conscription.

He spread out his arms grandiloquently.

—Bring out your streamers, fools! Ring the bells! England's coming to inspect us. Us French, who discovered Canada! It's unheard of!

Josephine assumed a submissive air, not daring to protest too much because though she ruled the roost inside the house she cherished a blind respect for her husband's political views. She suggested:

—But, dear, it's embarrassing not to have a flag on the house when everything else is decorated. We look like naughty children. And to think that I have drawers full of lovely streamers! And then the Queen has such a beautiful smile. What's she going to think of us?

Théophile got up and paced the kitchen. He seemed amazed.

—It is you, wife, who spend your time singing about how St. Joan of Arc threw the English out of France! And now you want to deck yourself up to receive them!

Josephine folded her old fingers and for a few moments humbly considered this contradiction under the triumphant eyes of her husband.

—Well. It looks as though times have changed. I was reading in the paper that His Eminence dines with the King this evening before leaving for the Joan of Arc festival at Domrémy.

Théophile brandished his pipe:

—I can't understand it! I can't understand it! Father Folbèche didn't want a Protestant received in his parish, and now His Eminence dines with a Protestant king. The priests tell us to join the Society of St. John the Baptist, to stay French, to distrust the English, and yet at the least little visit the whole bunch of them dine together with good wine and good beer and fine speeches about loyalty.

—Keep your temper, husband. You know politics. I rely on

you. Someone was saying yesterday that the King was also the Protestant Pope. That's something. In any case, it's terribly complicated. Leave His Eminence alone, he must know what he's doing, no one's got a better head than him. Besides if we don't put out any flags it could harm you at *Christian Action*, for they're printing whole pages saying we're the sovereign's most faithful subjects.

Théophile's convictions now reached the height of earnestness. Political events being the only matters left on which he exercised any authority, he faced them now in his kitchen with an ardour all the happier because it released him from the stagnation of tedious days.

—You don't want to argue, wife, but you're racking your brains for a way to make me afraid and get your miserable streamers up. *Christian Action* belongs to the two-faced brand. When the English stay at home they point their fingers at them and say they're pests. They sing to us the year round that we should be separated from Confederation; that we should be a kind of small, Catholic France. The King arrives; they're as sweet as honey and translate *God Save the King* into French. But I'm not two-faced. My political ideas stand before my job. I'm against the King, that's why I don't hang up streamers. I won't put my nose out of doors to see him pass. I mean it!

Napoleon's face brightened. A vacant chair. He must make sure of it, in case Guillaume should decide to stay on the balcony. He combed his hair quickly, and went to stand stiffly before his mother. He clenched his fists, because his legs felt like cotton wool. Words in an embryonic state emerged from his mouth and produced staccato grunts of 'Ha'. Madame Plouffe was not listening. She was musing sadly over the collapse of her hopes for a display of banners. She dismissed her disappointment with a long sigh and went towards the balcony, murmuring:

—If Ovide had been here . . . Well, I think I'll sit here; Cécile there; Napoleon . . .

Her eyes divided up the seats on the balcony in the same way they cut the cake before relatives called.

—Mama!

Cécile, her greying hair frizzed out by a too thorough 'permanent', followed Josephine as far as the door.

—Save a good place for Onésime, she said, smirking. He has the day off. I invited him.

Madame Plouffe stopped counting, but didn't turn round.

—Cécile, come here.

—Yes, Ma, the old maid replied, joyfully, as happy to be able to add another small pleasure to her platonic idyll as to add twenty-five cents to her money-box.

Josephine glanced suspiciously towards the kitchen to make sure that no one was listening.

—Come and sit on the streetcar bench, she said, gravely. I want to speak to you.

Cécile, chilled by her intuition of the worst, stopped smiling, grew pale, and sat down beside her mother without looking at her. Madame Plouffe took out her chewing-gum, rolled it carefully into a ball between her old fingers, and stuck it under the bench. (The bottoms of the kitchen chairs were dotted with these adhesions, dried and blackened by the years.) She cleared her throat:

—How old are you, exactly?

—Forty-one, Ma, but I've scraped together a good bit of money.

—It's not money. It's about men. Haven't you a good boy in mind?

Cécile was clinging to a mental picture of Onésime as though to a tree trunk.

—You know very well, Ma, what the boys are like today. If you don't go out in a car with them they think you're slow. And then I always wonder if they aren't after my money.

She had $422.48 in the bank.

Josephine made sure her gum was stuck tight.

—I'm serious. Because Onésime's wife came to see me today. Oh, I know you don't do anything wrong, but, after all, he is her husband.

Cécile closed her eyes and folded her icy hands. Her mother made a fresh start.

—She complains that he always makes a bee-line for here and that she's always alone with the children and she's fed up with being laughed at. She says you want to squeeze her out. Put yourself in her place. She's right. There are plenty who talk to me about it and Father Folbèche asks me questions about it sometimes. I can't have Onésime coming here any more.

Cécile fastened her distracted eyes on her mother, unable to speak.

—Well, daughter, what do you think? Shall we put Guillaume here, you there, Napoleon . . .

Cécile did nothing to help her mother in this painful interview. Instead she sprang up, fled to her room, and banged the door behind her.

Filled with anxiety, Josephine chewed non-existent gum.

—Are you there, Ma? Napoleon smiled timidly, poking his head out. I want to tell you something.

Madame Plouffe, heavy at heart and wrung by anxiety, thrust her son aside as though he were one trouble too many, and went into Cécile's room. Cécile lay upon the bed, her shoulders shaken by sobs that ran through her contorted body and issued in sniffles.

—Mama! Mama!

—Oh, my little girl! Josephine cried, rushing to her. Cécile elbowed her angrily away.

—It's all your fault. I didn't marry Onésime because you wanted me to stay with you. I was your only daughter. You told me marriage only brought trouble so I didn't get married. Now you take my only friend away. You only think of yourself! You haven't got a heart!

135

Josephine shook off the feeling of being a monster.

—Be reasonable, little girl. You told me you were afraid to have children. You must see very well that now, feeling as you do, it's a sin for you to go on seeing Onésime. Get that into your head. He's married, and his wife is angry.

—All the same, I'd have made him a better wife than her.

—Cécile!

—Go away! You're heartless, you're heartless!

Overwhelmed by her daughter's paroxysm of grief and troubled by her reproachful accusation of heartlessness, Josephine retreated slowly, holding out her arms in vain to this child who, under her nose, had grown old and emotionless as a parrot. And now a cancer of the heart, asleep under the decay of boredom, was revealed by the wound of a word. Cécile was discovering love at the moment when she knew it to be inaccessible. And she was writhing on her bed and sobbing in the same way that she had done, long ago in her childhood, when her mother had given away Cécile's doll, with which she never played.

—What's the trouble? Théophile demanded, seeing his wife come back into the kitchen.

—Oh, nothing. Just a woman's affair.

—Ma, I want to speak to you, Napoleon tried once again.

—Well, what do you want? Nuisance!

—I forgot to tell you that I have a girl friend. I want to invite her on to the balcony to see the King go past. A nice girl, Ma, believe me. Jeanne Duplessis.

—It struck him all at once, Guillaume said. Seems she's the only girl in the world that isn't bad for athletes. You'll introduce me to her sister, eh, Viourge?

—That's right, Josephine burst out. Get married then, all of you, and leave your old parents in the lurch! Then you can't throw it in their faces that they hung on to you just to have a good time themselves!

Josephine held her melodramatic pose a few seconds. There

was a long silence, for Guillaume was killing flies with a cunning hand and Napoleon suddenly began to think of marriage with a blissful smile.

—What did you say her name was? Josephine asked, on the alert.

—Jeanne Duplessis. A fine name nowadays.

For a moment Josephine was thoughtful, then she swelled out her chest and announced drlyy:

—Fine or not, I don't want to see her dawdling around here. We had enough trouble with that Rita Toulouse. You can send her packing.

Napoleon was completely dumbfounded. Then a picture of Jeanne came into his mind. And for the first time in his life his small figure had the dignity of a great personage who has been insulted.

—You'll keep a seat for my friend Jeanne Duplessis. I mean that. I'm going out to buy a cone.

—That he's going to suck till it's dry! added Guillaume.

Josephine ran to the door:

—You're crazy, Napoleon. Think it over! Remember Ovide. . . . Oh! . . . Good day, Monsieur le curé.

Astonished by Josephine's vehemence, the priest eyed her from head to foot, then without a word, came in and sat down, twirling his hat between his fingers. Disturbed by this silence, Josephine searched feverishly for an adequate way of expressing her respect. Théophile, on his guard, had stood up and was stroking his beard. Guillaume went out hastily, for he was embarrassed in front of his parents and the priest because of certain sins he had confessed. Monsieur Folbèche took stock of the room.

—Is Ovide managing all right at the monastery?

—Oh yes! Josephine fairly bubbled over. If you could only see him! He's the one that opens the door. He has a beautiful black beard. Even the fathers call him 'Brother Ovide', just like that. And he speaks beautifully. Like a real priest.

Monsieur Folbèche seemed to have heard all this before; while Josephine was speaking he looked at Théophile, his eyes sparkling mischievously. Feigning artlessness, he asked:

—What are you waiting for? Aren't you putting up your streamers?

Josephine awaited her husband's reply anxiously. Théophile had noticed the mischievous gleam which shone in the priest's glance. He sat down, gripping the arms of his chair.

—No, Monsieur le curé. When I say I'm against the English, I'm against them for good. The King as well as the rest of them.

The priest, secretly delighted with this reply, hid his approval and continued with pretended anxiety:

—But the King isn't an Englishman from Ontario. And think, a king and a queen, what an honour for our parish! That doesn't happen every day.

—Just what I told you, Josephine said softly.

Théophile glanced furiously at her, then winked at Father Folbèche.

—Monsieur le curé, look here, you know more about it than me. The English are all alike. They come to Canada when they need something, when there's something up. When there's no war, the King doesn't bother about us here. But now they're making fools of themselves! The firemen have been sprinkling the Pente Douce garbage dump for three days because the procession is going to pass by there. As for us poor beggars, we can breathe that for twenty years, and nobody cares. Everybody's going crazy, if you ask me!

The priest coughed with good-humoured severity.

—I, myself, hung some flags on my trees. It wasn't any hardship.

—No, it isn't the same for you. You have to obey the orders from His Eminence, Théophile added, hastily embarrassed.

—And His Eminence knows what he's doing, Josephine added.

—You're right, Madame Plouffe. It happens that we don't

always understand the subtle tactics of our bishops. We can close our eyes. They're bringing our ship safe into port.

But Monsieur Folbèche hadn't closed his eyes, and his gaze had met Monsieur Plouffe's for some moments. Théophile was radiant. He understood. The priest, burdened by his responsibilities, could not say what he thought and came to him, Théophile, to make him say aloud the words that a priest, in the circumstances, had to repress. Théophile pulled up his chair and said in a conciliatory and familiar tone:

—Monsieur le curé, look me straight in the eye. We're the same age; we can talk together. His Eminence aside, you're a real Canayen. Hundred per cent, eh?

Monsieur Folbèche softened and looked down with a protesting smile. Théophile pulled his chair closer.

—Do you think that a good Canayen like you, one of our farmers' sons, and all you men, the good priests who taught us how the English invaded us, how they tried to make us lose the Faith, and our language; how you fought them, how you kept us what we were; do you think that a good Canayen like you is going to make me believe he's in favour of the English King? Come, come. You have to obey, of course. And I respect you, now I know how you think.

Monsieur Folbèche, moved by patriotic feeling, sighed:

—Indeed, we have struggled, and we're still struggling. Sometimes obedience is hard for proud hearts. It's necessary to make sacrifices to achieve one's aim, and our bishops know what means to take in order to succeed.

Théophile winked at the priest. He felt he was penetrating the recesses of Monsieur Folbèche's heart, and believed he could read his most secret thoughts. Dazzled by this intimacy, he saw himself taking the priest's arm and rising with him in a stately flight above great fields of French Canadian grain. Josephine was looking at the two men in ecstasy. Théophile laid his hand on Monsieur Folbèche's knee.

—Dear Monsieur le curé, here's a man speaking to you who would die for you. You, our parish priests, you have preserved us and have never changed our ways. It's simple: we have been, we are, and we shall always be against the English. It's more complicated for the bishops. You know the history of Canada by heart. Remember 1837. The disorders; you priests, you were with the people; you hid us in the churches; you fought for Canada's independence. Then, all at once, bang! The bishops decided it was better to remain loyal to the British Empire. Then they turned against the Americans. I wonder why. Perhaps the bishops thought that, because the English are across the water, they have fewer chances than the Americans to come and meddle in the affairs of Quebec province. That could very well be.

Monsieur Folbèche held out his arm sternly:

—Tut, tut, tut, Monsieur Plouffe. Don't ever risk such insinuations. You must learn that the Church is One. Madame Plouffe, you see what microbe is sprouting in your husband's mind. Do you know where it comes from? From that American minister I have thrown out of the parish, from that thirty-nine-year-old whipper-snapper who pretended to be a good baseball player.

—Oh, come now, Monsieur le curé, Théophile protested. Him, influence me? He was against bicycling!

—The devil busies himself with all the sports, Monsieur Plouffe. Let that teach you to be on guard; and leave our bishops alone. There, I must be going. Good night.

He went out stiffly.

—You see! Josephine said to her husband.

Théophile laughed confidently.

—Come, come, old girl. Don't you see that he thinks the same as me, underneath?

Josephine ran to the balcony and tried to guess the priest's state of mind by his bearing. He was making his way carefully along the boards of the pavement like a man who ponders knotty problems. Monsieur Folbèche was at least not walking angrily. Josephine would have heaved a more decisive sigh of relief if she had seen his smile, which was so broad that it made his thick lips looks positively thin.

Monsieur Folbèche was satisfied. So the people were rallying to them, these humble priests who did not teach at the University and would never become bishops? The flock was astonished to see the Archiepiscopate differing from the lower clergy on political matters. The old priest was upset for a moment by this obvious division in the clerical hierarchy, but the pleasure of having public opinion on his side made it easy for him to tolerate it. The unity of the Church was safe, since the Episcopate never insisted that the parish priests should follow the line of conduct adopted in high places in the relations of Quebec and England. Unity in division! That was the power of the Church. Monsieur Folbèche inspected the few flags hung in his trees and shrugged his shoulders. Naturally, he liked neither the English nor their sovereigns, as Anglo-Saxons, but these banners, after all, signified homage to the sovereign line of St. Louis, which owed its greatest eras to Christianity.

Madame Plouffe lost sight of the priest. She glanced around enviously at the beribboned fronts of the neighbouring houses and felt the need to scold someone.

— Guillaume, how often I've told you not to play in the street. You hear me!

The pitcher seemed very busy with his practising. Planted on the pavement, he was engaged in enigmatic manœuvres with his partner, who was posted on the other side of the street. His arm pointed to an imaginary vehicle.

— Suppose the car is coming. It's there. Now it's here. It's going to pass. Bang! I throw. See? That'll wake him up. All right! I'm coming, Ma!

At this moment Napoleon arrived, armed with his ice-cream

cone. As soon as she saw him, Josephine was assailed once more by Napoleon's love problem. He crossed the kitchen swiftly. He was pale, and his tongue was not attacking the ice-cream.

—What's the matter? Josephine asked.

His voice almost dying away, he groaned:

—I've got an awful stomach ache.

Josephine shrugged her shoulders and said sadly:

—Now the trouble's beginning!

*　　　*　　　*　　　*　　　*　　　*

Napoleon was very sensitive. His indigestion kept him a prisoner in his room all the evening so that he could not run to his usual rendezvous. He was in despair. Jeanne, that great lady, would never forgive him for having kept her waiting. It would break up everything. He couldn't sleep that night. At dawn, as usual, he was up. His face drawn, rings under his eyes, he prepared his breakfast but did not touch it. He paced the kitchen, stopping often to listen to the snores and sighs of his sleeping family. Their bodies, on the verge of waking, kept turning in their beds.

Napoleon couldn't stand his uncertainty any longer. He ran down the stairs and hopped on his bicycle. It was a beautiful spring morning. The air was cool; the new leaves curled on the trees, the sun climbed over the clear horizon, and the town, washed by the night, had the smell of freshly laundered clothes. The flags seemed to be waiting for the wind and the royal procession. Napoleon veered past a couple of milk wagons and made for the Pente Douce, in the direction of the Upper Town, where Jeanne Duplessis was maid-of-all-work in a Jewish home.

The collector had met this girl three weeks before when, to celebrate the spring, he was making his first bicycle run on the Grande Allée. He had been struck by the uncertain walk of a solitary promenader. And suddenly she had collapsed. Napoleon's first impulse was to flee from this upsetting sight, but as the street was almost deserted at that hour, he was the only one to see the woman faint. He propped up his bicycle carefully against a tree and, with clammy hands, helped the girl to stand up. She had clutched at his arm with a frightened gesture and Napoleon, stiff with embarrassment, had given her nervous little pats on the back.

— You'll soon be all right. It's like that sometimes. Our legs go back on us.

That was the beginning of Napoleon's great love. Holding his bicycle handlebars with one hand and Jeanne's arm with the other, he had taken her home. They saw each other again, because, from then on, Napoleon rode along the Grande Allée every evening. Confidences weren't long in coming. Jeanne was the eldest of a brood of nine children; she was thirty, her face looked tired, and she had beautiful manners that intimidated Napoleon. In 1931, during the depression, her family had left Three Rivers to live on some uncultivated land about thirty miles from Quebec. Poverty, more than Jean Rivard's writings, had prompted Papa Duplessis to establish himself as a settler. He was one of those fatalists who had been convinced by crusaders of the back-to-the-land movement that they had the solution to unemployment; the necessary experience and knowledge of farming would doubtless be supplied by spontaneous generation, or by a colonizing missionary's blessing.

Grappling with an unprofitable soil, not even suspecting either the variety or the amount of knowledge essential to a colonist, surrounded by children in rags, he lost heart and took to drink. To relieve that poverty and escape from that hell, Jeanne had left for Quebec, where she had been working for five years as a servant for twenty dollars a month. This money she sent to her mother, not spending one cent on herself, even wearing 'Madame's' old clothes.

When Napoleon first met her, she was tired to the point of tears by her loneliness and her drudgery. He had appeared like a saviour to her. He was a man, a support, a little dynamo of devotion. The world was complicated; Napoleon was simple. She could close her eyes and rest her tired head on his shoulder, without his saying a word. Now that a woman had usurped the place of photo albums, sports statistics, and ice-cream in his heart, he meant to give himself to her completely for the rest of his life. Jeanne sensed it and she clung blindly to this faithful log which would permit her to float for as long as she lived.

Napoleon rode through a zigzag of streets lined with bungalows, his body bent, his head thrust forward. The pleasure of telling Jeanne that he had obtained a seat for her on the balcony was gradually chasing away the remorse that gnawed at him for having missed his rendezvous. He rang the door-bell. Accustomed to rising as early as a sexton, he believed that everyone did the same, except his own family whom he called lazybones.

Inside, along the hallway, came the sound of slippers rapidly approaching. Jeanne Duplessis appeared, holding her dressing-gown across her flat chest. She was tall, with slightly stooped shoulders. Her thin lips without make-up, her blue temples, the pink spots on her cheekbones, her high, bulging forehead, and her auburn hair accentuated the glassy brightness of her blue eyes. Astonished, then anxious, she let him in.

He sidled into the hall and said quickly:

—I got you a beautiful place on the balcony right beside me. Right above the King.

Jeanne stood still and her arms fell limply to her sides.

—And you come at six o'clock in the morning to tell me that!

Napoleon, stammering an excuse, tried to coax back her smile:

—I was in a hurry to please you.

—Not so loud, you fool! The family is asleep! she exclaimed, seizing him by the arm.

Upstairs, a bedspring creaked. The girl glanced fearfully towards the stairs. There was silence again. Relieved, she led Napoleon to the kitchen. Awed by the morning calm and the attitude of his dearest, he sat down cautiously, examining the electric stove with the furtive eye of a conspirator. Jeanne turned her back to him and said in a reproachful tone:

—I waited for you until eleven o'clock last night, you wretch!

—Don't say that! I'm not a wretch. I was ill.

—No!

She turned around quickly and looked at him with the anxious solicitude of a woman accustomed to suffering for others. He shook his head and smiled.

—I'm better. Blasted indigestion. Don't know what gives it to me! It bothered me that you didn't know. I felt badly about it. But now I've told you about the indigestion and the King, is it all right?

She came near and took his hand lovingly.

—Poor boy. You eat too fast.

—Listen, is it all right now?

—Yes! I can't wait to see the Queen. I have my afternoon off. If you could see the pretty outfit that Madame doesn't want any more. I'm so happy, dear! There!

She kissed his forehead mischievously. It was the first kiss. He gave a start and fixed his eyes on the staircase as if this kiss might have roused the household. Because he had only been kissed by women in dreams and because he was sure of not waking up out of this dream, he looked for a diversion, for he could never speak of his dreams, still less of one from which he had not wakened. He noticed the mop leaning against the sink and hastened to say:

—Do you wash the floor?

Jeanne frowned and coughed, putting her hand over her mouth. She seemed displeased.

—No. It's waxed. Madame likes me to do the downstairs floor before she gets up.

Napoleon was concerned, and looked morosely at his friend's pallor. He imagined himself in Madame's place, letting Jeanne sleep and doing her work. The mop, which in spirit he was already wielding vigorously, wiped away these thoughts and revealed beneath them Mother Plouffe's remark: 'Get married then, all of you!' His face lighted up.

—Jeanne, if you were married to me, you could sleep till noon and I could do the work before leaving for the shop. It wouldn't take much time. You'd get fat.

She looked down, and blushed. Napoleon, drawing in deep breaths of the fragrance of future conjugal happiness, jumped to his feet.

—I start at eight o'clock. I've time. Sit down. I'm going to wax your floor.

Jeanne protested in vain. Napoleon always finished what he undertook.

CHAPTER TWO

THE royal procession was due to arrive in a few minutes. The murmur of a well-behaved crowd awaiting an important visit added festivity to an atmosphere already charged with the magnificence of the imperial legend.

Crowns and sceptres, and a parade on such a scale as to defy the imagination, would pass before them. Clusters of heads jamming the windows were turned towards the horizon. From houses fortunate enough to have balconies, decorously joyous spectators overlooked the parade. A few daring cyclists, who had threaded red, white, and blue crêpe paper streamers through the spokes of their wheels, were zigzagging along the asphalt now become an endless ceremonial carpet in the crowd's impatient eyes.

French Canadians are not all, like Monsieur Plouffe, Anglophobes or rabid nationalists. During elections, however, they like to attack the English from the platform, because it is political tradition and in resisting the ancient conquerors they enjoy the same sensation as braggarts who have the reputation of not letting anyone get the better of them. But let there be a fine parade, and 1760 exists no more; hurrah for the procession! Brought up in a province where a mint of money is spent on pomp and circumstance, nothing pleases them more than circuses and confetti. Roman at heart, Norman in mind, they are a complete mystery to foreigners who try to understand them. They are, at one and the same time, French and American, simple and complicated; are happy to be so, and wittingly let themselves be drawn into vicious circles with a knowing smile.

A young man, satchel in hand, suddenly burst into Montmagny Street. It was Denis Boucher. Smartly dressed, preoccupied, he was the picture of the young reporter who looks casually at people and things as though they were guinea-pigs. Pushing his way through a group of loiterers, he asked point-blank:

—Hasn't this puppet-show begun yet?

He did not wait for a reply. In the course of a year, Denis Boucher had developed. As a drifting adolescent, with no prospects of a career, he had believed in a vague internationalism; his own province had seemed little more than a picturesque background. Since he had become secretary of a branch of the Society of St. John the Baptist, however, he had made straight for the very thing he had once avoided: narrow nationalism. Just as he had despised parochialism and admired everything else, so, now he was beginning to make his way, he praised his parish and native town to the skies, regarding the rest of the world as of no account. His occupation had brought him into contact with some young intellectuals who were publishing a patriotic paper with fascist tendencies: the *Nationalist*. They had welcomed his fiery spirit, and Denis, flattered by such a welcome from university people, had responded eagerly. In their debates and in their paper, these young people settled economic, political, and social questions by ignoring them, cutting off Quebec province from the Dominion and re-establishing it as a completely exclusive and self-contained community. So, tired of the saccharine tone insisted upon by the editor of *Christian Action*, Denis contributed satirical articles to the *Nationalist* under a pseudonym.

For a few moments, his clinical eye roved anxiously along the rows of heads, the packed balconies, the cyclists, and the streamers; then he gave a slight smile of satisfaction as he noted the nakedness of the Plouffe house. He looked at the skyline, at his wristwatch, and then rapidly climbed the steps.

—Your balcony's worth something today, Madame Plouffe.

Josephine smiled importantly as she leaned over the street and murmured.

—Napoleon's not in a hurry to bring his Duplessis girl.

—Did you say something?

—Oh, nothing.

She pushed her two teeth forward, closed her jaws, and made a smacking sound with her chewing-gum as she sat down on one of the chairs placed at the end of the balcony. Having glanced down at Guillaume who was idly tossing a ball to his partner stationed across the street, she turned towards the screen door behind which Cécile's rigid silhouette was visible.

—Come on and sit down, Cécile. Hurry up, I tell you. Get a good seat before they come.

—No, no, no, the old maid repeated obstinately.

Inside the house the floor creaked under the swaying of the rocking-chair. Denis leaned forward and, seeing Papa Théophile, went in.

—Good day, Monsieur Plouffe! Aren't you going to see the King go by?

Théophile stared at him in exasperation.

—No. I don't need to tell you that. You know why.

Denis, his jaws tense with sudden indignation, looked down and heaved a long sigh.

—You're right. We're a fine lot of quibblers. Do you know that I've been asked to report the parade in this district?

—I know, Théophile replied, shrugging his shoulders. You'll talk about cheers, flags, mounted police, the King and the Queen, with words as sweet as sugar. I could die of shame!

Denis ground his teeth.

—There's no way out of it. You know the password at *Christian Action*: 'the most faithful subjects of the rulers'. We know where that comes from. But I'll get even! he exploded.

Théophile waited for an explanation, then grumbled:

—Everybody says that! 'We'll get even.' That takes time. I don't want to wait. You've seen there isn't one streamer up here, eh?

Denis could keep his secret no longer. He looked furtively at the balcony then, in a kind of whispered shout, he said to Théophile:

—I'm writing two accounts of this disgraceful parade. You'll see in the *Nationalist* tomorrow an article signed 'Hindu'. That's me. Do you understand? he exulted. Look out for squalls.

Théophile had ceased rocking and looked at the youth with mingled joy and disbelief.

—Are you serious?

—I certainly am. O.K.?

—It certainly is. Give 'em the works, the rotters! That's the stuff.

For the first time Denis enjoyed the praise hitherto addressed to his pseudonym.

—And what if that wasn't all, Monsieur Plouffe? You've heard about the Irish Republican Army posters being found almost all over the town? We did that, the newspaper gang. You know that during the passing of the King and Queen spectators are forbidden to throw flowers, or use a camera? The authorities are afraid of bombs, like Hitler! And the royal limousine is supposed to have shatter-proof glass. It's absurd! Can you imagine Napoleon or Guillaume throwing a bomb?

Théophile, open-mouthed, was looking admiringly at the young reporter.

Denis burst out laughing and slapped his thighs.

—Did you see the article in the London paper saying that the people of St. Sauveur put the Union Jack upside-down and flew it along with a lot of religious emblems that don't go with the King's religion?

—And did you see our paper? Papa Plouffe said exultantly. They splurge all over the place that it's not true; that we are loyal subjects; that we love the King like a father. Ugh!

—Théophile, Josephine called.

Her body wedged in the doorway, she was looking eagerly towards the street.

—Théophile, come and see this. Napoleon with his girl friend. Just as I thought, a stuck-up thing. They look like Mutt and Jeff.

Théophile stood up, irritably, while Josephine let go of the door in order to receive the couple at the top of the steps. Jeanne Duplessis wore an elegant brown suit which made her look really fashionable, and Napoleon, trotting along beside her, might have been a little umbrella. When he had almost reached the top of the steps, he fixed his eyes admiringly on his friend, who was intimidated by Mother Plouffe's prying glance, and said:

—It's Jeanne, Ma. She's been anxious to know you.

Josephine did not immediately reply, and continued to scrutinize this tall girl with the friendly smile as if she were some kind of specimen. And suddenly the saucy face of Rita Toulouse, when Ovide had introduced her on the 'Pagliacci evening', flashed through her mind. Ovide's joy had prevented Josephine from recognizing a hostile woman at first sight, an enemy who had upset the family and sent Ovide to the monastery. Spurred on by this bitter recollection, Josephine's vague antipathy regarding the newcomer asserted itself. She said coldly:

—You were as anxious as all that?

—Good day, Madame Plouffe, the servant girl stammered.

She blushed under Josephine's searching glance as if the latter had caught her cheating. It was certain that Napoleon's mother had noticed that the suit had been given her and that it fitted her badly. Jeanne felt that her legs were excessively long and she feverishly pressed her handbag against her flat chest. Her inspection over, Josephine concluded that this girl was too tall and too well-dressed for Napoleon; that she would ruin him and lead him around by the nose if she became his wife.

—Well, anyhow, come and sit down.

Jeanne Duplessis, discomfited by this icy reception, cast confused glances at Napoleon who was running around among the chairs like an ant, for movement made him forget his embarrassment. Jeanne was shaken by a fit of coughing. Josephine stared suspiciously at her; for she was terrified of germs, which she imagined as large as lice on people she disliked.

—You have a bad, hollow cough! A cold in summer's not normal. You must take care of yourself.

—It's bronchitis, Ma, Napoleon said nervously, guessing, for once, his mother's thoughts.

Jeanne Duplessis, overcome by sudden weariness, wished she were in a kitchen, alone, waxing a floor. Josephine turned to Théophile who, shrugging his shoulders at his wife's bad manners, held out his hand to Napoleon's friend.

—Good day, mademoiselle, he said, bowing.

—Oh! yes, this is my husband.

—A grand champion, Napoleon added quickly.

Théophile gave the girl a shy smile, which comforted her; then, as he was in no humour to recall his exploits as bicycle champion, he took his leave and went back to the kitchen. Madame Plouffe looked round for Cécile, but the latter had fled to her room when the couple arrived. She put an end to the silence that was settling over the company.

—There are still some vacant chairs. Don't go thinking there weren't a lot who wanted to sit on them! My company haven't come yet. Oh! just an aunt and three women I play cards with, for money, in the afternoon. (Josephine was determined to let this well-dressed girl know she played for stakes regularly, and that to win or lose meant nothing in her life!) Do you chew? she asked, abruptly, holding out a stick of gum.

Jeanne shook her head timidly and Josephine, because of her bellicose state of mind, froze at the refusal. Napoleon leapt at the opportunity afforded him.

—No, Ma, he said, taking a bag out of his pocket. We've got some honeymoons, Jeanne and I.

Napoleon had intended the sweets for Jeanne and himself, and so he now offered them only to his friend.

—Don't you like them, Madame Plouffe? Jeanne ventured.

—No, let him keep them. It's his money.

Cécile's silhouette approaching noiselessly came out from behind the screen door.

—Well! So you smelled the caramels! Josephine said.

The old maid, motionless, scanned the bag of sweets covetously and looked at Jeanne Duplessis as an adulterous woman might jealously regard a girl who is free to love as she pleases. Jeanne, blushing, mouth full, lips tightly closed, didn't dare suck the sweet under Josephine's devouring gaze. But Mother Plouffe, enjoying the discomfort of a woman who dared threaten the peace of her family, had not yet finished with her victim.

She regretted most bitterly not having given Rita Toulouse the welcome she had deserved. Here was a chance for revenge. In a clumsy attempt to be spiteful, she exclaimed in honeyed tones:

—What beautiful clothes you have! It must cost you a lot to dress yourself!

—No, not much, Jeanne murmured weakly.

—Napoleon couldn't pay for stuff like that on his small wages, that's sure!

Aware of his mother's intention, Napoleon said impulsively:

—No danger, Ma. Jeanne doesn't spend a·cent on dressing herself. That's 'Madame's' cast-off clothing.

Haggard, Jeanne Duplessis stood up in protest and glanced distractedly at the collector.

—Napoleon!

She began to cry. Not knowing what to do next and quivering with shame, she walked to the steps and disappeared down them. Cécile, at her look-out, suppressed a smile.

—You stupid woman! bellowed Théophile from the kitchen.

Josephine was on the point of weeping with mortification. How could she have done such a thing? Napoléon seemed petrified as he watched Jeanne's flight through the groups of spectators.

—Viourge de Viourge! he burst out all at once.

He sprang down the steps, almost knocking over Onésime Ménard, who was calmly preparing to climb them. Luck was with Madame Plouffe: a new problem always came to her aid when she was perplexed. She called out:

—Go and fetch your wife, Onésime, or you'd better not come up!

He raised his head and looked open-mouthed at Josephine's harsh face.

—She's minding the children.

—You mind your own business, Mother!

Cécile had pushed open the door abruptly and was running to meet Onésime. She fumbled in her blouse and drew out a letter.

—Don't speak. Go and read that at home. You'll understand. Go on.

And she went up the steps without turning round. Onésime, overwhelmed by this incident, respectfully examined the pink envelope and immediately thought of the word 'correspondence'. It was paper which doubtless had smelled of lilac at the time Cécile, fascinated by the idea of writing a letter on such sentimental paper, had committed a wild extravagance. She had tried in vain to think of a correspondent: she had never thought of Onésime. Scratching his ear, Onésime retraced his steps under Madame Plouffe's appeased gaze.

Throughout this scene Denis Boucher had paced the sidewalk impatiently. The crowd became more dense and in the fever of waiting, disputes arose between first-comers and last-comers who were pushing and elbowing their way to obtain the choice places. Monsieur Folbèche hesitatingly passed from group to group, addressing trivial remarks to this person and that as though put out by not being, for once, in the procession.

In his nervous pacing to and fro Denis bumped into Guillaume who, motionless, was solemnly turning a baseball around in his fingers.

—What! You're not on the balcony? Watch out the Mounties don't take you for an anarchist! If they see you with a ball in your hands ...

Guillaume had not time to hear the end of this prudent advice. An excited murmur rose from the crowd, and the fronts of the houses seemed to turn with all the turning heads towards the horizon.

—There's the King! There he is, everybody whispered.

The crowd was transfixed in a silence tense with curiosity. At last! On the school lawn the little school choir prepared to stand at attention, for their conductor, the Principal, had raised his violin to his shoulder.

The royal procession appeared in the distance, a mass of scarlet. Like a long, tame serpent it crawled rapidly along the asphalt trail, its red and gold scales glistening in the sun, and soon its component parts could be clearly seen. First came a detachment of the Royal Canadian Mounted Police, the red uniforms moulding bodies that seemed all the more statuesque by contrast with the prancings of the magnificent horses they rode—for these had the proud and reckless mien that is proper to every horse so privileged as to escort a king in an automobile.

Behind this detachment glided the long, open limousine containing the royal pair. Another group of mounted police brought up the rear. All along the route there was a little spatter of clapping from women because the Queen, standing up in the car, wore a beautiful blue dress, smiled continually, and looked to them like a French Canadian dressed in her Sunday best. As for the King, he looked young, worn, and ill at ease as he made this formal appearance before an unresponsive crowd.

For indeed, the male spectators on the whole maintained a disappointed silence. They had hoped for a grandiose and completely unimaginable parade, and all they got was a few splashes of vermilion, rapidly disappearing without even a trumpet or a drum. In Quebec one is accustomed to slow and ostentatious processions with allegorical floats, fanfares, choral singing, and stops by the wayside!

And now the police of the advance guard, in their scarlet uniforms pipped with gold stars, impassive on their proud mounts which shone under the triumphant May sun, were approaching the Plouffe house. Denis Boucher was hastily scribbling notes. The Principal gave the signal and, to the sound of the violin, the little choir began to sing *Un Canadien errant.*

Guillaume made a sign to his catcher and flexed his muscles. The horses paraded along, prancing. The car was only twenty feet from Guillaume. He slowly raised his arm. The Queen, who seemed worn out with smiling at a silent crowd, appeared relieved by the children's singing. The nose of the limousine came into Guillaume's field of vision.

Whe—ew!

And the baseball, skimming the windscreen, sank into the mitt of the catcher, crouched across the street. The crowd gave a stupefied shout. The chauffeur put on speed, frightening the horses of the advance guard. Guillaume had no time to rejoice over his exploit. There was confused shouting:

—Look out, Guillaume! The police!

Four policemen of the rearguard, revolvers in hand, sprang from their mounts and ran at him. When they siezed him he seemed to become a lump of clammy flesh.

—Let him go, you bullies! Madame Plouffe, alarmed and furious, screamed from her balcony.

A large, noisy mob collected around the four policemen who were shaking Guillaume so that his head bobbed about in all directions. A car carrying provincial detectives was following the procession. It drew up at the kerb and the rear door opened wide ready to swallow up the nerveless prisoner. Monsieur Folbèche who had not been able to squeeze through the tight rows of onlookers, planted himself in front of the gaping door, thinking he could stop the policemen from taking Guillaume away by spreading out his hands solemnly, like a Moses separating the waters of the Red Sea. Then, incensed by the impatient gestures of the giants who attempted to wave him off, he took a firm stand and said sternly:

—Let him go. Let him alone. He's a poor, harmless boy, one of my parishioners. Why, he's not dangerous. He did it for a joke.

But the policemen, English Canadians from the west, were now preparing to take hold of the priest and push him aside. Before the impending sacrilege the onlookers changed into assailants. Threatening shouts of 'Don't you touch him!' broke out. The circle of angry men pressed around the enemy. The policemen hesitated, then said to the priest:

—We don't understand. He is an anarchist. Mind your own business. Get away.

Then the priest, looking proudly at his parishioners, dug up his English which he spoke as badly as he spoke Latin.

—It is my business. It is my parish, you know. Him a good boy. I order you to give liberty to Guillaume. Understand?

—Are you going to let go my Guillaume? You confounded great oafs! Josephine yelled, as she flew out, brandishing a heavy poker.

One of the police tried to subdue her, but, filled with maternal rage, Josephine defended herself with her nails, her two teeth, her two feet, and her two hundred pounds of flesh. At this moment, one of the detectives who was sitting in the automobile decided to get out, after having hesitated a long time because of Father Folbèche's intervention. This detective had secured his job from the Duplessis government, whose sympathy for the clergy and the nationalists is well known. The Quebec officer had a short conversation with the members of the Mounted Police; and Father Folbèche smiled, for it seemed that the good Quebecker was explaining to the red giants how unwise it would be, in the circumstances, to arrest a French Canadian without his priest's permission.

The Mounted Police, having talked this over, turned to Guillaume and curtly demanded his name and address; then they released the anarchist-in-spite-of-himself, sprang on their horses, and rode away. The crowd clamoured enthusiastically as it surrounded the victim and the triumphant priest, who was saying in English, 'You see; you see!' Denis Boucher, fired by the idea of the report he intended to write for the *Nationalist*, ran off to shut himself in his room.

— Théophile, get a glass of cold milk ready, Josephine called, breathless.

She was helping Guillaume climb the steps. Papa Plouffe, with the glass of milk in his hand, waited.

— So you wanted to hang out flags for those pigs?

— Oh, the damned English! roared Josephine.

She had no time for a further display of anger. Guillaume, ghastly pale, fainted. He had just contracted a disease which spreads terror: fear of the police.

CHAPTER THREE

THE next evening, Denis Boucher, exultant, ran to the Plouffes, waving the *Nationalist*.

—Monsieur Plouffe! he called.

He remained standing on the doorstep, the smile frozen on his lips, looking in vain for an answer to his call.

—Oh! it's you! Josephine sighed.

She assumed a dejected air which made her jowls sag more than ever. A sense of desolation mingled with the characteristic odour of the house, and the furniture seemed older and shabbier than ever.

—Hasn't Monsieur Plouffe come home yet? Why, it's almost eight o'clock! Denis remarked with forced astonishment, unwilling to have his ardour subdued by the despondency which weighed down the atmosphere.

—No, Josephine continued with a sigh, mechanically opening the lid of the sewing-machine. He must have stopped at the tavern, I'm very much afraid. But that doesn't happen very often nowadays. Something may be bothering him, or he may be celebrating something or other.

Denis's feeling of triumph revived.

—He's celebrating, Madame Plouffe! It's very simple. He's seen my article in the *Nationalist*. Listen to this! he went on excitedly, forgetting the limitations of his audience.

THE ROYAL MASQUERADE

As certain expensive visitors were passing along Montmagny Street a comical incident took place which gives a clear indication of the feelings of our good people towards those whom our

*imperialistic papers designate 'Our Beloved Sovereigns'. Our
people, whose humour is known to be without equal, had decorated
their houses with the emblems most capable of making the victims
of British haemophilia understand that we have been, are, and
always shall be French Canadian Catholics. There is no need to
mention the Union Jack. It was perhaps hanging out to dry on
somebody's clothes-line. Now, one house was conspicuous by the
absence of all decoration. It belongs to a compositor on the* Daily
X, *a man of such solid patriotic convictions that they have
remained unshaken by the threats of organized authority. However, the outstanding fact in all this is not his high-principled
honesty, which merits our entire admiration, but a comical incident
which indicates clearly that our race is ready to thumb its nose at
perfidious Albion: the fact that the printer's son, who is probably
the best baseball pitcher in our city, as a Gallic and inoffensive
gesture, threw a magnificent 'strike' across the bonnet of the royal
limousine.*

Denis's self-conceit was pierced by his listener's incurable
indifference to literature and politics. He lowered his tone, looked
about him, then became silent, biting his lips. Madame Plouffe,
who lent the same ear to Denis's reading as to Ovide's operatic
selections, looked in the direction of the lavatory.

—You can come out, Guillaume. It's not the police. It's Denis.

The door with the red glass panes opened an inch, allowing
Guillaume's suspicious nose to poke through.

—That child there has been through a lot since yesterday! He
doesn't want to go out. As soon as he hears a step he hides.

The child came out of his hiding-place. Guillaume was almost
twenty years old. His build was that of a grown man, and a fine
down, which looked more like an actual beard, darkened his face.
But Madame Plouffe persisted in calling it 'down' because Guillaume wanted to start shaving and because she feared to see her
Benjamin join Napoleon, Ovide, and Théophile in that hard and
unresponsive period of life which, for a man, begins with beard
and razor. At a loose end, Guillaume crossed the kitchen listlessly

He disarranged the oilcloth table-cover, pushed the chairs around, and rattled the handles of the stove.

—Will you sit down and be quiet, nuisance! Josephine said impatiently.

Sulkily, he seized his cat and began to stroke it confidingly.

—Denis, do you think the cops will come back to arrest me? They took my name and address.

Denis Boucher was not cured of his desire to appear important.

—You never know! he replied, shaking his head.

Josephine was indignant.

—Don't be a fool, Denis! He's upset enough now. You know very well, Guillaume darling, Denis loves to joke.

Her anxious eyes begged Denis to soothe him. Guillaume was worried. He let his cat fall and, forced to do something forbidden in order to forget his obsession, he walked towards the parlour door, which was closed. He looked at his mother before turning the knob.

—I guess I'll play Ovide's records.

—Never! she cried, frightened at the impending sacrilege. When Ovide comes back he must find the records and the parlour just as he left them!

Her face paled suddenly at the thought that Ovide might very well never come back and that then the parlour would always remain closed as though for a death. She returned to her old theme:

—Isn't anyone ever coming home? Will you tell me what your father's up to, all this time?

Denis stood up and looked at his watch.

—I'll come back later, Madame Plouffe.

—No, no, don't go away. He'll be here any minute now.

—Gee, this is getting me down! Guillaume lamented, having given up the idea of playing the records.

Josephine took a newspaper from the sewing-machine and thrust it into his hands.

L 161

—Read, read, read the pages where there aren't any pictures. You'll see how interesting it is. Practise reading. You're not more stupid than anyone else. Look at Denis! He's educated, he writes. He makes a good living too. It's a year since you left school and you're not working. You never read. If you go on like that, you're going to forget your French.

At these words, Cécile burst out of her room, holding her head proudly, a rusty pen in one hand and her pink notepaper in the other.

—Yes, learn to read. Find yourself a job. I've helped support you long enough and sacrificed myself for all of you! I've just about had enough!

—Mind your own damn business, you old skinflint! Guillaume retorted, and laboriously applied himself to reading the front-page article: 'Strained Diplomatic Relations between Germany and France.' Loftily, Cécile went to the cupboard and unearthed the ink bottle. Before settling herself down at the table, she remarked:

—Mama, we ought to have a desk here. It isn't right, me having to do my correspondence in the kitchen.

She began to find fault with her mother over the pen, the thin ink, the rickety table, and life in general. At this moment they heard Napoleon fussing in his room. He appeared in the kitchen and glanced mournfully at the clock. Josephine who, since Jeanne's flight, felt she had wronged her son, said affectionately:

—Aren't you going to buy your cone, Napoleon?

He shook his head sadly, closed his eyes, and said feebly:

—I don't eat them any more.

—It's about time you economized, Cécile threw at him, interrupting the torture she was inflicting on the notepaper.

—Mind your own business, Cécile, Josephine cut in severely. Oh, Napoleon, did you catch up with your girl friend yesterday?

He turned around towards the chest that held his photo albums. After a silence, he murmured:

— Yes. But it wasn't any use. She's gone for good. And it's your fault, he added softly.

— She wasn't the girl for you, said Josephine, excusing herself.

Napoleon turned round vehemently.

— You don't know that! We got along wonderfully. I helped her with her work, we told each other everything, and we went for a walk every night.

— You can walk out with other girls! That one was too tall. You looked like Mutt and Jeff.

This comparison seemed to stun Napoleon. He stammered:

— Is that all you care about me, Mother, laughing at me in front of outsiders?

He did not look at Denis who was following the scene with interest. And suddenly Napoleon did something he had not done since he was a baby and felt thirsty. His bewildered expression changed into a pained grimace. Napoleon, who had not even groaned when the dentist had pulled out all his teeth, who kept a serene face when his mother removed his boils with the neck of a bottle, Napoleon was crying. His eyes were wide open, just as when he laughed.

— I'm fed up. I'm going away from here. I'm going away from here!

In his eyes, open and full of tears, the mirage of a solitary hut in the wilds was dancing; a cabin where he could spend his life with his photo albums, and with Jeanne, who would sleep till noon.

— All right, go away, Cécile remarked. You behave like a baby! But me, if I'd left home every time I had some trouble, what would have become of you?

— Napoleon, dear, don't cry, Josephine pleaded, over-whelmed.

She took off her apron mechanically as if suddenly confronted with a distinguished visitor. The collector wiped his eyes on his sleeves and walked towards the door.

—Let me alone. I'm going.

He left for the Grande Allée, where, perhaps, he would find Jeanne tired to death, discouraged by her pitiful attempts to be happy with a man's help, and unwilling to see him, preferring to face the future alone.

Motionless, Josephine did nothing to hinder her son's flight. Denis Boucher got up abruptly and looked out.

—I think Monsieur Plouffe is back.

—He is? Well, I'm waiting for him! Josephine shouted, regaining her self-assurance.

She took out her gum carefully and stuck it under a chair. She had scarcely turned round when she gave a stupefied cry on seeing Théophile.

—Why, look at him! His suit's covered with mud!

His cap jammed down about his ears like a drunken man's, his face and his jacket mud-stained, his pipe hanging from moist lips, and his right arm crooked around some packages, Théophile did not dare to enter the house. He attempted to smile engagingly at his wife. His pipe fell out. Denis hurried to open the door for Papa Théophile. Josephine, hands on her hips, did not budge. She said slowly:

—I suppose you're going to tell me you come home at eight o'clock because you've been shopping!

Théophile assumed a martyred air and accentuated the trembling of his hands as he placed the packages on the table.

—So you don't love me, wife? I thought you'd cry when you saw me, like the time you did for Ovide. And I bought you some beautiful presents.

—What, Pa? What? Guillaume burst out, springing at his father and kissing him on the neck, something he had not done since his escapade with Rita Toulouse.

Inspired, Théophile held out his arms to his wife. She drew back with fright.

—Blood! Blood on your hands!

—Raspberries, I s'pose, Pa, said Guillaume.

Théophile stretched out his hands and looked at them.

—Oh! it's nothing! My bicycle needed repairing. The fork is a little bent. My wheel got caught in the track and I fell on some glass.

Josephine was no longer upset.

—More likely it's your own fork that's getting slack. Aren't you ashamed, you, the father of a missionary! Get a move on! You've got to be washed and then your nap. You know what the doctor told you about beer and your kidneys!

Denis Boucher, disappointed at Monsieur Plouffe's drunkenness, was nevertheless waiting for an opportunity to show his article.

—Before you lie down, Monsieur Plouffe, I have something interesting to show you: the *Nationalist*. My article on yesterday's parade. I give it a rap, you'll see.

Théophile, swaying in front of the table, eyes half-closed, and whimpering, seemed sinking into a drunkard's despair.

He shook his head feverishly and began to undo the parcels from which Guillaume had already removed the string.

—Listen, wife, I love you all right. Love me a tiny, little bit, won't you? I'm growing old, you know. Look, this is for you. A book about St. Joan of Arc.

—Oh! you old rogue! Josephine exclaimed, seizing the book. He knows how to get around me!

Guillaume had already grabbed his present: a baseball.

—Here's something for you, Cécile, dear. A beautiful set of perfumed notepaper. I don't think yours has any smell left.

The old maid took possession of the box and went off to hide it in her room.

—There! That's for Napoleon's girl friend. A lovely gold compact. She felt bad yesterday.

—He doesn't go out with her any more, Cécile gloated, coming out of her room. That's mine. I need one, right now.

Plunged in a deep reverie, Josephine was looking at the cover of her book.

—There's something you're not telling us, dear. The only time you ever brought me a present was when you were young and you weren't tight!

They all looked at Théophile. The tearful look in his eyes disappeared. He walked backwards slowly to his rocking-chair and fell into it. His lips were so heavy that little sobs came from them when he spoke.

—I've lost my job at *Christian Action*. They say I'm too old! Too old! Can I help that! Love me just a little bit; I love you, I do. I bought you some presents.

Josephine took a long breath and cowered against her stove. She said nothing and her distracted glance clung to her beloved furniture, for bailiffs had seized the household effects of one of her acquaintances when the husband lost his job. Cécile had stopped fingering the compact and gone back to her room saying:

—Now I see I was right not to get married.

Guillaume, almost cheered at the idea of having a companion whom he could tease all day long, tapped his father's shoulder gently:

—Don't worry about that, Pa. It'll be more fun with the two of us here.

From the crumpled mass that was Théophile, groans mixed with 'too old' emerged.

But it was Denis Boucher who was the most troubled. While listening to old Plouffe's confession, his eyes had rested automatically on his article. In a flash, he understood. His forehead became clammy. He got up, hiding the *Nationalist* behind his back.

—Don't be discouraged, Monsieur Plouffe. In the first place, they can't discharge you. They haven't the right. You do your work well and you haven't reached the age-limit. And aren't you a member of Catholic Syndicates? The traitors! They've thrown you out for another reason, and I know what it is. They fired you because you didn't put any flags out for the parade. The swine! Well! I tell you, they're going to take you back, or there'll be a strike. Leave it to me and have a good sleep. I'll go and see to this right away. Good night.

Once in the street, he clapped his hand to his forehead.

—It's my fault, it's all my fault! Why in the world did I write that damned article? But I'll make it right. Positively! This'll teach me to be a Smart Alec!

Denis's desire to occupy the limelight was beginning to give him trouble.

CHAPTER FOUR

D ENIS BOUCHER was burning to make amends. He walked rapidly, unaware that Théophile had trouble to keep up with him. He talked volubly and was over-solicitous because of his guilty conscience.

—It won't be long. You'll be back at your job.

—Yes, that's what I want, Théophile muttered. It's for my wife's sake, you understand.

Théophile was sweating and puffing but dared not ask Denis to go more slowly.

—Look, Monsieur Plouffe, my friends the nationalists have lent me the key to their office. It's a fine spot for our meeting.

That ought to be all right. By the way, has anybody replaced me yet?

—Nobody.

—Did the boys at the shop seem upset?

—It's as I told you, Monsieur Plouffe, everybody misses old Théo. You could see at the shop that nobody feels like working. He may be old, they keep saying, but there isn't a young man able to take his place.

—I miss them too, Théophile murmured sadly.

—We mustn't get soft, Monsieur Plouffe. We must work quickly and strike while the iron's hot. Today I made the rounds of the stereotypers and compositors and notified them of the meeting about your case this evening.

—There are still some decent people, the old man said, his hands trembling more than ever. I'll be glad to see them.

He felt the same emotion as on the day he had learned accidentally that his family were preparing to celebrate the twenty-fifth anniversary of his marriage.

They boarded the streetcar which went as far as Couronne Street. It was already getting dark. The two men were silent, Théophile moved at the thought of seeing his fellow-workers, and Denis uneasy at the idea of the venture he was undertaking. On leaving the streetcar the reporter scanned the front of a distant building.

—Some of them are here already. They're waiting for us.

A neon sign flashed on and off overhead, its glimmering light giving the group of men a mysterious appearance. Not a word was said as Denis and Théophile joined them. They exchanged furtive glances, for this half-clandestine gathering made them feel like conspirators. It was only when they were finally in the office of the *Nationalist* that they gave vent to sighs of relief, and slapped Théophile on the back as though they had not seen him for a long time. One man, big, florid, and fair-haired, with a neatly knotted tie, merely extended a flabby hand to Théophile with the words, 'poor friend'. He was Eustache Lafrance, known for his zeal on *Christian Action*, his large family, and the numerous societies of which he was an active member: St. John the Baptist, Lacordaire Club, St. Vincent de Paul, League of the Sacred Heart, and the Zouaves.

Greetings over, the men began to inspect the room. The place had the look of a merely temporary lodging. There were a few rickety chairs, the floor was littered with cigarette stubs and, the walls were covered with photographs of Mussolini, Hitler, Franco, Salazar, Codréanu, Degrelle, and other personages of dictatorial and violent temperament. A long table filled with pamphlets and newspaper clippings added to the clandestine look of the place.

Worried, Denis settled himself behind the table and listened for a moment to the workers who stood making wisecracks about the photographs. Out of patience, he thrust his head forward and counted aloud:

—One, two, three, four, five, six. Only six of you, gentlemen. Twenty promised me they'd come, didn't they?

The looks levelled at him revealed the incompatibility of old printers and young reporters. Phil Talbot, a stereotyper of about forty, and evidently the swaggerer of the group, shrugged his shoulders, looked at Eustache Lafrance, hesitated, then said in a bantering tone:

—You fell for that, young fellow! You thought they'd all come, didn't you! A job is a job, don't forget.

The reporter made a wry face and looked at his audience with misgiving. Suddenly, he felt very small, disarmed and powerless before the giant he intended fighting: a great newspaper. He was all alone with his twenty years. Théophile made no attempt to come to his side to spur on his flagging boldness. He huddled among his friends, moved to tears and fearful, like a banished son who has been joined secretly by his brothers.

—Let's wait ten minutes longer, Denis decided curtly. If no one else comes, we'll begin.

He mechanically glanced through the *Nationalist*, but seeing his article, he pushed the paper away sharply. He listened impatiently for footsteps on the big wooden staircase of the building. A discouraging silence answered him. He could hold out no longer and said feverishly:

—Come on, come on, take your seats, gentlemen. We'll start straight away. There are enough of us.

With the exception of Lafrance, they pushed forward, smiling like children, and settled themselves at the table as though preparing to spend a pleasant evening gossiping about everything except the stand they proposed to take against their employers. Contentedly, they stuffed their pipes, Théophile more slowly, feeling somewhat left out. Denis shrugged his shoulders. He had before him five fifty-year-old boys who had come to the meeting for entertainment, and in addition, Théophile Plouffe and Eustache Lafrance, whose gravity formed a contrast to the carefree expressions of the others. What motive had brought Lafrance here? A mania for meetings? Or was he a spy from *Christian Action*? Lafrance crossed his arms and legs, and waited. Perplexed, Denis looked at him for a moment, then began to speak:

—Gentlemen! You know why I have brought you together tonight. You seem to forget that Monsieur Théophile Plouffe, your fellow-worker for twenty-five years, has been discharged on the pretext that he is too old. What do you think about it?

Their gaiety disturbed, the five boys put away their pipes and looked at Théophile, dismayed at being asked to consider his misfortune. A heavy silence fell. It was evident, by the looks they exchanged, that the presence of Lafrance had put them on their guard and was keeping them from saying what they really thought. Phil Talbot, the most daring, shook his head:

—I don't understand it. He is still a good man and he works well. I wonder what's come over them.

Lafrance, twelve years younger than Théophile, chuckled comfortably.

—To hear you talk, you'd think it was us fellows here that employ the bosses. Théophile is a good compositor, it's true, but it's also true that he is growing old and that he might break down any minute. Of course, it's hard, I know.

—I like to work, I do, Théophile muttered, tears in his eyes. I like it. Though that's not the main thing. I have a wife and children.

—Don't worry, old man, said Talbot, patting him on the back commiseratingly. You there, Lafrance, what tells you you won't have a heart attack tomorrow?

Denis's enthusiasm began to revive. He knocked on the table.

—Monsieur Lafrance, that's your name, isn't it? Are you so indifferent to the misfortunes of others? You have a family to support. If you were thrown out tomorrow because you were too old, wouldn't you be glad if your friends stayed with you and defended you?

— Yes, yes, the other five exclaimed. We won't let you down, Théophile.

Lafrance flushed, then said aggressively:

— But what does it all add up to? What can you do about it? Théophile's family is grown up. He has children who work.

This unexpected opposition frustrated Denis's plans. He had pictured himself haranguing the indignant workers and inciting them to revolt. He clenched his fists.

— Oh! so that's it! Your idea of working is to depend on your children for food. Don't you appreciate the rightful pride of the man who wants to be self-supporting, or the joy felt by the craftsman who loves his calling? Aren't you aware that in depriving Monsieur Plouffe of a chance to practise his trade, you deprive him of his means of livelihood and turn him into an old man before his time?

— Yes, that's right! Try to deny it, Lafrance, they agreed, with a variety of indignant gestures.

Lafrance set his fat jaws and said nothing. Théophile, his eyes riveted on Denis, began to smile proudly. Denis Boucher was discovering a new pleasure; that of winning a meeting over to his opinion. And he adopted the illegitimate child of this pleasure: demagogy. He spread out his arms:

— Oh yes, gentlemen, you're quite right to find the cowardly trick of *Christian Action* unjust in Monsieur Plouffe's case, even though you, Monsieur Lafrance, seem to find it justifiable. I'm not as old as you and haven't your experience; I have no children to support; I'm neither a stereotyper nor a compositor, but when I went into Monsieur Plouffe's kitchen last night and saw his despair, I understood how the loss of a position for a man like him is as good as a death sentence. Wouldn't it be the same for you, gentlemen?

His audience, round-eyed, necks craned, listened to him as if he were showing them depths hitherto undiscovered within themselves.

—This is how it is when French Canadians stand together, Théophile declared in a quavering voice.

Throwing back his head like a popular leader, Denis glanced around at his listeners. Lafrance, eyes lowered, sat pinching his nose.

—You say nothing can be done? Denis went on. What about the Catholic Syndicates you belong to?

The illusion of strength left them. Their faces became anxious and discouraged. Talbot grumbled:

—The Catholic Syndicates and *Christian Action*! They work together. They'll promise to do their utmost for us. And then we'll hear no more about it.

—It might be embarrassing, you know, for the Catholic Union to make trouble for *Christian Action*, Lafrance suggested smoothly.

—But, good heavens! Boucher's anger burst out. What do you pay dues for? You do pay your dues, don't you?

—I'll say we do! they sighed.

—And get no protection? That's ridiculous. And yet you have to belong to the Syndicates! No, no, I refuse to believe that in our province the Catholic Syndicates serve as a screen for exploiters.

—You're going a little too far, young man, Lafrance broke in, drily. Aren't you afraid of losing your job for talking like this?

—Yes, watch out, Denis, Théophile advised, for he wished to resume his position without any clash.

—Let him speak! Let him speak! Talbot growled. He's right. All the employees at *Christian Action* think the same thing but no one dares say so. You know very well, Lafrance, that we can't choose our union. That's the way it is when one works for God around here.

Denis Boucher stretched out his arms.

—Let's be calm, gentlemen, let's be calm. (He was recapturing some of the flights of oratory muttered in his bed the night before, while he lay sleepless.) We must not go too far. As for you, Monsieur Lafrance, believe me, I'm not here to refute all your arguments systematically. It may be that you are right on certain points, but, on the other hand, you'll grant me, if you are honest, that I'm right about certain other ones. But that isn't the question. Let's not, above all, lose sight of the purpose of our meeting, which is to have Monsieur Plouffe reinstated through the intervention of the Catholic Union. I grant you, *Christian Action* is the last place where the Union would want to start a strike. But, faced with a scandal which might rouse public opinion, I think some of their officials, men of good faith, would take stern measures and go on strike if necessary. Yet, would they do it if the paper refused to take Monsieur Plouffe back because he is too old? I don't think so, because it's an individual case, which doesn't endanger their authority.

—If nothing can be done, why are you wasting our time, then? Lafrance interrupted, getting up.

—But that's the point, there *is* something to do! Denis cried.

He was silent a moment, staring intently at the fascinated workers. Then his two fists came down on the table with a crash.

—What if, for example, *Christian Action* had dismissed Monsieur Plouffe for other reasons than they say, reasons that would make you wild with anger?

Eustache Lafrance resumed his seat. Théophile gasped.

—Such as? they murmured.

Denis pulled himself together and continued coldly:

—Before answering you, I'd like to ask you a question. Are you, or are you not, sincere French Canadians who don't like the English any more than you have to? Do you graciously accept having to give your money to pay for a reception that cost millions, in honour of these damned English sovereigns? Is that the sort of thing you like?

The printers said nothing but looked grim. The agitator was enjoying his success.

—No, you don't like the English. I know that. Well now, do you want to know why your old comrade, Monsieur Plouffe has, lost his job? It's because he didn't dirty his house with decorations in honour of the sovereigns who were passing his door, and not because he is too old.

Leaning towards them, his face flushed, he watched eagerly for their reaction. He delighted in telling them this news, forgetting that he himself was probably responsible for the discharge of Monsieur Plouffe through having published his bit of braggadocio. Like an animal that has just been stung, the five-headed audience stiffened and gazed, stupefied, at Théophile.

—What? It's not true? That isn't possible!

When anyone talked about the English, Théophile was always angry, whether he could afford to be or not.

—As true as you sit there, he exclaimed, swelling out his chest and waving his hat. I had said I wouldn't put up any flags. I always keep my word and *Christian Action* isn't going to make me afraid.

—If what you say is true, we work for a bunch of stinkers, Phil Talbot growled, clenching his fists.

Denis Boucher was quivering with excitement. But Lafrance, who had listened to all this without stirring, shook his head doubtfully.

—Look, boys, don't let yourselves get carried away by a kid who makes fifteen dollars a week. It's hard to believe that *Action*, which is one hundred per cent with the St. John the Baptist Society, *Action* that spends its time fighting the Ontario Orangemen, would dismiss a man because he hadn't put out flags for the King. Come, come, we're not fools!

He looked down and closed his eyes, his expression as innocent and delighted as when he had delivered the fatal blow to his friendly adversary in mock debates staged by his parish priest under the heading of 'Catholic Action Forums', in which communism, anticlericalism, and Protestantism had been torn to pieces with an altogether parochial virtuosity and wealth of argument.

Denis Boucher bit his lips. He realized that it would be unwise to show them his article as proof. Concerned, he watched the hatred disappear from their faces to make way for relief. The printers looked thankfully at Lafrance, hoping he told the truth; for, if Denis were right, they would be obliged, all the same, to earn their living by working for *Christian Action*. Old Plouffe's Anglophobia was not so easily staggered:

—A newspaper that runs down the Ontario Orangemen. Right; but at the same time is capable of translating *God Save the King* into French.

—It is also true, Eustache Lafrance interrupted sharply, that the King and the Queen, who are English, addressed us in French, even if it enraged the Ontario fanatics.

—They're here so we'll enlist for the next war, Théophile retorted. They know they're going to get what for from the Germans if the 22nd Regiment isn't there.

Denis silenced him and gave his listeners no time to rally definitely to Lafrance's opinion. With an angry gesture he sent the pile of pamphlets in front of him flying.

—Gentlemen, it's my turn to speak. First, you, Monsieur Lafrance. I must say you seem rather pleased that Monsieur Plouffe has lost his position, and you seem to be doing all you can to prevent him getting it back. Would you be looking for a job for a friend, by any chance? And why did you come here? I'm young, it's true; I earn fifteen dollars a week, that's true. But I'm going to give you a little lesson in Canadian history.

—Oh! You flatter yourself that the King spoke to you in French even if those Ontario gentlemen didn't like it. The idea of enlistment brought out by Monsieur Plouffe is one of the reasons. But another one exists, one which is far more important.

Are you blind? For two hundred years, racial hatred has divided Canada and, today, despite the efforts of naïve apostles of good-will, the situation has hardly eased at all. Who is interested in seeing this division perpetuated? England. Because a united Canada, a real nation, would quickly get out from under her thumb. And what is England's trump card in the game of division? The Catholic province of Quebec. Our conquerors use our nationalism, our Catholicism, and our French blood to foment this misunderstanding. Again, our good bishops, desirous of assuring the survival of our race, must, by one of those distressing paradoxes of history, employ the same tactics. If Canada became an independent, united nation, then our admirable Catholicism, our incomparable traditions, and our French spirit would be swept away. Because, once the drawbridges of the province were lowered, we should be devoured swiftly by the materialistic Anglo-Saxon monster which our clergy have fortunately been able to keep in check at the frontiers of our province. The London Foreign Office, diabolical as always, has for a long time realized the identity of its interests with those of the Quebec clergy. And through it English diplomacy offers our higher clergy an abominable collaboration. Our bishops accept this collaboration in the good faith of exalted feeling which characterizes the apostles of a religion of love. Our bishops hope to assure our liberty and our life through this association, whereas, in reality, the English use it to keep us slaves of the Empire. A victim of its own sincerity and lofty aims, our Episcopate is thus the dupe of the English. Fortunately, the heroic members of our lesser clergy, ignorant of these subtle tactics, continue to disparage England and are astonished to see our admirable Cardinal receiving the English sovereigns with open arms. And, as you know, *Christian Action*, being the mouthpiece of the Archiepiscopate, cannot, in circumstances like the royal visit, do anything but proclaim aloud our loyalty to the sovereigns and discharge Monsieur Plouffe, despite the fact that, actually, this newspaper is as anti-British as you or I. So, believe me, the directors won't put up much resistance if the Catholic Syndicates demand the reinstatement of Monsieur Plouffe. The King isn't here now and they will have saved face. Do you understand?

—Well spoken, well spoken, Théophile applauded, sure now of taking up his work on the morrow. How happy my wife will be! I didn't have a leg to stand on any longer at home.

The others, open-mouthed, eyes dimmed by the efforts of laborious thinking, were looking at Denis who, enraptured by his speech, was convinced that he had installed a definite light of understanding in the printers' skulls. He looked proudly towards the photographs on the wall as if asking their admiration. But Lafrance, who at the word 'clergy' had ceased to understand, rose with dignity, buttoning his coat.

—I won't stay here to argue with a young upstart who dares talk about the priests! If you want to be sat on, you can come to our Catholic Action forum on Sunday; we'll put you in order, little communist!

He went out, closing the door quietly behind him.

—There's a friend for you, Théophile remarked scornfully.

—Well, well, everybody sighed anxiously. What did he come here for?

—Do you think he'll go back to the paper and tell them what I said? asked Denis, who had grown pale.

—What, are you afraid too?

They started to get up, then sat down again, not knowing whether to stay or to follow the runaway. Lafrance had shaken them more by his departure than by his arguments.

—No, I'm not afraid! Denis shouted fiercely. Those are my ideas. I'll repeat them to anybody. And you men, are you courageous enough to support them?

They sat with bowed heads, turning their hats in their hands and murmuring:

—It's not that. We have families.

—Oh! Fine guys, you are! Be men! Let the cowards go, the rest of us will stick together and help our old comrade. I'm not asking you to do the impossible. Then it's understood, you're going to see the union officials and ask them to take back Monsieur Plouffe?

When he had their wavering approval, he gave a sigh of relief. At bottom, he was no longer so sure that *Action* had discharged Monsieur Plouffe for any other reason than his age, because he felt that, in spite of all his little schemes, the paper would not take the printer back. But, in case his article in the *Nationalist* had been responsible for the dismissal, Denis had done his utmost to redeem his error. Denis Boucher absolved himself, and recovered the lightness of heart on which he depended for his success. He did not keep it long.

CHAPTER FIVE

WHEN Josephine Plouffe learned that her husband had lost his position, she foresaw a catastrophe that would reduce the family to fantastic poverty, strip the home of its furniture, and force her to take in washing. However, the furniture was still in place and they still had plenty to eat. The catastrophe was not this poverty on which her imagination dwelt so freely, but Théophile's pervading presence in the house all day long. He nosed about everywhere, doing his wife's housework after her; he insisted on setting the table and washing the floors, for by keeping busy he chased away the spectre of unemployment which was beginning to frighten him. After two days of this régime, Josephine lost patience completely.

The evening of the day after the meeting, Théophile, without news of Denis, was waiting about nervously. He approached his wife who, with both hands plunged in the dish-pan, seemed to be jostling her elbows among an invisible crowd.

—Where are the tea-towels? he asked anxiously.

—For goodness' sake, let me do my own work, nuisance. You're a regular plague. If you go on bothering me I'll have to go out to work myself. I'm tired of having you under my feet, you and our handsome Guillaume.

Théophile sank down heavily into the rocking-chair.

—You put up with me better when I was working. If I could die, you'd be rid of me.

—Don't be so tragic. Go out for a bit, that'll be a change. Still got your bicycle?

—I'll have to check up on the fork, first.

Since his discharge from *Christian Action*, he had not dared mount his famous racing bicycle for fear of falling. Before, when he went to work on his bike, his arthritic legs kept their old sureness and the way from the house to the shop seemed a practice track, on which a dying cyclist could have ridden without falling. But from now on, although he would not admit it, even to himself, Théophile feared the ride and began finding defects in his machine. The old man began to whistle *It's a long way to Tipperary* and looked out of the window. At this moment Napoleon, hair untidy, eyes staring, collar open, rushed out of his room and made quickly for the door.

—Where are you going, Napoleon? Josephine asked quietly.

He stopped dead, but did not turn around. His voice was flat, as though untuned to his feelings.

—To run a bit.

He pushed open the door. Josephine detained him by a plaintive exclamation.

—What's the matter, son? Why don't you talk to us any more? We've done nothing.

—I've nothing to say.

He went out. Josephine pulled back the yellow curtain a trifle and looked out at her eldest son who was running across the fields, elbows glued to his sides, on a race with no other goal than to outstrip the dusk. Now that Jeanne Duplessis refused to see him any more, he would run, every evening, until he was out of breath, as if by running he could leave his grief behind.

Josephine sighed and shook her head.

—He worries me. He's terribly in love. But it's better that way. She's a sick girl and she's going to die young, and besides, she'd cost him every cent he has.

—It will pass, said Théophile, who had only loved once, himself. Napoleon has a good wind. I shouldn't be surprised if he could win a race.

—Do you know what's in my head, dear? I'd like to go to the

monastery to see Ovide tomorrow, and tell him all about it. He can find a way to make them take you back on the paper.

—Don't do that! Théophile exclaimed in fright. That will upset him and he'll think he's obliged to come out to help us.

He had always considered Ovide as a sort of family magistrate who had spared his father simply because he never flunked work. The old man hastened to add:

—Besides, I'll be taking up my position again one of these days. I told you about our meeting yesterday. If you could have heard Denis! A regular M.P.! The boys have to speak to the union first, you understand. That may take a couple of days.

—Let me tell you, dear, Denis is a lad that talks big. But I don't trust any of it, your unions and your meetings.

Josephine bent over, stretching her neck in pursuit of an idea that kept eluding her.

—Heavens! I'm stupid! Monsieur Folbèche! Of course! He's the one to see. I'll cry if I have to. I'll get dressed right away.

Théophile's eyes shone hopefully. He saw himself setting out for the shop the next day.

—Good idea! The union and the priest too, and I'm all set. But don't go and cry. He'd take us for a couple of beggars.

—We're no better than beggars as it is.

As Josephine was leaving to go out, Cécile rushed into the kitchen, holding her new compact open at the height of her nose and powdering her face. The wings of her nostrils closed, and without raising her eyes she put out her hand and stopped her mother.

—Wait, Mama, I'm going to church. We'll walk together.

Josephine straightened her hat and looked her up and down.

—You write and pray so much lately that it's really beautiful to see! It's the best way to forget our troubles, and it keeps our minds off other things. Are you ready?

—All but my gloves.

Cécile ran to her room, a smile hovering at the corners of her lips. Her parents were not very bright! She fooled them as she pleased. But she helped them so much! What would have become of her family if she had married, if she had not economized? What a good thing she had sacrificed herself; she kept the household in order with a shower of tart remarks and disinterested advice. Just now, she was going to meet Onésime who was waiting for her at the church.

When they were gone, Théophile surveyed the kitchen, which appeared to him in a new light. He examined the rooms and the furniture, like a delighted owner visiting the furnished house he has just won in a lottery. Everything was marvellous! He shifted a chair, pushed back the table, opened the cupboard, and there was no shout from his wife. The old printer stepped across into the parlour and strummed *En roulant ma boule*. The sounds filled the house, and the music was for him alone. He stroked the trophies on the piano and felt proud of Guillaume; fingered his armchairs, and admitted that he had a fine set of furniture. Théophile smiled at the portrait of himself on his bicycle, then went back to the kitchen. Before the big cabinet which held Napoleon's albums he reflected, reached cautiously for the handle, then drew back his hand. He tiptoed to the window and, poking his nose through the curtains, made sure that his eldest son was not coming back from his running. Then he went back to the cabinet, opened it, took out an album and spread it on the floor. He squatted, down and looked for photos of cycle champions.

—Monsieur Plouffe, said a stifled voice.

Denis Boucher, pale eyes almost haggard, was framed in the doorway. He was pressing his lips together to keep them from trembling and wiping his forehead as if it were covered with sweat. Théophile closed the album furtively. His hands began to shake.

—Well, are they taking me back?

—Monsieur Plouffe, put the news on the radio. I've lost my position myself. Oh God! What'll my mother say!

—What!

Denis slumped into a chair. His words were so broken with his emotion that they seemed to emerge in pieces.

—Yes, on account of last night. It's Lafrance that sold us. They accuse me of being a communist.

—Then, they won't take me back? Théophile stammered.

Denis Boucher protested feebly.

—Is that all you can say when I've been let out of my job for trying to help you?

—It's not that, Théophile excused himself with a pleading look. You're young. You can do something else. You're educated. I'm sixty-two.

A surge of courage straightened out the long, listless body of Denis Boucher. He was shouting because, in his excitement, he could scarcely hear himself speak.

—Yes, I'm young and, more than that, I have a cause to serve. So *Christian Action* wants a fight. It'll cost them a lot. Do you think I'm discouraged? Far from it. What about my friends on the *Nationalist*? They're real men. They'll help me. Now I'll be working openly for the *Nationalist*! It's straight sailing.

His smiling eyes shone with the hope of the captive watching a friendly army rush to his aid. In his mind, the faces of his nationalist comrades became extraordinarily beautiful because of their fraternal arms held out to him.

—Perhaps you could manage to get me a place on that paper?

—Maybe. But I've thought of something. It's *Christian Action* that prints the *Nationalist*. Didn't you ever notice it? We're not rich enough, you know, to have our own shop.

—Ah! sighed Théophile, to whom a printed page meant merely its lay-out. Then there's only Father Folbèche left.

Denis began to think that if the *Nationalist* was not rich enough to have a shop, it was still less able to pay a journalist other than the paper's editor, whose patriotic and fiery enthusiasm fanned the generosity of voluntary contributors. They would give him ten dollars a week, at the most, perhaps less, whilst he had earned fifteen at *Christian Action*. Denis wanted to keep his fine self-confidence and stopped thinking of these disagreeable details, for he had to face his parents.

—I told you to put the news on the radio, Monsieur Plouffe. A general strike has been called at *Christian Action* because they have discharged all the others who were at the meeting, except Lafrance.

—What do you mean?

—Yes, they've accused them of holding communist meetings and have discharged them. That's made a pretty stink. Except for a few zealous workers, all the pressmen, all the compositors, and all the stereotypers have left their jobs as a protest. The Catholic Syndicates is supposed to call a strike tonight.

The lines smoothed out on Théophile's beaming face.

—And you didn't tell me!

The realization that his old friends would be at home and bored at the same time he was, that they would endure the same kitchen torments all day long, took away his loneliness and made him feel he had found a job whose employment consisted in not working for a time. He said triumphantly:

—There! That's French Canadians for you! And you didn't tell me!

The strike that Denis had wished for so much yesterday now left him indifferent. It was as out of place in his depressed mind as a long-desired pleasure on a day of mourning. This printer's strike did not gather him up as reporter on the lap of its solidarity, it left him groaning in vain on his little, individualistic footstool. He, who credited himself with common sense and with a clear idea of the hierarchy of values, was relegating to second place an important social issue in order to torture himself first over a reduction of five dollars a week in his salary.

—Let's have the news, Théophile said gaily, walking over to the radio. And you didn't even tell me! Hurrah! We're on strike!

As the waves of sound grew louder, Denis felt afraid to listen to words that would increase his sense of humiliation; discussed over the radio, this printers' strike would assume an importance that must force Denis into yet deeper oblivion, down into the limbo of stillborn reporters.

He went out without saying a word, his eyes clouded and his heart heavy at the sight of his father's house which appeared like an impregnable fortress to him. He gazed at the familiar landscape without seeing it. From the school hall, children's voices were singing *O Canada*. Denis Boucher pricked up his ears, and comfort flowed into his heart. His nationalist friends would stand by him. He was no longer alone: he had his union. Denis entered the house, his mind made up not to break the news of the loss of his employment to his parents until he should be engaged on the *Nationalist*. Just to assure himself of his own strength, he turned on the radio and listened as the blurred voice of the announcer became clear: 'The officials of *Christian Action* assure us that this strike is of no importance and that, with the collaboration of the Catholic Syndicates, this slight dispute will be settled in a few days. This news has come to you through the courtesy of . . .'

The young reporter heaved a sigh of relief and took a cigarette. Well, he was having his lesson. In future he would act more intelligently. He had scarcely drawn two puffs when he pricked up his ears again as the announcer, in a happily melodramatic voice, continued: 'A special bulletin from the Canadian Press has just arrived. By order of the Minister of Justice, the Royal Canadian Mounted Police have raided the offices of the *Nationalist* newspaper, which had been accused of secret activities and the publication of virulent articles calculated to threaten the safety of our sovereigns. Because of the course that international events are taking, this paper is henceforth banned, for the democracies need to unite their forces to face the menace of Hitlerism which becomes greater every day.'

In a rush of anguish, thoughts clashed with such rapidity in the young reporter's brain that his forehead was wet before the announcer had finished his script. Denis turned off the radio, put out his cigarette, and walked up and down the parlour. All his fine dreams of the future were collapsing—burning controversies, journalistic fame, fortune, and the imposing figure he would cut as a well-known personage. He was again reduced to obscurity, to the despair of useless applications to newspaper editors. He would die of old age, a proof-reader. Another anxiety was born from this confusion. His article was responsible for everything. He recalled the words 'the victims of British haemophilia', a literary find which had delighted him. Perhaps there would be arrests? Fortunately he wasn't dealing with fellows like Lafrance, but with real friends, with true nationalists. They would not give him away, even under threat of punishment. Discarding the idea of arrest, he thought of the loss of his position in another light. What a blow to his prestige in the parish! Unemployed! And his parents; especially his mother, who made him put on a clean white shirt every morning because she was so proud of him. What would his father think, who told everybody how glad he was that his son was a journalist! Denis wiped away the tear that glistened on his lashes and lay down on the couch. His head buried in his arms, this man of twenty stifled a heart-shaking sob.

There were three sharp knocks on the door. He leaped up, ready to fly into another room. His mother, who loved receiving letters and visitors, eagerly ran to open the door. As he slipped furtively into the kitchen, Denis heard:

—Does Denis Boucher live here?

—Yes. Yes, monsieur, his mother said, hesitatingly.

Out of the corner of his eye he saw two enormous members of the Royal Canadian Mounted Police. His heart almost stopped beating and he was hypnotized by his mother's pallor as she stared at him anxiously.

—Run along, Mama, he managed to order airily. It's about some articles.

She went out, smiling at her absurd fear. Nervously, Denis pointed to the couch.

—No need to sit down, said the one who was a sergeant. Was it you who wrote that?

He handed him the *Nationalist* and showed him the article signed 'Hindu'. The young reporter, limp with fear, stammered and tried to deny it, but he saw it was useless.

—Who told you that?

—It wasn't a little bird. Your good friends at the *Nationalist* were delighted to give us your name and address and have assured us they don't share your ideas.

Open-mouthed, Denis looked stunned with surprise.

—They told you that! he finally articulated. The skunks! The cowards!

—Pipe down, pipe down, my boy. We've just come to warn you we've got our eye on you, understand? You'd better toe the line and keep your mouth shut, see? It's for your own good. Good night.

When they had left, Denis sat down and, laboriously, tried to put his emotions in order.

—Simpleton! What a simpleton I've been! Fool!

He struck his forehead violent blows, making his hair fly up. He would have liked to leave, then and there, for Montreal, to begin a new life, even as a bus boy, if need be. 'Misfortunes never come singly', says an old proverb. There was another knock on the door.

—This is it! he breathed in a mournful voice, getting up like a drunken man. Another blow.

A big fellow with a pasty, beardless face, who could just as well have been taken for twenty as forty, stood before him, eyeing him up and down haughtily and swelling out his chest like a male intent on showing off his virility.

—Monsieur Boucher? The voice ranged in quality between tenor and contralto.

—Yes. You want *me*?

—Don't you recognize me?

Embarrassed, Denis tried to remember this face among the thousands of his victims all over the world who, doubtless, were waiting their turn to enter his door.

—It does seem as though I've seen you before. Frankly, I can't say where, though.

—I'm Stan Labrie. Does that mean anything to you?

—Stan Labrie! Oh! The baseball pitcher!

—Exactly.

With a grandiloquent gesture, his solemn visitor delicately unclipped a fountain-pen from his inside pocket. Denis, who did not yet understand, but dared not forget his irrational fear, laughed awkwardly.

—You look different without your baseball clothes. Sit down.

—No, monsieur. If the clothes are changed, the man isn't. The man whose character you insulted.

—What do you mean? Denis stammered feebly, unable to recall having insulted Stan Labrie, but already accepting the responsibility for every crime committed in the town.

—Hypocrite! You don't remember! The baseball game against the Protestant pastor last year. What did you say about me to that idiot, Guillaume Plouffe?

Denis closed his eyes, blinded by the recollection that gushed up in his memory. Words said for their picturesque effect returned like a boomerang to stun him with the accumulated pressure of twelve months. He remembered precisely what he had said about Stan Labrie's impotence in order to pacify Guillaume Plouffe. He spoke falteringly:

—Frankly, I don't follow you.

Stan Labrie, flourishing his pen in his large, plump hand, his behind waggling like a matron's in a hurry to get to a sale, crossed the parlour, infuriated by the innocent look Denis wore.

—I'm going to refresh your memory, then, he shouted. You told Guillaume Plouffe I was a queer, so you could turn Rita Toulouse against me. Today, she's my fiancée. That's a good one, Stan Labrie a queer! Why, I've had my private flat on Caron Street for five years and I've had mistresses and thrown more parties than you'll ever throw in your life.

Suddenly, Denis got angry.

—So what! Shut up! Get out or I'll put you out!

Stan Labrie, instead of becoming speechless with rage, spoke softly with honeyed politeness, face now all smooth curves.

—That would be bad for you and good for the lawyers. Your father has a nice house and nice furniture. I can see that. What would you think if I told you I was going to sue you in the Supreme Court for attacking my reputation? Ten thousand bucks, is that enough?

Slyly, he watched his victim turn paler. Denis gasped, his eyes hard. What? Through his fault, throw his family into the street, make his decent father a derelict, that humble unpretentious labourer, who had worn himself out in the task of acquiring a real family home, who stood aside for the sake of his growing children, who was tied to a thankless job twelve hours a day, who did without his beloved tobacco and walked to work so that his children could take the streetcar to the commercial school? No! No! It was impossible! He shook his head angrily and sobbed in spite of himself.

—You can't do that. I was young and I didn't say it seriously.

Stan Labrie gloated, hammering out his words distinctly:

—A reporter who doesn't know what he says! Listen! It's not over yet, see? This is serious, boy. At first, I was going to smash your face in. But it's better to go to court. For your information, I asked Madame Toulouse yesterday for permission to marry my fiancée, Rita, and I was refused. I wanted to know why. Then she told me the frightful thing that she had always been too embarrassed to tell me: that Guillaume Plouffe had told her on the quiet that I was not like other men, that I could never marry, and that I had a woman's physique, and so on. . . . She has asked me for a doctor's certificate into the bargain. What an insult! And you'll pay dear for it. I went to see that young idiot Plouffe, but he isn't responsible, he's a fool, and his father isn't even working. You're the one that's guilty and you're going to pay up.

—What a disaster! Denis groaned, scarcely able to breathe. He was beginning to feel, as though they were his own, the misfortunes he was causing others, and he would have liked to carry the whole burden so that none should be his victim.

—If you like, he suggested, pleadingly, I'll go and see Madame Toulouse and tell her that I was just kidding. Leave my father out of this; it would kill him.

The victor's lips set in a thin line.

—That's a good one! You want to get off too easy. 'Madame Toulouse, I said that for fun.' And she'll think you're siding with me to help me out.

Denis was becoming more and more conscious of his victim's plight.

—But if you take it to court it will make you look ridiculous. It would be so easy to get a doctor's certificate.

This suggestion, instead of exasperating the visitor, seemed to soothe him and lead to a compromise.

—A guy that's had a flat for five years doesn't need a doctor's certificate. That would be stupid. No, you're going to sign a statement for me that I can show to Madame Toulouse. If she's satisfied with it, then I might let the matter drop.

—I'll sign anything you want, you're very kind, Denis cried out hopefully.

Then Stan Labrie, flourishing a paper like a herald, began to read the proclamation in his high-pitched voice:

I, the undersigned, Denis Boucher, declare that I told Guillaume Plouffe an infamous lie regarding the physical character of Monsieur Stan Labrie. I admit saying that Monsieur Labrie was impotent, through ignorance in the first place and also because of my jealousy of him. I was jealous for two reasons: because of his success with women and because I was fond of Mademoiselle Toulouse and wished to take her away from him. I wish, therefore, to make honourable amends and state once more that what I said about Monsieur Labrie's impotence is false and inspired by jealousy.

Signed: DENIS BOUCHER

He held out the pen to the reporter. But Denis, at last emerging from his stupefaction, shouted:

— Do you think I'm a fool? Sign my own condemnation? Get out! You can do what you like!

Denis Boucher remained standing a long time in front of the door as though awaiting the next accuser. His face was burning, his eyes were blurred, he caught the everyday sounds in a kind of confused murmur like a diver coming out with his ears full of water. Then all at once, sounds, objects, thoughts, everything became clear. He heard the beat of his panic-stricken heart. But instead of the gentle warmth that follows torpor, a kind of cold sweat chilled him through and through.

He flung himself into the armchair, sobbing. His pride was in tatters. His future was ruined, he would be the butt of jeers and the shame of his parents. His enemies would abuse him and his friends forsake him. He sat up, his fists clenched. A fierce need to be consoled and encouraged took hold of him. He had always been self-sufficient. That was over. To whom could he cling? His father? His mother? He did not wish to add to their worries. The nationalists had betrayed him. The priest would lecture him. The youth felt as if this were the end of everything, and his sobs became more and more hollow. Suddenly, he stood up, his face lighted by an unexpected thought. He almost shouted:

— Ovide!

Ovide, whom he had gone to see only once at the monastery,

through curiosity, as one goes to see the famous specimens of misfortune in a waxworks museum; Ovide, who had filled his childhood with romantic legends and bits from operas, who had always confided his griefs to him and of whom he had begun to make fun, secretly, when he was seventeen. He would go to see him immediately. Denis looked nervously at his wrist-watch. He had two hours. The monastery did not close until nine o'clock. How could he get there most quickly? Papa Plouffe's bicycle came to mind and he ran to Théophile's without stopping to think that the Plouffes, who treated all their possessions like relics and never lent a thing, would hesitate to do him this service.

Denis went in without knocking. Théophile, who was coming to the door, seemed disappointed to see him.

—Ah! It's you. I thought the boys were coming in to talk over the strike.

The old man turned around, looking towards the toilet.

—Guillaume, you can come out. It's Denis. What do you think? A big fellow came here threatening Guillaume with the police about the gossip over Rita Toulouse. He made quite a hubbub and said he was going to see you.

Denis closed his eyes as if that could help him to overcome his humiliation.

—Forget about it, Monsieur Plouffe. He's crazy. I've settled that. Monsieur Plouffe, I've come to borrow your bicycle.

—Eh? My championship bicycle?

—Yes, I must go and see Ovide right away. It's important.

Annoyed by so unwarranted a request, Théophile took refuge behind a polite refusal.

—My poor boy, you know as well as I do that a champion's bicycle isn't loaned. And then it needs an overhaul. There are some cracks in the fork that worry me.

Wild anger blinded Denis, relegating his troubles to second place.

N　　　　　　　　193

—Monsieur Plouffe, just what sort of man are you, then? To help you get your job back I lose my own. I want to go to see Ovide about something important and you refuse me your bicycle. Whether you like it or not, I'm taking it.

He rushed down the steps and ran to the shed.

—Watch out for the tracks and the street corners. Check the tyres! old Plouffe called.

Bowled over by the sacrilege, he was still more concerned with the immediate danger to his bicycle.

But Denis, crouched over the handlebars, his head pointing like a greyhound's over the front wheel, was already disappearing into the distance. He was rushing to Ovide; he was going to throw himself into the arms of the lay brother.

CHAPTER SIX

—D ENIS!
Ovide's joyful surprise and his thin body burst forth
simultaneously from the tunnel of pale light revealed by
the monastery's open door. Standing on the sill, he seemed to
repulse the shadows that fell across him. His bony face was so
completely hidden by a black beard, already very thick and long,
that only the sparkling of his eyes and the broadening of his
scrawny cheekbones betrayed his wide smile.

—Good day, Ovide, Denis said awkwardly, without moving.

—Come in. It's good to see you, Denis, old man.

With a sort of skipping gait, the lay brother escorted the
young reporter to a huge parlour with bare walls and shining
wooden floor, whose only furniture consisted of a few straight-
backed chairs of severe design. Ovide, happy, straightened his
slightly rounded back. With his close-fitting red woollen cap, his
body adrift in an ample black habit, his black beard and pale
cheeks, he looked like an anaemic Jew in his ghetto receiving a
Gentile from French Canada.

—Don't you wear the robe yet? Denis asked, diffidently,
walking behind him.

—No, not before my novitiate is finished. That won't be long
now.

—It'll suit you very well.

They sat down facing one another. Ovide gazed at his friend
complacently as though he were a child grown bigger and
stronger in a year's absence.

Denis made a face, frustrated in his hope of not seeming like a
mischievous urchin in search of forgiveness or like a child borne

down by adversity looking for a breast on which to throw himself. He heaved a long sigh and in a low, almost broken voice, said:

—I have a whole lot to tell you, Ovide.

—Go ahead! Go ahead! Tell me about your career and your articles. Tell me you're as happy as I am here. I'll tell you my side afterwards. Go ahead!

Ovide clasped his hands in anticipation, his open mouth showing his yellow teeth shining with saliva, and his thin, tense frame quivering with happiness.

Denis eyed him suspiciously and drew back his chair. His wounded pride, revived by five miles in the open air, sensed danger once more. Who was this new Ovide? He wasn't the person whom Denis in his extremity had placed at the end of the path to the abyss, to keep himself from falling down it. Instead of the former grandiloquent Ovide; that puppet-like character; that Ovide who was easy to convince because of his vanity; instead of a crazy lover of opera on whom he had thought to unload his disappointments, Denis discovered a man who had unearthed another destiny than that for which he seemed destined, and who was radiant with his victory. Ovide was no longer the same; and Denis, who did not believe in such transformations because of his ignorance of the power of prayer, was distrustful. This distrust built up a wall between them; and the more it thickened and rose, the more firmly did self-pride encase Denis's heart, so ready a moment before to pour itself out. Even Ovide's way of talking intimidated him. His once affected speech had become simple, direct, careful. Angry with himself, Denis mumbled:

—Happy? Do I look it? Take a good look at me. And you, are you going to make me believe that you like this hole here?

Denis's question ended on a defiant note, which Ovide ignored.

—Do I like it? You won't believe me, but if you offered me a job at sixty dollars a week I'd refuse it. Besides, in this place, money doesn't count. It can't bring happiness anyway; sons of rich families, fine big lads like you, with classics courses and all that, who could have everything in life, enter our community, and are completely happy leading this life of sacrifice.

Denis choked back a malicious retort, and said:

—It's easy for them. At least they're priests. They say mass, and preach. But for you brothers . . .

At this moment a weasel-faced lay brother waddled across the room. Ovide glanced at him furtively with a hard light in his eyes which seemed to imply: 'What are you scrounging around for?' But he turned quickly to Denis and shook his head gently.

—You look at it from a worldly point of view. In a religious order self-respect takes on another meaning.

—Look here, you're still the same men, with two legs, two arms, a belly, and a head, aren't you? Be sensible!

Denis scraped the floor with his heel nervously. He could scarcely complete his sentences because, with each breath he took, the wild desire swelled up in him to knock over the chairs and cry: 'Ovide, Ovide, I've lost my job. Everyone's going back on me, jeering at me. Help me!' Frowning, the lay brother was occupied with something more precious to him than Denis's peace of mind.

—It's true, we are the same men. But we look beyond this life. It's true that our pride can be hurt. Take the little brother who just passed us, that's Brother Leopold. Ever since I've been here he's played all the nastiest tricks possible on me. There's no one more sneaky or detestable. He hides my shoes, fills my pockets with sand, pricks me with pins, deliberately dirties the floor I've just polished and calls me 'Brother Caruso of the gods' into the bargain. He's a Philistine, he added disdainfully. Ah! While I think of it, are you going to hear Pinza next week?

—No, Denis breathed, at the end of his tether.

Ovide mused for a few moments, then, waving his thin hand, said:

—To come back to Brother Leopold. He upset me at the beginning, you know. I went to the Superior, who simply laughed at me. 'Is that the way you stand unpleasantness? What would you do on the mission field, my dear fellow!'

—Do you want me to bash Brother Leopold's face in for you? cried Denis, leaping up and clenching his fists.

Threatening, breathless with anger, he was happy at finding a comrade bogged down in humiliation like himself. Ovide, frightened, made him sit down.

—Are you crazy? After seeing the Superior I understood. It's Brother Leopold whom they've made responsible for testing me to make sure of the sincerity of my vocation. He probably has the soul of a saint and suffers more from what he has to do to me, than I do, putting up with it.

—In any case, you're stupid to let that pie-face make a nuisance of himself.

—No. You see, the great joy, here, is to make sacrifices for Him who will not betray us.

—And suppose God, and all that heavenly shebang, weren't true? You'd have wasted your time.

The reporter watched the brother, anxious to confound him, to make him fall into his own slough of despond. Ovide stroked his beard and stared absent-mindedly at the wall.

—Denis, you're hiding something from me. When you bluster like that, it's because you're in trouble. I'll answer your question. Do you remember your crippled brother Gaston, who died? When you gave up your evenings to stay with him to make him forget his loneliness . . .

—All right, all right, Ovide. Don't be sentimental.

—Answer me. Did you do it for God? No. You did it first because you loved your brother. Your sacrifice made you more important in your own eyes, allowed you to have a better time the rest of the day. It was a pinch of salt in your reckless, gay life. You made that sacrifice as an amateur. For us, here, it's our daily bread. And that satisfaction you felt over giving up an evening, we experience from five in the morning until nine at night. It's a kind of gratification of the soul which strengthens it instead of exhausting it. It becomes changed. It expands to such a degree you might say our body is in our soul, like a chicken in the egg. And the more you feel your soul like that, the nearer you feel to some splendid One who is God, I'm sure of that.

—All that's just pride, Denis grunted, shrugging.

—Is it pride to choose one's way of life, one's ideal?

—All right then. But whom do you make all these sacrifices for? For others or for God?

—For both, old man. Because the more you love your neighbours, the higher you rise. I told you that, just now. Then, you begin to see the wonderful peak that the fog of your egoism hid from you. And you know, as soon as you see that peak, you want to reach it. Oh! Denis, if you knew the joy in making sacrifices to help a whole community, you wouldn't talk like that. It's only in that way you see that loving your neighbour is the path that leads to God.

—Well, what do you say about the monks who do nothing but pray and never go out of the monastery? What do they do to help their neighbour?

—They pray for him. They are so spiritual from such close contact with God that, by praying in their cells for everybody, they obtain the same results as we who travel in the bush. These monks are the aristocracy of our religion; our experts, if you prefer.

Denis smiled.

—Somehow, I can't see you at all in the bush, facing up to lions and negro jazz-babies. All the same you certainly have a good line. Where do you get all that?

Ovide looked down, blushing as he used to when told he was a connoisseur of opera.

—Our instructor teaches us pretty well, but I can say they're mostly my own ideas. Oh! I don't take any credit. That's our greatest problem here. We think of it all day long and we become specialists in sacrifice.

He burst out laughing, and struck the floor so hard with his heels that the roomy legs of his trousers, which hung loose from his bony thighs, shook like flabby flesh at his gust of hilarity.

—But I must not exaggerate, either. We have our good times. For instance, I'm in the choir and I copy out the music. The acoustics of the chapel are good, and I should like to try out one of my little pieces. It would sound well, I can tell you!

—Denis smiled sadly and put out his hand.

—Don't try to persuade me to come in here. I feel I'd die.

—Oh! No! I wouldn't think of it. If there must be humble lay brothers to help the mission fathers, there must be reporters as well.

—Ovide!

As though an abscess had just burst, Denis's heart was released from the pressure of self-consciousness. He was standing up, his chest heaving, tears in his eyes.

—What's the matter, my boy? Whatever's the matter?

Denis's voice, thrusting back his sobs, sounded muffled.

—I'm not a reporter any more, Ovide. Everybody's let me down. I've nobody but you. I don't know where to turn.

Ovide, with an air of authority, raised his hand.

—Denis, don't be discouraged. Your good old Pagliacci orders it. Now, let's hear all about it, he added gently.

Denis began a feverish recital of recent events.

—What! Papa's lost his job? Ovide exclaimed blankly, his back riveted to his chair. Good heavens! However will they manage?

A confessor learning that his father has been murdered by his penitent would have just the same reactions. With horror-stricken eyes, he kept repeating:

—Papa's lost his job. And I'm not there any more.

His terror was increasing because, having quickly taken stock of the disaster, his mind seized upon its most terrible result: the sale of his records, as luxuries, to pay the debts.

Heatedly Denis went on, with an account of the meeting, his

speech, and finally the appalling catastrophe of his dismissal from *Christian Action*. Then he told of the betrayal of his friends of the *Nationalist*, and the threat from the Royal Canadian Mounted Police. He did not relate the humiliation he had suffered from Stan Labrie, for Ovide was too depressed to help relieve him on that score.

—Your article is responsible for all this, Ovide said, shaking his head.

—You mean the political hypocrisy of *Christian Action*.

—And even if it were! Ovide replied indignantly, striking his brow. All these fine words won't pay the rent. Cécile and Napoleon earn next to nothing. And Guillaume doesn't work.

So Denis's predicament meant nothing to Ovide, either!

—Of course! When I lose my job on account of your father, and have nothing to look forward to, you're not even interested. As soon as the Plouffe tribe is affected, friends don't count any more. If somebody wants to borrow your bicycles, they're smashed. And when I needed ten cents you refused me on the pretext that one should never lend money to friends, yes, you, supposedly my greatest friend. Well! Cheer up! The Plouffe clan is saved. The employees of *Christian Action* are on strike since this evening, and they won't go back to work until your father and his friends who were at the meeting are taken back. Now you can pity me. I don't belong to the union and they're not going to take me back.

—You think they're going to take Papa back?

His serenity recovered, he once more turned a graciously compassionate eye on Denis's troubles.

—Look, Denis, be reasonable. You can't hold a grudge against me for worrying over the state of my family when I know that you, with your intelligence, can earn a living any time.

The discouragement of the unemployed is a compelling emotion, made up of hopes paralysed by the debris of failure; over it the mind has no control. Denis looked down, and said obstinately;

—No, no, I wanted to be a journalist. Now it's quite impossible.

—Well, now that they've called a strike, and *Christian Action* is going to take my father back—the strike will be effective, I suppose—let's get busy with your case. In front of me is Denis Boucher, who has just lost his job as reporter and who, apparently, hasn't a chance of another place on a Quebec paper because of the Mounties. This young man is of superior intelligence, is good-looking, and has no match in literary ability. What course will he take to become somebody in life?

—I feel like turning communist, Denis asserted, anxious to be convinced by the other's optimism.

Ovide crossed his hands behind him and began to walk up and down.

—Is it possible that our Denis could come to that? Communist!

—Find me another solution. The nationalists' principles aren't strong enough to keep them from betraying me when the police threaten them. The motions of *Catholic Action* are like those of marionettes when someone pulls the strings . . .

—Be quiet, Denis! What a fool you are! I understand so many things, since I came into the monastery. Haste is like love, it makes us blind. You're in too much of a hurry. You want to succeed too quickly. Because your ambition meets obstacles you accuse our Catholic faith and your countrymen, and then the gentleman turns communist, if you please! You ought to accuse yourself first.

—That's right, lecture me; that suits your calling. You've nothing to lose. . . .

—Mock at me as much as you like. But you seem to forget that I, myself, have suffered a good deal, and before you did. My poor Denis, I played the fool too; for example, Rita Toulouse. If I'd wished, I could have had her. Instead of being foolishly discouraged, trying obstinately to force my tastes on her, I should have pretended to share her own. That particular evening, I should have sung some American songs instead of singing

Pagliacci, and I should even have asked her to show me how to dance, to jazz. And then I should have gone to the Pente Douce with her, in place of Guillaume. Instead of making fun of me at the factory she would have praised my kindness, and in the long run she would have come to like opera.

—And you wouldn't be here. Very interesting, Denis said.

He followed Ovide's gestures with astonishment, not missing a word of his excited argument. Ovide stopped, embarrassed, the blush hidden by his beard betrayed by his ears and forehead. He mumbled:

—Then I wouldn't have been Ovide Plouffe. We are what we are before becoming what we become, and we never become again what we were.

—Obviously.

Ovide's face contracted.

—Don't think that I came here through discouragement, like your wanting to turn communist. No. It was my vocation. Now that I've found my way, I understand all my past mistakes and I know why I made them now that I'm free of them. I want you to open your eyes and profit by my experience.

—And opera? You could have become a great singer.

—No. I haven't absolute pitch, Ovide breathed, suddenly dreaming. But I'm telling you about the experience gained here. Yesterday my brother Napoleon came to see me and, with tears in his eyes, told me about his love troubles. It concerns a servant, Jeanne Duplessis, who doesn't want him to see her on account of circumstances that I can't tell you about. Did I suggest that he forget her and look somewhere else? No, I advised him to be patient, to pick flowers and to take them to her every day, to smile and then go away. I'm sure he'll win her over.

—But what's that got to do with my bad luck? I'm not having any love troubles, Denis answered impatiently, wearied by Ovide's laboriousness.

Ovide raised a finger.

—I'm coming to that. Like myself and Napoleon, you got off to a bad start. Remember the means you took to climb in society and become a reporter. First you went to university and disowned your poor Lower Town friends, and whenever you spoke to me you used to give me a look that was like a slap in the face; I've told you that before. Then you met a Protestant pastor and showed our family to him as if we were something funny. And then you used all of us to fool the priest, and forced him to find a place for you on *Christian Action*. Don't try to deny it; I understand all that, I've had time to think about it. Then there is still the fact that you used my father in writing a provocative article which did honour to your reputation as a journalist. But all that has fallen on your own head today and you are lost. Why? Because you have used others like steps to rise in life.

—What can I do now? There's no other way of getting on.

—What can you do? Instead of trampling on other people's hearts, trample on your own.

—Right now, other people are taking care of that. Give me a chance.

Ovide, with a brotherly gesture, took his friend by the sleeve.

—Poor old chap, I understand. You were so right to come to see me. Listen, look me in the eye.

He sat back in his chair and said with a triumphant smile:

—Denis, do you want to get over all this? Didn't you win a literary prize two years ago? Write a novel.

Ovide kept his mouth open after the word 'novel' as though he had pronounced the name of a cure for tuberculosis. Denis, astonished, reflected a minute, then shrugged his shoulders.

—To say what? Add a drop to the flood of love stories we're deluged with? I couldn't face it. I want to be someone, I tell you

Ovide examined Denis as a psychiatrist his patient.

—I've already told you your disease is that you want to succeed too soon. Haven't you ever thought of writing a story about your life and the parish where you were brought up and the clever minds you've met? What wonderful sentiments, what noble sacrifices you could portray!

—That's true, too, Denis said, almost inaudibly, dazzled by the ideas that struck him.

Seeing his friend's body stiffen with excitement, Ovide treated his proposition seriously, as though he had presented genius to a writer on a silver platter. As elated as though he had reached a high note, he saw, in the brilliance of his advice, thousands of sparks flying off from his idea of a novel. He imagined Denis carried away by the description of lofty feelings, decorating his parish like a superb wedding cake, with himself, the extraordinary Ovide Plouffe, planted like a glowing candle in an icing of attractive personalities. He said, his voice trembling:

—You would have to sacrifice a year without salary, I grant you. But afterwards you would win fame, the kind that journalism will never bring you. And you would have acquired it without hurting a soul. A novelist, Denis, think of it!

Denis had risen suddenly and was striding up and down the room, driven by the burning ambition Ovide had created in him. He spoke in a low tone, his teeth almost chattering.

—It's tremendous, Ovide, all the thoughts that come to me from that idea. My head is bursting. My novel is building up in this very moment like a house one builds in a dream. Ovide, Ovide, you've saved me!

Pale with joy, the lay brother still had his mouth open, and a drop of saliva he had forgotten to swallow ran down his beard. He was listening to Denis who, in his exaltation, seemed to be clasping an invisible being in his arms.

—I see them, my characters, they are there, wonderful, splendid.

Ovide closed his mouth and his eyes and bowed his head, blushing. Denis had come to a standstill and was smiling ferociously at the phantoms he had tried to seize. What a beating he would give to Stan Labrie, to *Christian Action*, to the nationalists, what a memorable picture he would paint of the Plouffe specimens!

—And you'll be able . . . Ovide began.

—Stop! We won't talk about it any more, Denis said gravely, or we'll spoil the idea. I'm going away now.

—Denis, stay a little while, Ovide begged, as if the idea of the novel had made them Siamese twins. Tell me news of the town and everybody. When my family come here they always tell me about their parish curates and about girls who are going into the convent.

Denis came slowly back to his friend, his lips still curling with the ferocious smile of a few moments before. By a strange reflex, his imagination, set in action by the pressure of joy, was transforming the events which just now had crushed him into fictitious adventures that he could dismiss or direct as he wished.

—Ah! You want news. You mentioned Rita Toulouse a little while ago.

—Have you seen her? Ovide asked indifferently.

The picture of Stan Labrie calling him a fool came before Denis's shining eyes.

—Oh, yes, I saw her walking along St. Joseph Street.

—If you had known her better you could have asked her how she was.

—I did speak to her.

—Oh! Is she married?

—On the contrary! Wait till you hear this! That Stan Labrie, pitcher for the *Canadiens*, you remember, was engaged to her, but he's a queer. It came out two months before they were going to be married. There's been a lot of talk about it. It was found out that he isn't any twenty-five-year-old but thirty-four at the least, and that he's an impostor who tried to trick two other girls before Rita Toulouse. She's finished with him!

—If she hadn't told you that, perhaps she would have mentioned me, ventured Ovide, not interested in the impotence of laymen.

Denis, brimming over with generosity, did not hesitate to invent.

—Yes, she spoke to me about you.

—She made fun of me, as usual, I suppose, Ovide said, with a sad smile that his hungry eyes contradicted.

—Not at all. She's changed a lot, you know. More serious, and now she's thinner, looks really beautiful. She told me she regretted bitterly not having realized, right away, how fine you were. She said she had been a little scatter-brain, but now, after what she's been through, she sees things in another light.

—She told you that, Ovide breathed softly.

—Of course. And then she sent you her best wishes. She wants you to forgive her foolishness, and to believe that she feels friendly towards you.

—I forgive her with all my heart, Ovide exclaimed. What shall I do? he asked himself. (He was suddenly filled with consternation, as if somebody he could not see were drowning beside him, in the dark.) Listen, he whispered, going close to Denis, tell her . . .

The sound of a bell made him jump. Brother Leopold rushed in, swaying about like a marionette and repeating through his nose:

—Visiting time is up, Brother Ovide; time is up. It's time for prayers.

He spread out his arms as though he were shooing hens. Denis went out, leaving an indignant Ovide to struggle as Brother Leopold propelled him towards another door. The youth drew in great breaths of the early summer air, full of the fragrance of freedom; the ephemeral freedom of those who do not choose their own fate. He was happy. He mounted Papa Plouffe's bicycle and bowled along peacefully, whistling. He would soon be famous.

Quebec gleamed in the distance.

CHAPTER SEVEN

—Not bad, not bad, Denis Boucher murmured, putting the last period to the first chapter of his novel. That'll make them sit up.

—A letter from the United States for you, Denis.

In spite of his eagerness to read the letter, the aspiring author took it from his mother with a casual air. He had had no difficulty in convincing his parents that within a year he would be a great man, even if during that time he did not bring a penny into the house.

—Mama! You won't regret your belief in me. My book is progressing and soon I'll be famous.

He did not catch his mother's ecstatic glance but went back to his room and hastily opened the letter. He frowned. The Reverend Tom Brown?

My very dear friend,

Most of the big American papers have reported the recent sensational events that took place in Quebec during the visit of the British sovereigns. French Canada is a very curious country and never ceases to astonish us Americans. You don't know how sorry I was not to have been with you when Guillaume Plouffe, that extraordinary lad, threw a magnificent speed-ball past the nose of the British sovereign, who owes his throne to an American woman.

The publicity given to Guillaume Plouffe's exploit has amused and intrigued our baseball fans. That boy's phenomenal ability can help him carve a great future in Uncle Sam's country. Consequently, I have spoken about him to the manager of the Cincinnati Reds, who is a great friend of mine. He's tremendously interested to meet him and he's keeping his eye on him. In two weeks' time I shall be in Quebec City with my wife; two scouts from the Cincinnati club will be with me to give young Plouffe a try-out. If he lives up to our hopes, we will offer him a contract.

You can, my dear Denis, announce this news in the papers; being a reporter, you know the value of publicity.

See you soon,

REV. TOM BROWN

—Terrific! My future's made!

Denis was radiant. Not because the letter announced the tremendous luck which had befallen young Plouffe but because it assured the realization of his own ambitions. A marvellous world really did exist, then, beyond the borders of his province; a world in which fortune might smile at everybody, even a Guillaume Plouffe. Denis, too, would leave this province of Quebec, this filthy hole where he could scarcely breathe.

He ran with the glad news to the Plouffes.

*   *   *   *   *   *

At the very same time, Monsieur Folbèche was hurrying along Montmagny Street. He looked troubled and, out of the corner of his eye, was watching Madame Plouffe as she made a timid motion from the end of the balcony to attract his attention. The priest feared to meet Josephine because he had failed in his effort at *Christian Action*. They would not take the compositor back; in fact, they had as much as told him to mind his own business. What, then! Had the lesser clergy so little influence? Were they being sacrificed to royalty? He quickened his pace. Josephine yielded to her desire and called after him:

—Monsieur le curé! Have you any news? Monsieur le curé!

He stopped and looked up.

—Too late! You should have let me do it alone. I would have arranged everything. Your business of a strike has spoiled it all.

Josephine leaned over farther.

—We must stop them, Monsieur le curé. They're having a parade this evening to rebel against religion. They have placards and speeches ready. My husband is like a madman. It's a regular revolution!

—Let them have one. I wash my hands of it.

And Monsieur Folbèche went on his way, shaking off the responsibilities with which people wished to burden him. A revolt against *Christian Action*, which had completely ignored his existence, a revolt against the bishops who left the priests to do the chores while they paid court to the English; so much the better! Monsieur Folbèche would await calmly in his parsonage the aristocracy of the clergy and would receive them with a superior little smile when they came to beg him to correct their mistakes, to soothe the flock and bring them back, submissive, into the bosom of Holy Church. He caught sight of Denis Boucher running, a letter in his hand.

—Are you taking part in the parade against *Christian Action*, too?

Breathless, Denis stared at him with a mocking smile.

—That's right. I'd forgotten about that. I'll certainly have to take part, although it won't do me any good.

The priest turned this over in his mind, forgetting his hurry.

—You've lost your place yourself. If you had minded your own business. . . .

Denis threw his head back proudly.

—I mind what I like. Besides, I'm glad to be out of that stinking hole.

—Nevertheless, you can't deny that you struggled pretty hard to get in, the priest retorted.

—I was young then, sir. I didn't see anything else. But now, my eyes are open. The future is in the west; here it's starvation. The United States is big and generous. They've a fine literature, too. And I'm strong, and I think I have some talent.

He was growing excited, his smile came and went as his voice vibrated, now with joy, now with defiance.

—I'll tell you a secret. I'm writing a great novel about the parish. It will be a success, I'm sure of that, and the Americans, who are extremely interested in our customs, will read it and welcome me with open arms.

His eyes shining naïvely Denis Boucher was secretly comparing himself with Guillaume Plouffe. The young reporter, unappreciated at home, would become the pet of New York, the exotic genius discovered in the Quebec bush. Monsieur Folbèche was less optimistic. Ears pricked up, nose to the scent, he bent towards Denis and said anxiously:

—A novel about the parish! What can you find to write about?

His distrust of literature equalled that of old fishermen who find their sons buried in books. Isn't reading as alluring and as treacherous as the sea, which robs people of their children and never gives them back?

—What do I write about? Denis replied slowly, rejoiced to see the priest's concern. I talk about you, your mission, the great souls you have formed, and of the splendid family you have brought up, in short, of our wonderful parish.

The priest, who had looked as suspicious as an old Norman, now sighed:

—Frankly, if I were you, my boy, I'd give up the idea. I'd prefer not to have anybody speak about the good I've done. Do you imagine the Americans will read it? They're not interested in us. They're simply Protestants who don't like Catholics because we beat them all along the line, even at baseball. You saw the minister last year; I beat him, eh?

—The Americans aren't interested in us? Denis shouted, waving Tom Brown's letter. Here, read this, read it!

Monsieur Folbèche slid his spectacles to the end of his nose and began to read, puffing out his lips in a reproachful and sceptical pout.

Triumphantly, Denis tried to gauge the priest's dejection by his eyes.

—Now! What did I tell you!

Monsieur Folbèche made no answer, and forgot to push up his spectacles. The weariness against which he had been fighting for some time bowled him over, all at once. How he wished for a chair in which to seat his old body, tired out with struggling. He was beaten; his parish was no longer impermeable but full of holes, and he inadequate to fill them up. For the first time he longed to be appointed canon, or failing this, chaplain of some monastery, far from his parish, where he would keep intact at least the memory of the big family he had raised, and where he would not have to see it disperse. But hopelessness does not keep us long from things we have made and loved. Monsieur Folbèche straightened up, refusing to admit that if he were failing in his task it was his fault. He recalled the triumphant welcome accorded the King of the English against the wishes of the priests, he reviewed the mistakes committed in the name of tolerance, and the future of the Church, by ecclesiastical generals who read too much, compromise with politicians, and do not sufficiently heed advice from humble corporals like himself, the astute and clever Monsieur Folbèche. He plucked at a hair in his nose, sneezed, wiped his glasses, then said with an odd smile:

—It's true the English and the Americans are beginning to invade us. I know who are responsible. But I'm waiting for them on my little side road, when they come complaining and ask me to fix things up for them. . . .

—Who are 'they'? Denis demanded naïvely, although he knew very well.

—You're too young to understand, grumbled Monsieur Folbèche, never dreaming that a layman could find his way through the winding paths of the clerical labyrinth.

He began to hum dreamily the *Dies Irae*, then said in a patronizing tone:

—You can tell the pastor that I'll allow him to come. I even invite him to visit me at the rectory. As for your novel, if you really want to write it, you can bring me some chapters from time to time. I haven't written a novel but I took my course in classics and perhaps I could help you. And then if you unwittingly said distasteful things about the parish, we could take them out. It's always better to wash one's dirty linen at home.

—Of course, Monsieur le curé.

Denis Boucher, smiling sardonically, watched Monsieur Folbèche as he went off sick at heart over the concessions made to the enemies of his parish; literature, the Americans, and the English. How could he do otherwise? His sentiments were those of the father of a family who is anxious to preserve his children's virtue: he prefers to invite the boys to his home rather than see his daughters go to meet them secretly.

*　　　*　　　*　　　*　　　*　　　*

—Perhaps blood will flow, but they've asked for it!

In voicing this threat, Théophile Plouffe felt himself a fully fledged striker. The more horror-stricken Josephine looked, the more gruffly he spoke, the more frightfully he rolled his eyes. He never dared get angry with his wife but, by the law of compensation, he could indulge in anger towards others.

Hands on his hips, his mouth distorted in a mocking grin, he watched Josephine run to the balcony and question the priest. When he heard 'We must stop them, Monsieur le curé, they're having a parade', he burst out into an almost hysterical laugh which broke over Josephine when she came in again, dejected by her failure and dumbfounded by the priest's attitude.

Théophile folded his hands over his belly to control his laughter.

—You're like wet hens, all you women. You're afraid of everything and then you jump head first into your priest's skirts, like ostriches. And yet you want to lead us about by the nose, us men who make wars and revolutions.

Flat on the floor, Guillaume was reading the Sunday comics in *La Patrie*, and Cécile, at the end of the table, head on hand, pen in mouth, was searching for the right word to make Oné-sime understand she loved him and was tired of not having him call any more.

Josephine set her fourteen stone of flesh in motion and stumped over to the stove, not daring to show her anger for fear of crying. Seizing the poker, she rattled the grate sulkily and turned round:

—We're cowards, are we? Bringing a child into the world is worse than going to war. As I've been through it twenty-two times, it's no wonder if my courage is a little worn out.

Théophile, who from modesty did not like talking about such things before his children, said hurriedly:

—Speaking of war, I know you'll trot out your everlasting St. Joan of Arc. But you can read her story a hundred times, you won't settle the strike, nor save Canada from the English. Any-way, that's not the issue. *Christian Action* has played a dirty trick on us and we're on strike to get our jobs back. Run along, wife. Go and get me my big leather belt that I use when I go fishing. If there's going to be any rough stuff, I want to be ready for it.

Guillaume looked up suddenly and said with enthusiasm:

—If Tarzan was with you fellows, Pa, you'd sure win, you betcha!

—Goodness! How grown up you are for your age! Cécile said bitingly, then went back to her writing.

Despite her anger, Josephine instinctively went to look for Théophile's belt.

—If you'd let Monsieur Folbèche alone he would have settled the whole thing without a strike. Today you'd be working and we'd be leading our quiet little life. It's those politics!

Théophile gave his wife a long, discouraged look. Would she ever understand?

—I've already told you, wife, that Monsieur le curé couldn't do anything in this case. It's higher politics. When everything is peaceful in the world and going along all right the priests have a great deal of influence. But war's going to break out any minute between the Germans and the English, and the Cardinal knows it's no time for fooling.

Josephine caught her breath.

—War?

—Yes, war, Théophile responded, delighted to have the floor. They're getting ready for it. Didn't I tell you the King came in order to get us to enlist? And if I didn't put out flags and if I lost my place and if there's a strike, it's because I refuse to see my children, especially that one, who isn't twenty-one yet, serving as cannon fodder for the English.

Théophile's raised arm emphasized his point. Guillaume had risen to his feet and Josephine rushed to put her arms around him.

—Your father's only joking. Don't bother your head about it. We two will go on the way we always do. Tomorrow we must be off early. The strawberries are getting ripe.

—Well! Théophile observed, rubbing his hands. Go and get me my belt.

—If Ovide was here, things would be better than this, Josephine whimpered, weak at the thought of her darling dressed as a soldier.

Armed with a broom which he shouldered like a gun, Guillaume aimed at his sister.

—Bang! One gossip gone!

Théophile squeezed in behind the stove to see if his banner for the parade was ready. He had cut it out carefully from cardboard and nailed it to the end of a stick. Napoleon, who was expert at block lettering, had painted in red, under his father's supervision and dictation, 'Down with the English dictatorship!' Théophile

laid the placard flat on the table beside Cécile's writing-case.
Cécile gave a grunt. Théophile threw a glance around the
kitchen.

—Well, the gang ought to be here any time. Now, then
where's Napoleon?

Josephine came back with the belt.

—He's gone to pick his little bunch of dandelions and daisies
just the same as every night, you know that.

—Yes. He can't think about anything but this girl business.
Anyhow, girl or no girl, flowers or no flowers, he's my eldest son
and I want him to go with me in the parade.

Josephine shrugged.

—Poor boy, loving that kind of a girl, stuck-up because she
works in the Upper Town. Ah! I'm not sorry I told her off.
And Napoleon's growing thin and doesn't eat ice-cream any
more and doesn't cut out pictures. He picks flowers for her like
mad, and when he takes them to her she won't even open the
door. Look in his room! Nothing but withered bunches of
flowers hanging from the shelves like old dish-cloths. Oh . . .

She lowered her voice, embarrassed, for Napoleon came trotting in looking distressed.

He ran to put away the flowers he was holding and came back
saying eagerly:

—Quick, Mother, my sweater. I have to cycle to St. Etienne.

— This evening? Josephine said, incredulously, holding up her
hands in surprise.

—Yes, right away. It's still chilly out of doors at night. It's
twenty-five miles there. Jeanne is ill. She's gone home.

Josephine's arms dropped heavily.

—Don't tell me that you're fool enough to ride fifty miles for
a girl who doesn't even open the door to take your flowers?

Napoleon, fallen into the trap, blushed and floundered, then
stammered:

—That's because I was too shy to ring the bell. So I came

back with them. This evening I gritted my teeth, and I rang. Another servant told me about her.

He was smiling.

—It can't be serious. A country girl won't be ill long. She coughs a little but I'm going to tell her about a remedy right away. A chap told me she must inhale manure fumes. Quick, Ma, my sweater.

—A consumptive! Oh dear! Josephine cried, holding her head between her hands. A stifling silence ensued, in which the room seemed closing in on them. Théophile's unrelenting, dominating voice shattered it.

—There's always an end to playing the fool, Napoleon. Start at eight o'clock for St. Etienne! You haven't your father's legs. You're not going to St. Etienne, you're coming with me to the parade; you're going to follow your father to battle.

—I'm going to St. Etienne, Viourge!

He sprang backwards to the doorway and faced them, ready to spring again, his face distorted, his eyes bright as though with tears.

Then Théophile Plouffe, trembling with melodramatic anger, walked slowly towards his son, brandishing his broad leather belt.

—Are you going to defy your father and disobey him?

—Wait, Napoleon, I'll go and look for your sweater. Josephine was crying.

Obstinate and ferocious as a beast cornered by a hunter, Napoleon waited for his father.

—I'm old enough, he snarled. I know what I'm doing. I'm thirty-three.

—The age of Jesus Christ our Lord when He died, observed Guillaume.

—Come on, Father. I'm not afraid of you with your little belt. But don't ever strike me.

At this moment Cécile intervened. She leaped up and placing herself between Napoleon and her father, shouted:

—Will you let that boy alone! Nobody's allowed to love the way he wants in this cursed house. Here, here's your sweater, Napoleon, she finished, taking it from the hands of her tearful mother. Go on, and see the one you love.

Napoleon fled, leaving Théophile nonplussed by Cécile's feeling for justice. She marched back to the table like a victorious soldier and with a grand sweep threw all her writing paper to the floor. Hands on her hips, she confronted them:

—I'm fed up with writing letters. You'll let Onésime come back, or else he'll take your streetcar bench away first thing tomorrow. It belongs to him, doesn't it?

—Let him come and take it then, said Josephine, for once coming to Théophile's rescue, since their authority as parents was at stake.

—What! The streetcar bench!

Papa Plouffe did not seem to understand. The streetcar bench on which he sat to warm himself for long hours in the sun; on which for ten years he had smoked his pipe after supper and looked vaguely into space; his streetcar bench, spirited away to land on another balcony! His anger melted, and he looked at Cécile pleadingly.

—Onésime couldn't do that. We're old friends.

—Théophile, don't you give in! commanded Josephine, who preferred her rocking-chair.

—Yes, he'll come for it tomorrow, Cécile threatened relentlessly, and that's not all either. I've drawn forty-five dollars out of my bank since you lost your job, Father. That's enough, you won't get another cent except for my board.

This time it was Josephine who was panic-stricken. The husband and wife gave each other a long look and Josephine yielded as she said in a low, shamed voice:

—All right. Let him come, but only when I'm here.

—That's better, Cécile said stiffly, for she always found it hard to relinquish her indignation. I've had enough of that. When I see that little, twenty-year-old parasite playing ball, tossing rings, and going off to pick strawberries, not bringing a penny into the house it gives me a pain in the neck!

—Ma, she's picking on me again, Guillaume threatened. If you don't stop her . . .

—Hi! Don't quibble about money any more. Your fortune is made!

They all turned around and saw Denis Boucher waving the pastor's letter.

—You're rich!

—Did you buy some lottery tickets? Josephine asked in a weak voice, clutching at her heart.

—Better than that, Madame Plouffe. Guillaume's going to be one of the greatest baseball players in the United States.

—How, tell me? Josephine asked, defensively.

—Me a big player? Guillaume asked naïvely. Listen, Cécile, better take back what you said about me being a boaster.

Denis Boucher read Tom Brown's letter aloud triumphantly.

—Never! exclaimed Josephine, edging Guillaume off into a corner. I'd rather have him out of a job than that. A little while ago it was the war, now it's exile to the United States, that country of wild parties and actresses! Guillaume, you're staying here, I tell you! and she pointed her finger emphatically towards the floor.

—But, Madame Plouffe . . .

—You, Denis, you, she replied, furious. I've had enough of your Protestant pastors and these crazy ideas you come putting into my children's heads. I'm boss here.

—Just a minute, Théophile interrupted with the important air he wore when he was speaking of his bicycle championship. This is serious, this business. Wife, our son has the Plouffe blood in his veins, champion's blood. It's time he became known in the outside world. It's time to prove that us men of the Lower Town can climb to the top, even abroad.

Denis went further.

—Your husband is right, Madame Plouffe. If Guillaume plays with a big club in the United States he can earn five hundred dollars a week. You'd all be rich.

Cécile, who up to now had merely shrugged, went off into fits of laughter. She could not conceive that her mother's pet, whom she considered the biggest hypocrite on earth, could earn the sum, in one week, that she, Cécile, had taken ten years to save.

—That's good, that is! she managed to say. Five hundred dollars a week! Him! I could die of laughing.

And she went away and threw herself on her bed, rolling with laughter. Guillaume came out timidly from his corner and asked, incredulously:

—Five hundred dollars a week? That'll pay some board, Ma. Apart from that, I've wanted to buy an Angora cat and a racing bicycle for a long time.

Théophile threw out his arms.

—No need to get excited over this. You'll spend that money as we decide, Guillaume. Besides, for some time I've had the idea of starting a little printing plant.

—You make me sick, all of you, Madame Plouffe exclaimed. That's right, go away, go to the dogs, desert me. . . .

And she retired into her room, carrying her apron with her.

—Listen! Here they come, Théophile said, cocking his ear. The steps resounded with the heavy tread of a number of men, shouting and waving their banners as if they were playthings. Théophile threw out his chest and waited for them.

*   *   *   *   *   *

The meeting which preceded the parade took place on Charest Boulevard opposite the office of the Catholic Syndicates.

In front of a temporary platform placed on a shed roof, a crowd of men were muttering anxiously. There were between five hundred and a thousand men there, forming a tumultuous

rearguard to the strikers of *Christian Action* who clung with
waning indignation to their heroic banners: Down with Dictatorship; Long Live the Catholic Syndicates; Away with the English;
Long Live the Cardinal; Are we Slaves? They don't want
Syndicates.

The sympathizing spectators, curious to test at last the effec-
tiveness of their union, were showing a fresh anger that their
scapegoats, the strikers, had exhausted in their kitchens during
the sixty days of the strike. It was the end of July. Darkness was
falling and car headlights cut swaths of light through the mass of
men that blocked their way. Streetcar bells and honking horns
clamoured above the crowd. From car windows, furtive, mocking glances rapidly scanned the men and the platform. Who were
these idiots, these simpletons, these crackpots, trying to climb
ladders without rungs! The Catholic Syndicates calling a strike
against *Christian Action*! The fools were blocking the road into
the bargain! And the horns and bells dinned insistently.

But the crowd didn't hear them. The speakers settled themselves on the platform. Clapping broke out. Whistles split the
air, paving the way for cat-calls. The staring strikers clutched
their banners, forgetting to moisten their dry throats. They had
been protesting for too long, without success, in a silence which
did not even give back an echo. They were not built for idling
and grousing, they were men who wanted to work and mind
their own business.

Besides, what good is it to struggle with an adversary who
controls our weapons as well as his own? Without having really
begun, the battle would end with this droll comedy, this demon-
stration of orators and microphones. But Denis Boucher, standing near Théophile, who was radiating anger because of his hate
for the English whom he held responsible for all his wrongs,
kept badgering them, inciting them to fight: their only response
was the mournful gaze of men who are beaten.

Five men were seated on the platform, their knees pressed

together, like spectators who have got on to a stage by accident. The union chaplain, a tall, bald man with hard but sympathetic features, gripped the microphone with one hand and stretched out the other for a silence which was already there.

'My dear friends,' he began, searching for the right words, 'in my position as chaplain of the Catholic Syndicates, I cannot judge whether your strike is legal or not. Your officials are here for that. The duty that is mine is to watch over your character as Catholic workers, to help you to be workmen esteemed by your employers, workmen like those Pope Pius XI wished for in his encyclical *Quadragesimo Anno*. You are aware that Catholic Syndicates was founded to hold certain unions in check whose sole aim is to upset society with a view to bringing about communism. We want to do away with the obstacles between employers and employed, in place of widening the breach that these other unions are making; we want to have you model workmen, not rebels and revolutionaries. A strike is always an unfortunate event, especially when it breaks out between two groups organized by the Church.'

—So *you* think! someone in the crowd called out.

One of the speakers on the platform poked his head forward to detect the source of this uncalled-for remark. The chaplain coughed, looked down, and continued:

'Up to now, we haven't been too unlucky; except for the strike at Dominion Textiles, which His Eminence succeeded in settling amicably with the directors of that big company, we can congratulate ourselves on having avoided quite a number of labour conflicts by bringing the employers to an understanding. Now it is a great misfortune for the Church that the syndicates have to fight *Christian Action*. I ask you, also, to mitigate as far as possible the effects of this conflict because our higher clergy suffer from them a great deal.

'You're going to parade through the streets of the town—then be dignified, go quietly like men, like Catholic workers. Above

l, don't forget to pray, because God, who through Moses
ivided the waters of the Red Sea, is also able to reconcile divi-
ons of opinion.'

—Amen! interjected the same mocking voice.

There were a few scattered laughs, but the strikers, pale and on
dge, did not turn their heads, seeming to be transfixed by the
haplain's frown as he came back to the microphone.

'My friends, as you can be quite certain, there are agents of
evolutionary unions dispersed among you who will try to incite
ou to reprehensible actions. I have confidence in you; you should
now how to rid yourself of them.'

Smiling, he waited, but the crowd ejected nobody and re-
ained motionless. At this moment, a youngster climbed on to
e platform and handed a note to the priest.

'My friends,' the chaplain said, 'I've just learnt that your presi-
ent is kept at home by illness and cannot come to this meeting.
e offers you his best wishes for success.'

Denis Boucher, standing beside Papa Plouffe, called through
is cupped hands:

—A fine time to choose! When was he ever ill before?

The chaplain, very dignified, took his seat. Then a large man
ith a loose tie, whose coat scarcely covered his thick chest, left
is chair and walked with a heavy, firm step towards the micro-
hone as though approaching an adversary. He had scarcely risen
hen the crowd called out hopefully and threw their hats in the
r:

—Long live Jos Bonefon! they shouted. Hurrah for a good
an! He has won his epaulettes!

Without smiling, Jos Bonefon pulled out a huge handkerchief
nd mopped the red brow of his enormous head. He fumbled
tently in his pocket, and managed to produce some notes.

—No need of paper, Jos. We know you. Speak from your
art.

He opened his mouth and was beginning to speak when a

hubbub occurred. Some tearful women, apparently come b
agreement, had sought out their husbands among the strike
and were begging them to leave.

Then the stentorian voice of Jos Bonefon rang out:

'Women, let your husbands alone and go back to you
kitchens. Your husbands are here to carry out a strike and they'r
going to do it. We're not cowards. I know the foreman of ou
workshop went to your house when your husband was away an
told you that if he didn't return quietly to work he wouldn't b
employed any more and your family would die of hunger. W
know their dodge. You won't die of hunger,' he shouted at th
top of his voice, 'because we're going to win our point and mak
them take back Théophile Plouffe and the other five who wer
thrown out like old dish-rags for reasons that have nothing to d
with their professional duties.'

The crowd was electrified. People shouted, gasped, an
applauded. Blushing and submissive, the wives let go their hol
on their husbands and with folded hands listened to the big
uncouth man who hypnotized them with his bulldog air and hi
reverberating voice.

'Boys, it's not necessary to tell you about my past. You al
know me! I was a compositor, you chose me as an official of th
union. And I assure you that I filled my office as representativ
just the way I did my job as a type-setter.'

—Go on, Jos, let 'em have it.

'First of all, why are we come here this evening? To protes
with all our strength, as honest men. We're here to deman
justice. This strike is legal. *Christian Action* hadn't the right t
discharge Théophile Plouffe, because he hadn't reached the ag
limit, and it had no right either to discharge five other employee
who met to discuss his case. That's dictatorship. Do we live i
Moscow, or in Berlin?'

—It's worse than that. We live in Quebec! someon
shouted.

Stimulated, the orator took off his tie.

'In any case, we have a union and we're going to use it. The rike has now lasted sixty days. We've hardly advanced at all. *Christian Action* obstinately refuses to submit to arbitration, to which we have the right. And what does the Department of Labour do, whose duty it is to enforce this arbitration? It doesn't udge. It's afraid. Who of? Who of? Why aren't the labour laws nd the unions doing what they should for us? It's time to hold up ur heads and insist on our rights. *Christian Action* is a sworn nemy of trade-unionism. Even in the ranks of its employees here is a Gestapo that informs the management about everything nat goes on.'

—We know who they are, Jos!

Carried away, Jos Bonefon raised himself on his toes and, raving his arms in the air, shouted:

'And the most disgusting thing is that the paper's coming out ust as if we were still there. Who's replacing you, you fathers who have children to feed? Kids of sixteen and seventeen, raciously supplied by a Quebec orphanage which owns a print-ng shop. And because it's *Christian Action*, they ask us politely ot to picket. It's pure slavery. In 1916, the strikers were replaced y nuns; today they're replaced by orphans'.

—Shame! Shame! the crowd roared.

Fists were clenched, shouts struggled to escape from con-racted throats. The other speakers, ill at ease, fidgeted in their hairs and looked disconsolately at the chaplain, who was shaking is head. Jos Bonefon mopped his brow. He continued:

'Remember the strike at Dominion Textiles. *Christian Action* denounced the lack of collaboration of that company with the unions under eight-column headlines. Yet that company agreed o arbitration and took back all its employees, thanks to His Eminence, whose orders *Christian Action* ignores today.'

—Long live the Cardinal! they shouted.

'It's uplifting, isn't it, this rebellion of a Catholic paper against

its chief? A chief who is well respected. A man to whom th
Revue des Deux Mondes of Paris devoted a long article latel
saying that despite his honours and ecclesiastical rank, he ha
remained a man of the people, on the side of the people, settlin
labour disputes and proving that he is the champion of th
working class. It's time, gentlemen, that this dictatorship wa
ended. Parade through the streets of the town, shout you
demands, and for our part, we of the union will put pressure o
the government and we'll beg His Eminence to intervene in ou
favour as he did in the Dominion Textiles strike.'

The rising clamour that came from the ranks of the spectator
and the ovation given Jos Bonefon after his speech, did not di
down in time to give the following speaker the cold receptio
that the meeting had kept for him. Shouts of enthusiasm change
into whistles and boos. The general excitement simply change
its tune.

Azarias Bégin was well dressed, and patient. He held th
microphone calmly while waiting for the crowd to be silent. H
was the type of union official who, at a meeting, shows himsel
more anxious about the opinion of the majority than about th
interests of the workers. If a strike seemed lost in advance to th
workers, he would turn employer's tool at the heart of the union
After a motion of impatience from the chaplain, partial silenc
was restored and Azarias Bégin started to speak in a steady voice
Spending some minutes on vague considerations of the prin
ciples of the Catholic Syndicates, he continued:

'In theory, of course, as an official of your union, I am hear
and soul with the strikers. But in the present situation I fough
the idea of striking and I still think we have been wrong to strike
I beg of you, let me speak! As Catholic workers we haven't th
right, whatever our motive, to go against Christian leadershi
for higher spiritual interests are at stake . . . Ow!'

A rotten tomato, hurled with force, squashed over his left eye
The general indignation manifested itself in a great burst o

laughter, then in a slow surge towards the platform. Angry comments were heard:

—And our children's bread? I suppose that, and our liberty, are lower interests?

The banners wavered in the trembling hands of exhausted strikers who were being carried along towards the platform by the angry crowd. The speaker, busily wiping his face, had managed to take refuge behind the chair of the embarrassed chaplain. Fortunately, at this moment, a telegraph messenger brought an envelope to the priest, who had scarcely opened it when he rushed to the microphone and opened his arms like a heavenly peacemaker. The crowd stood still in breathless silence.

'Brethren, friends! I've received a message this very moment from high authority. The strikers are ordered to return to fold. The case of the six rebels will be settled in a couple of weeks' time. Pardon assured for all!'

The crowd released a sigh like that of a collapsing balloon. Most of the strikers brandished their banners and shouted with joy, but the five men who had been discharged for having supported Théophile Plouffe bowed their heads, two of them bursting into sobs, and went off dragging their banners behind them. The crowd was about to disperse with a murmur of 'same old thing' when the voice of Denis Boucher rang out stridently, with all the strength that a good, indignant, twenty-year-old chest can summon. Eyes flashing, he challenged the crowd:

'Stop! Are you going to let yourselves be fooled once more by this shameful comedy? Will you always fall for blessings and high-sounding slogans? These six men won't ever be taken back, and you know it. Can't you see that financial interests are driving us like slaves, using our nationalism and religious faith as screens? Rebel . . .'

He got no further. Two tall, strong men in civilian dress, whom he recognized as the Mounties who had visited him, rushed at him and tried to overpower him. He fought back, dealing out blows with his fists and his feet, and stunned the sergeant with a hefty swing, but the other policeman struck him with his baton. They led the staggering youth to their car.

—We told you to keep quiet. We told you we had our eye on you!

Intimidated by the brutal force of this intervention, the silent crowd made way for the three men. Suddenly, the raucous yelps of an old man trying to shout made them turn around. Their astonishment changed to stupor. Théophile Plouffe, eyes staring out of his head, foam on his lips, was brandishing his standard as he howled. Petrified by the idea of displaying his anger before a crowd, when he had never done so except before his wife, he now managed to splutter the scraps of sentences that were strangling in his throat:

—Stop them! Stop them! It's the English! They're the ones that run *Christian Action*. They're the ones that will make us starve. War's coming, they want us to enlist. I mean it. I mean it, believe me. These damned men on the platform are all traitors except Jos Bonefon who's being tricked. I myself, Théophile Plouffe, he bawled, slapping himself on the chest, I didn't put out any flags for the King, that's the reason they threw me out. I don't care a hang for their job, he added, hurling away his banner. I'm through with the strike. I'm independent. I have a son who is a world champion. I'm going to start a little printing business, and I'll write and shout until I die, 'The cursed English!' And you there, on the platform, you traitors, you can go to the devil with those like you! Long live Guillaume II. Long live France! Ah! . . .

Papa Plouffe had suddenly grown very pale. He staggered, and his jaw, still open from his last word, sagged to the left. His extended arm twisted; the clenched hand opened, and the outspread fingers stiffened into marble. Then he collapsed, and the crowd closed in on him. An anguished murmur floated up; then, from those nearest, a cry was heard:

—Poor old soul! He's paralysed. He's paralysed.

With one accord all the faces, stamped with tragic accusation, turned towards the platform. The chaplain climbed down and ran towards the sick man. Azarias Bégin went to the microphone and said, in an altered tone:

—Take him home, some of you. Now you see, my friends, that *Christian Action* did discharge this man because of his age. And you see also how heaven strikes down those who rebel against its institutions.

The brief silence of the crowd gave way to a roar of indignation.

* * * * * *

—God in heaven! exclaimed Josephine in a faint voice when she saw the men come in, carrying her husband. Deathly pale, she first backed away to the sink and then rushed towards Théophile, who was being laid on the table. She held his head lovingly, straightening his hair.

—Oh, dear! It can't be liquor; he doesn't smell.

The men looked down in embarrassment.

—He's paralysed, madame. You'd better have the priest here, and the doctor.

The mask of distress that came over Josephine's face at these words was soon replaced by the confident, almost boastful look of the wife who has met trouble before.

—Huh! Him paralysed! Tomorrow it won't even show. He's limber, that man, he's been a champion, he's as strong as a horse; I ought to know. Besides, I'll look after him. I know what to do to bring him around, better than the doctor. Guillaume! Guillaume! Wherever are you? Come and help me carry your father to bed.

She ran about, turning here and there, not knowing which way to move, wiping her pale face and looking for Guillaume. The latter, on seeing his father, had approached him curiously and then, hearing the men declare so gravely that Théophile was paralysed, had fled into his room. With the help of her husband's friends, Josephine carried Théophile. He still had a speck of foam on his mouth, which was open and twisted to one side. Prompted by a vestige of his former dignity as head of the family he tried to move, and succeeded in blinking his eyes defiantly. Then he made a superhuman effort to speak, and they thought they heard him say:

—I won't die. I'm not a chicken. Go on, wife, scold me; what are you waiting for?

They laid him down on the bed. Josephine appealed to the men:

—Do you hear that? Scold him! He's like an emperor, that man, in his own home. He has only to lift his little finger and everyone does what he says.

She accompanied the workmen to the door and listened with close attention to their story, her face screwed up as she struggled to retain her confidence in Théophile's recovery. Thanking them, she nodded her head importantly.

—Yes, he's an orator, he is. Ah, if only the English hadn't been in his way, he could have been prime minister.

She went back quickly to the room and fussily set about undressing Théophile, promising to sew on a button, to buy him another shirt. She began singing, in a cracked voice, 'When I was eighteen, I came out of church, it was the first day of my marriage.' Théophile was purring softly. Except that their bodies were old and wrinkled and sick, they might indeed have been back in the early days of their marriage, when Théophile would linger in bed on Sunday morning while Josephine went around singing happily.

When she had tucked him in, after making fun of the temporary stiffness of his left side, she took down the crucifix from the wall facing Théophile. It had been taken from her father-in-law's coffin, and she feared it might suggest to her husband that this tiresome paralysis would lead him to the grave.

Théophile's tongue, which was recovering a little of its elasticity, tried to wag, knocking jerkily against the roof of his mouth, for he was snug in bed and his wife was singing.

—I made . . . good . . . speech . . . crowd . . . howled . . .

Josephine gaily arranged the curtains.

—Yes, so it seems. Everybody's talking about it. I'm not surprised.

She began singing again.

—Going to start a little printing shop, Josephine!

—Yes, my dear?

—You're very nice. Come and give me a kiss.

She moved towards him and timidly kissed him on the forehead.

—Josephine, don't let anyone touch my bicycle.

—No one will touch it. You're the master here. Just a minute, I'll be back. It's eleven o'clock and Napoleon and Cécile haven't come in. I don't see Guillaume either.

She went out on the balcony and peered along the street. Thoughtfully, she turned and, planted in the middle of the kitchen, looked at the wall as though trying to recall the date of an appointment. Then she slapped her brow:

—Heavens! Did I pay the premium on his policy?

She ran to the cupboard where she kept her important papers in a large soup tureen that was never used. This preoccupation with material matters indicated no hardness of heart. On the contrary, insurance policies and wills allow men, who are all born more or less tradesmen, to look at death as a business arrangement, and so almost forget the terror of the grave. Consequently Josephine intended to be wholly prepared, in the event of an ultimate transaction, to avert the unrelieved fear reserved for those who die without testament or insurance. She could not complete her search, for at that moment Cécile came in beaming, holding the hand of Onésime who blushed like a nervous schoolboy. It was only now that Josephine's grief found expression. She threw herself into her daughter's arms, sobbing:

—Your father! Your father! Paralysed!

—Oh, oh! Cécile cried, weeping in turn on Josephine's shoulder. Where is he?

Onésime, his arms dangling, gazed open-mouthed at this distressing scene. Standing on the back of the black horse which was woven into the mat at the door, he was the very picture of the embarrassed knight.

—You must rub him with cherry juice, he said. That's good for paralysis.

Hearing Onésime's voice, Cécile drew herself out of her mother's embrace and sniffed up her tears with all the energy of a woman who has had many troubles and numbers of children but has remained strong.

—Let's go and see Papa, Onésime.

They went into the room on tiptoe.

—Well, Papa, Cécile murmured, bending forward graciously like a nurse. Don't be discouraged. We're with you, Onésime and I. You'll come to see him every evening, eh, Nésime?

The streetcar conductor, who was jingling his money in the bottom of his pocket, smiled broadly.

—We'll sit on my bench. I've decided to give it to you.

—You see how it is, Papa, Cécile observed, glancing fondly at Onésime. Do you hear that? He's giving it to you. And then, if you need any of my money for treatment, you can take all you want.

The paralytic seemed not to be listening. He was sweating and puffing as if he were struggling to lift a vast weight. He gave a cry of distress.

—That's that! Can't move my arm for my pipe!

*　　*　　*　　*　　*　　*

—Here I am!

The victorious cry came from the kitchen into which Napoleon had burst like a whirlwind, breathless, his face beaming with happiness.

—Mother! Mother! I found her, my Jeanne; she's in a sanatorium about five miles from Quebec. Whoopee! I'll go and see her often and I'll pray so much that, before long, she'll be cured. Isn't anybody here? Are you all in bed?

—Napoleon!

Tragically, Josephine called her son and showed him Théophile. Troubled, and ready to defend his love, he approached cautiously, caught sight of his father, and then looked up questioningly at his mother who stood immobile, her arm still extended towards the bed.

She spoke in snatches so that her tears should not overcome her words.

—Paralysed! Ill!

Napoleon turned pale, but only for a moment.

—Viourge! That makes two patients for me! he said, swelling out his chest like a man who accepts his responsibilities with a will. Don't worry. Everything will be all right. When I pray to St. Anne it always works.

They were silent, surrounding Théophile who, groaning, was discovering moment by moment, degree by degree, the extent of his helplessness. The kitchen floor creaked. Guillaume, drawn by the silence, was approaching. He hesitated at the door of the room and then, in one bound, was kneeling beside the bed.

—Poor Papa! Poor Papa! I love you so much. I'll give you all the money I earn, it's all for you.

He buried his head in the pillow, for he was sobbing too hard to say more.

CHAPTER EIGHT

THE vanquished are faced with an immediate problem, that of becoming accustomed to their defeat. It is an easy task for those who lose often. Thus, even though the five comrades had not been taken back at the shop, the rest of the employees who, for their sake, had gone on strike, submitted to their employers with no other regret in their hearts than that of having lost two months' pay for nothing.

And because it is true that a group accustoms itself more quickly than an individual to misfortune, Papa Théophile refused to submit to the paralysis that bound him. His rigid tongue expressed in furious gibberish his interminable abuse of the English, his own recalcitrant limbs, and his family, who soon accustomed themselves to his state in order to devote themselves more completely to the demands of their egoism. Guillaume began to caress and tease his father as he would a big cat, but the other three felt no need of Théophile's presence. Mother Josephine had a freer hand in the kitchen and Napoleon and Cécile could enjoy their respective love affairs more peacefully when they had dumped the paralytic like an old parcel on the streetcar bench on the balcony, to bake himself in the sun and grumble at the neighbourhood children and the sparrows.

It was August 1939. News from Europe threatened the world with imminent war. The distressed populace had already forgotten the King's visit and the strike on the religious paper. To stave off their anxiety they lavished their attention on lesser problems and, frightened by the tremendous events which were darkening the horizon, devoted their energies to the establishment of a Canadian independence. Rumours of participation in a war by the side of the English were already circulating, and French Canadians forced themselves to believe in their freedom by making the most of every incident that flattered their whim of provincial autonomy.

In Quebec, as elsewhere, it is sport that gives rise to the most ardent displays of nationalism. Who would have believed it? It was Guillaume Plouffe who was to become a symbol to many of his countrymen. The news that his fame had crossed the border and that he was going to be given a public try-out by the talent scouts of the Cincinnati Reds, lit a fire in hearts made heavy by the threat of war. Press and radio lent such support that this particular Sunday, although the test was announced for three o'clock, the fans were crowding the baseball grounds by noon.

*　　*　　*　　*　　*　　*

Napoleon Plouffe ran down the steps and bounded into the street, smiling blissfully at the colourful scene unfolding like a fan on the baseball diamond. His most beautiful sports dream was taking place before him. Josephine appeared on the balcony.

—Poleon, you haven't eaten your bread-pudding.

—Not hungry, Ma.

—Never mind. You'll see the Americans tuck into it later on.

She spoke loudly, because the curious were crowding the sidewalk in hopes of seeing Guillaume appear. Josephine went in. Napoleon, now awakened from his dream, no longer breathed in the exhilarating murmur of the impatient crowd. Napoleon was in torture. He had to choose between the happiness of paying his first visit to the hospital to see Jeanne and the joy of witnessing his brother's triumph. For Jeanne had been in hospital for a week in the free ward, which could not be visited in the evenings. This being Sunday, he could see her between two and four o'clock, and the game started at three. It was a tragic dilemma for Napoleon. Tensing his muscles and wrinkling his brow, he gave himself up to its solution. He had not seen Jeanne since she had fled from the Plouffe house. Suppose she should die? A tear glistened on Napoleon's flat nose.

He mounted the bicycle and, without turning around, pedalled off to the sanatorium.

*   *   *   *   *   *

—Viourge! How big it is! he murmured, wandering down the endless corridors in the hospital.

He sniffed all the odours, stared at the sisters who passed, and exclaimed with delight over the cleanliness of the floors, like a child sent to look for Alice in Wonderland. It was the most beautiful place in the world, this hospital, and he was astonished that the people he met could look so sad, when Jeanne was there somewhere, in the remotest wing of the building. He would have wandered a long time if he had not discovered that the chocolates he had in his pocket for her were melting. Then he began to hurry down stairways and go up again in lifts, questioning orderlies, nurses, and sisters on the way.

When he finally reached the waiting-room on the third floor, he began to tremble. He had never felt so short nor so tongue-tied. Napoleon was about to push open the door to the ward when he saw a tall sister, with an ascetic face, who for some moments had been watching his strange antics.

He was afraid, but he smiled at her.

—I'm going to see Jeanne Duplessis.

—What did you say?

—You know, my Jeanne, Jeanne Duplessis. Well, I must go in, my sweets are melting.

He gave the imperturbable sister a bright smile and, in his nervousness, swung his bag of chocolate as if he were ringing a small hand-bell. The sister maintained her majestic air.

—Is she your sister?

—Cécile? Not on your life. It's Jeanne, I tell you. She's my girl friend.

Astonished by Napoleon's attitude, she inspected him again from head to foot. This little man's actions seemed unusual, so unusual that she determined not to let him upset her patients' peace of mind. She frowned and said coldly:

—Your girl friend? I'd advise you not to see her. We prefer that the treatment of our young girl patients should not be counteracted by useless sentimental worries. Worldly pleasures have harmed them enough without men coming here and bothering them all over again. Our hospital is a retreat for the soul as well as for the body. Why don't you go home, monsieur, and leave Mademoiselle Duplessis alone?

Napoleon thought, at first, that he had misunderstood. But as she went on speaking, he set his jaw. Then he thrust his head back into his shoulders, stiffened, and clenched his fists as he had done when his father tried to prevent him from going to St. Etienne.

—I suppose it's Mother who warned you to stop me from seeing her? I tell you that I'm going to.

The dumbfounded sister changed her tactics.

—Compose yourself, monsieur. And be respectful, I beg you, she said, toying with her crucifix. We're responsible to God for our patients, and as the anxieties of love are fatal for them we keep men out as much as we can. For instance, we protect them from contact with the male patients of this hospital and, as far as possible, we prefer them not to receive visits from young men who aren't related to them.

—I agree with that absolutely, Napoleon exclaimed. But it's not the same for me. I receive Holy Communion every morning for Jeanne. And apart from that, I'm Guillaume Plouffe's brother, do you know that? And my other brother, Ovide, is a White Father.

He swelled out his chest and gave a little side-glance at the sister like one member of a secret society identifying another.

—O.K. Right? Can I go in? My sweets are melting. I won't be long.

He walked round the sister and, slyly, as though they had been accomplices, he pushed the door open. Amused by the little man's manners and disarmed by his confidences, she let him do it. The mouse that profits from a cat's complacence could not have sprung into his hole more quickly than Napoleon into the ward.

Two rows of heads rising from their pillows were turned towards him. Stopped by twenty-four pairs of astonished and already mocking eyes, he stared along the shining floor, fascinated. His shadow, enormously long and thin, lay stretched there. A single discreet laugh summed up the silent mirth on every face. Napoleon's eyes gazed ahead as if to avoid seeing the sides of the room. With one hand, clammy from nervousness, he squeezed the bag of sweets, and ran the other over his little round head. Stifled giggles could be heard. 'Viourge!' he murmured with fright. He took a few cautious steps, as if he were walking on a skating-rink.

—Here, Napoleon!

St. Paul, encountering the vision on the road to Damascus, cannot have undergone so quick a transfiguration.

—Yes, Jeanne, here I am! he exclaimed, with a caper that swung him round to look into all twenty-four faces.

He slid and almost fell full length on seeing Jeanne who, sitting up in bed, frowned at the gymnastics he was executing in order to recover his balance. But he had short legs and his feet seemed to go all ways at once. When he had succeeded in not falling again, he performed two or three dance steps, smiling and bowing to all the patients, who burst into laughter. His capers brought him as far as Jeanne's bed. He did not look at her. Eyes cast down, he laid the sweets on the foot of the bed. Was she going to chase him away by reminding him of Josephine's attitude at the time of the royal procession? Wasn't Jeanne going to say anything at all? He began to recite all in one breath:

—I thought I'd come here and tell you that Guillaume was to have his picture in the English papers. The Cincinnatis are here to try him out. Thousands of people. Journalists, Americans. Wonderful for a Canadian. But I wanted to see you.

—Napoleon, look at me.

Moved, a sad smile on her lips, she gazed at him. A woollen shawl over her shoulders, head wreathed with braids, her face thin, but rested, she saw only her Napoleon, this man-child, this pure being that she had given up from love. The bright joy in her clear eyes contradicted the weariness of her smile. Round about them, ears strained in an inquisitive silence, for no one as yet had a visitor.

—Take a chair, she murmured, seizing him by the hand with tender abruptness.

—What! You're not going to send me away?

He was breathless; he wanted to cry because this exceeded all the joys, even the joy of sport, that he had experienced until then. The sick girl blushed; all the tears she had not shed filled her eyes. With an effort, she controlled herself.

—Why did you try to see me again? What good will it do you? Your mother was right. I'm very ill, Napoleon.

Livid, he stamped with indignation; he leaned feverishly against the bed as if he wished to take it in his arms and carry it to the end of the world, to the place where consumptives, perhaps, recover.

—You, ill? Don't say that.

She put her hand on his mouth, begging him to speak more softly. He glanced suspiciously at the neighbours and assumed a husky voice like that of a conspirator.

—Not true, Jeanne, can't be. You'll get well. I miss you so much. If you had seen all the flowers I picked and that you never smelled. You, ill? That's a good one. Listen. You know, a champion, to win, has to stick it. At home, we're stickers, we Plouffes. Try that. You've got to be a champion. You've got to win, and I'm sure you have nothing to worry about, anyway. Look, I'm going to ask the others if I'm not right.

—No, don't do that, she pleaded.

The delight with which she had listened to Napoleon's speech suddenly changed into fear.

—I can see you don't know what a sanatorium is. Those who are very ill will tell you that my case is serious, even if it isn't true, because they want to get better as quickly as the others. You heard them laughing a moment ago, it's because they want you to talk to them as much as to me.

—Ah!

Napoleon stole a glance along the ward as if Jeanne had pointed out strange beings. The tubercular take great pride in not coughing, especially in front of healthy people. So, a heavy silence, devoid of conversation, reigned in the room. A few girls, glued to the windows, were waiting wistfully for a possible visitor, in case some relative or friend should sacrifice this magnificent summer day for them. Others, with toilet articles on their knees, were doing their hair, making themselves lovelier and lovelier for the good-looking boys who would never come.

Napoleon sighed, shaking his head.

—Well, it's just too bad! Suppose I brought a gang of boys from the factory.... They could visit them. Everyone would like it, everyone would cheer up. Well, now, he concluded thoughtfully, for he suddenly remembered the sister's advice.

—You mustn't bother about the others, she replied, shaking her head almost joyfully.

The moment of emotion had passed. Lovers like Napoleon do not dwell forever on sentimental matters. They show their love by telling anecdotes about their trade or in confiding their ambitions. So talk turned on Guillaume, Théophile's paralysis, and the money Napoleon was banking.

On leaving the room, he came face to face with the gigantic sister. He was going to avoid her by skilfully bowing his way out when she stopped him:

—Dear me, monsieur, why do you persist in troubling that

girl? You'll hasten her death, for she has only a few months to live.

—What!

Petrified, he tried in vain to shake off the despair into which the sister had thrown him. She was not Cécile, the fibber, this tall woman, so grave she never laughed. And that black dress she wore cast a gloom over the whole place! He managed to fall back a step.

—Not true! Not true!

—Alas, monsieur . . .

—Yes? All right. I'm going to St. Anne. You try to stop *her*!

He dashed out of the sanatorium like a whirlwind and pedalled madly towards the town which must be crossed. When Napoleon, lying forward on his bicycle, heard the far-off clamour of a delirious crowd, and when his anguished eyes perceived the broad tumultuous fan whose axis seemed to be a silhouette raised at shoulder-height, he realized that Guillaume had emerged victorious from the try-out by the Cincinnati Reds, and that the Plouffe family numbered, henceforth, a baseball champion. He thought he would faint. His heart, as man and sportsman, wedged between the sorrow caused by the possible death of Jeanne and the pride of seeing Guillaume reach the top in sport, thudded quickly, then seemed to stop. His gaze clouded over. Jeanne's body, ghastly pale, placed itself between him and the playground, which drew him like a magnet. His love for Jeanne was the stronger. He continued straight ahead with meteor-like speed and did not even turn his head.

However, he might have seen from the corner of his eye something that would have pleased him. Pastor Tom Brown, Denis Boucher, Father Folbèche, and two Americans in plaid shirts were heading a triumphal march, sporting enormous cigars and chatting enthusiastically about Guillaume's game which he had played with unparalleled calm. Guillaume, from the height of his bulwark of shoulders, waved nonchalantly to his many fans.

Stretched on the streetcar bench, the paralytic cried with joy over his son's triumph; and Josephine put her arm around his neck, because the newspapermen were aiming their cameras at the balcony.

Napoleon did not see a lone girl who, from afar, was gazing with dreamy eyes at the reflections of all this glory. It was Rita Toulouse.

PART III

SEPTEMBER 1939

CHAPTER I

O N the 2nd of September 1939, America at first took refuge behind its ocean barrier. But this nation of sight-seers, sportsmen, reporters, and champions quickly resumed its place on the grandstand, excited by the sensational news that burst upon it. What a World Series! What a wonderful game! Would it beat the records of the first great war? Without fear, a man could light his cigar, or eat his hot-dog, for the Atlantic and the Monroe Doctrine kept watch. Babbitt rejoiced so much in his security that he failed to see the great Roosevelt discreetly exploring the arena.

The Canadians were more nervous, tradition and the economic interest of the country requiring them to stand ready. Faced with this state of emergency, when each of the nine provinces must yield many of its rights to the federal government in order to consolidate national unity, the different provincial factions of our bilingual country made the most of their last opportunities for disagreement: the ultra-imperialists of Ontario clamoured for all-out participation, and the Quebec separatists proclaimed loudly their total refusal to don the Allied uniform.

On the morning of the 4th of September, the Prime Minister announced that Canada was declaring war on Germany.

Quebec was in a fever. It was Labour-Day Monday. There was a strong wind, warmed by an ardent sun. The air buzzed with anguished rumours. The *Athenia* had been sunk the night before; Germany was martyrizing Poland, and the Quebeckers were going to the Provincial Fair to forget their sorrows in the hubbub of circus barkers, trumpets and race-tracks, and the odour of fried potatoes. This crowd, impressed by the Prime Minister's action, was almost proud of belonging to such a fine country. The

Maginot Line was protecting France (which had the misfortune to be the ally of England) and the Liberal Party had promised that there would be no conscription. So turn, little merry-go-rounds! One could enjoy oneself in peace.

But the nationalists were watchful. They organized their Resistance. They claimed that the politicians had tricked them. These apostles of Anglophobia ran about the town and the province trying to prepare a country of fatalists for a bloodless revolution.

*   *   *   *   *   *

—Denis Boucher!

The youth who was striding along the wooden pavement turned around sharply. He walked slowly towards Monsieur Folbèche who was approaching quickly, face pale, breath short, and hands fidgety. With the nation in danger, Monsieur Folbèche forgot his self-control and almost shouted:

—Have you heard the news? It's shocking!

—Yes, Monsieur le curé. I was expecting it. But there's nothing to be done.

—What do you mean, nothing to be done? Why, Denis! what will happen to us?

The old priest stiffened in surprise tinged with fright, not wetting his thick lower lip as in ordinary conversation; and the eye that some people said was glass seemed to shine with entreaty. Denis made no reply and maintained an abstracted air. The priest misunderstood his silence and smiled affectionately.

—Look here, I know you better than you think. You can talk without fear. You know, I've never told you that I read your articles in the *Nationalist*, and I thought they were good.

Denis looked at the ground and began to whistle. Young men were passing, hands in their pockets, thinking of the tragic tomorrows this era was offering them. They looked sullen, and if they spoke at all, it was to say: 'What a life! Unemployed or cannon fodder!' These lads had lost all thought of flirtations, although the girls had never been so agreeable. Compassionately, the priest watched them pass. He had the same fatherly feelings for Denis because, without telling him so, he had always considered him as a favourite son.

—Listen, Denis, we must protect them. In the name of all this youth of our French Catholic population we must defend ourselves against British schemes to enlist us and exterminate us. War is too easy an excuse. Now is the time for us to gather and demand our rights. You are with us in this, aren't you?

—No!

Denis Boucher looked sullenly at the dejected priest. Then he lifted a lock of hair and uncovered the scar of the wound he had received at the strike meeting. He smiled derisively.

—Look! Look! See what I got for defending our race! The nationalists not only didn't defend me, they gave me away to the police, the cowards! *Christian Action* sent me packing, and you reproached my boldness when you thought it was useless. Well! That's all over. My political party, now, is myself. What interests me is carving my own future. A new world's beginning, and I'll be with the strong.

—Denis!

—Excuse me, Monsieur le curé. But that's the way I see it. I've seen too much unemployment; I've seen too many blind and useless sacrifices made in the name of a sham ideal. There aren't enough of us, and there are too many of them. The struggle only succeeds in impoverishing us. The only ones who get anything out of it are . . .

The lad did not feel he had the courage to inflict a last cruelty on the old priest, whose eyes were filling with tears.

—Good day, Monsieur le curé.

Denis Boucher hurried away, his eyes raised to the Cape, towards the old fortifications, their openings rammed with outmoded cannon. The world-wide catastrophe, instead of overwhelming him, opened up broad and mysterious paths to his ambition. Instinctively, he felt a presentiment of the disappearance of thousands of men now enjoying life; a terrible economic upheaval; a harvest of opportunities of which he could easily gather his share. The economic and social barriers that had kept him prisoner were open; their guardians were busy escaping, or killing each other. At last the great adventure was opening its arms to him. Denis quivered with joy, for the terrible era that was unfolding also allowed him, without loss of self-esteem, to give up the novel that he had begun. He had read too many fine books.

Monsieur Folbèche, shoulders sagging, feet turned in, looked after him for a long time. Then he shook with anger.

—They let Protestant pastors into the University, they welcomed the King of England with open arms and they dined with him. They laughed at the advice of their old parish priests like me, and that's the result. The parish is breaking into smithereens, the young people are deserting. I was right.

A gust of wind suddenly raised the dust on the street. One fold of his cassock moulded the priest's thin legs, another fluttered in the breeze like an old flag the storm threatens to carry away. Monsieur Folbèche, his heart consumed and his body battered by the elements, seemed to sway for a moment. But his Norman tenacity prevailed. He caught at his hat nervously. His chest swelled in defiance, resisted all the assaults of the whirling dust; head high, teeth clenched, he looked at the sun.

—Well! I'll fight all the same!

*   *   *   *   *   *

Josephine Plouffe slowly crossed the kitchen, giving her husband and her children the look an anxious general gives his beloved sleeping soldiers. She paused in front of the calendar, tore off the month of August with a sullen gesture, and inspected September 1939 as though it were a military map.

—Poor children, she sighed. Poor old world!

She was thinking fearfully of Guillaume's departure the next spring. He had signed a contract as a new member with the Cincinnati Reds and was to hold himself ready to join his club the following season. How could such a tempting offer be refused? The Plouffes were poor and the Americans had paid a thousand dollars in advance.

Josephine felt quite alone. Everybody was leaving her. First it had been Ovide; then Cécile had defied her over Onésime; then Napoleon, foolishly enamoured of a girl suffering from a contagious disease. Paralysis had taken her Théophile, and now the United States was carrying off Guillaume.

That country seemed to her like a giant merry-go-round on which cigars, six-shooters, hot-dogs, actresses, gangsters, and cowboys gyrated, filling her mind with surrealist images. She was all at sea. Even the world that had been hers was disappearing. Her foot, shaped by the high boots of 1900, could not step into the new age. Her yellow cheeks puffed out with nostalgia while she thought tenderly of the babies that had not been born alive, whether because of a fall down the steps, or a violent squabble with Théophile, or because of a danger which had threatened either Napoleon, Cécile or Ovide; of the babies that today would be grown up and, perhaps, would not be leaving her like those for whom she had sacrificed them.

The bubbling of the boiling water drew her out of her musing and she ran to the stove.

—Guillaume, my pet, what would you like to have for lunch?

Since the public try-out, and especially because of the thousand dollars which he had hidden in his room, Guillaume, more than ever before, was the little master in the house. Leaning forwards, his mother waited patiently for him to look up. He was absorbed in reading the letters that littered the table. Many fans of both sexes were writing to him, and Guillaume, never one to be upset by glory, found in these testimonies an opportunity of teasing his sister.

—Guillaume! Josephine begged once more. Do answer! What would you like to eat?

He seized another letter and ripped it open ostentatiously. At this moment Cécile, who was in her room deciding on a dress, rushed out into the kitchen, wearing her rose slip.

—Mother, she burst out angrily, I'm going to have steak. You think that because of his thousand dollars and his championship, that little brat can boss us all.

Josephine, her face worn, looked at her daughter and said nothing.

Guillaume put down the letter which he had not yet read and smiled discreetly.

—Is it you or me that has the thousand dollars? You'll eat what Guillaume tells you to eat. You're nothing but a poor old hag who never gets any letters. Nobody knows you.

Cécile was so angry that she sneezed. Guillaume advised her to blow her nose. The old maid was as prickly as though she were a cactus dressed in a slip.

—You think you're the centre of the universe, eh? There are plenty left that are smarter than you, you'll find out. I'd like you to know that Onésime's been made a bus driver. You couldn't do that, little ball pitcher with the swelled head. That'll put you in your place!

—So that's why you spend your time riding around in a bus? the champion concluded.

Under Josephine's alarmed and inquisitive eyes, Cécile, who thought she had carried off the victory, went haughtily to her room.

—You could fry some potatoes, Ma, Guillaume ordered, plunging into his reading again.

While Josephine went to question Cécile as to the bus rides, Napoleon, who was pacing the kitchen gravely, stopped in front of his hero and mechanically sorted some envelopes.

—You ought to start an album. You must paste these letters in order of size and date. Take me, for instance, I've kept your pictures from the papers. It's convenient. Later on we can look at them. When someone doesn't believe us, we bring out the album and we're all right.

Guillaume assented, but without listening to him. The letter he was reading seemed to interest him to a marked degree. From Cécile's room Josephine's voice could be heard remonstrating sharply. Cécile replied in a defiant tone that she was free to choose whatever bus she liked.

Napoleon, seeing that Guillaume was not listening, changed the subject.

—Are you going to the circus this afternoon? You can see the fat woman who weighs four hundred pounds. She's healthy, no need of a sanatorium for her.

Guillaume got up from the table, beaming, and waving the letter he ran to his mother who was coming back into the kitchen.

—Ma! Do you remember Rita Toulouse? She's written to me, she congratulates me!

Josephine stopped chewing her gum and her jaws seemed to turn to stone. But she said nothing and closed her eyes. She no longer felt equal to the struggle. Formerly, when confronted by a difficulty, she had put her foot down. Now, every family difficulty corroded her energy like an acid.

Napoleon who, since Jeanne's entry into the hospital, had been paying attention to his mother to bring her around to his love, approached and offered her a stick of gum. She backed away in consternation.

—You! Don't you let me catch the germs that you cart back from the hospital. Haven't you any heart at all? Doesn't it matter to you if you contaminate us? For goodness' sake, leave her to die in peace. You'll kill yourself getting all tired out with these pilgrimages!

Napoleon tossed the gum into a corner of the kitchen and looked at everybody with bitter hatred. Then he went out, banging the door. Josephine shrugged her shoulders and announced:

—It's shocking what goes on here. The more that happens, the more I think that Ovide has made the best choice. He's a man, he is. It's easy to see that he's not here. Otherwise things would be different.

She glanced listlessly at Guillaume who was tickling his helpless father's nose with the corner of his letter. Then, overwhelmed, she went and polished the stove mechanically, but all she saw was an idiotic image on the convex nickel plate. Since her husband had been helpless and she no longer received any money from him she felt less the mistress in her own home. Something had changed, as if she too had become very old and paralysed. Irritated by Guillaume's trick Théophile grumbled angrily, letting his pipe fall.

— Oh! Let your father alone! Josephine called impatiently.

Guillaume sat down again at the table and gazed at Rita Toulouse's signature and Madame Plouffe replaced the extinguished pipe between the paralytic's four loose, yellow teeth.

The last two days Théophile had seemed fidgety. He grumbled incessantly. He had never suffered so painfully from the confines of his prison. The war that he had predicted had been declared, and no one in the family spoke about it. There he was, dumb as a blockhead before their insignificant quibblings, when he could have been pacing the kitchen improvising clever speeches about his prophetic political mind and the present armed conflict. Théophile looked sadly at the calendar, which advertised a famous brewery. In the first days of his paralysis, when everyone was full of kind intentions, he had made superhuman efforts to speak as clearly as possible; but they very soon grew tired of staring their eyes out in order to understand him, and as nobody listened any longer he unblushingly muttered his unintelligible sounds. What was the good? He was only a father who no longer brought home any money! He was only a bicycle champion who could not even walk any more and whom they treated like a sick old dog. Suddenly, Théophile almost struggled to his feet as the priest came into the kitchen solemnly and held out his hand to him.

—Good day, Monsieur Plouffe; good day, my friends.

His voice was grave and he gazed at the Plouffes as though they were statues he was about to destroy.

—My friends, Canada declared war with Germany at six o'clock this morning!

The great calamity had finally reached the Plouffes. When they had learned that Poland had been invaded they had done nothing more than pity Europe for its quarrelsome spirit. Monsieur Folbèche, eyes half-closed, waited for their reactions with a patriot's firm stance. Théophile, the veins in his neck standing out, raised an old face smoothed out by the complete triumph of his predictions. The paralysed man gripped his chair in an effort to raise himself and the words he would have said ran down in saliva on his trembling old chin. Silent, standing with her back to the stove, Josephine seemed to be waiting for an aggressor. Her jaws clenched, her eyes venomous, she scowled ferociously at the world that was bringing her disquieting news. The Plouffes scarcely breathed, and now, as if the muscular effort could defend their egoism against the contagion of world-wide misfortune, they stiffened. Monsieur Folbèche, standing motionless on the black horse on the rug, waited for the explosion of their fear. It was Cécile who made the first move. She burst into the kitchen, still pulling her skirt down over her hips.

—Do you think that men who have flat feet will have to go to war, Monsieur le curé?

The priest was disconcerted.

—No. In view of the threat that hangs over our heads, it would be better if all French Canadians had flat feet.

—I thought as much.

The old maid heaved a deep sigh and walked quickly to her room, proudly recalling her Onésime whose feet stuck to the ground like a blotter to an ink blot.

The paralytic gave vent to some incoherent sounds. Then, pale with anger at his helplessness, his brow furrowed and his free foot scraping the floor, he rolled his tongue between his open jaws and succeeded in pronouncing:

—I told you. The English have fooled us. Conscription?

In her anguish, Josephine took off her apron. The priest stared at the paralysed man.

—Conscription? No, not yet.

—Ah! Good God! That's what I was afraid of!

Josephine seemed deflated. She closed her eyes a moment and thanked heaven. Then she hurried forward and offered the priest a chair. Monsieur Folbèche crossed his legs and filled his nostrils with snuff.

—Don't rejoice too quickly. No conscription yet, but if we don't defend ourselves the government will put one over on us. And our young men, the future of our French-Canadian race, will be mown down on the battlefields of Europe.

He pointed gravely to Guillaume. The latter, dreamy-eyed, his hands in his pockets, got up from the table and began to prowl around the priest.

—Just the same, he said, I wouldn't hate going to war. Wonder what I'd be worth with a rifle.

His mother gave him a thump on the back.

—Don't you ever say that again, you lout of an imbecile. Your place is in the United States, next spring. That's the end of that.

She wanted to find some sign of approval, and looked at the worried priest who was thinking enviously of the easy task of the American clergy. Josephine mistook his silence.

—Oh! Never fear! Monsieur le curé, I've warned Guillaume not to let himself be roped in by the actresses. No danger. He's such a good boy.

The glance she gave Guillaume was moist with maternal pride; and Guillaume bent over, pretending to tie his shoe-lace, so as to smile without being seen. 'That's what you think, Mother,' he said to himself, picturing the young girls of the United States. The paralytic fidgeted in his chair, then succeeded in laughing sardonically.

—The Germans will rip the guts out of the English.

—Don't say that, my dear, Josephine expostulated. Don't forget France is with England. It's a pity St. Joan is dead. She'd have dealt with the Germans.

The priest coughed as though beginning an important sermon.

—Stop there, Madame Plouffe! You don't know all the evil that's been done in France. You've only to listen to Lucienne Boyer and Tino Rossi singing. It's lewdness turned into song. God has had enough of it. France must pay for her sins.

—Exactly, mumbled Théophile, who had never had occasion to deceive Josephine but who hid himself in the parlour to listen to *I have Two Mistresses*.

Frightened, Josephine thought of those passionate love songs that she hummed by heart every day without dreaming of evil, and wondered if they were not the cause of her misfortunes. The old maid burst out of the room from which she had been listening to the conversation. Head up, looking very virtuous, she put in her observations hoping to gain the good graces of the priest who had lectured her about Onésime at confession.

—You're right, Monsieur le curé. It's not up to us to get killed for the wicked doings on the other side.

The atmosphere was at last established. The old priest felt within him a fever that, with a temperamental despair, he had thought lost forever.

—Yes, my friends, he said, lifting up a voice trembling with patriotic fervour, is it right that this population of Quebec province, this population which is, thanks to us, the most Catholic in the world, should be spoiled by contact with these English and these French, whose sins are only too well known, under the pretext that it is necessary to save democracy? In 1918 our soldiers returned with miserable ailments and were, to cap it all, anticlerical. Ought we to fight for a victory that would cost us the salvation of our young men? An agonizing problem, to which Christ gave the only answer: 'What profit hath a man if he should gain the whole world and lose his own soul?' But that's not the most serious side of the matter, said he, turning mysteriously to Théophile who opened his mouth like a child being given something to eat. For three hundred years the English would have liked to have seen us disappear and they have always missed their aim because we were there, we the clergy, at the head of the Resistance. The United States, a true democracy, isn't going to war! Why should we . . .

— We'd be with the United States now if the bishops had let us alone in 1775!

Théophile had shouted, for he could no longer subdue his voice to the required intonation. Monsieur Folbèche's body seemed to fuse with his chair.

— Monsieur Plouffe, you don't understand the great political problems. If the United States had had us, I think that would have been worse than being with the English. The Province would be covered with buildings higher than churches; the priests would have no more influence, because religion in the United States is of no importance. You saw the Protestant minister? A baseball player! He doesn't save souls, he discovers pitchers! Wait till you see your Guillaume, when he comes back with a cigar in his mouth, married and divorced three or four times, with his head full of Protestant ideas and his mouth full of O.K.s and Yeahs. But I've warned you about all that.

Josephine stared at her son with her large eyes flashing over her spectacles.

— Guillaume, do you hear what Monsieur le curé is saying? Over there, no girls, no cigars.

— O.K., Ma.

Inside Théophile, the demon of politics was at grips with the demon of paralysis. The old man's tongue emerged almost victorious:

— In any case the English shan't have us. We'll defend ourselves with guns.

256

—Oh! my dear! You can speak again! Josephine shouted joyfully. Monsieur le curé, if this man wasn't paralysed, think what speeches he could make!

—He is with us at heart, that's sufficient, madame. We, the priests, are still here, and we are going to put the population on guard, with all our might, against the threat that hangs over it.

His speech was interrupted by Guillaume, who sprang up and said:

—Ma! Here's somebody!

Silence fell, and all stared at the door. Cautious steps padded softly over the loose boards of the balcony, making the same indescribable noise as Guillaume's cat when he prowled about at night. A shadow, wearing a bowler hat, passed across the drawn blinds. 'Who can that be?' Josephine muttered. The screen door was slowly pushed open.

—Ovide!

His smile was crooked and his eyes were dim with distress. His face appeared all the paler and all the thinner because he was wearing black, and had shaved off his heavy beard.

—Everything all right, you people?

Nobody replied. The staring eyes of old Josephine looked as though they would run to meet her beloved son. Mouth agape with embarrassment, Ovide stayed in the doorway and looked at the astonished priest. Then he put down his valise and raised his hat like a timid salesman uncertain how to present his merchandise.

—Not so bad, Vide. But we weren't expecting you, Guillaume admitted gaily.

—Ovide! My Vide! Josephine's bare gums clashed together with happiness. But she could not stir, she was so completely overcome with joy. It was the priest who was first to recover from this ecclesiastical surprise.

—What? Does the Community give you holidays?

Ovide grew even paler, took a long breath, and let fall the response that had taken away his appetite for three days.

R 257

—Yes, I came out for a little while. I don't want anyone to say I entered the monastery to escape the war. Do you understand?

As though Ovide had pulled a trigger, the priest exploded. He stood up and, almost purple in the face, he choked:

—What? What? It's incredible! Why, you should be doing just the opposite! Now or never is the time to stay in the monastery. Perhaps you don't know that we're against enlisting?

Ovide's first impulse was to curl up in the doorway like a beaten dog. But the smell of the kitchen had already acted on him like a tonic. He was in the very atmosphere which during twenty-five years had seen his authority supreme in the family.

Ovide airily threw his hat on the table.

—Monsieur le curé, I've consulted my conscience.

The priest's controversial mind controlled his blind anger.

—You call that conscience, to desert Christ's army for one that betrays the nation? Be honest with yourself!

He was silent, and looked at his family. Guillaume frowned as though passing judgement on him. Josephine pouted reproachfully and Théophile, trembling all over, looked up at his Ovide, in hope of a greeting. The words that the priest had to say to Ovide could not be said before the laity. Monsieur Folbèche moved towards the door and ordered, in a solemn tone:

—Ovide, I want to see you without fail at the rectory tonight, after church.

He went out, brushing his hat furiously. Then Josephine threw herself at Ovide, drew him to her ample bosom and hugged him lovingly.

—Vide, you know your own business. This is your home, more than ever.

Ovide stiffened, embarrassed by feeling his mother's flabby breasts against him.

—Poor mother, he said, smiling awkwardly.

He pushed her away, stroking her grey hair, then turned to the paralytic and took him by the shoulders.

—Papa! My papa! I'm going to have you looked after. You're going to get better.

Father Théophile threw back his head and the joy on his ashen face acted like sap, puffing out the white hairs of his beard. With his free hand, the old man gripped Ovide's forearm and his moist eyes shone with a wild hope. He had come, the saviour, he had returned to bring order out of family chaos and restore to Théophile his title of man and father.

—At last! he stammered.

Ovide sensed the whole situation. He straightened up, inspected the kitchen like a judge, and announced:

—I think it's about time I got back. You need a head here. Everything will go better, from now on. Guillaume, take my suitcase into my room.

Guillaume swelled out his chest like a champion who has been decorated.

—Yes, chief! With all my pictures in the papers and that arm you see there, I'm no ordinary porter!

Josephine folded her hands.

—It takes a priest to get attention like this.

Ovide made a face. Then Guillaume came back from the bedroom and pointed out the pile of letters to Ovide.

—You know my fan mail keeps me busy. Matter of fact, I've had a letter that you'll get a kick out of. Rita Toulouse.

Ovide walked over to his brother, and absent-mindedly tested the steadiness of the table. Then he snatched the letter out of Guillaume's hand. As he began to read, Cécile's voice made him look up.

—Hello, Ovide. Have you come out for good?

—Why, hello, Cécile. I can see you're as calm as ever. You haven't changed a bit.

The old maid glanced towards her mother and said ironically:

—Just have to be calm, here. This house is like a real convent!

Ovide was immersed again in his reading, but Josephine, irritated by Cécile's remark, drew him out of it.

—Don't try to get Ovide on your side. He'll stop your goings-on with Onésime, he will.

—What! Isn't that affair over yet? Ovide said severely.

—Over! Josephine went on triumphantly; why, she spends her evenings riding in a bus.

—So what! Cécile retorted, tight-lipped.

She was defying Ovide, this usurper, this ghost who seemed to reclaim his old authority.

—Cécile, he said firmly, I must speak to you confidentially about this. You'll see that it must stop.

—I don't owe you any explanation, she replied. While you were gone we all paid our board here!

—Be quiet, Ovide bellowed. You're all going to behave properly. And you're going to learn not to go out with married men, and to respect your parents.

The old maid banged the door and disappeared. Ovide had forgotten his anger and continued reading Rita's letter. Then he threw it back carelessly on the table. Josephine went up to him, took his arm, and carried him off to the parlour, showed him the piano, the records, and the phonograph, and in the quavering voice that, in a few years' time, would ordinarily be hers, she murmured:

—I told you nobody would touch them. I knew you'd come back.

Ovide enthusiastically patted her cheek, then took off his coat, threw it on the sewing-machine, rolled up his sleeves, and sang a few loud notes in a baritone voice.

—What would you say to a Georges Thill before dinner?

He was flourishing the record, *May a fair one charm my senses for a moment*, when he blushed and took a look at his mother. He thought better of it and put on Bizet's *Agnus Dei*.

Théophile, in his rocking-chair, muttered his approval as reinstated father.

CHAPTER TWO

THE first rays of dawn touched Ovide's eyelids. A fly tickled the sleeper's nostrils and he grimaced. Next, in the kitchen, the tinkling of a spoon broke the silence. Ovide woke suddenly, opened startled eyes, and leaped out of bed, groping for his shoes. Then he stopped. His glance ran round the room and finally rested on Guillaume who was snoring beside him. The two shoes fell back on the floor and Ovide went back to bed, smiling blissfully.

—Ouf! How stupid of me! I thought I was at the monastery.

He buried himself in his pillow with the pleasure of a milkman who realizes that it is a holiday and he can sleep until ten o'clock. He frowned. Let's see. Where was he in his dream? They were at a concert, Rita Toulouse and he. She was pressing his hand gently and murmuring her regret for having misunderstood him. Ovide turned on his left side and curled up in an attempt to return more easily to the land of dreams. No use. Its doors were definitely closed. His disappointed eyes fell on the plaster crucifix hanging on the wall, immediately lost their dreamy languor, and dimmed with anguish. Ovide! Deserter!

The sight of the crucifix aroused in his spirit a surge of remorseful fear. A year of sacrifices, prayers, and mysticism loomed up to accuse him of desertion, to heap scorn on the worldly pleasure now recovered in the trivial preoccupations of a lay sinner. What must God think of his flight, God, to whom he had felt at times so near? But Denis Boucher had come and had spoken to him of a new Rita Toulouse. How shameful to dream of Rita in this fashion! He was on the point of despair. He had leaped from a transatlantic liner to swim towards an island he thought held paradise. But there he found only pygmies, familiar pygmies, who again bound him hand and foot in their absurdities, while the liner, already far away, went on steering its difficult course towards greatness.

Ovide's downcast glance fell on Guillaume's striped pyjamas. Ovide crossed his fingers, cracking the knuckles. The previous evening there had been a dispute between Guillaume and his mother. Guillaume wanted to sleep naked, as usual, and, because of Ovide, Josephine had made him muffle up in this red and white garment in which now he looked like a barber's pole, so much had he turned round and round in his sleep.

Ovide rested his chin on his bony knees. Rita's mocking smile, her letter to his brother, and Denis Boucher's words at the monastery danced before his eyes. Then he understood. That was it. He must burn all the bridges to his monastery life; he must cheerfully become an ordinary man again, since it was now too late for him ever to rejoin the far-off ship. In a flash, Ovide again saw the grieved face of the Father Superior when he had announced his departure with the hard words: 'I've had enough of this desiccating existence where love is lacking most of all.' At that moment he had thought of Brother Leopold's spitefulness and of Rita's hair. And he had gone out almost banging the door in the silent Superior's face. Ovide suddenly remembered with hallucinatory clearness the speech that he had given Denis on the love owed to one's neighbour. He shrugged his shoulders impatiently. Why soften himself by these recollections? He had to face up to a more pressing problem. What attitude should rightly be taken towards his family, who were treating him like a clergyman on holiday? What a poor opinion, unacknowledged among themselves, they would privately have of him if he assured them he preferred to come back to the everyday scramble; if he confessed that monastery life oppressed him! And would he not finally forfeit their remaining respect when they found he had become his old self again for the sake of Rita Toulouse? Ovide knew his family and his friends. They would think him a Luther, for, in their eyes, an unfrocked priest, unless ill-health were the reason for the unfrocking, seemed almost as great a renegade as a layman who has not gone to mass for ten years.

Ovide struck his pillow an angry blow. He was imprisoned in a halo and there was no getting out of it without being accused of cowardice, even by his mother who spoke to him as if he were a holy Canadian martyr. She anticipated his slightest wish, was always using religious expressions, and had already enforced a clerical discipline in the house. Napoleon could no longer say 'Viourge', and she had forbidden Cécile to go about the kitchen in her slip. Oh! Yes! He must speak to Cécile about Onésime. What should he say?

The church bells were ringing for six o'clock mass. Ovide slipped into his clothes with alacrity. God was calling him to meet Him. God wished to tell him to regret nothing, that He would save him, just the same. Avoiding the sight of the crucifix he went almost joyfully to the kitchen. Napoleon, barefoot and in his drawers, leaned on the table, stirring the sugar in his coffee; he turned round and blushed on seeing his brother.

—Viourgemarie! Pardon! One moment! I'll go and put on my trousers.

In an access of modesty, he was about to rush towards his room. Ovide looked impatient and ran his long, hairy hand through his untidy locks.

—No, he said sharply, stay in your drawers. What do I care?

Napoleon gazed at him in amazement, then smiled timidly, blinking his eyes, for he liked to eat his breakfast barefoot and half-dressed.

Ovide paced up and down the kitchen, then glanced into each room to make sure the others were still sleeping. The two brothers kept looking at their feet, avoiding one another's eyes, and nothing disturbed the silence except Théophile's catarrhal snores. Napoleon ran to the stove. His toast was burning.

—It's unusual, he said, for priests not to be over-scrupulous. But you, Vide, have never been like other people.

Ovide ran his thumbs nervously up and down under his braces.

—Look, Napoleon, I'm not a priest or a brother. I've never worn the cassock nor taken vows.

Napoleon took a mouthful of coffee and raised his eyes with that nonsensical look one has when eating.

—It's funny. But you're not as you used to be. You seem like a priest even if you're not one. A person can see it's your vocation and that you'll go back to it when the war's over, this winter.

Ovide was overwhelmed. Why hadn't he told his family he had come out for good? But there had been the priest's unexpected presence. Ovide would certainly not go to see him at the parsonage! He walked over to the window so that his back would be turned to his brother.

—Napoleon.

—Yes.

—Tell me. Would it matter to you if I told you I wasn't going back to the monastery? Would you mind?

Napoleon respected his brother. His little teeth nibbled the toast with great speed. He dared not confess the disappointment that such a possibility caused him.

—I don't know how Mother would take it. When she chats with the women, she boasts she has a son who is a priest. Perhaps, underneath, she'll be satisfied, after all. Father and Guillaume will be all for it. But Cécile? She's sure to be against it. She was telling me last night she could scarcely wait till you went back. She says you're like a young widower who comes back to take his place in his father's house. That's hard on the other children. Once you've left, you've left, she says.

—Ah! Ovide murmured, perplexed. But how about you? What do you think, Napoleon?

—Me? Well . . .

—Go ahead. Don't make any bones about it.

—To tell the truth, it makes more people in the house. With you here, we feel safer.

There was a pause. Ill at ease, Napoleon looked in the bottom of his cup. Ovide stared at him.

—Go on.

—Don't get angry, Vide. There's just one more thing. I think that the sister at the hospital lets me see Jeanne often because you're a White Father. You understand, if you aren't any more . . .

—So it's true, Napoleon. You're in love as much as that?

The collector put his cup down and studied his brother's back for some time. Josephine must have instructed Ovide to break his relations with Jeanne. Always the same underhand conspiracy. He wiped his lips.

—Jeanne? No two ways about it. True love, for keeps, and Catholic, all sincere, nothing low-down. Nobody can stop me.

Ovide turned round and smiled gently.

—Then don't worry. I'll go and see that sister and I'll talk to her. Is your Jeanne getting along all right?

Napoleon left off eating. Surprise and happiness made him get up and run over to Ovide.

—Yes, she's putting on a little weight. That's my pilgrimages to St. Anne. You mean, you're not against it?

Ovide examined his brother's short, hairy legs.

—Against it? Are you mad? We only live once. And, seeing you're lucky enough to find the real thing, give yourself up to it completely, without troubling yourself about others.

Napoleon's eyes were wide with surprise. One weeps openly in the morning. A tear ran down his flat nose. Through Ovide's words, his love for Jeanne was at last defined. He knew he would die for her.

—Thanks, Vide, he stammered. Then some Sunday you could

come and sing for the girls there. They have a dull time. There's a piano in the ward.

In their emotion, the two brothers were silent with embarrassment.

—I'll go, Ovide promised, at last. Now, pull yourself together. I won't go back to the monastery. I'm staying here. Do you still mind?

Napoleon shook his head gaily. His eyes laughed.

—Are you coming to mass? Ovide asked.

They walked briskly off to church. Two unfortunates, making a team, would obtain what they wished from God.

* * * * * *

During those unhappy days, when the threat of conscription hung over the people of Quebec, the church was filled to overflowing at early mass. Monsieur Folbèche had sounded the alarm to his parishioners and composed a Prayer for Peace which he recited at every service; a prayer which dealt, vaguely, with fighting for the independence of the province, repulsing British forays into French-Canadian ranks, and resisting incorporation with the sinful armies of England and France. This invocation ended with a call for complete confidence in the Pope, who knew the secret of a peace in which there would be neither conquerors nor conquered. But, as the belligerents were paying no attention to the Pope, Monsieur Folbèche felt justified in acting for him to the extent of encouraging among his own people a comfortable neutrality, without any possible accusation of cowardice.

Ovide quickly broke away from the crowd which, from the open doors of the church, was dispersing along the street. A number of persons scrutinized him and whispered: 'There's Ovide Plouffe, he was with the White Fathers, you know!' 'Why, there's that brother of Guillaume Plouffe, the champion. He's the opera singer!' 'Théophile's son?' 'Right, too skinny for Africa, I suppose.' 'Or did something bad, perhaps.' 'He has nothing to risk, they'd never take him for the army. He's a regular stick!' The tongues wagged on, and some of their spiteful remarks reached Ovide's ears.

He was weary. The atmosphere of the church had not restored his peace of mind. He had sought in vain for the serenity so easily found in the monastery chapel. The atmosphere of this parish church, preoccupied with budgets, construction plans, repairs, and collections, and containing so little true piety, offered no freedom for the wings of prayer and quelled in the heart the impulses of an exacting faith. In the middle of mass Ovide had wanted to go out. All these stares fastened upon him crushed him like so many accusations. And hadn't the curé looked at him severely when giving him the Host?

Ovide felt skinnier than ever. What had he done to them? They hemmed him in, reproaching him for his way of life, whichever direction it took. When would he be free to make his own decisions? Ah! If he could only bring together the people of the parish, including the priest, in an immense meeting, and tell them all exactly how he felt. 'To begin with, mind your own business. This is my affair. And in the second place, you've got to understand that if I was intended for great things, I haven't been granted the wherewithal to reach them. I always come down with a bang to Ovide's wretched body and Ovide's unhappy heart.'

He perceived that he was speaking out loud, and blushed, for a housewife leaning on her broom was looking, open-mouthed, at him. He hurried along faster. A desperate wish to see Denis overtook him. He wouldn't be astonished; he could understand, and tell him more clearly what it was that Rita had said about him. Had he begun his novel?

Surprised at seeing Ovide, Madame Boucher at length succeeded in saying that Denis had just left for the Citadel where, he said, all the bright lads hung around in war-time.

—I warned him not to enlist, she said. I'd rather see him out of work.

Ovide felt lost. The school term had begun and children kept jostling against him. September's splendour had touched the trees and, in the brightness of the leaves, busy sparrows seemed like birds of paradise. Ovide absent-mindedly picked a leaf and chewed the stem. It was time to leave for the factories, and working girls, still sleepy, came stumbling down the stairs. The men were so deeply buried in their newspapers that they kept bumping against houses and slackening their pace. What now? War had been declared six days ago and the French, strong as they were, had not yet invaded Germany. What were they waiting for?

Arriving in front of his father's house, Ovide set his foot on the step, then paused. A new worry had just added itself to those that tortured him already. What was he going to do at home? Sit in the kitchen between a paralytic and a baseball champion while the others went out to earn their daily bread? At the monastery there had been the daily routine, the dishes to wash, floors to polish, and the religious services. Here, nothing but idle, aimless dawdling. What had he been thinking of to desert like this?

He walked on among the workmen, his back bent and his hands in his pockets as when he used to go to the factory on a cold morning. But it is hard to create the illusion of a goal. These others had doors to open, machines to start.

The rapid clacking of high heels caught up with the listless crawl of his disillusioned steps. Cécile, with her everlasting umbrella under her arm, passed him, her small head, shaken by the haste of her mincing walk, allowing him a sisterly nod.

—Oh, Cécile, wait.

At this moment she was a godsend to him. He had something to say to her. He had to persuade her not to see Onésime any more.

—I haven't time.

He clutched at a straw.

—It's serious, I tell you.

—What?

She had stopped dead and was looking at him. Ovide felt himself grow taller. The struggle against this frightful uneasiness was over. The intellectual of the family was gaining the advantage, the kitchen despot finding firm ground again. He was happy. He smoothed back the lapels of his coat.

—Oh! You know very well what I want to talk to you about. That's why you keep out of my way and why you're eager to see me go back to the monastery, but I waited to see you alone, out of consideration. In fact, it's about your relations with Onésime . . .

—We don't do anything we shouldn't.

The old maid hugged her umbrella like a close secret and, with eyes closed, waited for the storm. She felt that the real enemy of her love was neither Onésime's wife, nor gossip, nor Mother Plouffe, but Ovide, wearing his halo of religious severity. His voice grew softer, its sternness tempered with the unctuousness of a sham confessor. Words that he had muttered when he had gone to bed too early as a novice, sentences he had mulled over when he imagined himself confessing, one by one, the most beautiful sinners in the world, came to his lips.

—I know. You're not a passionate woman, and I trust these meetings are still platonic. But with St. Augustine and Paul Bourget, I believe that long friendships between men and women always end in forbidden caresses. Wait! I haven't finished.

But a hen condemned to death does not heed the soothing sounds made by her butcher. Every feather ruffled, she defends herself, with cries of distress.

—We're good Catholics, Onésime and I. It's his wife who has had six children. Not me. He hasn't even kissed me. Not ever. I just feel happy when I'm with him, that's all.

Ovide raised a finger.

—Ah! Ah! You see. I believe you when you say there hasn't been sin between you and him. But you feel happy when you're beside him, you desire his company. Evil is like a fruit. While it's green we can resist it. We tell ourselves we'll never touch it. And then it ripens all at once. It has only to be touched and it will fall. And it's almost impossible to see a ripe fruit rot on the ground without . . .

Cécile felt as though a knife were at her throat. Her brother Pagliacci had her in his clutches. She uttered an incoherent excuse and looked at her wrist-watch.

—A fruit. An apple, a pear! Oh! It takes him the devil of a long time to ripen. I've known Onésime for twenty years!

Ovide backed against the wall to make way for a dog that was chasing a cat. His steel-grey eyes, like those of a hypnotist, held Cécile prisoner.

—Twenty years? Then the fire isn't very hot in either of you. But you're ripe at last for evil. I feel it. I see it in your eyes. Why do you persist in threatening his hearth, in dishonouring your family and spoiling your future? Remember the woes of the adulterous woman.

Cécile stopped her ears, her eyes staring out of her head.

—Ovide! Ovide! A priest! With thoughts like that!

He hardened his voice, then softened it as he went on speaking.

—It's the truth, I'm opening your eyes, blind one. See here, little sister, listen to me. Have nothing more to do with Onésime. There are other boys, cleverer than he, who love opera, symphonies, and beautiful things.

Taken aback, Ovide stopped, for the tears were spilling from his sister's eyes, tracing transparent streaks on her white face. Then, with a stifled sob, she managed to exclaim:

—But, Ovide, you don't know Onésime! And then, you know, I'm forty-three years old!

She fled, straightening her hat with one hand and wiping her face with the other, the umbrella now wobbling absurdly under her arm.

Ovide stood watching in amazement. His mouth fell open.

—Well!

The cords of his neck, which had swelled out with importance while he lectured his sister, resumed their usual shrivelled look. He felt a tightness in his throat. He was discovering a tragedy in this Cécile, his sister, who had scarcely meant more to him than a piece of household furniture. As far back as he could remember her, she was always the same, going and coming from work, always discontented with the meals, talking with Onésime on the balcony and going to bed at ten o'clock.

How many things had happened since the evening of *Pagliacci*! The lives of Napoleon, Guillaume, Cécile, Théophile, Ovide himself, had been turned upside down by events. Only Josephine, steadfast in the ktichen, had resisted their impact.

Dreamily, Ovide continued to stroll along. Was it consciously that he began to walk around the factory where he had been employed, the factory where Rita Toulouse must still be working?

*   *   *   *   *   *

Ovide would not admit to himself that he wished to speak to Rita Toulouse that day. But he carefully calculated all his chances of meeting the girl. The surest one in Ovide's opinion was to stand not far from the office-workers' exit. And, as it happened, a jeweller's shop provided, in its show-window of watches, exactly what is necessary to an innocent stroller who wants to affect surprise at meeting a lady friend. He gazed, examining each watch for so long that the jeweller began to glance suspiciously at him and to take note of his appearance; for, with his furtive looks alternating between the factory and the showcase, Ovide looked like a burglar planning to make a haul.

The noon whistle blew. The swing doors opened to let out the chattering group of young office-girls, laughing, straightening berets or hats, saying good-bye or hastily putting on lipstick Ovide's heart thumped. Ah! He had recognized her at once,

Rita, with her blue raincoat and the belt that held in her waist so well and emphasized her breast, her shoulders, and her beautiful legs. But it was the tilt of her chin, and her beret worn jauntily on the back of her head, that most clearly distinguished her in the eyes of this anguished man. How demure she seemed from this distance! She waved to the others, absent-mindedly, and, stuffing her hands in her pockets, sauntered off in the direction of the jewellery shop. Ovide started to move away, but first made sure, by consulting his reflection in the window, that his hair was combed and his tie knotted properly. Then he turned. But, in his nervousness, he mistook his direction and walked to meet Rita Toulouse. He was looking at his feet as though he had not walked for a long time. She didn't see him, then! How anxious and almost sad she looked! He plucked up courage:

—Why, it's Mademoiselle Toulouse! What luck!

She looked up at him with astonishment and her eyes widened as she came slowly out of her dream and recognized him.

—Monsieur Ovide! But . . . you . . .

He smiled humbly, embarrassed, shaking his head as if she had discovered him to be a colonel covered with decorations instead of the dull and commonplace civilian she had once known. She examined him with curiosity as though disconcerted by what he was wearing. Then she grew pale. The sight of Ovide suddenly recalled to her mind the ridicule that she had showered on him and the embarrassment she had felt when she learned of his entering the monastery. The presence of this thin, pale fellow with the burning eyes confused her, for he looked lost in his suit and she was accustomed to think of him draped in a spotless robe. It made her remember her silly behaviour as a nineteen-year-old, her infatuation for Stan Labrie, and then the ridiculous drama in which her engagement had ended.

—I thought you were in the monastery, she stammered.

He shook his head wearily, still finding enough patience not to reply curtly to this unwelcome reminder.

—No. The war, you know. The only crusade that matters now is the victory of France and the Allies. I intend to enlist.

—You?

She inspected him again as if this reply obliged her to see Ovide from a new angle. He was going to enlist, when so many men were fighting shy of it. This little man would wear a uniform, shoulder a gun; this little man, whose almost feminine mannerisms she had ridiculed, was perhaps going to a hero's death? All at once, she felt very small before him. She shook her head.

—What you must think of me!

Ovide's whole body expressed his generous denial.

—Think badly of you? What for? For having laughed at my ignorance of women's hearts? At my affected poses and my ridiculous pretensions? After all; you did right. And that letter I wrote you? Wasn't I stupid!

She gave a deep sigh of relief. Her face lighted up first with gratitude, then with trust. She felt inclined to tell him all her troubles, for from this man there emanated some of the prestige of the monk who is able to console and to forgive.

—I was a little fool then. But life hasn't spared me, since. I think I've changed.

He interrupted her with a magnanimous gesture.

—Oh, yes, I know. Denis Boucher told me. But I forgave you a long time ago.

Rita's face contracted.

—What do you mean, Denis Boucher?

—You remember, when he met you and you asked him about me?

—But I never did meet him! And a good thing for him I didn't! I detest him!

She had turned very pale; her mouth tightened and her eyes shone with anger. The hateful name of Denis Boucher reopened the wound, scarcely healed, of her disappointment. Instead of being grateful to him for having warned her of Stan Labrie's infirmity, she unconsciously held him responsible for her misfortune, as if a man's sexual impotence could have been as easily ignored in marriage as a misdemeanour of his boyhood.

—What! You never met him?

He backed away, apologizing, as if he had mistaken her for someone else. At that moment he recalled Denis's cold, inattentive face at the monastery when he was describing his meeting with the girl. All a lie! And that lie had overwhelmed his dedicated heart to the point of making him give up his vocation to run after a girl who had forgotten him! What a farce! All Ovide's tragedies turned into farces. And all this time, Denis, with his hands in his pockets, was strolling around the Citadel, his chest stuck out, his glance triumphant.

—Pardon, Ovide stammered, his eyes closed.

His embarrassed attitude astonished the girl so much that she forgot the sudden anger Denis Boucher's name had aroused in her.

—Pardon for what, Monsieur Plouffe? He lied to you, that's all. He lies to everybody, the skunk!

—He lied to me! To me, of all people. Why, I've known him since he was little.

—A chap like him! She shrugged her shoulders. He'd hang his own father. Look here, don't you fuss about that. It doesn't matter, seeing we've met each other.

She tightened her belt a notch, crushed down her beret, and added a touch of coquettish encouragement to her polite smile. Ovide held his head up and tried to smile back understandingly.

—Why, yes. Since we've met.

They exchanged bright glances. Ovide and Rita did not perceive that instead of reviving disagreeable memories during a commonplace meeting, they were already beginning to combine their feelings and were mutually astonished at the result. Hazy, mysterious feelings in Rita and, in Ovide, feelings that were direct, acknowledged, and overwhelming. Circumstances had so tossed about these two diverse beings that they now met at a crossing where they might stop, and exchange words and looks. Tall, handsome, bold men had let Rita down so often that she now felt attracted to a little, skinny, timid Ovide, who was still stamped with ecclesiastical dignity and reserve. Rita did not realize that the new man she was discovering in Ovide filled her with as much sympathy as respect. She came to meet him this time intending that he should find her sweeter than he had ever dreamed.

He hesitated. He dared not believe in the world of hope of which he had caught a glimpse in her eyes. He had been too greatly disillusioned. He spoke again of Denis Boucher.

—It's incredible! A lie like that.

She frowned impatiently, in a motherly way.

—Oh! Look here, don't let's talk any more about that chap. Get over it, you'll soon forget all that. You can get over anything, you can even get out of anything. Oh! Excuse me. I didn't mean that.

He was so delighted to hear her speak like this that he understood her blunder only a long time after she had apologized for it. He shook his head and laughed with the warmth of a man who is happy.

—Oh! That's nothing. Please don't worry about it. You're right, we get over everything, we change. That's life. Oh, excuse me, I talk and talk. I'm keeping you.

—Not at all, she protested. It's such a long time since we saw each other. So many things have happened. I'll hurry with my dinner, that's all.

Ovide reflected, hesitated, then dared to say:

—I can take you home if you like.

—Limoilou is a long way . . .

He took hold of her arm politely. She smiled and continued to protest, mentioning that they would have to take bus 14, and describing the route with childish excitement. This recalled his conversation with Cécile.

He hastily rid himself of the thought and glanced swiftly and tenderly at his companion's saucy chin.

—I was forgetting, Rita said suddenly. Don't you think your brother is a credit to us? Some pitcher! Were you at the public try-out? He was super!

—No, I wasn't there, Ovide replied coldly.

She looked at him and frowned.

How stupid she was! She ought to have remembered. All at once she recalled clearly the *Pagliacci* evening, her escape with Guillaume to the Pente Douce, the storm, the mist that rose from the moist asphalt, and the kisses on the flat stone. Then she shook her head laughing.

—Just imagine! It was only last year that I was such a little fool. You mustn't blame me any more than you would a baby, Monsieur Ovide. I was an ignorant kid looking around for other kids to play with. But the world isn't a big doll's house to me any more! I've gone through a lot.

She grew sad again and her lip pouted wearily, denoting a secret, lasting sorrow. Ovide felt brimming over with manly assurance.

—Look, don't make yourself unhappy. Would I be speaking to you like this if you were still a child? Raise that chin, little girl. Smile. Life's beautiful. Look at me. Haven't I changed too?

—Oh! Yes!

She smiled at him trustfully, and Ovide set his jaw and threw superior glances at the passing cars. Then shaken by an unexpected inspiration, he made her stop and looked ardently into her astonished eyes.

—I've changed so much . . . I don't know if I should . . .

—Go on, tell me!

--If I invited you to come dancing at the Chateau Frontenac, tonight, would you come?

—Pardon? Dancing?

The girl repeated this word as if she couldn't make any sense out of it. Not only could she never imagine Ovide, the fanatic opera-lover, abandoning himself to the mercy of jazz, she could not conceive of being folded in the arms of a dancer who held her, now, with such a look; a look that recalled the brilliant gaze of certain priests through the grating of the confessional. Once again, she saw Ovide draped in a long, white robe.

Ovide's hands tightened and his eyes closed. His ears were throbbing. He might as well give up at once if she were still seeing the monk in him.

—Yes. He spoke very distinctly. Dance at the Chateau. They have a good orchestra. We can have a couple of cocktails. We can tell each other things. It's a good way to spend an evening.

The thought of the dance floor at the Chateau Frontenac finally vanquished Rita's astonishment and preconceived ideas about Ovide. To dance at the Chateau, in the intoxicating atmosphere of that smart hotel reserved for Americans and rich girls holding their first ball! She didn't dare think of it! Ovide was a magician casting spells.

—You're not joking? Do you really want to take me there?

She seemed to suspect a trick. Her disbelieving eyes watched Ovide's lips intently. The cry of joy he was longing to utter translated itself into a gesture of satisfaction.

—That's why I'm asking you. Then it's agreed. You'll come?

—Swell! Yes. You bet I will! Oh, dear! What dress shall I wear? My blue, no, my black and my patent-leather slippers.

She quickened her step, imagining herself already dressed, her hair done in an unusual way, promenading about in the sumptuous atmosphere of the Chateau Frontenac. Ovide, a fatherly smile on his lips, gazed at her, shaking his head, as if a dance and a cocktail at the Chateau were an everyday matter to him. He did not know how to dance, but this obstacle had not occurred to his mind, so fully was he savouring the victory just gained. They arrived at the bus stop. Rita took his hand and they pushed through the crowd that surged towards the bus door.

All at once Ovide grew pale. The driver! Onésime! Seated as though on a throne, he presided pompously over the destinies of his bus. St. Peter at the gates of paradise is not, in the minds of the devout, more conscientious towards mortals than was Onésime towards his passengers, inspecting and distributing tickets. Ovide mechanically looked for Cécile, as if it were inevitable. Seated at the front, near the driver, she was gazing almost ecstatically at her Onésime on duty. What a man! Then she saw a hand which drew another along with it: Rita Toulouse, and Ovide.

Ovide was caught in the trap. Brother and sister gave each other a long look, without smiling, not a muscle moving in either face.

CHAPTER THREE

The flower that you threw me, in my prison . . .

—WHATEVER is the matter with you? Josephine smiled, holding a steaming pot and stopping to let Ovide pass as he pivoted from the sink to the mirror, singing and waltzing.

In my prison, this dry faded flower is with me . . .

Ovide was happy. In an hour he would be at the Chateau, dancing with Rita Toulouse. And Cécile had said nothing at home about their meeting. She had contented herself with staring at him during the meal. That didn't mean much. What a discreet girl! He had misjudged her. Fine! His beard now. The usual ceremony. The shaving-brush attacked his face, masking him with white foam, except his lips which smiled secretly. Then his left hand, tense, went over his head and pinched his right cheek, offering it to the glinting razor. Josephine continued on her way to the stove.

—You can see that religion makes you happy. Look at your brother, you others. That will teach you a real lesson.

In the mirror, Ovide met his sister's stare. Her features were still impassive. Napoleon, his elbows on the table, held his head between his hands. He seemed overcome with anxiety and had eaten almost nothing. His mother's remark reached his brain like the confused echo one hears without attempting to understand.

But Guillaume sprang to his feet all at once and announced blandly:

—Ma, I know why Ovide is happy.

279

The razor paused above the lather. Ovide stiffened. He felt quite cold. And, still looking in the mirror, he saw Guillaume mysteriously giving him a big wink and tipping his head as an invitation to go into the parlour.

Ovide longed to cry out 'Just you dare!' but he took no chances and went instead to the parlour, saying roughly:

—Still another of your pointless jokes, I suppose. Hurry up, my lather is getting cold.

Whistling, Guillaume followed him. Josephine looked fondly after them as if they were two children having fun. There was happiness in the house since Ovide had returned. That would last at least until his next departure for the monastery. She began to hum *When I was eighteen.* . . . Guillaume closed the door behind him and whispered:

—I know why you're happy. Rita Toulouse. I saw you together at noon. I was on my bike.

Ovide leaned back against the piano. Mechanically, he struck the highest C. He felt faint. He nodded towards the kitchen.

—Did you tell them?

Guillaume threw out his chest, and his lips set in offended dignity.

—Are you crazy? We're Americans or we're not. I'm no tell-tale.

Ovide heaved a long sigh. In a fatherly fashion he pulled the hairs that adorned Guillaume's chin, as if they were medals for bravery.

—There, I see you're a man. You'll do us credit in the United States.

But Guillaume winked and interrupted him with the famous hand whose fingers and wrist could give such deceptive spin to a baseball.

—Well! I'm a man and I like to go to bed naked. I won't say anything if you tell Mother not to make me put on those damned red-and-white pyjamas. I nearly die of the heat in them.

Ovide burst into a loud laugh and patted his brother's shoulder.

—It's a bargain. You sleep naked and keep your mouth shut. And above all, don't be thinking any evil. You'll see, old chap, one day, that the woman question is complicated. The important thing is that Mama doesn't know. It would upset her.

He went back to the kitchen triumphantly and, while passing Napoleon, shook his sagging shoulders.

—Buck up there, old Napo! Be more cheerful. Life is wonderful. Difficulties don't count. You can get over everything. It'll come out all right.

The collector raised a face full of doubt and sadness, then smiled.

—I want to speak to you, Vide. Five minutes.

Ovide patted his arm absent-mindedly.

—Yes, after. I'm going to shave first.

Josephine, seeing Ovide come back into the kitchen, lowered her voice because Ovide did not like *When I was eighteen*. Then she stopped singing and exclaimed:

—Faith of St. Joan of Arc, Vide, you've put on your grey suit and your beautiful calf shoes. You look as though you were going to a Eucharistic Congress!

Ovide made no reply and began shaving. It would have been impossible to say whether the anxious lines on his brow were caused by the exigencies of shaving or by his reflections. His mother, by an innocent remark, had a genius for disturbing his happiness, bringing into the foreground the uncertainties that he had concealed behind a superficial joy. With cruel intuition, Josephine chose the paths leading to the inmost depths of his being, as if she had known them for a long time, even before him. Pensively, Ovide wiped his razor with a piece of newspaper.

At this moment, Papa Théophile, like a motionless bronze statue in his chair, begged his protector, with monotonous persistence, to read the latest news to him. The pleading timidity

with which the paralytic had begun to enjoy Ovide's kind services had rapidly changed into the despotism of a spoiled invalid.
Any excuse was good enough to call Ovide: a fallen pipe; an
annoying beam of sunlight; matches; glasses of water; a change
of position. The old man lived only to hear the paper read. He
kept eight o'clock every evening for that; just as he had when he
worked at *Christian Action*, and, healthy but tired, had got up
from the table and slumped down in the rocking-chair with the
paper. But the old man was worried. It seemed as though Ovide
wanted to go away without thinking of the news, at present so
disappointing but sure to bring, some evening, echoes of a
gigantic battle in which thousands of Englishmen had been killed.

—Yes, Father, I'm going to read to you, but let me shave,
Ovide said shortly.

—You're in a bad humour, all at once, Josephine remarked,
worried.

Most of the violent scenes in the household had broken out
when Ovide, Napoleon or Théophile were shaving, as if the
soapy make-up and the blade created a dramatic atmosphere.
With a hasty movement, Ovide turned on the tap, filled his hands
with water and washed his face, making a weird splutter with his
nose and mouth. Having dried himself off vigorously he kept the
towel in his hands and remained motionless, his face puckered
and his eyes lost in thought, suspended on the brink of an important decision. All the family were watching him. Suddenly he
threw the towel on a chair and, with his back against the sink, his
arms crossed, looked at his family, one by one.

—Listen. You can stop treating me like a priest on holiday.
Today, I decided not to go back to the monastery. I haven't the
religious vocation. I mean it.

He waited eagerly for their reaction. It was unexpected. Four
knowing glances, scarcely suited to the occasion, and a joyous
cry from his mother were his answer. Napoleon, Cécile, Guillaume, and his father did not laugh, but looked as though he had

confided to someone in their presence a secret which they already knew. Ovide was baffled. Was this a conspiracy? Since supper, only their eyelids had blinked, like night signals, in reply to his statements and his actions. But Josephine had both her eyes wide open.

— So, it's over? You're going to stay here for good, really for good?

She didn't know what to do with her hands, nor how to smile, for Ovide's decision had just crowned the secret hope that she cherished of keeping him with her forever. In addition, she was so conscious of her happiness, knowing so well the inmost recesses of her heart, having studied them in advance, that she did not know to what degree she should show it. This anticipated joy, the evidence of which embarrassed her, encouraged Josephine to take refuge in a mood which would allow her more spontaneous relief. The joyous expression that twisted her face gave place quickly to a cross, discontented mask. She turned round sharply and wiped up the blobs of soap that Ovide, from nervousness, had dropped on the floor. Disconcerted, Ovide frowned.

— What? Does that annoy you, Mama?

She shrugged and did not answer. Ovide was almost pleading.

— Oh, I see. You're going to be ashamed of me now?

— That's not it, Josephine grumbled at last. Whenever I had an argument with your aunt I could always put it up to her that I had a son who was a White Father. And then they all call me 'Madame Plouffe'. I've been somebody ever since you went to the monastery.

Ovide grew pale. His tragedy of failure was made up of all this pettiness. His fate was conditioned by what people would say! He needed all his strength and the memory of Rita Toulouse to shake off the weight that was crushing him. He went up to his mother, put his arms around her sagging shoulders, and spoke so sweetly that Josephine shivered and wanted to cry.

—Look, Mama, don't you love me more than that? Do other people's opinions mean more to you than your child's happiness, your Vide's? Come, now!

—You're trying to get round me, eh?

Josephine steeled herself mulishly not to sink back into tenderness, for since Ovide's return she thought she had found her former energy again. She pointed to Cécile:

—And who's going to stop her from following a married man on his never-ending bus trips, if there isn't a priest any longer in our family to prevent it?

Ovide instinctively looked at his sister. Her burning eyes defied him. Beaten, he bent down and caressed Josephine's hair.

—Cécile? Let her alone. It's not serious. Onésime is an old childhood friend. She has to have a little diversion.

Josephine straightened up, her face brightened.

—Do you think so?

She asked nothing better than to believe Ovide, since the Cécile-Onésime problem was preying on her mind. And her false alarm, once recognized and classified, reassured her of her authority, for one never feels so helpless as when one tries to solve a problem that does not exist. She took Ovide by both arms and shook him as though he were a baby she had frightened and wanted to make laugh.

—Big silly! Are you blind? Now I'm happy! It's unbelievable that you're going to stay with us all the time.

—You're good, Vide, Guillaume said placidly. You're almost as good as St. Joan of Arc.

Cheered, Ovide drew himself away and distending his Adam's apple fastened his collar button.

—Get ready, Father. In five minutes, the news! Well, now, I'll need ten dollars. I have to buy some things tonight. Guillaume, can you lend me it?

Guillaume, who had been busy playing with his cat, seemed not to have understood and walked towards the door.

—I think I'll go for a walk.

Nonplussed, Ovide stared at the closed door for a long time. When he had invited Rita Toulouse to the Chateau, the question of finance had not worried him; his twelve months in the monastery had accustomed him to see money as manna easy to harvest, and he had been free to consider, above all, the moral aspect of a problem. So, if the unquestioned authority which he exercised in his family allowed him to control Guillaume's actions, it must also justify him in managing the pitcher's money, which the latter counted indefatigably every night before going to bed. Josephine's voice roused him from his torpor.

—I'd willingly lend it to you, Ovide, but I paid the rent and only have a dollar left. If you don't mind waiting till tomorrow, I'll have the board money then. You mustn't be angry with Guillaume. He treats his money like gold. He gives me ten dollars a week. He hides the rest. If only I could find it.

She walked towards Guillaume's room, watching Cécile and Napoleon from the corner of her eye. Ovide felt panicky. What should he do? The vision he had had of life since his departure from the monastery was shattered once again. Money and the suffering that its shortage entailed took their revenge on the one who for a year had ignored them. And Rita Toulouse, all dressed up, must already be waiting for the fine gentleman who was taking her to dance at the Chateau.

—Vide! My paper. My news, Théophile's jerky voice insisted.

Overwhelmed, Ovide was imagining a slow walk in the street where, looking down with anxious eyes, he would, perhaps, find ten dollars. Then he inspected the sewing-machine, and looked at the pedestal of the plaster Sacred Heart, where Théophile, when he worked, had put his money, pocket-knife, and watch before going to bed. Nothing! Oh, money! Suddenly Ovide stiffened. Cécile, at the doorway of her room, was winking and beckoning to him just like Guillaume, earlier. Cécile! It wasn't possible! She was too stingy. She disappeared into her room, signalling to him to come. He began pacing up and down the kitchen so that it might appear he was entering Cécile's room for want of anything else to do. As he finally went towards it, his heart thumping, and mechanically murmuring a prayer, 'God let me find this ten dollars', Napoleon, who for some time had been watching for the opportunity to take Ovide aside, seized his arm and carried him off to the parlour.

—What next? Ovide muttered impatiently.

He was so agitated by his own anxiety that he failed to be touched by the trembling mouth, by the little, round eyes filled with distress.

—Vide, I don't know what to do. I don't think Jeanne loves me. Yet I make pilgrimages enough. You told me when I spoke to you about it that you approved of my visiting Jeanne and not to bother about other people.

Ovide looked at his watch. He was like a doctor deeply in debt who is consulted by a bankrupt patient.

—Why do you think she doesn't love you any more?

Napoleon was full of his trouble, which he explained passionately and with many gestures. On each free afternoon he went by bicycle to Ste. Anne de Beaupré to pray for Jeanne's recovery and then, as speedily as possible, rode to the sanatorium and hurried to Jeanne's bedside. Breathless and anguished, he first of all asked her, 'Do you feel cured?'

—This afternoon, when I asked that, she began to cry, then she got angry and said to me, 'Leave me alone, you upset me. I'd like to die.' Do you think she still loves me, Vide?

His eyes pleaded behind a glaze of tears. Ovide looked at him steadily, then shrugged his shoulders.

—She has plenty to upset her. Put yourself in her place. Pray for her, but don't talk about it to her. It's irritating to feel that someone is waiting for us and we can't catch up with him. Look, cheer up; Jeanne loves you, but she's ill and it upsets her not to be as well as you would like to see her. Understand? Don't talk to her any more about health, or prayers. You'll be amazed what happens. There, I'm in a hurry.

He left Napoleon alone with his problems in the dim light of the parlour, and went into Cécile's room. She was waiting for him, solemnly, one hand resting on the dresser.

— Did you wish to speak to me? Ovide said, as though he had just remembered.

— Yes. You need ten dollars. Here it is. You can pay me back later.

Ovide's suspicious glance went from the bill to the stiff, averted face of his sister. He took the money and suddenly felt frightfully embarrassed, as if he had just signed a contract pledging himself to favour Cécile's forbidden love and to pave the way to adultery. But Cécile had seen him holding Rita's hand. Looking down, he backed out of the room.

CHAPTER FOUR

THE English having taken Canada from France in 1760, and the Quebeckers having obstinately remained French in their customs, language, and architecture, the conquerors seem to have thought it well to challenge such resistance by erecting an edifice, on a strategic spot, to mark their victory: the Chateau Frontenac. This enormous and luxurious Canadian Pacific Hotel, whose most important shareholders, so they say, are Anglo-Saxons, crowns Cape Diamond with its massive brick turrets, admires its own reflection in the St. Lawrence, and looks coldly down at the ships that come and go. Placed on the top of a mountain, facing east, above the shoulders of a town that runs down the slope behind it, the structure turns to the sunrise a rigid mask, completely disguising the turbulent face of Quebec. This pacific fortress is perched so high that it exceeds the most audacious steeples by a hundred cubits and casts a shadow over the schools, the Archbishop's palace, the monasteries, and the convents.

An hotel like the Chateau Frontenac is designed for the reception of kings and their retinues, princes, prime ministers, and cardinals. But as such important persons do not arrive every day, it is necessary to secure a more stable clientele: American tourists. They are attracted by the quaintness of the conquered country: French characteristics, fortifications, narrow, winding streets, miraculous shrines, an eighteenth-century orchestra, and cuisine to match. The clients from the south flood across the border in noisy, colourful crowds, establish their headquarters in the Chateau Frontenac, and roll up their sleeves. They hasten to take inventories of the picturesque and historic features of the town, which they rapidly evaluate in terms of feet, seconds, and dollars. Reinvigorated by this pill of condensed knowledge, their conscience soothed by a rapid bus tour in the course of which they distribute a few nickels, they speedily return to their rooms and open some good Canadian whisky, already smacking their lips over the juicy stories they will share with the women who are with them. The average American, more often than not a Puritan in his home town, comes up to Quebec for the same reason he runs down to Mexico: to have a good binge. The historical charm of these cities justifies his trip, gratifies his curiosity, and enables his scrupulous conscience to hide in the misty veils of a noble saying: Travel is education. And hence a striking paradox: the very Catholic city of Quebec, sometimes mischievously compared to Port Royal, becomes the rendezvous of tourists dying for an orgy they dare not have at home.

The authorities of the Chateau Frontenac do their utmost to please this precious clientele. The Americans not caring, perhaps, for negroes, the latter are not welcomed at the hotel. Nor does the management waste time kowtowing to the Quebeckers in summer, for, though it accepts their money during the slack season, it does not like the natives to rub shoulders with the spectators of June and July who have paid to see them. It is quite enough that they should flock, on Sunday evenings, to Dufferin Terrace which surrounds the Chateau, in order to contemplate at least once a week, from the top of the Cape, their big, beloved river.

This was the hotel which, that evening, Ovide, stiff as a ramrod in his well-pressed suit, entered with a dazzled Rita Toulouse on his arm.

The two young people, accustomed to walking on linoleum, asphalt or wood, seemed to sink at each step into the springy carpet of the immense rotunda, across which there streaked, in every direction, the gold braid of page-boys and porters. Groups of American travellers, in plaid shirts and holiday mood, were clustered around the entrances talking at the top of their voices, as though at a picnic. Most of them were very tall, and Ovide anxiously measured the number of inches he lacked by comparison. He pressed Rita's arm more firmly, for a page-boy, whom Ovide took to be an important official, was looking at them suspiciously. Rita welcomed his pressure with satisfaction, blending it into the deep sense of belonging with which she was now pervaded. The Chateau was opening its doors to her, bathing her in the glow of its chandeliers, welcoming her to the atmosphere of luxury that her fair beauty deserved and, until now, had been denied. In this sumptuous hall she would receive, so she thought, by general acclaim, the great distinction due to her by virtue of her coiffure, her dress, her shoes, and the locket set with glass beads which she wore around a neck tanned by the summer sun. Smiling at her success, head held high, eyes glistening with happiness, she walked with undulating hips, clearing a path, as though in triumph, through all the masculine scrutiny to which she believed herself subjected.

The couple emerged from the motley crowd and found themselves in a long corridor which echoed softly with dance music.

—Men are all the same, she sighed. They have eyes that undress you. It's embarrassing!

Ovide blushed. He had never even imagined Rita undressed. Nor had he noticed the complacent way she looked at everyone, having been too intent on deceiving the page-boy's inquisitive eye by trying to look like an American.

—These strangers, you know, when they see a pretty woman, their eyes brighten.

He was as awkward with compliments as with the carpet. He felt himself a stranger to the ordinary Ovide, and searched for phrases to match the surrounding atmosphere.

—All the same, Rita smirked, I'm only a little Quebec girl.

In order to re-establish himself, Ovide had to resort to his former nationalist and religious vexations. At this moment, without realizing it, he saw the American as the giant with a bird's brain, that legendary figure created by disappointed Europeans in order to depreciate the achievements of the builders of the New World.

—Exactly. They come here, thinking they'll meet strange characters, and they see women like you and men like me. So they're charmed and astonished. I don't like them myself. They're too brassy; they think money buys everything. No intellect. Just overgrown children. Yes, overgrown; abnormal, even.

—Don't say that, Monsieur Plouffe. They are handsome men.

She smiled slyly as if she had already arranged a secret rendezvous with one of them. Ovide looked down sadly and crumpled the ten-dollar bill he held in his hand.

—I should have done more gymnastics and less music, then I should have been taller.

Rita examined him, and a tender light veiled her eyes. She took his arm with both hands and drew close to him.

—Now, now, Monsieur Ovide. If you only knew it, big men don't excite me. Often they're not up to much. I've found that out. I'll tell you some day. And then what I like about you is your elegance, your intelligence, and your fine forehead.

Ovide already felt comforted. However, he knew he was thin and scraggy. But at twenty, when he had realized that his body would never be muscular, he had given up inspecting his stature in the mirror. And that was how he had come to attach a fanatical importance to music, to things of the mind.

—Look! Rita exclaimed.

Two Canadian Army officers, smug with the sudden importance war was giving them, came from the ballroom, their chests puffed out, peaked caps jauntily tilted on their heads. Fascinated girls hung on to their arms, basking in their reflected glory. These young men seemed more conscious of the smartness of their uniforms than of the peril of death for which their dress marked them out. When they had passed, Rita whispered:

—To think you'll be in uniform soon. I can't wait to see you. Won't you look smart!

—Yes! he said, without conviction.

They had reached the entrance where tickets for the dance were sold. While Ovide paid with Cécile's ten dollars, Rita, her eyes as round as those of a child who is going to the circus for the first time, eagerly watched the couples dancing. Ovide joined her. He stopped beside her and glanced curiously around the room. The glance grew distrustful, and he frowned. But Rita, excited, led him along, for the head waiter was coming to meet them, smiling, and summing them up with the quick eye of an expert. The girl was too enraptured, and this little, lean man was too careful of his least movement. They were Quebeckers, sure enough, clerks in a store, probably, who were treating themselves to a grand evening at the Chateau. Their tips would not be lavish. This diagnosis gained the couple a table nobody wanted because of its proximity to a column.

Ovide sat down and folded his hands underneath the table, after wondering whether it was preferable to fold them on top of it. Then he ventured to glance quickly around him.

Almost at once he looked severe. Since his entrance, in the wake of the head waiter, he had been absorbed in his anxiety to look like a regular patron; so apprehensive about the first steps in dancing with Rita, and so concerned about the few dollars that remained in his fingers, that he had no time to absorb the atmosphere surrounding him. Opposite him, Rita was scanning her beauty in her half-open compact, feverishly, as if she were afraid of missing something. On the tables of couples who had gone to dance, the straws stood crookedly in the almost empty glasses. In front on a low platform, an orchestra in uniform, nonchalantly conducted by a leader with a drooping lip, rendered a syncopated lament which bore the docile and languorous couples along at the mercy of its eddies, now slow, now impetuous. A singer took possession of the microphone, embraced it as though it were a woman, and began whispering into the chromium-steel disk, like a dying man still striving to make love, a melody which, hiccoughed in this way, would have made the blood of a sane man in the eighteenth century run cold. But the couples hummed with the singer, and now danced cheek to cheek.

—Does monsieur wish something?

The waiter stood beside them pencil in hand, bending slightly. Ovide, who thought his smile ironic and his tone curt, became flustered. What drink should he order? He was unfamiliar with the names of cocktails. He consulted Rita with a glance.

—Scotch?

She shook her head and suggested, eyes sparkling:

—No, Monsieur Vide. A Singapore Sling. Haven't you ever tasted one? They're marvellous!

Ovide hesitated, then pretended to recognize the name.

—Make it two . . . Singapore . . .

—Slings! Rita added with childish glee. Wait till you see how sentimental it makes you! You feel all sorts of ways, and then you want to say a lot of nice things to each other.

The girl waved her hands; she was all smiles and glances, her pleasure coquettishly exaggerated for the benefit of two elderly men whose eyes she felt upon her. They were sitting at an adjacent table, having come there to lighten their boredom with the silvery gleam of gin and the sight of young people dancing. Rita was giving them their money's worth—Rita, who had imagined the ballroom at the Chateau to be a paradise where even old men with corporations had the features of young gods. Unaware of the byplay, Ovide was looking sulky and muttering to himself, 'A lot of nice things?'

—What, aren't you happy, Monsieur Plouffe? Rita asked, inserting an expression of anxiety between two smiles.

Ovide looked down. No, Rita was telling him about 'a lot of nice things' and he was not happy. His whole being protested against the dance-hall atmosphere that he was trying in vain to assimilate. His opera-lover's soul was on guard against dance music and, in spite of his wish to please Rita, he could not climb the barricade. His year of privations, prayers, and dedication had not changed him. He was still the same Ovide who, in his father's parlour, used to weep while singing 'On with the Motley', and pour scorn on American jazz. Having retained his youthful modesty, he averted his eyes at the sight of women in evening dresses that revealed the line of the breasts. And he no longer understood how Rita could remain at ease in this atmosphere which made him indignant. She was an inaccessible stranger. Then why did he wish for her?

—Aren't you happy? she repeated. More troubles? Come, forget them. We're in a dream.

He shrugged his shoulders listlessly and his voice was lost in the noise that rose from the dance floor. Then he yawned, almost dislocating his jaw. His eyelids were heavy. It was ten o'clock and he was sleepy. At this minute, in the monastery, he would have been snoring.

—Frankly, this ballroom doesn't appeal to me. The evening dresses are too low, and everybody looks idiotic.

She surveyed him with astonishment, as though recognizing in him some other person she had met. Chin between her hands, her brows wrinkled, she was trying to solve a difficult problem. Her face brightened suddenly.

—There are the Singapores! Oh! I can't wait!

The waiter set down the glasses and held out the bill; two dollars. Ovide paid, adding a tip. He yawned once again.

Cécile's ten dollars were disappearing rapidly, more rapidly than the humiliation of accepting them as the price of a shameful silence. Rita was already sipping greedily, her eyes still lost in the same difficult problem. Then she looked up vivaciously.

—I have it! I have it! I know why this shocks you. You're too used to the monastery. It's still in your blood. It's not long enough ago. It'll pass, for sure, you'll soon be yourself!

Ovide woke up. Pale and on his dignity, he touched his chest with his forefinger.

—Me, shocked? It would take more than this to shock me.

A dance was ending. The couples came back to their tables, brushing Ovide's elbow in passing. He drew his chair in, politely making himself smaller. He continued to protest:

—I've been around, you know. I'm completely free of the monastery. Waiter, two more Singapores. You'll see. Watch me slip this one down, and tell me if I have any scruples about drinking.

He clasped his glass, pulled out the straw, and drank with the same feverish haste with which, a year ago, on the evening before he entered the monastery, he had downed glass after glass of beer. Rita laughed and applauded.

—Wonderful! Don't drink too fast. You'll get too much of a kick.

Ovide pushed his glass away airily and coughed.

—A kick? Nonsense! You don't know me very well. It takes more than one drink to affect me.

Rita, her mouth searching for the straw already tipped with lipstick, tossed her head and winked.

—Not me. You'll see presently, at the end of this glass. It's just as though I went all soft and my heart sort of opened up.

Ovide did not react immediately to this confession. He was too busy holding himself stiff, defending himself against the gentle torpor which, starting from his stomach, was filling his chest and rising to his shoulders. He frowned suddenly and stared suspiciously at her.

—What? You've had this sensation before? You drink? Did you . . .

He was in anguish. He dared not continue his questioning for fear of discovering in Rita a woman with a past, for whose sake one does not leave a monastery, and for whom it would be ludicrous to suffer so much. It was true she had humiliated him.

He forgave her for that. And that she had been Stan Labrie's fiancée could be excused, since she had broken it off. In Ovide's fanciful mind the association of Rita and Stan had had a formal and official air because of the word 'engagement' and Stan Labrie's physical handicap. Embraces and kisses were out of the question, as they would have been if he, Ovide, had been the fiancé. But, how did she know about the Singapore? How had she felt soft and woolly already? How had she opened up her heart? Jealousy, with the fumes of the Singapore Sling, took hold of Ovide. This jealousy was developing in its own good time, just as later, the moment of desire for possession would come. He was ripe for this torture, now that he had crossed the first barriers He leaned forward in anguish, no longer seeing the ballroom. At his question and his fiery, searching glance she stopped drinking and became quite sad.

— Yes, Monsieur Plouffe. But if you knew what it brings back to me, you wouldn't speak like that. Oh! When I think of it, I could cry!

And indeed, at these words, her eyes became moist. Ovide sighed with relief. He felt strong, joyous, able to comfort. People's tears reassured him of their goodness. Bad people do not weep. All this time the alcohol was accomplishing its upheaval. It was making a happy girl cry and changing a hesitant admirer, petrified by scruples, into a triumphant lover.

— Come, Rita, what's the matter? he said tenderly.

She wiped away a tear.

— You just reminded me of a terrible thing in my life.

Ovide was caressing her hand now and waiting magnanimously for her to recount this sensational affair. Come to think of it, she had told him, that morning, that she had suffered and that she had changed. Ah! Life was wonderful!

— Tell me everything, you poor, dear little girl. We have to confess now and then in our lives. It takes a load off your heart. Oh, here are our Singapores.

The waiter was coming back with two more glasses. Rita pushed away her first, which she had not finished, and seized the full glass with the nervousness of the smoker who throws away a half-smoked cigarette while taking a fresh one. Excited at the thought of the approaching confidence, Ovide clinked glasses and then closed his eyes, expectantly. Rita did not speak. He reopened his eyes, looked at her, and said persuasively:

—Let's drink first to our future, to your future, should I say, dear?

At this word, Ovide's lips became scarlet as if they had just been kissed. Rita put back a rebellious curl, then began drinking eagerly. She almost emptied her glass at one gulp. Ovide's eyes were riveted on her, and he too swallowed his drink without knowing he did so. At last she began:

—The whole business started with that precious Denis Boucher. Stan and I had been engaged a week. We hadn't told anybody. Then, one evening, Stan decides to see Mama and announce our engagement. Oh! It's awful. I can just see it all over again.

Rita put her hands over her eyes. Ovide moved his chair nearer.

—Go on. Be brave.

—Mama went white and looked at us both, for a long time. Then she began talking very fast with her eyes shut. 'I have never been able to bring myself to speak to you about something very serious that stands in the way, monsieur, nor to you, Rita. But since you wish to marry we must settle this matter first. Monsieur Labrie, before I allow you to have my daughter's hand I insist you show me a doctor's certificate stating that . . .'

The girl, a frightened look in her eyes, did not finish her sentence, and emptied her glass without the aid of the straw. Ovide looked like a child who is being told a detective story.

—You never saw anything like it, not even in a novel. Mama said that a certain Denis Boucher had told your brother Guillaume, who came and told it to her, that Stan Labrie was impotent and not able to marry. Imagine what happened! I was so mad and so ashamed, I just shook! I wanted to smash everything in the house. I had my ring, and our furniture was bought. We had made all our plans. I was surprised because Stan was always bragging about the way he stepped out before he knew me. Mama was crying. Then I said to Stan, 'Let's get out of here. Let's look for a doctor right away.' But he put me off, and gave a little laugh as if nothing were the matter, and said: 'Madame, how can they say things like that about a man who's had a flat for five years in St. Olivier Street?' Oh! Monsieur Plouffe, I can't talk about things like that. Mama flew up in the air when she heard about the flat; she told Stan he was thirty-five years old, that people had told her so. Instead of going to a doctor Stan just argued. I was all worked up by this time. I wanted to go away with him, get married, and never see my parents again. Stan was good to me. He bought me presents, and never quarrelled with me. And then he was a good pitcher. Oh! How unhappy I've been, Monsieur Ovide!

Speechless with astonishment, Ovide waved his hand mechanically to a waiter who was not there. He was thirsty; his head was burning. He loosened his tie. Tears, aided by intoxication, dropped like beads on Rita's cheeks.

—Then Stan went to Denis Boucher to make him sign a statement instead of going to a doctor. He didn't want to, Denis didn't, the beast! Stan thought of suing him but he was afraid of the publicity. Then he came back to our place, and ordered me to choose between him and Mother. I banged the door behind me and followed Stan. He was whistling, sort of a sad tune. He looked all mixed up as if he didn't know where to take me. I was all out of breath and I kept sobbing: 'We'll have to sleep with each other right away, so they'll know it's not true.' I was right, wasn't I, Monsieur Plouffe? We had the right, because, under the circumstances, it wasn't just for the fun of it. Knowing about religion, you can realize that. (Ovide, looking down, shook his head conscientiously.) Then he said to me, 'Let's have a drink.' That was how we came to drink a Singapore. In a Chinese restaurant.

Rita was now weeping bitterly, to the astonishment of the old gentlemen and some couples seated at the tables nearby.

—Look here, Rita, cheer up, do. People are looking at us.

But the girl could not control herself.

—Well, Monsieur Plouffe, you might as well know that what Denis Boucher said was all true. After three drinks, Stan told me everything. It was frightful what I went through! Just as if Stan had put on a dress and nylon stockings and said to me, 'I pulled a fast one on you. I'm a woman, after all.' I ran out of the restaurant, alone, I've never laid eyes on Stan again, and I cried for two months!

Rita's head fell forward as though she were overcome, and her chin sank to her heaving breast. Stricken, Ovide forgot to savour his triumph.

—Poor little soul! One gets over everything. You said so yourself. Cheer up, I'm here. I'll always be here.

Rita sobbed softly while the room became animated once more. The couples crowded on the floor, invited by the orchestra which began playing *East of the sun and west of the moon*. All at once, Ovide felt himself filled with the languorous rhythm. At first astonished by this strange sensation, he offered his arm enthusiastically to the girl and carried her off to the dance floor. His bristling rancour against jazz and the atmosphere of ballrooms was melting into complacent relish for surroundings which but a short time ago he had abhorred. There were so many couples that Ovide was able to dawdle instead of dance. Head held high, he thought his look of lofty superiority in some way minimized the forbidden pleasure of Rita's embrace. The Singapore triumphed. Misfortunes forgotten, the girl placed her fair head tenderly on Ovide's shoulder and, hesitatingly, felt the length of his back, sliding her hand from his neck to his waist.

—I feel you're a man, Ovide dearest!

Ovide's look became more and more lofty. His back quivered under the caress. He said, with the assurance of a connoisseur:

—It's true. There is something in dancing, in jazz; a kind of mysterious intoxication.

—Oh! Ovide! Ovide, I've suffered so much. Don't enlist, stay with me.

—I've suffered myself, and because of you. At the monastery, I couldn't think about anyone else but you. I love you.

She pressed harder against him. Ovide wanted to cry, now, himself. All his past failures assailed his tender heart.

—Oh! Hold me tight! he murmured tragically. I've lacked love so much.

—There! Rita said, her voice fading away languidly. I feel all soft. And I'm warm. Suppose we leave here and go and sit on the Plains above the river.

—Oh! Yes! he exclaimed theatrically. There are too many people here. Let's go! Solitude awaits us!

They disentangled themselves from the maze of dancers and made their way to the exit, no longer conscious of the Chateau nor even seeing the people through whom they pushed. Their goal, solitude, compelled them. They walked straight ahead with no thought of anything else, their quivering bodies pulling their minds in tow. They hurried towards seclusion, where the pleasure for which they thirsted awaited them. In silent haste they made for the Citadel. Suddenly, Ovide stopped, his face bright with an unexpected thought.

—There's a better place than the Plains. I've a wonderful idea!

—Not a room in a hotel? Oh, no! I know just what would happen. I'm asking you, Ovide; protect me, you're the strong one.

The strong one opened his mouth wide, aghast at the thought of an hotel, which would never have occurred to him. Then he quickly suppressed his astonishment and smiled.

—No! I should think not! Do you remember the steps, last year? At the top, there's a Franciscan monastery to the left. It has a cement wall around it. Then there's a little patch of grass and beyond that, the Cape. We can sit on the grass with our backs against the wall and the town at our feet. That'll show you that monasteries don't mean anything to me any more.

—And we can make up for the kissing we didn't do on the steps!

—Oh, that, he said, with a mysterious look.

They were soon ensconced in a taxi. Rita snuggled up to him, pressing her mouth against his neck. Ovide made no move and, despite his bewildered senses, gave himself up to careful but inconclusive calculations on the possibilities of a little carnal pleasure. For him, it was not a question of accepting or refusing, but of knowing where to begin, so much surface did Rita, stretched out beside him, present for his exploration. And Ovide, in order not to look like a fool who fails to grasp the good luck that chance holds out to him, hummed in a slightly Gregorian rhythm the melody of *East of the sun*, the whole of which now came back into his memory.

They arrived at their destination and as yet Ovide had come to no decision. 'Presently', he said to himself, by way of excuse. As if she had suddenly become very weak, Rita hung on to him and only spoke in snatches, faintly.

—Are we there?

—It's over there, Ovide replied feverishly. Do you recognize the steps and the third landing we missed? How stupid I was! See the monastery at the left and the cement wall around it? Let's go up this path.

He guided her along the ribbon of flattened earth that other lovers had helped maintain. The tall grass that met across the little path parted with a soft rustling before them. They finally discovered a patch of turf and stretched out on it after Ovide had carefully spread his handkerchief as a matter of form. Their heads

touched the monastery wall and their feet followed the slope of
the Cape. At their left, the long flight of steps looked like a dis-
mantled accordion in the darkness. Below, the town slept under
its crust of roofs. Except for the lighted steeples, which stood out
from the anonymous mass of houses, the Lower Town seemed
flattened out. Ovide raised himself on his elbow, took a long
breath, struck, his fist on the monastery wall with pleasure, and
glanced victoriously at the steps.

— Is it really true? We're free beings.

— Yes, free, Ovide.

She moved closer, touching him with her knees and playing
with his tie. Now that the desired and at the same time dreaded
moment for kisses and embraces had come, Ovide was seized
with a sudden need to talk, to hold forth brilliantly on love, life,
and death.

— To think that while we're having a quiet talk, men are
killing each other in Europe, the monks are praying in this monastery, women are suffering in the poor houses at our feet.

She pressed herself unreservedly against him and said in a wail:

— Don't talk any more, Ovide. Close your eyes. We're here,
that's all that matters. Oh! I told you I felt all soft. Well, I've an
idea. Shut your eyes a minute.

He closed his eyes and tried to guess what Rita was doing with
her hands. She must be moving her shoulders because her locket
tinkled. All at once she grasped his head and kissed him, whispering feverishly:

— Hold me tight! Tight! Tight!

If he opened his eyes, it was only to close them again, for confronted with the dazzling immodesty of the spectacle before him
his gaze, accustomed to the sober tints of his bashful dreams, at
first plunged back, frightened, into the depths of scruple. But the
flash sufficed for the devil of the flesh, that ruthless fisherman, to
catch Ovide's virtue like a silly trout. His conscience numb and
his vision blurred, he thrust his burning cheek against Rita's

breast, which was now triumphantly free of her unfastened dress. Feverishly, he pressed her against him and gave her a long kiss. It was all he dared, his pleasure being extreme.

Alcohol changes a man. But its effect is brief. Especially when, like Ovide, one is a novice in the art of drinking and loving, one tastes a first glass and a first kiss too quickly.

He shivered and stiffened in the embrace. Then he raised his head slowly and looked towards the sky.

—Ovide! Ovide! Kiss me again, Rita insisted in a seductive murmur, as if the fate of the world depended on another kiss.

Spurred by vanity, he attempted to summon up his ardour of a little while ago, and sought Rita's mouth passionately. How cold his lips were! His forced passion subsided and he said uneasily:

—Don't you think it's getting rather chilly?

—Quick, warm me again, she whispered, raising pleading eyes.

But the coolness of the September night now stole through Ovide's body, taking the place of satisfied longing and dispersing the last fumes of the Singapore Sling. Slowly, he was becoming the pre-Singapore Ovide, severe and puritanical. Like a diver coming to the surface, his personality reasserted itself as it climbed the distance separating it from its own atmosphere. His ears buzzed, his blurred eyes discerned a clearer sky, and his whole being gradually discarded the ballast that had carried him down towards the whirlpool of drunkenness and pleasure. His eyes, which in embarrassment shunned Rita's, suddenly fell on the girl's naked shoulders. He grew pale and recoiled, frightened.

—Ovide! she cried out in frustration.

His teeth chattered, his eyes stared fixedly as though set in terror. That sight, which doubtless would have dazzled him still, had it not become so dark around them, now made him shudder. It had the effect upon him of an ice-cold shower; in an instant he was once more the old Ovide.

And that was all that Ovide could do—Ovide the novice who, scarcely a week before, prayed every night on his knees on the wooden floor to dispel the unworthy thoughts that hounded him in his sleeplessness—about the bare, palpitating breast of an infatuated woman who was offering herself to him.

—Ovide! Kiss me again, please, Ovide, she begged, almost in tears.

—Cover yourself up, quickly, it's frightful!

His trembling mouth gasped out a few broken words. His eyes were closed and his bony hands repulsed the devilish vision. Rita Toulouse drew back and began to cry like a disappointed small girl. Her faint, insignificant sobs were lost in the deep silence, above the sleeping town. Ovide suddenly turned a face like a hunted animal's towards the monastery.

The bell sounded midnight. Then a wailing chant flowed over the walls and spread like a mist in the air. The monks were beginning the wistful midnight service.

Ovide began to tremble all over. His misty eyes conjured up ghouls with rotted teeth who laughed mockingly through the chinks of the wall, preparing to seize him and carry him off to hell and plunge him into a sea of boiling oil filled with the bodies of the lustful. He was powerless to rise; his legs gave way under him, just as when he was being pursued in a dream. Languorously, pleadingly, Rita renewed her request:

—Come on, Ovide! Be nice to me. A little kiss, just one!

Suddenly he felt in himself the intransigence of a Savonarola, as if chastisement of the sin he had just committed could transform the spectres grinning from the wall into smiling angels of mercy.

—Dress yourself, little devil! he screamed.

Dazed, she got up mechanically and fastened her dress. Suddenly she burst out crying, then darted along the little path and ran down the steps. Ovide was still unable to move. The tapping of her high heels on the wooden steps diminished, but he did not listen for them to die away. The monks' singing took hold of him again. The spell of the Gregorian chant raised him above this sickening, sudden lapse and swept him into the ethereal regions of mysticism, prayer, and remorse. He pressed his hands to his head:

—Oh God! Forgive me!

All the torment and contempt that, at the monastery, was promised to the lustful, broke over his conscience. He was damned. His soul was beginning to rot. He felt sick. Oh, if he could only confess. He could never pass the night in this state. Like a drunken man, his eyes fixed on the distant steeples, he managed to walk to the steps. Then, all of a sudden, as though freed from the grip of the monastery, he went running down the steps, in the hope of escaping the thousands of devils that pursued him. He had put evil into Rita's mind. And Cécile, on the point of adultery, had bought his complicity for ten dollars! What punishment would God not have in store for Ovide? The Pope himself would be compromised in giving him absolution! Unconsciously, he was heading for his parish church, all the while breathing incoherent prayers. He arrived in front of the rectory, breathless, and almost cried out with joy. The light was burning in the priest's office. Not stopping to think, he rang the bell.

— Ovide Plouffe?

Old Monsieur Folbèche, his face still wearing an intent expression, for he had been absorbed in reading, led him to the office impatiently, like a scholar interrupted during his research. Ovide was panting.

—I want to confess, Monsieur le curé.

The old priest listened with half an ear and sat down behind his varnished oak desk. He looked for a long time at the page of an open book, which he closed slowly. He gazed wistfully at the title: *The Call of the Race*. A little radio was whispering last-minute news of the war. Poland was conquered, but nothing stirred on the Maginot Line. No development was announced regarding possible conscription in Canada. The priest turned off the radio. Ovide, on the extreme edge of his chair, bent forward

U

and, hands clasped feverishly, watched him in anguish. The priest pushed back his chair and leaned his chin on one hand while, with the other, he turned a globe on its axis.

—Brother Ovide Plouffe, he said at length, you do keep people waiting. Moreover, you come to see me at an hour when priests are either asleep or praying. Yet, I told you the other day to come and see me, immediately; the other day, when you deserted the monastery and our patriotic ideas.

—I haven't come about that, Monsieur le curé. Will you confess me?

He had sprung forward and was kneeling before the priest's desk, his haggard eyes raised to the crucific and his clasped hands resting on the papers that littered the desk.

—There certainly is reason for you to confess, Monsieur Folbèche grumbled. A man like you, the cleverest in the family, comes out of the monastery when it's the time, if ever, to stay there. And why? Why? So it wouldn't look as though you shut yourself up in the monastery in order to avoid enlisting. That's the crowning touch! Stupid, proud fellow! But our cause, and we're proud of it, is precisely for us oppressed Catholic French Canadians to find all possible means to escape from English domination. In 1917 I was proud, myself, of being a priest and so avoiding conscription. The more there are in the Church, the more victims snatched from the English guns. There are several I have not been worrying about. Guillaume will go to the United States; Napoleon is too old. Others have weak hearts or flat feet. But there are still others to protect. To think that you are giving up your shelter in order to take up arms. It's incredible! Silly, proud fellow that you are! I hope you will go back to the monastery just as quickly as you can. And that other traitor, that Denis Boucher, who deserts the national cause, who has dealings with army officers and the Mounted Police. It's enough to make one believe that all clever people are abandoning nationalism and religion.

The priest was breathing hard. Ovide's clasped hands trembled on *Time* and *Christian Action*, which jostled each other absurdly.

—I've just committed a terrible sin, Ovide stammered. With a woman. The sin of the flesh. Ask God to forgive me.

The old priest, heedless in his irascibility, rejoiced.

—I knew it would turn out like this! National betrayal leads to the worst debauches. If the Canadian cause had been dearer to you, you would have stayed in the monastery, where you would have been protected against sins like that.

He walked up and down, hands behind him.

—And then, you want to confess, to confess! You can come tomorrow morning. I don't feel like giving absolution tonight.

Ovide, his eyes haggard, moved backwards to the door. On the step he finally managed to say:

—I didn't come out of the monastery on account of the war. It was for her, the woman. I loved her. I'm desperate . . . damned. And I'm party to another's adultery as well.

His voice strangled in a sob. He rushed out and plunged into the street, almost running. The old priest, astounded at such a confession, seemed to realize its full import as the door banged behind his visitor. He rushed out on the veranda and called after the fugitive in an anguished voice:

—Ovide! Ovide, my son! Come back so I can confess you, so I can forgive you.

His last words died on his lips. Ovide was already far in the distance. He had not heard the priest's call, immersed as he was in his fixed idea of damnation.

*   *   *   *   *   *

Drunk with distress, Ovide staggered along in the direction of home.

—What will become of me? Oh God! Who will forgive me? he murmured.

He reached a street intersection where a group of adolescents were boastfully recounting their pranks. On seeing Ovide they were quiet, except for a few mocking laughs. When he had passed them, they began to shout:

— Go to bed, fake priest. Did you leave your cassock over your girl friend?

A cold sweat chilled his forehead and he braced himself against the impulse to dash off blindly towards the surrounding country, beyond the range of fear. But his mother, who had caught sight of him from the balcony, exclaimed in relief:

— At last! Here you are, Vide. What were you doing? I was beginning to worry.

This voice freed him from his nightmare. He coughed, ran his hand through his hair, and mounted the steps.

— Just loafing. It's such a lovely night.

The words did not come easily, for he was concentrating all his efforts on masking his feelings. Satisfied, Josephine preceded him, heavily, into the kitchen.

Nobody except Théophile had gone to bed. Napoleon, Cécile, Guillaume, and Josephine were still up at this late hour, like captives awaiting every night a liberation that never comes. Ovide eyed them glassily. The Plouffes! Kitchen prisoners for life! Napoleon was massaging Guillaume's back and bare arms and growling:

— You come in too late for a champion. I'm your trainer. You must listen to me. I've waited two hours for you. In the States you'll have to go to bed early.

Guillaume paid no attention and glanced mischievously at Ovide. Cécile was rocking in her father's chair at a bored and dignified rate. Seeing Ovide, she stopped and looked at her mother like a soldier warning his comrade that the signal for battle is about to sound. Josephine bit her lips and could not bring herself to speak until Ovide had his back to her.

— Oh! While I think of it, Vide. We were talking about it, Cécile and me. For the sake of talking, you know. Are you going back to the factory, seeing that you're out of the monastery for good? It'll be tiresome for you, hanging about all the time.

Cécile's voice cut in relentlessly on her mother's:

—In this life, one has to work by the sweat of his brow, to earn money.

The two assailants stopped talking and waited for the retort that did not come. The crazed, dejected glances of Ovide were fixed on the patterns of the table-cloth.

—We know very well, Josephine went on, you don't need to worry, a man like you. I think you could give up the factory. Cécile said that you could be a sacristan, but I claim you can work in an office and make a lot of money.

—Pooh! Not like on a bus, Cécile interrupted. I could try out Onésime, who has influence with the bosses. Perhaps he could get you in. Of course, you would be on the streetcars for some years to begin with. For the experience, you know.

Ovide emerged from the hypnotism of the patterns on the cloth, and his eyes looked utterly weary with the visions evoked by his mother and sister. Go back to the factory, to be crushed by the jeers of fools about the 'fake priest'? Admit the failure of his life before those boors? Never! Be a sacristan? Ring the bells, handle ciboriums, chalices, monstrances; decorate the church with banners of mourning or festivity; light the tapers and extinguish them; go back into that world, a renegade? Ridiculous to the point of disaster. Work in an office? Magic prospect! Nothing but a mirage. What did he know how to do? Recite Latin prayers, cut leather, assume lofty poses, quote pieces from opera, and the singers' names. And streetcars! Like Onésime. What a farce! The saraband of pictures ceased, gone in a flash of perception. Ah! He understood! It was Cécile who, all evening, had prompted his mother to suggest to him that he go back to work. Contemptuously, he walked over to her.

—You're afraid you won't see your ten dollars! You heartless wretch!

—Business is business, Cécile muttered. She felt troubled on seeing her brother walk to his room.

Before disappearing, he said in a tragic voice:

—Tomorrow morning I'll find a job. A real one.

He went into his room and thought he heard Josephine reproaching Cécile for having persuaded her to speak to Ovide. Then Napoleon's voice said:

—Let him alone. You feel confused when you come out of a monastery. It's like a hospital. Let him rest. If you need money I'll earn some.

Ovide stifled a sob, and two tears refreshed his dry eyes. He looked at himself in the mirror while taking off his tie. Then he caught sight of the Christ hanging on the wall and, out of doors, the dark night. The tune *East of the sun and west of the moon* was playing in his throat. He chased it away. Then the Gregorian chants filled his head and buzzed in his ears. The dreadful anguish of the last two hours enveloped him anew and cast him, trembling, upon his bed.

CHAPTER FIVE

I F Werther had suffered Ovide's despair he would have committed suicide during the night. Ovide was less fatalistic; and, the instinct for preservation aiding him, he chose instead a dramatic action that would not commit him to die immediately.

He had made up his mind to enlist.

His features drawn with sleeplessness, and his eyes consumed with a noble fire, he went into the kitchen where he washed himself in a manner already stiff and military. His mother, busy preparing the toast for Cécile, who was waiting impatiently, watched him out of the corner of her eye. Josephine had always been satisfied to admire her Ovide; never having understood him, she was continually expecting him to achieve great things. Consequently, she felt anxious, seeing him worn from lack of sleep. She held her breath when she saw him go towards the door.

—Aren't you going to eat, Vide?

He turned around slowly.

—Eat? What for? Those condemned to death have no need to eat.

He had assumed his deep voice, used on the mornings he felt gloomy, when he imagined himself a radio announcer and was hearing the echo of his words.

—How do you mean, condemned to death? Josephine mumbled, for she disliked this kind of joke.

Ovide cast a black look at Cécile who had stopped eating her toast.

—Yes. You told me plainly enough last night to look for a job. As for those I owe money to, they needn't worry; I think I've found a good one.

At his son's last words, Théophile let his pipe fall and gave a kind of anguished groan.

—Don't ever join up! D'you hear?

Ovide, frightened by his father's perspicacity, did not wish to mar the quality of his sacrifice by preliminary arguments which would lessen the intensity of the consternation into which his family would be plunged, once the tragedy was achieved. So he made no reply and walked haughtily to his heroic fate.

As a matter of fact, once past the climax of his distress the night before, Ovide had become dizzy when confronted with the melodrama of his problems and had fallen, head first, with a clownish abandonment, into the idea of enlisting in the overseas army. Besides, melodrama had allowed him to suffer all his life without growing embittered. As soon as his troubles could be turned into dramatic posturings, he felt a strange comfort like that experienced by an artist who becomes reconciled to his woes by the works of art they have inspired. So Ovide, before dismayed onlookers, had played the noble part of a hero who leaves secretly for the front, and he was reluctant now to spoil this effect.

He rushed down the stairs. Nothing could stop him. Joséphine and Cécile called to him from the balcony; Guillaume was practising a new spin in the yard; but their calls and the sight of their useless occupations made no impression at all on the mind of this hero called to the battlefield. With what dramatic intensity he felt himself vibrating! What a sensational moment! What a grand finale, when he would return home announcing: 'It's done. I am a soldier.' Ovide was jubilant.

His conscience did not dare to intrude its faint remorse at failure and unfrocking upon the sublime transports of a hero. For the time being the resources of acting isolated Ovide in a cloud of irresponsibility. He charged along the street and, in his exultation, vaguely imagined himself buttoned up in a brightly coloured uniform, in particular that of Don José in *Carmen*, which he had seen in Montreal in 1937. Warlike tunes crowded his breast, and it was *The Regiment of Sambre and Meuse* that he began to hum.

Animated by such a spirit, he soon found himself in the centre of the town. It was cool, and the houses seemed to huddle docilely under the mild caress of the September sun. This is the month in which things look like themselves: bricks are bricks, asphalt is asphalt, cars are cars. It is extreme cold or extreme heat that spurs or deadens the imagination, putting between the thing seen and the seeing eye the distorting prism that begets the false picture. This too is the month, in Quebec, in which people are the most sensible, because the temperature agrees with them.

A car that nearly ran him down brought Ovide back to everyday life.

—Well! he murmured, Couronne Street hasn't changed!

The bracing September air began to affect him. Openmouthed, like a sleepwalker who wakes up in the middle of the street, he gazed at the happy, jostling crowd. Then he began to look with curiosity at the shop windows and to dawdle before each one.

Strange sensation! What was happening to him? Away from his home and his parish, life appeared to him under another aspect. Why, exactly, should he enlist? He began asking himself if his craving for valour was not somewhat abnormal, since no sensible Quebecker could wish to be killed for his country. He was trying to persuade himself that it was not necessary to enlist because on leaving a monastery one has kissed a woman or because one is neither accountant nor store-manager, when his eye fell on a scene which made him grow pale. A priest, his hands behind his back, rocking backwards and forwards on the soles of his feet with a slight air of scorn, was reading a large notice: 'Canadians, enlist!'

The September air lost its tonic quality. Ovide was steeped in anguish again. The combination of the cassock and the word 'enlist' seized him like a pair of tongs and dropped him back into his drama. His imagination took but one leap, and he was back on the stage, well protected by the footlights from the pettiness of men and their reproaches. Furthermore, the third act wsa beginning, and a threatened France was calling for help. 'Come! It's time to go!'

The thin little man, stepping like a gunner, attacked the Côte d'Abraham. He was not aware of the spy at his heels. For Josephine, alarmed, had sent Guillaume after him.

*   *   *   *   *   *

The army headquarters were on St. Louis Street, close to the Citadel. These barracks, big stone buildings, which, since the end of the first Great War, had thrown a bleak and desolate shade round about, had since the beginning of September radiated a feverish activity. The Sleeping Princess had awakened. The guards at their sentry boxes felt they belonged to the present events and showed an air of authority characteristic of soliders in war-time. From offices hastily set up came the click of typewriters and the impatient shouts of peace-time officers, who had studied war in their manuals and, versed in the red tape of the Department of Defence, thought themselves already on the battlefield, with forms and subordinates for enemies. In the large brick yard separating the sentry boxes from the barracks appointed for enlistments and medical examinations, soldiers who, only last week, had been unemployed, were showing off their uniforms and boasting about their adventurous life to some of this week's unemployed civilians. The latter were listening attentively and glancing uneasily at the medical office. Occasional loud bursts of laughter issued from a group as someone told, with great gusto, details of the general examination in which different categories of wholly naked males, their clothes under their arms, form a line in front of the army doctor's office.

Amidst this puppet-like soldiery, bewildered extras awaiting the rehearsal of a badly produced play, officers went about like stage-managers who expect the worst. They were well shod, well groomed, and their lips were pinched together in a pout of chronic disdain. What wretched human material! Some twenty men shuffled about for hours before bringing themselves to sign the enlistment form. And then, out of ten men who presented themselves for examination, five, six, and sometimes eight were refused. The Beau Brummel recruiting officers, zealous apostles of a military régime which revives the fashion for fine uniforms, shrugged their shoulders and glanced impatiently in the direction of St. Louis Street. Their looks revealed a cherished dream of transforming the Houses of Parliament, nearby, into an immense training camp and booting out these pacifist Quebeckers, commencing with the civil servants. But, alas! There it was. Enlistment was voluntary in this country. Politicians and tradition demanded that it be so. And the recruiting officers champed at the bit, waiting for the occasional volunteers; for, in spite of their fine uniforms, they were still in the position of commercial travellers soliciting custom.

Clothed in his only new suit, leaning back against the steps leading to the medical office, one leg thrown casually over the other, Denis Boucher offered an American cigarette to a captain who was listening inattentively to the explanations of the former reporter.

—No, as far as I'm concerned, I shall be more useful to the army by not enlisting immediately. As I've told you, I intend to render certain very secret services to the Department of Defence. But to come back to the nationalists. Being a former nationalist myself, I can assure you I know what they're up to now. They're working up an intrigue against you military, you know.

His peroration was interrupted by the sudden silence which filled the yard. All heads were turned towards the sentry boxes.

—Why, it's Ovide! Denis murmured, amazed.

At the entrance to the yard, Ovide was pulling away from Guillaume, who had him by the arms and was shouting:

—Don't go there, I tell you! Mama doesn't want you to! No!

Ovide, who had begun to struggle without conviction, succeeded in freeing himself with a sharp blow when he felt the presence of onlookers. Breathless, holding himself straight, smoothing his hair in place with a trembling hand, he approached the guards and, as though delivering an ultimatum, demanded:

—Gentlemen! Do I enlist here?

The guards laughed and pointed to the registration office.

—Thank you.

Eyes burning, head high, he stepped into the yard, bending his shoulders as though he were about to climb a mountain. But his climb was interrupted at the outset by Guillaume who, disconcerted for a moment by the sight of the armed guards, renewed his attempt, pulling his brother back by the sleeves. Ovide stumbled.

—Will you let me alone! What do you know about war? This isn't baseball!

Blindly obeying his mother's injunctions, Guillaume began dragging Ovide off towards the exit. The soldiers and the unemployed, their hands in their pockets, were laughing heartily. But the recruiting officers were in no mood for nonsense and had no intention of allowing a precious customer, however thin and puny, to be kidnapped before their very eyes. Three of them rushed at Guillaume and, before he had had time to make a move, the champion pitcher was thrust out into St. Louis Street by some well-placed kicks. His heart wrung by seeing his brother ill-treated in this way, Ovide at first felt like leaving the yard haughtily and giving those inhuman soldiers a piece of his mind.

On the other hand, these men had protected his freedom of action, and quite an audience was admiring his courage in thus withstanding the wrath of his family. Besides, an actor, on the stage, has no family. He is there to satisfy the crowd. The theatre won the day. Ovide recovered his composure, straightened his suit, and announced:

—Thanks, gentlemen. France first, family second.

At these noble words, the laughter of the unemployed and the soldiers doubled.

—That's all very fine, but you just want to make a dollar thirty a day, like the rest.

Dumbfounded, as though a group of hecklers had been organized against him, Ovide glanced around anxiously. Cécile's ten dollars, streetcars, buses, monasteries, bits of opera, and a girl's breast began to jostle each other in his bewildered mind. But a recruiting officer took his arm and led a meek Ovide to the enlistment barracks. Ovide was aware of no one, not even Denis Boucher, standing near the door that the officer opened with a shrug as if to say 'We must take them as they are.'

For a long time Denis gazed at the closed door. Why was Ovide going to enlist?

Denis had of course learned that Ovide had left the monastery, but he had not ventured to go to the Plouffes to find out the reason. Since the tragic events that had turned him against the nationalists, Denis felt ill at ease with all those who had known him from childhood and preferred to avoid them in order to cut explanations short. He had entered a new era in his life, one in which his former friendships, his youthful habits, were nothing but embarrassing memories. The visit he had made to the monastery had filled his heart with bitter recollections; further contact with Ovide might interfere with his plans for advancing himself by means of the war. But at the scene which had just taken place before his eyes, his calm indifference collapsed, giving place to an uneasiness that came back to him like a bad after-taste of what he had felt at the time of the King's visit and the strike at *Christian Action*.

Denis Boucher had always tried to repulse the feeling of guilt that attacked him when he visualized Papa Théophile's paralysis. At this very moment, while he was staring at the barracks door, he felt remorse more keenly than ever. Actually, hadn't his ambition been responsible for all the misfortunes into which the Plouffe family had been thrown? It was the arrival of the pastor, Tom Brown, in the parish that had started it all. Denis Boucher wanted to be a reporter. The sorrows of the Plouffes had been the price of his success. Now, following some mysterious tragedy, a haggard Ovide came to enlist. Denis began nibbling at a match. Who knows? Perhaps it was because of him that Ovide was

317

suffering to the point of wishing to become a soldier. He decided to find out, and waited for the return of the former novice.

The hero appeared at last. He closed the door behind him cautiously, as though he would have liked to leave unseen. Ovide was crushed. Of course, he had been turned down. His physique destined him, at most, to the role of patient in a training hospital; and he would have been overwhelmed still more to have seen himself accepted, for a spark of common sense glowed beneath the theatrical exaltation which had inflamed him since morning, assuring him that he ran no risk in playing a hero's part. Now the act was finished and, crestfallen, he was forced to revert to the ordinary Ovide, with all his distressing problems. For a few hours, at least, he had believed in the comedy that he had played for his own benefit; thanks to the theatre, he had suspended an intolerable moral torture. A long hand seized his arm.

—Hi! Private!

—What . . .? Is it Denis?

—As you see. In the flesh. How goes the brotherly love?

They shook hands. Denis, on his guard, smiled cautiously. Ovide almost danced with joy. An inexplicable happiness suddenly illuminated his depressed being. Denis Boucher!

—Quick! Let's get out of here, he spluttered. Tell me about yourself. Is your novel progressing?

—The novel? I'll be working at that later. Something more important keeps me busy. We'll have to talk about it. Suppose we go and sit in the bar at the corner. Do you mind?

—Of course not. Oh, dear old chap, how happy I am to see you! At last I can talk about something intellectual.

Ovide was grinning broadly and looking his friend up and down with delight. He had met Denis at the very moment when thinking himself devoid of all hope through an unbroken succession of disillusionments, he no longer expected salvation unless the impossible should happen. Ovide did not know himself very well. The first happy accident would be the 'impossible' for him.

Since Denis had not been involved in Ovide's recent adventures, and was associated in his memory with the fine hours that Ovide once had spent, his sudden appearance symbolized in the poor fellow's eyes the miraculous intervention that turns a lost cause into a possible triumph. Ovide rejoiced. Denis did not share his exuberance, but endeavoured to show a corresponding pleasure.

At the door of the tavern a blast of men's voices met them; voices raised in vigorous discussion. War is a wonderful subject for conversation, when brimming glasses of beer sparkle with a golden light and smoke envelops you in an amber halo. In the tavern men feel sheltered. Separated from women by the barriers of the law, they give themselves up to orgies of talk which reveal the multiplicity of opinions that even the most ordinary individual can express.

—Two beers! Denis ordered, choosing a table and looking at Ovide questioningly. You'll have one?

Happy, Ovide shrugged and sat down, laying both hands flat on the marble table-top.

—Look here, Denis, you know your old Vide. Five glasses, ten, if you like. For all the effect it can have. That's nothing, compared to a Singapore.

He looked mysterious. Denis glanced up.

—Singapore?

Ovide smiled dreamily, his lips moist.

—My poor boy! Wait till you've seen something of life. Your old Vide's experienced, you know! Hm! The Singapore, dear Denis, costs a dollar a glass and you drink it with a beautiful woman.

Denis was more and more curious. He could not connect Ovide's language with the attempted enlistment of a few minutes ago. Was Ovide drunk? Ovide was tipsy with the joy of the prisoner unexpectedly set free. All the suffering, endured from the time he had left the monastery until his sudden meeting with Denis, found an unforeseen reward in this tavern, where, facing his dear Denis Boucher, he felt his whole being swim in an

319

indefinable peace. The past was no longer important, seeing that it was merging at this very moment into this pause, this halting-place where, together, in front of two glasses of beer, sheltered from everything, they talked to their hearts' content, before plunging into the unknown which awaited them outside. Ovide's smiling lips were still moist and his hand caressed the surface of his glass absent-mindedly. He was thinking of Rita, last night in the taxi, then on the grass when she had asked him to close his eyes for a minute, and then when he had opened them again. Ah! He bit his lips in order to restrain his sharp desire to see Rita again. Denis drank slowly, his eyes riveted on Ovide.

—A woman? Did you go out with a woman?

Ovide settled back in his chair.

—Yes, yesterday evening, to the Chateau. We danced. That doesn't mean I approve of jazz. But the Singapore! An elixir! It makes you soft and crazy.

—And then what? urged Denis, who was twenty-two.

Ovide threw back his head, laughing with pure satisfaction.

—And then, everything that can happen afterwards. But don't let's talk about that. You know my principles. I've always protected women's honour.

He began humming *East of the sun and west of the moon*. Denis was baffled; he sighed and smiled, visualizing the metamorphoses of Ovide. He saw him again, as he had seen him two months before, in the hall of the monastery; Ovide, floating about in an ample black robe, wearing a black beard and a cap. Denis's ears were still ringing with the pious words that Ovide had pronounced on sacrifice, the love of God through the love of one's neighbour. He looked up suddenly.

—I bet it was Rita Toulouse!

Ovide's arms fell down at the sides of his chair. A reticent hero who sees that his exploits are an open secret is not more joyously resigned.

—I can't hide anything from you! How clever you are!

He leaned on the table with his face between his hands and became confidential.

—We're growing older. A few years ago you were a child; and to think that now I can confide men's secrets to you. For you *are* a man . . .

—Alas! Denis interjected quickly, unwilling to check the flow of Ovide's confidences. Ovide's fingers thrummed on the marble. His intonation conveyed a friendly reproach.

—Denis, I've a bone to pick with you. You knew I had come home. Why haven't you been to see me? It's not nice. I'm your best friend.

The battle was commencing. Denis felt it. At last his curiosity was going to be satisfied, his uncertainty confirmed or removed. He would know the events that had upset Ovide's life to such an extent these last few months. Denis hooked his feet on the chair rungs and explained calmly.

—Out of consideration for you, Vide.

Open-mouthed, Ovide cocked his head to one side.

—Yes, I was being considerate. I thought that a serious reason had made you leave the monastery and that enough people had already asked you questions that made you suffer. I knew that you needed some seclusion in order to readjust yourself. I waited. And there you are, I meet you at the exact moment when I should meet you. That's the reason.

—Two beers! Ovide called out in a husky voice.

He bent his head sadly. His lips had become dry again.

—Now I see your big-heartedness, Denis. Thanks. Alas, there are so many who don't understand.

—I know you've suffered, but don't let's talk about it, Denis said, generously, content with the turn the conversation was taking.

—Yes, I've suffered, Ovide said in a low voice.

—Ovide, tell me. I want to ask you a question. You've always been an out-and-out nationalist. Why on earth did you come to enlist a little while ago?

—Enlist? said Ovide in a far-away voice. Oh, yes, that's right. He mentally traced the course of his emotions, starting with the shame he had felt at finding himself naked in front of the army doctor. Since coming out of the monastery he had travelled through such a long sequence of different states of mind that, in visualizing them, he felt like an old man recalling the important stages of his life. Everything passed through his mind: his despair the night before; his decision to become a soldier; his unsuccessful confession; the scene of his transgression; the dance floor at the Chateau; Cécile's ten dollars; and, far distant, almost beyond recall, his meeting with Rita at the factory door, when they had spoken about all manner of things, had even talked about Denis.

All at once, Ovide put down his glass carefully and intercepted his friend's anxious glance. How was it, when he had met Denis just now, that he had not remembered what Rita had told him? In the storm of feelings that had transported him since his meeting with the girl, he had forgotten his indignation against Denis. Ovide's desires had subsequently been so entirely gratified that his anger had vanished. He now tried to recover this anger, but Denis looked so astonished and so sympathetic that he only succeeded in assuming a tone in which reproach was drowned in sadness.

—Are you asking me, Denis, why I went in to enlist? It was your fault.

—That's right! Always my fault!

—Obviously, you forget your lies, even if they break up other people's lives. Remember when you came to the monastery to be comforted? By way of thanks you told me you had met Rita Toulouse. You said she had spoken about me, asked you for news of me, said she was sorry. That was all untrue. Oh! Denis, what harm you did me. You came and threw the seed of desire into my soul, which was so well protected. You took me from the happiness of my vocation, in which I felt so much at ease before your visit. Well, then! Yes, from that moment I thought only of her, wanting to see her again because she had spoken to you about me and was sorry for the grief she had caused me.

—Two more beers! Denis ordered, wiping his forehead.

—Do you want to know why I wished to enlist? Listen. In the first place, it was because of your lie that I came out of the monastery, in the hope of getting Rita back.

Wide-eyed and breathing hard, Ovide recounted the storm of events which had cast him on the shores of despair, from where he had crawled to the army barracks, attracted by the mirage of a redeeming heroism.

He stopped talking, lowered his eyes, and drank slowly, in little sips. He must go to see Rita at once to ask her forgiveness for having incited her to evil. The thought of having made her cry became unbearable to him. He started to get up. Impatient, Denis made him sit down again. Denis could not endure an anguished tension long. He clasped his hands together and drew himself up against the chair back.

—Well, how could I know? I yielded really to a good intention. I wanted to please you.

Ovide had the advantage.

—Good intentions! Pooh! Hell is paved with them.

Boucher got up brusquely and banged the table with his fist.

—Stop your vestry moralizing! It doesn't go down with me. And you may as well know that I don't regret that lie. It helped you. It allowed you to see yourself clearly, to see that your religious vocation was spite, transformed into a false mysticism. Look here, my friend, it's Providence that made me meet you today to stop you from playing the fool again. After all, you love this girl, why are you making a fuss over kissing her? Haven't you got enough money to marry her? Suppose I helped you to make some easily?

—Do you really think so? Ovide asked, impressed in his turn. Waiter, two beers!

The full glasses, topped with their caps of white foam, reflected the gold of the beer and the rising bubbles of fermentation—a picture of the feelings that now rose in their hearts. Ovide was already imagining himself arm in arm with a Rita Toulouse who would be his forever. He could see himself paving the floor of the family kitchen with ten-dollar bills. And Denis was seeing in Ovide a useful assistant in the strange ventures that he was planning. Ovide protested; it was too good to be true.

—But just think of it, Denis, it's frightful what I did with Rita last night, a week after coming out of the monastery. And her, what about her? Poor little thing!

—Wake up, stupid! Men and women have kissed for centuries, and had children. Do you imagine your midnight kisses are going to change the course of history?

—But what about the priest, who heaps reproaches on me? And all the family, who want me to go back to the factory? And the kids who jeer at me in the street?

Denis shrugged impatiently and swallowed the rest of his beer.

—Drink. That'll do you good. The priest? Don't mind him! He only sees the world through his parish and his political whims. Your family? They're not fit to hold a candle to you, you know. Go on being the head of the house and see to it that they don't discuss your actions. And the kids and the fools around us in this parish? Ah! let's be patient, we'll show them our superiority, because . . .

—You're right, Ovide agreed, conscientiously attacking another glass. I think my first move will be to go and see Rita and make her understand that because of the Singapores last night, I acted like a cad.

—That's right. But before you go, listen, Denis insisted, more anxious to propound his plan. I spoke to you about making money. You've noticed that, with our nationalist ideas, we always stayed poor. And the strict education we received in the parish only helps to prick our consciences and make us remorseful. You've had the proof of it. All right. I know you're clever.

324

—I do my best.

—Do you know what I've thought of? Suppose the two of us formed a secret service agency, a kind of Intelligence Bureau? Well?

Ovide's eyes had never been so round. Denis moved nearer and lowered his voice.

—Yes, a secret service. We could offer to work for the Department of Defence. It pays. We'd have to keep the authorities conversant with all the subversive movements that aim to undermine the war effort. We'd need to mix with the nationalists, or fascists, if you prefer, and keep ourselves posted on their activities and their plans. It's less complicated than enlisting. Pretty sharp, eh?

Ovide gazed at Denis in fear.

—Have you gone mad? Me, work against the French Canadians to help the English? Do you realize it's treason, Denis? Why, you're planning to have us assassinated! No, Ovide Plouffe will never have anything to do with it and I hope my Denis won't make this mistake. Just go on writing your novel. I gave you some good ideas for it, anyhow.

Ovide made this dramatic declaration and looked at his watch. Denis did the same.

—Then you don't want to make money?

Ovide seemed busy with a more pressing problem. He walked to the door, answering briefly:

—Not like that. Besides, I'll think about the money later on. It's a quarter to twelve and I have to meet someone at noon. Do you want to come a little way with me?

Denis shook his head and sighed. He was vexed with Ovide.

—No. Go and see your Rita Toulouse, since you're in such a hurry. We'll talk about this plan another time.

The five glasses of beer had made Ovide jovial. He laughed, said good-bye, and began to walk rapidly towards the Lower Town. He would arrive just in time to meet Rita at the factory exit.

CHAPTER SIX

OVIDE's heart beat more quickly. Rita Toulouse, hurrying along, was nearing the corner where he waited. From the moment the wish to see the girl had taken hold of him, while listening to Denis Boucher, he had completely thrown overboard all emotions and thoughts alien to that wish. He scarcely remembered Denis's last remarks. He forgot the humiliations of the morning. He even forgot his remorse for having put evil into Rita's soul and his resolution to ask her forgiveness. Once more, because of the beer, he felt the blind well-being of desire. He dashed from his corner like a youngster and planted himself squarely in front of her.

—Monsieur Plouffe! I . . .

—Hush! Hush!

Ovide smiled and, standing at attention, gave a military salute.

—Good day, dear.

Embarrassed, Rita looked obstinately at the pavement and stammered:

—You . . . you're well?

—Well? Better than that. I feel like the king of the world. May I go a bit of the way with you?

She was so astonished, and at the same time so intimidated, that she walked beside him mechanically, saying nothing, groping in the pockets of her raincoat with fidgety fingers. Ovide felt his boldness growing. His voice rang out, serious, yet gay.

—Rita, I've come to speak to you about my stupid behaviour last night.

She blushed, and stammered.

—It's dreadful, what I did, Monsieur Plouffe. You must think...

—Tut, tut, Ovide interrupted, amazed by his unwonted

breadth of mind. I acted like an idiot. I must tell you that your famous Singapore turned me completely inside out. I don't want you to think I'm the sanctimonious type; because, you know, I don't make a habit of refusing to hold a pretty woman in my arms. Well, once again, it was the Singapore. And I've come to apologize for that stupidity. Ah! If I had been sober!

His hand sketched a wide circle of implication. Rita looked dismayed. She managed to interrupt him.

—That goes for me, too. It was the Singapore. I don't know what was the matter with me. I didn't sleep all night. I hope you don't think I'm fast, and all that!

Ovide did not think that at all. Indeed, he felt such a sharp desire to improve on his kiss of the night before that he failed to notice Rita's present state of mind.

—Look! We were two human beings. We were kissing each other, like millions of others in the world. And a little kiss in front of a monastery won't change the course of history. God doesn't attach great importance to what we call the sins of love, you know.

—Monsieur Plouffe! What's come over you? If I'm crying, it's because of the Singapore, and all the things I told you. I made a fool of myself! Please, tell me you believe me when I say I'm a good girl, not in the habit of carrying on like I did last night. God! I feel awful!

Ovide gaped at her as though he had been paralysed by a shower of cold water. Rita dabbed at her eyes with a handkerchief. Ovide tried to recover the feelings of remorse and forgiveness which had filled his mind since last evening. The transition was too sudden. He fell back on a commonplace.

—Yes, I believe you. Surely you realized I was joking?

—You shouldn't joke like that. Oh! I'm so sorry about the way I behaved.

People were approaching. She put her handkerchief back in her pocket and, her face set, head high, turned to leave him. Distressed, Ovide lost no time.

—Must see each other again, Rita, eh? We'll go to the Chateau again. We won't drink any more. I don't know what possessed me to speak to you like that. Believe me, I wanted to ask you to forgive me.

She bowed to him with the dignity of offended virtue and said, very low, her voice breaking with emotion:

—Yes, but not now, Monsieur Plouffe. Later on. When you have a better opinion of me. Excuse me, I must go to dinner.

She went away quickly. Ovide wiped his forehead. He felt dreadfully alone.

—Now what will become of me?

He said this to himself in a dull voice. Everything was leaving him; he was like an empty sack. His last hope had failed him. Under what star had he been born? He compared himself to the hand of a watch that is out of order and never tells the right time; if he wasn't slow, he was fast. Bewildered to the point of idiocy, he confessed his bad luck to the dirty bricks of the houses, to the asphalt of the street. He must still eat, sleep, face his family, and endure his mother's reproaches because of the bad treatment he had let others inflict on Guillaume at headquarters. He must go back to his home crestfallen and inglorious, after having threatened his persecutors that he would sacrifice himself on the altar of enlistment.

He followed the direction of the wind, which was blowing towards his parish. As he came into Montmagny Street he saw some agitated housewives talking together and pointing at his father's house. A vague anxiety seized him as though a fire had broken out there and he had arrived just before the fire brigade. He passed the housewives quickly and thought he heard them saying, 'She was very fond of him, you know'. He looked up at the kitchen door and almost ran. The instinct for family preservation made him forget his own problems. What was happening? Still, no smoke escaped through the windows, no ambulance waited at the door. Just as he was putting his foot on the step, he heard a heart-rending sob. Cécile? His heart congealed and he climbed the steps four at a time and rushed into the kitchen, obscurely pleased that the mysterious drama which was about to unfold afforded him such an entrance.

Standing, open-mouthed, near the sink, Guillaume and Napoleon were gazing at the sad sight. Ovide remained rooted to the threshold.

Cécile was sobbing, her head buried in the curve of her mother's shoulder. Josephine rocked her, murmuring incoherent words while Cécile moaned as if, by so doing, to rid herself of the torment under which she writhed.

—You must listen to reason, little girl. It's God who has taken him. It was his time to go, Josephine added, pressing Cécile more firmly against her as though to put her to sleep.

—It's not true! Cécile gripped Josephine's shoulders convulsively. I won't have it! I saw him just this morning! Oh God, I'm all alone, I wish I could die myself. Mama! Mama!

Ovide, guessing the tragedy, asked discreetly:

—Was there an accident?

Josephine looked up.

—Thank God! He's come back! A little longer and I'd think you dead, too. You're not a soldier, eh, Vide?

With a bleak look, he shook his head and pointed to Cècile. Josephine tried to make Ovide understand, with grimaces, that Onésime had been killed that morning. Cécile, straightening up as if she had heard, pushed her mother away savagely. She stood up.

—It's not true! I won't have it!

Suddenly, she saw Ovide. Her face swollen with crying, her eyes wild, her hair dishevelled, she stretched towards him a hand like wax, the veins standing out upon it, and shouted hysterically:

—He's the one that killed him! I know it. He cast a spell over him. Wicked sorcerer! Go back to the monastery! Look at his eyes! Go away!

She fled, running into her room where they heard her fall on her bed. Very pale, Ovide slid along the edge of the table like a fugitive hugging a wall. His bewildered look met the fixed gaze of Théophile, which said: 'Ungrateful son, you've betrayed your country, you went to offer your services to the English!' Guillaume gave him a furious dig in the ribs with his elbow, muttering: 'You'll pay up for those kicks.' Ovide drank a glass of water, thirstily, while his mother told him about the accident in which Onésime Ménard had lost his life.

Onésime had been driving his bus along the usual route when, all at once, an enormous transport truck had come right at him. Taken by surprise, he had clutched the wheel, forgetting to turn it, and had accelerated with a foot trained to press the bell of a streetcar. Driving a bus had been, for Onésime, a kind of honorary position; it was normal that, in such an unexpected situation, his reactions should be those he had repeated for fifteen years. It had not even occurred to him to swerve around the truck and the two vehicles had met head-on with a horrible crash. Some had been injured, two were dead; one was Onésime, whose chest had been crushed against the steering-wheel.

Josephine sighed, and then looked towards Cécile's room.

—It couldn't last. I told her it would turn out badly.

Ovide drank another glass of water. He could not banish the sight of Cécile accusing him of Onésime's death. 'Look at his eyes, he's the one who cast a spell.' A hand took him gently by the arm and led him away to the parlour. It was Napoleon. The little man was over-excited.

—You see, Vide, he whispered, his eyes round. Life is very strange. Onésime was healthy, never coughed, never in the hospital. And he's dead. Take Jeanne, she almost never coughs now, she's getting fatter. In a little while, she'll be well. I think we're going along fine.

He smiled as he spoke, his eyes fixed complacently on Guillaume's trophies which cluttered the piano and tinkled whenever a heavy vehicle went along the street, shaking the houses.

—Wouldn't you feel like paying her a little visit? She would like to see you. And the other girls too.

Ovide felt a sudden need to weep, to roll on the parlour floor, shouting, as if by doing so he could become a new man whose past brimmed over with victories. But he neither wept nor shouted. Napoleon's words buzzed in his ears, and his eyes measured out the place where his coffin would be put, if he were dead.

Cécile's moans began again, worse than ever, in the next room, moans which rose in a new cry of distress.

—It's the unfrocked priest that killed him! Oh, God!

His face twisted with terror, Ovide clapped his bony hands over his ears. Napoleon examined his brother in astonishment. Suddenly, his lips began to tremble; behind Napoleon's low forehead, through the narrow channels of his simple brain, Ovide's distress had just penetrated, drawn by the magnet of a loving heart that had suffered.

—Viourge, Vide. You'd better come with me. You're feeling terrible. I know a White Father at the sanatorium, who got tuberculosis in Africa, Father Alphonse. You must talk to him right away. He'll understand you. He's the one who encourages Jeanne and me. Let's go now.

—Oh, let me alone, all of you! Ovide burst out, throwing himself into the armchair and burying his head in his hands.

He was shaken by heart-rending sobs that sounded like a pump sucking from an empty well.

Napoleon, his throat dry, hesitated, then sprang at his brother and seized his wrists with his short, strong hands. He pulled Ovide to the front door.

—You must come out of the house. Viourge, come, I tell you.

—What's going on here?

It was the priest's voice. Entering the kitchen, probably with the idea of finding Ovide, he broke in upon Cécile's tragedy. Ovide stopped resisting and allowed Napoleon to lead him out.

They were in the street. Round about them children played,

some with marbles, some with balls. Ovide reflected that it is overshooting the mark, ever to grow up. The autumn wind blew, betraying his thinness in the flapping suit. He felt lost. Napoleon was more optimistic. He was talking with tremulous volubility. His love for Jeanne, for which his family reproached him, allowed him to hold out to Ovide the only hope capable of saving him: Father Alphonse. Napoleon was delighted. He was killing two birds with one stone. He was helping Ovide and at the same time was bringing his intellectually superior brother into his inner world, that world which no one had tried to enter except through banter or contempt. And his love for Jeanne, which no one, except Father Alphonse, understood or approved, would receive, thanks to Ovide's visit, the approval of the whole line of Plouffes, an approbation Josephine had refused for fear of microbes. Napoleon was thinking that, whatever we say or do, our loves always seem guilty when parents disapprove. He steered Ovide toward the shed where the bicycles were kept. He was talking about Father Alphonse as if he were a friend who had played an outrageous trick that was laughed about still.

— You'd think he was a hundred years old. Has a beard as long as this. Chews tobacco and sometimes it runs into the white hair. Seems that the sisters at the hospital wanted him to cut it. They're used to seeing our priests without beards, you understand. He doesn't want to; laughs at them. Gives him something to stroke, that's what he says. Seems that the sisters have asked the Cardinal to make him cut it.

— A White Father, did you say? Ovide murmured, a wan smile on his lips.

— Yes, with a big white robe, Napoleon ran on. Been thirty years in Africa with the negroes. Seen more lions and snakes than you'd believe. He's a truly good father. He's bored at the hospital. He's not a reader. Spends his time visiting the patients. They even confess to him. Almost all of them. Especially the dying. The hospital chaplain, who is big and healthy, doesn't like that. You see, that leaves him only the sisters to confess, the sisters who don't like Father Alphonse's beard. Seems as if the sisters are tiresome to confess. Jeanne confesses to Father Alphonse. Yes.

There was a pause. Napoleon coughed, swallowed, then glanced sideways at Ovide, who was silent, his eyes unseeing like a judge meditating over a sentence.

—You know, Father Alphonse encourages me to go and see Jeanne and to marry her when she is a little better. I think he's right.

Ovide did not reply. He was thinking of Napoleon who, in his simplicity, was happy; of Napoleon who, like a persistent ant, was attacking with blind fervour all the obstacles separating him from happiness.

—Vide, Napoleon continued patiently. After seeing Father Alphonse, suppose, just for one little minute, you would come and see Jeanne. She'd be pleased.

Ovide agreed, with a nod. This acquiescence made Napoleon jump joyously into the shed. He eagerly brought out the bicycles into the yard.

—It's not true, eh, Vide, you haven't enlisted? That would be crazy, and it would kill Father.

—No, I'm too thin, Ovide said dolefully.

Napoleon then spoke of Onésime's death, concluding that it was very sad for Cécile, that something must be done to comfort her, but that it was too soon, yet. The two cyclists began pedalling. Napoleon, with his back hunched, his head emerging from between his shoulders like a large wart, crouched over the handlebars. He knew where he was going and what he wanted. Ovide, body sagging, hands slack, and legs flabby, seemed to be mounted on an illusive machine which threatened to give way under him like all the dreams on which he had ridden.

Change and trouble were restoring a scale of values among the Plouffes. Napoleon was the eldest and he had no need to get angry to prove it.

CHAPTER SEVEN

FATHER ALPHONSE'S room was in the wing of the sanatorium reserved for private patients, but it had not the clean and elegant appearance that priests' rooms usually have in a hospital run by a religious order. The old missionary had lived too long in a tropical climate where he had accustomed himself to doing without even the bare necessities. He could not acclimatize himself, at seventy years of age, to the little attentions of the sisters who, on his arrival, had overwhelmed him with courtesies accorded exclusively to sick priests. The nuns, chilled by his rebuffs, had quickly taken him to task about his beard. The blunt manner of the old campaigner for Christ would, however, have been forgiven him, in the long run, thanks to the feelings of clerical charity with which the nuns of Quebec are particularly endowed. But, unforgivable fault, Father Alphonse stretched himself out on the white coverlet of his bed, fully clothed, shoes and all. During the rest hours he smoked interminable pipes that scattered innumerable grains of tobacco and sent a thick smoke filtering through the cracks of the door. These smoke wreaths floated along the corridor, making the little sisters sneeze as they nosed about from room to room insisting on obedience to regulations. And when some audacious nun ventured to point out that it was forbidden to smoke during these hours he would draw his pipe slowly from the hairy cavern of his mouth and retort:

—I don't give a fig for the cure, my good Sister. I smoke; I'll smoke even after my death, if God lets me.

He would thrust his pipe into his toothless mouth and suck at it furiously, sending out big puffs in all directions. Feet spread out, robe turned up, his head leaning back against the bars of his bed, he would recite his rosary, staring at the wall for hours. Father Alphonse chafed under restraint. Impatience was killing him. Man of action, colonizer of souls and of the bush, he seemed to give himself up to prayer as to a last resource of the apostolate. He knew too well the difficulties with which his brother missionaries were at grips in Africa; he knew too much about their poverty and the practical aid that they need to enjoy the cosy atmosphere in which his superiors had confined him.

Sharp, agitated knocks shook the door.

—Come in!

Napoleon's puppet-head appeared.

—I'd like to speak to you a minute.

Father Alphonse sprang off his bed with visible good humour.

—Of course, come in and have a pipe.

He knew that Napoleon did not smoke, but he said this to all his visitors, and even, in fun, to the nuns. Napoleon turned to Ovide and whispered quickly:

—Wait for me in the passage a moment. Won't be long.

He tiptoed back into the room, turning his head towards the door as if someone might surprise him in the act of robbing Father Alphonse.

—Is there a lion at your heels? the missionary asked, surprised and amused.

—No. It's Ovide, my brother, who was a White Father. I told you about him.

—And you left him outside? Bring him in.

Napoleon, looking like a conspirator, exclaimed rapidly:

—Very discouraged. Cried at home a while ago. Don't know what's the matter with him. Brought him to you because you White Fathers know what to do. He'll have to recover his spirits, eh, Father? I'll get him.

He went out with all speed. Father Alphonse, suddenly concerned, had a premonition about Ovide's tragedy. He laid his

335

pipe on the dresser and went to the door. He was small and bald; his eyes shone like glass above the hectic flush of his cheeks. With his closed fist he suppressed a dry cough, and his long, white beard stirred like foliage around the cross that shone on his hollow chest. Ovide, pushed by Napoleon, who remained in the hall, entered with his eyes fixed anxiously on Father Alphonse's smiling face.

— Come in. Make yourself at home. Come and smoke a pipe.

*   *   *   *   *   *

Napoleon began to pace the long corridor full of numbered doors. Because of the silence which the polished floor seemed to render more artificial still, he started to whistle a gay tune very softly, and his little, round eyes looked like a diaeresis above his capital O of a mouth. Napoleon never sang and was not interested in music. But today, warm gusts of melody transported his whole being. He felt the joy of the innocent prisoner whom Justice has acquitted. His love for Jeanne, imprisoned in his heart behind the bars of family incomprehension, was in the process of being freed by Ovide's visit to Father Alphonse. Today, tomorrow, next week, he could speak openly of this love to all his friends, to his parents, the way one talks about a lawful affection. What a beautiful day! A nun suddenly popped out of a door which seemed as though it had always been closed. In this hospital the sisters loomed up like this, all at once, at the very moment when one least expected it. She stood still a moment, looking inquisitively at Napoleon who had quickly changed his whistled joy into a long sigh.

Head up, stiffened by the starchy look fixed on him, he slid, rather than walked, along the floor. Reaching the end of the hall, he turned back and saw that the sister had disappeared. How anxious he was to see Jeanne! Ovide had been a quarter of an hour already with Father Alphonse. As he neared the door of the missionary's room, Napoleon slowed up, hesitated, then bent his ear to the keyhole. He straightened up with fright. He had nearly heard a secret of confession. Ovide's rasping and hurried voice had reached him:

—Father, I accuse myself . . .

Napoleon resumed his walk at the rapid pace of a man who has had a narrow escape. But the sister whom he had seen a moment before now appeared, sailing towards him, for as her ample skirts hid the movement of her feet on the glistening floor, she seemed to be floating on water. She smiled like a figurehead.

—Are you looking for someone, monsieur?

—No, I'm waiting for my brother Ovide, who's confessing to Father Alphonse.

She shrugged her shoulders and continued to sail along the calm sea of the corridor towards the port of bottles, thermometers, and paternosters, murmuring:

—Aren't there enough priests in the town?

At the end of an hour's wait, Napoleon, with tired feet and eyes enlarged by the hallucinating sight of the polished floor and the closed doors, decided that Ovide's confession had been over for some time and that the two men had forgotten him. One never knows, with these White Fathers. They can talk for hours, as if in the pulpit, about wild beasts, Negresses, and all that sort of thing. But Napoleon wanted to see Jeanne. He could no longer contain himself, and after making sure that there was no nun on the horizon he went and put his ear to the keyhole, determined to go in if it seemed that the confession was finished. The complicated remarks he first heard did not permit him to conclude that a secular conversation was in progress.

—But, Father, Ovide was protesting, I've betrayed my vocation.

Father Alphonse's voice was slow in replying. He must have been pulling on his pipe.

—I tell you again that you can't betray a vocation you never had. You went into the monastery through spite, through pride.

Y   337

If you had known how to be truly humble, you wouldn't have suffered as you have.

Napoleon's head struck the door handle lightly, for he mentally agreed with Father Alphonse's opinion; the proud Ovide had always wanted to be master at home. Ovide's anguished voice reached him.

—But, Father, without that pride, one's only a rag.

—Excuse me, old chap, one is a true Christian, Father Alphonse interrupted gently. It's one of the most detestable forms of pride to believe that one is the victim of complicated and subtle spiritual torments. Our sufferings amount to very little when we have the courage to expose them to God's sunlight. It's also pride that makes us refuse the place that Providence assigns to us in society with the excuse that it isn't in keeping with our ambitions. And your place isn't in the monastery or, otherwise, the mere name of a woman wouldn't have brought you out. Here I am talking to you, just an old worker whose job has always been that of a missionary. Well! When you have a true religious vocation you feel as much at ease in the ministry as a carpenter in his workshop. A religious calling isn't in your line, old chap.

—Then what? What is there left for me? Society doesn't offer me any other refuge, Ovide wailed.

Father Alphonse burst out into such a shout of laughter that Napoleon withdrew his ear from the keyhole.

—Earn your living and get married! Get married! Furthermore, you show an excellent aptitude for that state if I can judge by what you've told me.

Father Alphonse continued to laugh and Ovide had to laugh, too, his eyes lowered modestly.

—Do you think so? Ovide's voice sounded brighter already. What makes me afraid, however, is that I should have to be content with a small salary all my life, and have to drudge so much to earn a living for my family that I shouldn't find time for beautiful things. Music, literature, and great ideas.

—Old chap, the most beautiful thing in the world is to do one's duty. And you know, if the arts are so important as all that, it's because millions of people like you, who drudge, who do their duty, love beautiful things. Look, stop being complicated and have confidence in God if you wish to find peace.

There was a long silence. Father Alphonse must have been pulling hard on his pipe because the smoke came through the keyhole, making Napoleon want to cough.

—Tell me, Father, Ovide asked, you can't have a very high opinion of me since I entered the monastery when I should have known it wasn't my vocation?

—Not at all. It is when one is hurt that one makes the worst mistakes. On the other hand, the way in which you acted shows that you have an honest mind. I know some lay brothers who, during the economic crisis, played the comedy of vocation in the community for the whole period of a difficult novitiate, the sole reason being to escape unemployment and to have an Atlantic crossing at our expense. Once landed in Africa they deserted us in order to seek adventure.

—Ah! the dirty skunks! Ovide cried, returning quickly to his problem. I thank you with all my heart, Father. I feel truly comforted. All that remains is for me to get rid of the anguish that comes over me because of the attitude of my parents and those who know I was in the monastery.

—Exactly, and I have something to propose which will cure you completely. It would do you good to travel for a bit and to get away from Quebec.

At this moment, Napoleon, still in the hall, gave a jump. His downward glance had just encountered the nun's skirt beside him.

—So that's the way you eavesdrop at confession, is it? she said sarcastically.

—No, no, Sister, he stammered, shamefaced. I . . . I was listening to see if it was finished.

Annoyed with himself, he began pacing the corridor again. Ah! He should certainly have taken Ovide to see Jeanne first, before introducing him to Father Alphonse.

*   *   *   *   *   *

Ovide stayed so long in the missionary's room that the hour for visiting patients in the public ward had passed, to Napoleon's despair. Coming out of the sanatorium beside his triumphant brother, he imagined that it was going to rain, in spite of the sun and the blue sky.

—Viourge! How disappointing! With all that, we didn't see Jeanne.

But Ovide, his eyes shining hopefully, gazed at the distant mountains.

—Napoleon! Do you know something? I'm leaving for New York, next week, by boat!

—What?

Ovide's tongue could scarcely keep up with the flow of words coming out of his mouth. Father Alphonse's nephew, captain of a merchant vessel which plied between Quebec and New York, would, on his uncle's recommendation, employ Ovide as kitchen help. Then, when navigation closed, Father Alphonse had promised to find a job for Ovide.

—Of course you'll go to see the World Series, Napoleon said.

—And the opera! Ovide added.

Mounting his bicycle, he looked like a convalescent eagle preparing to take flight. Life was wonderful! Rita Toulouse, on the quay, would wave her handkerchief in farewell. For some time he would be a sailor and would become the hardest of the hard. In fact, he would have to take the Charles Atlas correspondence course in physical culture and teach Guillaume how to become a man and a real champion.

—Are you going to Onésime's funeral? Napoleon asked, looking back towards the sanatorium.

PART IV

MAY–JUNE 1940

CHAPTER ONE

DUNKIRK: the end of May 1940.

The first cry of alarm, terrifying after long months of war without battles, long deadening months of indecision and stupefaction.

Dunkirk: the lash that suddenly ended the strange halt, drove terrified men helter-skelter into action, and set the Machine moving at last, to pile up disasters that would explain its slowness in getting under way.

Dunkirk!

Quebec, surprised out of sleep, turned anguished eyes towards Europe, towards Ottawa, towards the Archbishop's palace. Would the catastrophe reach Laurentia? During the preceding winter months, in the face of a war of paper and print, the Quebeckers, once their fears about conscription had calmed down, jeered at those loud-mouthed Europeans. Reassured by the aspect of the phoney war, they had almost forgotten that on each side of the Maginot Line there were soldiers waiting for a signal. But the Germans, without warning, had been the first to pounce, invading Holland, Belgium, pushing back the English to the sea and throwing their panzer divisions on a helpless France. And all that in only a few days.

Was this the end of an era? Alarming rumours came from Ottawa. The English provinces were clamouring for conscription, Mackenzie King, in an uncertain voice, was maintaining a weak refusal, and Ernest Lapointe was vainly trying to appease the fears of the French Canadians.

The Quebeckers were choked by uncertainty. Only a grand, religious ceremony could calm their anxiety. Providential coincidence: it was the time for the spectacular procession that is organized every year in homage to the Sacred Heart. This procession now assumed such an important place in everyone's mind that it seemed as though world safety were dependent on it. For nine days the display was ardently prepared, and the nearer the great evening approached the greater grew the fervour and hope.

Feverish activity stirred Quebec and the neighbouring country. The hotels were filled; long lines of cars and crowded trucks came in from the country districts. The faithful received Holy Communion; conversations went on and on every evening around the thundering radios and, in the kitchens, while their wives watched anxiously, the men waited with resolute faces for the signal of the great gathering.

*   *   *   *   *   *

Two hours before the procession. The stream of cars flowing into the town by all routes so definitely indicated the importance of the ceremony that an immaculate ambulance, threading through the streets of Limoilou, looked as though it were on its way to where the procession would pass in order to wait and collect the wounded.

The brakes squealed. The driver, pale and slender in his white uniform, leaped out and knocked feverishly at a door. Rita Toulouse, her head wrapped in a towel, opened it.

—Ovide! Come in. I'm just giving myself a shampoo.

The driver smiled broadly and shook his head.

—No. I just came to ask if you're going to see the procession. I want to march. We'll meet afterwards, at the City Hall.

—O.K. Whatever you say.

Rita was in charming disarray. Fair curls escaped from under the towel, which was twisted like a turban, and her dressing-gown had been fastened hastily. Ovide, his eyes shining, lingered.

—I'm sure we're going to have compulsory service. The procession can't do anything. The chap at the record shop is in perfect health. His job will be available and I'll get it. I have my rejection button. I've been wanting to give up the ambulance for quite a while. And then, as a record salesman, I would have a salary to marry on.

Ovide watched Rita eagerly. Coquettishly, she gave him a slight push.

—You think so? Ah! We know you, you men with your promises.

She accepted him then? Ovide laughed.

—We'll be tremendously happy, you'll see. No more kissing in the park. And to think it's the war that brings us good luck. Not to mention that everybody at home will be safe. Guillaume is leaving for the United States tomorrow.

—Buzz off, villain! See you tonight, she added quickly. My water's getting cold.

Ovide looked at the closed door for a moment, then, smiling ecstatically, settled himself at the wheel. After returning from his trip to New York, from which place he seemed to have brought back some mysterious experiences, he had accepted this work as ambulance driver that Father Alphonse had found for him. Secure in his position, he had begun to go out with Rita regularly and even to bring her to his home, to the great dissatisfaction of the grudge-bearing Josephine. Then he became obsessed with the idea of marriage, but his income was not sufficient for this venture. And so he began to detest his position and to covet the job of selling records.

Not only was Ovide tired of hearing groans behind him in the ambulance, but he had to suffer Cécile's nagging with respect to ambulance drivers. The sinister sight of the vehicle parked outside the house at meal-times recalled, for her, too lugubrious memories. Only Napoleon rejoiced over Ovide's position, for it produced in the family a hospital atmosphere in harmony with his love affair.

Marriage! Ovide's mouth watered. The ambulance rolled

along with unsuitable gaiety. A tall figure suddenly sprang on to the running-board and the tousled head of Denis Boucher appeared at the window.

—Jumpy, Ovide? Just a word. I've enlisted. Assigned to the propaganda service. Officer's pay. Good-bye.

—Enlisted? Are you mad?

But Denis had jumped off the running-board. Ovide quickly fell back into a luminous dream. Love, when you hold us. . . . All was going well. He would march in the procession, luxuriate in prayer, cry over the fate of Europe. But the procession could not prevent compulsory service.

All the luck was going Ovide's way. Even Guillaume had been called by his club and would leave for the United States tomorrow. For the champion, haloed by his glory, had recommended a flirtation with Rita which Ovide found exasperating.

Ovide smiled. He swung his ambulance expertly to the kerb, parked it without a sound, and climbed the steps. The blare from the radio turned on at full force burst out through the kitchen door. Ovide shrugged his shoulders. The old paralytic never tired of listening to news of the disaster of Dunkirk.

—Here's the undertaker, Cécile grumbled. Dressed in black, she was seated on the streetcar bench at the end of the balcony and looking with disgust at the roof of the ambulance. Since Onésime's death the old maid, whose grey hair was now turning white, spoke ceaselessly about the dead man, so much so, that after a few months she seemed to imagine that she had been his wife. Because of her innate sense of economy, Cécile drew from Onésime's passing the only advantage that his death presented to her: she could at last open her heart and speak of Onésime as of her husband without the family finding fault, and it was tacitly understood among the Plouffes that the departed was a kind of son-in-law or brother-in-law whose memory Cécile might daily conjure up with a widow's prestige. But for some weeks the situation had been growing more complicated, and the Plouffes considered that things were going too far. Cécile was insisting on adopting Onésime's youngest child, as his legal widow could no longer take care of him. The principal obstacle that she encountered in this plan was Guillaume who, jealous of his privileges as youngest, looked askance at the intrusion of this two-year-old child. Consequently, Cécile too was interested in American baseball.

Still grumbling, she peered eagerly through the screen door.

—Here he is!

—What now? asked Ovide.

An unusual activity reigned in the kitchen. Madame Plouffe's suitcase was lying wide open in the middle of the room, receiving woollen socks, drawers, medals, and scapulars, belonging to Guillaume, together with innumerable injunctions from Josephine.

Guillaume walked over to Ovide and handed him a yellow envelope.

—We've just received another telegram from the States, Josephine said.

All the Plouffes followed the rapid movement of Ovide's eyes as they swept over the telegram.

—Hum! he said, perplexed. It seems to me that in New York this word isn't spelled with two S's.

—What does it say? Josephine asked timidly. Do turn down the radio, Théo, so we can understand! she called to her husband who was turning the regulator with his good hand.

The paralytic beamed while listening to the news of the English defeat and, like a radio sports fan who relishes the explosion of triumph released by the victory of his team, was alternately decreasing and increasing the volume.

Josephine, ignoring his woebegone look, turned off the radio herself.

—What does it say?

—There's a word here that seems to be spelled wrong. I'll look it up. It's very important.

—What an ignorant fellow! Cécile said impatiently. Onésime would have told us right away. He didn't know how to write English, but he understood it.

—Do you want me to read it or not? Ovide threatened.

He went to his room to consult a dictionary. Since his trip to the United States they thought he knew English well, and his standing had gone up. While he puzzled out each word, Napoleon tried to restrain the impatience of the others in the kitchen.

—Sometimes a letter too few or too many can change everything in English.

—Don't show off, Cécile cut in. Go on with your statistics.

—Nothing will stop Jeanne from beating all records, her brother protested.

With his back to the window, Napoleon was sitting at the table in front of the ruled sheets on which he noted the history of Jeanne's illness; number of days in hospital, high and low temperatures, sedimentation, ounces and pounds dearly gained, daily, weekly, monthly; in short, a series of painstaking figures with which Napoleon cemented the edifice of his hopes.

At the word 'statistics' Josephine glanced irritably at the outspread sheets.

—You certainly like to waste your time.

But during the past winter Napoleon had strengthened his position a great deal. Staring at his mother, he stated calmly:

—Father Alphonse says that order in life is beautiful. He says that the sick are just like other people. Father Alphonse says that Jeanne is almost cured and she can get married soon.

Josephine had, for some time now, been finding Father Alphonse unanswerable. So she changed the direction of her impatience and looked towards Ovide's room.

—Oh, how complicated English is!

There was a short silence; all they could hear was the sound of a pen ruling lines and the humming of the radio, furtively turned on by Théophile. Cécile, looking down, smiled mysteriously.

Very amiable all at once, she spoke to Guillaume who was near
the sink, hands stuck in his pockets, waiting anxiously for
Ovide's return.

—Are you anxious to leave, to find yourself in the United
States? Aren't you afraid of being homesick?

The pitcher glanced sideways at her.

—Don't be a hypocrite. You're keen enough to see me go.

At this moment Ovide came into the kitchen, dragging his feet
and looking most depressed. He threw the telegram on the sink
beside Guillaume.

—Well! You're not going.

—What?

The exclamation burst from every mouth. Ovide, out of
patience, almost shouted:

—You're not to go. It's clear. They're cancelling your departure, putting it off until later, because of international events, I
suppose.

—Viourge! Father, turn down the radio so we can hear,
Napoleon roared.

In the explosion of collective astonishment, each reacted in a
different fashion. Napoleon left his statistics and began to walk
up and down the kitchen trying to put some order into the
muddle of his disappointed hopes.

—Viourge! That doesn't make sense. I'd trained you; you
were ready. And what about the articles and pictures that we
won't have now?

—A lot that matters! Ovide muttered, looking angrily at him.

Cécile had not moved in her chair. A bitter smile twisted her
lips. It wasn't surprising, nothing ever happened that she had
hoped for. She wouldn't be able to adopt Onésime's child, that
was all. Josephine, who at heart was rather pleased, realized at
this moment that family solidarity is impossible with adult children, the egoism of each bringing its element of disagreement.
She watched the faces of her children and guessed the reasons for

their disappointment. Josephine wanted to smile. She was winning a victory, since events prevented her flock from scattering.

—The good God knows what He's doing, she said. After all, you're better off with your mother, dear. Now, don't get upset.

Furious, Guillaume ground his teeth and, in his rage, kicked an empty carton until it finally landed on Cécile's bed.

—The good God, the good God, he grumbled. I'm a pitcher, aren't I? I'm better than ever at judging the distance, hang it all. And do you think I'm going to stay here in the kitchen? No. I'm too used to thinking I'm going away. I'll have to leave. I'm enlisting.

—Don't lose your head, Napoleon cried, startled. Mustn't get excited. It may work out all right yet.

Over the radio, the speaker was giving a literary version of the disaster of Dunkirk; the bombardment, as described by a graduate of the Quebec Seminary, seemed to have its repercussion in the Plouffe radio, which buzzed and crackled.

Papa Théophile, by his grimaces and his groans, by all the bodily contortions of which he was capable, tried to attract his children's attention in order to tell them not to be astonished at what had happened to Guillaume. Conscription would be imposed in a few days and the government would not allow young men to leave the country. But it was a long time since they had paid any attention to Théophile. He was very thin now, and his face was furrowed with deep lines. A tear formed on his lashes. He was an expert in making these diagnoses of war, and his children refused him the supreme consolation of conveying even one to them.

Suddenly Father Folbèche burst into the kitchen. Hat pushed back, breathless, handkerchief in hand, he nervously wiped his face.

—From the latest news, it seems that Ottawa is on the brink of voting on military service. You know what that means: conscription. England sees a chance to exterminate us at last. Don't forget

o march in the procession tonight. It's our only hope of safety.
You too, Guillaume, even if you're leaving for the United States.

—He's not going, said Josephine, who suddenly thought of
enlistment with terror.

They had scarcely finished telling the old priest what was in
the telegram when he declaimed in prophetic tones, his arms
outspread:

—Monsieur Plouffe, you cannot speak, but in your eyes I read
that you are the only one who has understood. Look at your
father, all of you. The gaze of this helpless patriot cries out to you
that a bloody era is about to descend on your young people. Do
you realize that Ottawa will send Guillaume into the battlefield
instead of the baseball field? We must defend ourselves. The procession is our last weapon. Seven o'clock! At the Church of
St. Roch.

He went out. The Plouffes looked at each other in fear. The
international situation, which had not greatly disturbed them
because of the excitement over Guillaume's departure, suddenly
assumed a place of first importance in their lives.

CHAPTER TWO

An intense Sunday atmosphere swept down upon that Friday evening when a hundred thousand persons came out from their ordinary week-day meal to attend a solemn evening celebration.

The heat was enervatingly humid and the city, under a heavy canopy of clouds, seemed doomed to a storm; yet nobody believed it would break, because of the power of the Sacred Heart

As the hour of the ceremony drew nearer the town underwent a curious transformation. The traffic stopped, or almost, and the few vehicles still moving appeared sacrilegious.

For a new order had taken possession of the streets. Faith was upsetting all the rules of topography. Wide streets were changed into blind alleys, and lanes had become royal highways. The streets chosen for the procession wound triumphantly from the Church of St. Roch to the City Hall, and were gaudily decked with flags and streamers, leaving the multitude of other roads in the shade and draining them of the lively crowds of people.

At seven o'clock the bells rang for the gathering of believers and patriots, and the exodus began towards the starting-point for the procession, the Church of St. Roch. Men, women, girls, and children surged out from everywhere, attracted to the lighted way. One was astonished that there were so many people in this peaceful city, just as one is surprised at the multitude of moths around a lamp on summer nights. Only invalids, the infirm, and the aged seemed still to inhabit a few of the houses, where radios were broadcasting the first reports of the ceremony.

Even the muffled hum that ordinarily rises from the town, especially at night when the streets and buildings are lit up, was changed into an immense murmur blended with hymns and veiled in a mist of incense coloured by the street lamps and neon signs. The city fell on its knees and began to pray that calamity might not overtake it.

From loud-speakers placed at strategic points along the way the mechanism whistled and crackled as it sent forth two tragic cries like streaks of lightning through the supplication that rose from the streets and over the rooftops: 'Hail, Sacred Heart'; 'Sacred Heart, save Europe, remove from us the spectre of war!'

The procession took form, responding to the call of its official leader, Father Lelièvre, a saint whose great love for the Sacred Heart equals the understanding he has for the anxieties of the people. He was already sounding his rallying cry inside the temple itself, where the heart of the procession began to beat, and giving direction to the flame of faith that as yet was sheltered inside four walls. But, presently, emerging from the Church of St. Roch, that flame would be transformed into a gigantic Greek fire of fervour which would sweep through the crowds right up to the City Hall.

The masses of people flowing along the streets in confusion towards the place of the ceremony seemed to obey a mysterious discipline when approaching the centre of the town. With faces become suddenly grave, the men separated themselves from the women and marched off to the church, while the latter took a last glance at their clothes and ran to crowd together on the pavements. The wives of the pacifists applauded the display of their menfolk with as much zeal as the wives of militarists cheer soldiers' parades.

While these lines of colour continued to grow along the sides of the square, some thousands of bare-headed men darkened the vicinity of the temple, shaken by the thunder of voices and of organs. They awaited the coming of the golden Monstrance in order to fall in line behind it and follow it on its extraordinary course.

The sale of badges, which usually brought an appreciable revenue to the organizers of this annual procession, lost its business-like aspect this particular evening, being almost unheeded by the surging crowd who paid and pinned without a second thought. Attitudes and gestures mattered little in the sort of mystical rapture that exalted every being, a state peculiar to crowds and now brought on by the suddenness of the European tragedy, heightened by the recent Novena and the imposing setting of the procession, and stimulated by indefatigable priests such as Father Folbèche. The latter spurred on their parishioners, brimming over with fervour, making them sing hymns that the loud-speakers wafted to the sky. When fifty thousand believers begin to sing like this, a town is no longer a town. One could have thought oneself transported, that evening in 1940, into a valley of Jehoshaphat, sublime and awful, waiting only for the trumpets of the Apocalypse to conclude that the end of the world had arrived. Would the earth open up, the buildings topple down?

No. In the great door of St. Roch was framed the throne-chair with its gold-embroidered canopy, used for the first time at the celebrated Eucharistic Congress of 1938, and now sheltering the apostolic vicar of James Bay, whose head and shoulders disappeared behind the golden sun of the Monstrance.

The fascinated crowd, quite motionless, gazed at this symbolic luminary that held the Saviour. The Hebrews, before the Ark of the Covenant which was shown to them at tragic moments in their history, were not more exalted than the people of Quebec in front of the Monstrance that glittered in all its fire. For it was not the God of ordinary Sundays who showed Himself this evening, it was the God of 1837, of 1917, and of 1940, the God of nationalism, the God of the people of Laurentia, the God of those great historic moments when the fatherland is threatened.

While the head of the procession was forming and the movements of the crowd, submissive to a mysterious order, were bringing them already into line, a priest of fiery speech, well known for his violent anti-British attacks and his nationalistic sermons, seized the microphone, left free by Father Lelièvre. The latter was on his way to the street altar at the City Hall to welcome the procession.

'As we all know, Europe is ablaze and covered with blood. We pity her and we pray the Sacred Heart to put an end to her suffering. But our participation must not go beyond that. Our young race cannot be allowed to expose itself to death on the battlefields. Don't forget that the political forces that encourage conscription for overseas are the very ones that wish to see us disappear. God forgive them! Come, young men, let us pray! The Sacred Heart is listening to us. Let us sing! Altogether, with a loud voice . . .'

The chant of these tens of thousands of anguished voices appealing to the Sacred Heart rose with such force that the ear could not judge its intensity. It seemed as though the town uplifted in a spiritual volcano, sought to pierce heaven with its cries. An atmosphere of catastrophe or miracle slowly replaced the pervading heavy tension. The excitement originating in the church communicated itself to the whole line as far as the altar in the City Hall, like a tornado that razes everything in its way.

'No conscription!' This watchword marked the departure of the avalanche of men. The gigantic crusade began to move, preceded by mounted police. In the vanguard, as if to clear the way for the throne-chair, marched the various religious orders; after them came the great cross of the procession, the clergy of the Senior Seminary, and the priests and curés of the town. Then followed the throne-chair, supported gravely by churchwardens in white gloves, who were relieved along the route by others. After them marched prelates, canons, and clergy of high rank. Then came the notables, the political personalities, and the enormous mass of anonymous laymen whose ranks extended and swelled like a tremendous tidal wave.

Towards eight o'clock the wind rose and pushed northwards, helter-skelter, the black clouds that threatened the town. Streamers, flags, vestments, dresses, hair—all blew together in the wind and beat, like the hearts, as one. It was too beautiful, too ardent, too imposing; surely God would hear. The volcano of St. Roch square continued to pour out its inexhaustible lava, whose flow of men, wave on wave, rolled towards the altar in a tumult of chants and prayers. As the canopy passed them, the women standing by the way knelt down, and looked, from afar, like multicoloured sheaves bent to the ground by the passing of a superhuman breath. Such a faith transported these thousands of men, who were carrying a Monstrance as their flag, that one had the impression of a hurricane of piety sweeping these beings like straws.

If some hundreds of church dignitaries preceded the throne-chair a few priests, even more ardent, were following it, spaced out in the interminable body of the procession. One could see them in their surplices, walking backwards, exhorting their parochial regiment to pray, to sing louder, still louder: 'Sacred Heart of Jesus, save us from conscription!' Then a new spasm of fervour would stir the procession which, with the noise of a cataclysm, pressed onward from street to street.

These tremendous phalanxes, moving rapidly along, offered a sublime sight. Armed with thousands of rosaries swinging like pendulums in time with the growing exaltation, groups of men all joined in the same adoration of the Sacred Heart of Jesus.

Among them there were frenzied Anglophobes muttering fervently. There were also the disheartened whose anxieties and hopes, transplanted into that collective fever, were transformed into questions of life and death, depending on whether the procession succeeded or failed. There were the people influenced by the political parties that had waved the bogy of conscription for so many years to obtain votes. For the fearful, this threat, like that of hell, tuberculosis, and cancer, constituted part of the basic heritage of fundamental feelings bequeathed by our brave forbears. And this fear, which in ordinary times gave place to preoccupations of secondary importance, passed from the chronic state to that of acute disease, once plunged in the burning fever that raged through the procession.

Then there were those, indifferent to racial struggles, who thought with terror of Europe's misfortunes. With tears in their eyes they besought the Sacred Heart to heal the world.

Finally came those who, holding their rosaries absently, were preparing themselves through meditation for the holocaust of the morrow. These were the innumerable young men who would soon swell the ranks of the 22nd or the Chaudière Regiment, either for love of France, or through a taste for adventure, or to put their muscles, now wasted by unemployment, to work, or simply through a strange and admirable need to give themselves.

Needless to say, some young men here and there, instead of lifting their gaze to the heavens, were watching the hundreds of pretty girls along the route whose dramatic emotion at the threat of conscription enhanced male prestige. Once the raised chair had passed, the more flirtatious girls could hardly reply to all the ogling glances they received. The other women, the Josephines, the Céciles, even if they were joining in the chants and the men's prayers, were satisfying their curiosity without neglecting their fervour. And indeed, what an incomparable spectacle! Swarms of men at a time! Many of the women accomplished the prodigious feat of examining them one by one, and the vision sank so deeply into their eyes that, by a kind of optical illusion, they were still seeing the parade an hour after the end of the ceremony.

And above all, what amusing faces they could discover! Certain homely men have such ridiculous faces when the faith that moves mountains deforms their features and makes their imploring mouths drop open. But the majority of the participants, released from their usual concern for their appearance, were oblivious to the spectacle they afforded. Ears buzzing, blood

357

throbbing at their temples, their eyes lifted towards the Sacred Heart, they were part of the frenzied avalanche. Dumpy or lanky, thin or fat, pale or ruddy, they were following the star.

And the flood of human lava rolled on towards the altar in ever-increasing haste. The pounded asphalt emitted a continuous, muffled protest under the trampling feet. The loud-speakers, lacerated by the shouts of Father Lelièvre's hoarse voice, seemed about to choke in an asthmatic crisis, for the saintly promoter of this procession, who was now conducting its immense orchestra of prayers from the City Hall square, was aroused to a paroxysm of ecstatic religious enthusiasm as the last movement of the symphony of the Sacred Heart approached. Such adoration, such confidence in God was heard in this voice that the oddest supplications took on an aspect of sublimity. The procession was his creature. Thousands of men, breathless with climbing the slopes, their necks craned and their eyes starting out of their heads, were responding to the call of his inspired voice. The psychosis was complete. What was about to take place?

Suddenly Father Lelièvre gave a cry choked with holy jubilation. 'The first contingents of the procession are reaching the altar, and in the square of St. Roch the crowd continues to swell the parade. Hail to the Sacred Heart! Sacred Heart of Jesus, have pity on our young men!'

A gust of exaltation shook the electrified marchers. The door of miracles was opening at last. The city, whose poles were now the Church of St. Roch and the City Hall, was sewn from end to end by a single human thread.

From this moment, the parade took on a new aspect. Its pace accelerated, because all were burning to reach the centre. The tight ranks broke and melted into the illuminated space before the altar. At the end of half an hour a tumultuous mass of heads darkened the City Hall park, its approaches, and the surrounding streets; and the procession, like a river, continued to pour its inexhaustible supply into the overflowing gulf. The multitude of men and women, lighted by beams from the reflectors and by the moon, which was just appearing, continued to sing and pray while waiting for Cardinal Villeneuve, who was to give the address.

These regiments of crusaders, vibrating with exaltation before the Holy of Holies which they had reached at last, awaited only the consent of the great leader of French Canadian Christianity to let free the victorious cries they could hardly restrain. The address was awaited with anxiety by men like Monsieur Folbèche, the nationalist priests who, tired out and covered with sweat, were going from group to group continually stimulating the fervour, increasing the general tension by feverish exclamations, as if to release a triumphal tidal wave that would roll right up to the feet of the Sacred Heart, sweeping away as it went all arguments and governments favourable to military service.

The enormous crowd, a single, moving mass, seemed dominated by a hypnotic power. Held at the topmost reach of fervour, it lifted to the sky the outbursts of supplication that came from Father Lelièvre. It was now nothing more than a gigantic medium in a trance. Helpful associates would suggest passionate invocations to Father Lelièvre who, in the candour of his jubilant saintliness, repeated them into the microphone before he had even grasped their meaning.

Suddenly a tremendous detonation shook the ground and rolled away like thunder to echo in the distance.

It was the 9.30 cannon.

A heavy silence descended on the multitude. War had presented its symbolical threat to the procession. The tragedy of the battlefields loomed above the altar.

At this moment, Father Lelièvre's broken voice, tremulously deferential, was transmitted through the loud-speakers. 'My brothers, His Eminence.'

The distinguished churchman raised himself from his prayer-desk and walked to the microphone. Though he was small of stature there emanated from his person a nobility and an impression of grandeur that commanded the respect even of great statesmen. For a few interminable seconds he gravely contemplated the immense flock of breathless sheep awaiting only a sign from his hand to shout with joy.

Flashes from the nickel-plated microphone played on his spectacles, and above his head waved the tricolour, the Carillon flag with its four fleurs-de-lis, and the white-and-gold flag of the Vatican. The Cardinal folded his hands and in a strong, sweet voice he began to speak of the Sacred Heart with a dignity which the purity of his language transformed into an artistic act of faith. His words, carried by the loud-speakers, floated serenely above the motionless heads. Then slowly his voice swelled out, vibrating with a proud steadfastness of purpose. The supreme moment had come. The crowd held its breath.

'We must all take advantage of these solemn prayers,' the Cardinal proclaimed, 'to ask the Sacred Heart to kindle and to spiritualize in us feelings of the purest patriotism, so that we shall be deeply affected by the ills that have fallen upon friendly nations and by the dangers that threaten all Christianity. The world has need of the riches of the Heart of Jesus, especially in these days when the most abstract ideas struggle in confusion with each other. It is fitting and proper to condemn those thoughtless spirits who weaken the Christian sentiment of right and of a just victory by their ill-considered or malevolent declarations regarding the upright nations of the world.'

Some of the ardent apostles in the crowd clenched their fists. The Cardinal continued:

'Cruel and sacrilegious potentate, murderer of women and children, Hitler represents treachery and the organization of evil. His adversaries and his victims represent patriotism and the right. The Pope, with discretion but also with unconquerable energy, has publicly denounced the barbarous audacity of a man who no longer respects humanity. It must be proclaimed aloud,

360

before the whole world and especially before the Adorable Sacrament of the divine Heart, that the flag of the allied armies is our flag. The Church does not bless war, but she blesses the sword of those who know how to use it for good. Those who are allied to us, by treaty, by blood, by language or by political solidarity, have the right to count on our good wishes, our prayers AND EVEN OUR SACRIFICES TO ASSURE THEIR VICTORY.'

The terrible blow had fallen. The numberless crowd wavered and let out an astounded sigh of despair.

Afterwards, the Cardinal spoke in English; but the dumbfounded crowd understood no longer. When the starry Monstrance was held aloft in the night it shone on thousands of bewildered men resigned to disaster, and on those few fierce apostles who, with clenched fists, prepared to fight for 'the race'.

CHAPTER THREE

Pensive and alone,
Dressed in khaki,
Crouched on the ground,
Hand on his gun,
A young Canadian soldier . . .

THE nostalgic melody floated through the Plouffe kitchen. Josephine's lips scarcely moved; it was enough that the terrible words should be pronounced in her broken heart. For Guillaume was submitting to his medical examination that morning in view of compulsory service.

Josephine dusted the table for the tenth time. Before the threat that hung over her household she clung desperately to the housework as if it could draw the family ties closer and make them indestructible.

—You never can tell, perhaps Guillaume has some little ailment, poor child. I should be quite content.

She looked at no one as she said these words in much the same tone as *Pensive and alone*. Furthermore, no one replied to her. Théophile had had his chair placed facing the door. He had insisted, with an invalid's caprice, that they put his Sunday clothes on him. Perhaps because he had solemnly said to Guillaume, before he left in the morning, 'Sign nothing!' His eyes were riveted on the door.

Cécile, bending over her work, threaded the needle in and out of the child's garment on which she was working. She looked up impatiently, now and then, at the stove and at her mother, for it was dinner-time and Josephine seemed to be giving it no thought. But Cécile said nothing. Napoleon was kneeling on the floor,

362

cutting accounts of catastrophe out of the paper; his partiality for statistics, affected by the universal upheaval, now inclined him to collect pictures of eminent politicians and reports of carnage. His features, which did not easily reflect his shades of feeling, expressed nevertheless a convinced 'Things are going wrong'.

The defeat, which had afflicted Canada like an epidemic, had smitten the Plouffes.

Following the failure of the procession, squalls of confusion, blowing from Europe, had broken freely over Quebec. The Plouffe ship, among many others, foundered, and the crew, dazed by the violence of the elements, made no move, awaiting the end in silence. The fall of France had paralysed all will-power. 'Paris capitulates', coming tragically from the radios, had sown a profound, mysterious sorrow in the hearts of all. Women of the uneducated class, like Josephine, who knew nothing of France except its language and its songs, had cried without knowing why. Tears came from a source deep down in their being. The men were silent; they set their jaws and began to feel a fierce hatred for the Nazis.

The struggle of political ideas changed fronts. The anti-British nationalists began to deify Marshal Pétain, the rest began to applaud General de Gaulle.

—There, I think he's coming! Josephine called out, rushing to the door. Everything's all right. He's whistling.

Théophile tried to pull himself up. Cécile's scissors and needle hovered in mid-air. But Josephine's shoulders sagged with disappointment. She went back to the stove.

It was only Ovide. Opening the door, he stopped whistling and tried to hide a joy which seemed brimming over. Oddly enough, he was not wearing his ambulance-driver's uniform this morning, but nobody noticed it. He began to walk up and down the kitchen and said in a firm tone, as if to hide a twinge of remorse:

—I've just been to see Denis Boucher off. He's sailing for

England. War is a serious matter for him. He volunteered. But for Guillaume, it's only for the defence of Canada. It's not dangerous.

—You think so? Josephine said. Just the same, Monsieur Folbèche seems to think that once our soldiers are trained, they will be sent overseas. But I don't think Guillaume will be accepted.

The old woman, her eyes half-closed, was smiling craftily. She had made Guillaume swallow four aspirins before he left. His heart would be so upset that . . .

—Vide!

The paralytic finally broke through his silence. Ovide did not seem to hear him, and continued to walk up and down nervously, looking at the door from time to time. Since his interview with Father Alphonse, Ovide had been feverish, as though gnawed by the fear of failing in the objective he had set himself; marriage. In a word, he still pursued his dreams. Once the marriage was consummated, he thought, peace and happiness would follow. And the nearer he came to his goal, the more his illusions absorbed him.

—Vide! Théophile called, more insistently.

Ovide clapped impatient hands over his ears.

—Yes! Presently, Father, presently! Give me a chance to think.

He went and shut himself up in his room and, armed with a pencil, tried to estimate the cost of the furniture necessary for a young couple.

Napoleon raised his head from his albums and looked searchingly at Théophile's angular profile. The collector had become an expert in the art of guessing his silent griefs. With an anxious air he walked over to his father and touched him on the shoulder.

—What is it, Father? Want your pipe?

The old man growled a few unintelligible words.

—What are you saying?

Théophile's eyes filled with tears, and then his voice seemed clearer.

—You never speak to me!

Napoleon's mouth felt dry.

—That's because we're not chatterers.

Théophile's good arm tapped spasmodically on the arm of his chair.

—My racing bicycle . . . I give it to you.

—Thanks, Father. I'll look after it, the collector stammered, unable to take his eyes off Théophile's hairy ears.

The old man turned his head with an effort, in order to attract the attention of his eldest son, who stood there stiffly listening to him without venturing to meet his gaze.

—Napoleon.

—Yes, Pa.

—Jeanne, marry her.

—Yes!

Napoleon's teeth began to chatter. A great joy possessed him, and his body was too small to contain it. It seemed to him that his chest swelled to an enormous size, yet, at the same time, he felt himself unsubstantial. Marvellous moment: Father had said yes. The collector was about to unburden himself by telling his mother this news when his eye fell on what the rest caught sight of at the same instant. Standing in the doorway, in a khaki uniform too big for him, was Guillaume, smiling.

There was a long, distressed 'Ah!' from Théophile; then a mournful exclamation from Josephine; and then a discouraged 'This is it!' from Cécile and from Napoleon, whose cry of triumph was nipped in the bud. Having savoured the success of his entrance, Guillaume clicked his heels together.

—Army salute! Salute! Forward! March!

He moved towards Josephine, who remained motionless. All at once, her eyes wide with indignation, she cried out:

—Isn't that absurd? That uniform's much too big for you! And a pocket all unstitched!

She ran to the sewing-machine, and hastily caught up a needle and a piece of thread which she moistened between her trembling lips.

—Come here and I'll sew it for you.

Docile, his arms dangling, Guillaume let her have her way. Napoleon revolved furtively around his brother and his mother kneeling at her sewing.

—So they didn't think your heart was beating too fast, she said.

—No fear! It seems my heart is so steady you'd hardly believe it.

—That's why he never gets worked up, ventured Napoleon, who never knew what to say at a dramatic moment.

Ovide had appeared in the doorway of his room. His back bent and his lips dry, he was rubbing his hands; a habit contracted at the monastery and not yet lost.

—Well, Vide, here I am in the army, Guillaume announced, throwing out his chest. I'm thinking of turning into a rifle champion. I leave tomorrow for Valcartier. That won't worry you much, eh, Cécile?

—Don't talk like that, you idiot, she answered in a muffled voice.

She hid her face in her hands. This surprising grief of Cécile's suddenly stripped off the shell of impersonality that Guillaume's uniform gave him.

The soldier dreamily began to stroke his mother's hair as she sewed more and more feverishly.

Napoleon's and Ovide's glances met, flashing the signal for grave decisions. Ovide walked to the window so that his back would be turned to the others. He cleared his throat.

—Mother, now that we know how Guillaume's examination turned out, we must be resigned. It's not dangerous, anyway.

I'm going to take advantage of this opportunity to tell you that I've changed my job. I've left the ambulance and I've obtained the position of record sales clerk that I told you about. The other chap is in the army now. I'll have a good salary. I think I'm going to decide to marry Rita.

Josephine's jaw clamped into a hard, smooth line from chin to ear, but she went on sewing. Ovide had opened up the way to confessions, for Napoleon's voice, in the same tone, followed that of his brother.

—Yes, we have to get married some time. I think I'm going to get married too. Father gave me permission a little while ago. Hospital's no place for Jeanne.

His eyes were closed but his ears were waiting eagerly for approval. Nothing came, not even support from Ovide, who was also waiting for his mother's reaction. Then Napoleon ran to the sideboard full of albums, brought out his big sheets of statistics, and spread them on the table.

—With records like these, don't you think Jeanne will make me a strong wife?

And now it was Cécile's turn to take the floor, for she had been eagerly following her brothers' announcements.

—Of course, if you go away from here, you three boys, we'll be all alone. The house is going to be empty. A small child would liven us up, it would do us good.

Guillaume gave her a ferocious look, then set his teeth; but it was Josephine's feelings that burst out finally. She was sewing feverishly, and the words that came out of her mouth, chopped short by vexation and her two loose teeth, punctuated the movements of her big, yellow, flabby arm.

—That's right. I suppose you won't forget to take away the sideboard, Napoleon; and Ovide, you'll take the piano, the radio, the armchair, the records, and the desk. And then Onésime's baby, he'll come and soil my curtains, and snivel all day long. Why don't you take away everything and let me die with my old husband, since the only one who cares about me is going away?

She buried her sobs, the sobs of an old, abandoned mother, in Guillaume's uniform—and Guillaume took her in his arms, kissing her forehead, her temples, her hair.

—Don't cry, Mama. And you won't die, nor Pa either. Eh, Pa? What about a little kiss on the neck, like old times?

He ran to the paralytic's chair and bent over.

—Ma!

He sprang back. Josephine gave a great cry.

—Théophile!

But Théophile had died at the moment Guillaume arrived.

EPILOGUE

MAY 1945

EPILOGUE

Quebec West, 8 May 1945.

Private Guillaume Plouffe,
22nd Regiment,
Holland, Europe.

Hello, Guillaume,

Here's your brother Napoleon writing you. You say there are good cyclists in Holland, what did I tell you, eh? If you have a chance, go and see the Princes' Park. That's where the *Tour de France* used to end. Try and get some souvenirs, especially some glossy photos of the best European cyclists, get them autographed, it makes them more valuable. Seems you're pitcher for the 22nd and the Dutch think you're pretty good. Don't be too proud, it's dangerous. Don't fall in love with a girl over there, even the most beautiful; you'd get married, then you'd have children, and good-bye sport. You wouldn't have the time any more. Meanwhile, take care of your arm. The big American baseball leagues are waiting for you.

Over here, it's V Day and we have a holiday at the munition factory. Tonight, fireworks on the Terrace. I've read all the bulletins about the 22nd and your name isn't amongst those who got medals. You must have earned some, but the English didn't like your never signing to go over to the other side. Don't worry, I've kept the pictures of the traitors at Ottawa who sent you to war on 23 November 1944, when you hadn't signed. They're in my album and I'm keeping them so it will be easy to recognize them later. I'm afraid that the munition factory is going to close down on account of the armistice.

Well, we're going to spend the evening with Mother. I must dress the three children. If you could only see what muscular legs they have. I think they're going to be good runners. They send you kisses, Jeanne too. She's still O.K. She weighs 170 pounds. Solid flesh. Good night.

NAPOLEON.

Napoleon carefully re-read his letter, addressed it in small capitals, and slid it into the envelope. He licked the edge generously with his tongue because he didn't send letters very often.

— Won't be long.

He gave a brief glance of apology to his wife, and to the children who were waiting patiently for their father to dress them. Jeanne, like many tubercular persons who have been in a sanatorium, was accustomed to leaving her husband to do everything in the house. And Napoleon fulfilled his role of housekeeper with a zeal rewarded by the regularly increasing weight of his wife. The kitchen shone with cleanliness and the floor was as well polished as a ship's deck.

Napoleon went trotting off to the only piece of furniture that he had brought from his father's house, the cabinet for the albums, and took out a notebook headed *Family Statistics*. He inserted the letter recently received from Guillaume. He smiled at his children while handling the album in which he had carefully noted their dates of birth: 'François, sired by Napoleon, birth 3 April 1941, in 35 minutes and 40 seconds. — Charles, also by Napoleon; birth 7 June 1942, in 28 minutes and 20 seconds. — Georges, also by same, birth July 12, 1943, in 22 minutes exactly.

At each birth, Jeanne's health had improved as much as Father Alphonse had predicted before his death in 1941. Having closed the cabinet door, Napoleon shook his head. He was thinking with fond regret of the wonderful life that Guillaume had had at Valcartier Camp, near Quebec, from 1940 to 1944. The commanding officer of the camp, an amateur sportsman, had retained Guillaume as cook in order to keep the netball championship, which was held by the Valcartier team thanks to Guillaume's skill. And then, the catastrophe. On 23 November 1944 the

King Government, driven to the wall by the Tories, had found itself obliged to extend the frontiers of Canada to Europe and to send some thousands of recruits to the front. Guillaume was not spared.

—I should like to see the fireworks, Jeanne said.

Her blue eyes shone serenely, and from her fresh, smooth face nobody could have guessed that, four years previously, it had been marked by death. Obedient to the wishes of her lord, she waited for his decision, rocking herself with the tranquillity of a generous corpulence. Frowning, Napoleon finished combing the curly hair of the little ones who, accustomed early to a strict discipline, submitted, in Indian file, to the last preparations for going out.

—No, wife, Napoleon said quickly. We must visit Mother. On account of Guillaume. There'll be a wonderful family gathering.

—You know what you must do, dear.

Jeanne went to the mirror and inspected her hair. Napoleon gave a long sigh. He did not wish to see the fireworks. Those sheaves of multicoloured stars reminded him too sharply of one of the anxieties brought about by the armistice; the munition works would not be slow in closing now, and he would be obliged to go back to the shoe factory.

—O.K. Let's go. Have you got out your money, Jeanne? We'll eat our cones on the way.

The children quivered with joy.

*　　　*　　　*　　　*　　　*　　　*

Napoleon and his family, carrying ice-cream cones, arrived at the old home at the same time as Ovide, his wife Rita, and their three-year-old girl, Berthe, who began to pull the hair of Napoleon's tots, too timid to defend themselves. Ovide and Rita were wrangling in low voices. On seeing his elder brother, Ovide straightened his tie and, out of the corner of his mouth, told his wife to be quiet. Like Jeanne, Rita had put on considerable weight; the Plouffe brothers, while remaining thin themselves, had a special gift for making their wives bloom.

Grandmother Plouffe came hurrying on to the balcony, holding out her arms triumphantly.

—Hurrah! The war is over! Guillaume hasn't been wounded. Come and give a weeny kiss to your granny.

There was an onslaught of kisses on old Josephine's cheeks and forehead, and all her wrinkles creased in happiness. What a beautiful day!

The streetcar bench, as always, occupied the end of the balcony, but its green paint, through exposure to rain and sun, was peeling off.

—Come in! Josephine exclaimed gaily, after the warm greetings. I've made some good maple cream. As it happens, Father Folbèche is here.

The latter came out.

—No, I must go, Madame Plouffe. It's seven o'clock and my May devotions wait for me. Good day, everybody. You boys remember that your income-tax returns are overdue. And don't hesitate, if you need any little receipts for gifts to charity.

Monsieur Folbèche had become an old, worn-out man with bent back and white hair. Even the soles of his boots were no longer as thick as in 1935 when his authority over his parish was absolute. The old priest's nationalist fervour, smothered by events, only manifested itself now on the occasion of income-tax returns, because the federal government accepted as deductions all gifts to charitable organizations up to ten per cent of income. According to statistics, the people of Quebec were never more charitable than during these years of magnanimity.

When the priest had gone, the children and grandchildren invaded the kitchen. Cécile, her hair parted in the middle, was rocking a six-year-old child, Onésime junior, who, seeing all the other youngsters, hid his face shyly against his adopted mother's breast while she whispered in his ear:

—Now, now, you're at home here. They'll be going soon. Then we'll be all alone with Granny. Don't worry about them.

While Josephine distributed sweets to the children, Ovide and Rita resumed their quarrelling, softly, in a corner of the kitchen. Rita was saying:

—If you think you're going to make me miss the fireworks by sticking here, you're mistaken!

Only a peppery whisper was heard by the rest of the family. Cécile closed her eyes to hide the contented light that shone in them, for these marital discords convinced her that she had nothing to complain about as a mock widow. Josephine's anxious glances went from her son to Rita. Ovide hid his hands in his pockets and clenched his fists. He was white with anger.

—Not so loud! They'll hear us. Go and see your fireworks, and all the soldiers in the world. You'll come back at midnight, as usual, I suppose.

Rita went out, an offended, fat blonde, and Ovide went to the tap for a glass of water. He was unhappy; his marriage had solved nothing. Old Josephine came up to him and murmured:

—What's wrong now? It's going to end up badly.

Josephine thought that the bonds that united her son and another woman could not be other than fragile and that the least dispute might break them. But Ovide felt himself bound so much more to Rita than to his mother that he tried to smile:

—Nothing serious, Mother. A stupid upset in our domestic affairs. When I arrived home this evening the little one had broken my *Dream of Love* sung by Schipa. Her mother spoils her. I must confess my temper has been on edge for some time. The record clerk will be coming back from the war. You understand? So I quarrel with Rita; and as she is a sensitive person, you see . . .

His back turned, Napoleon was gazing at the photograph of his father perched on a bicycle. His features quivered with pure joy. He had three children and not one even dared to open the album cabinet that he secretly intended to leave them as a heritage.

He winked at his mother, who was coming back thoughtfully to the middle of the kitchen.

—Jeanne has gained another two pounds, he said.

Josephine, who ever since Napoleon's marriage had tragically predicted the impending death of the bride, saw in the increased weight of her daughter-in-law a challenge to her infallibility as an experienced mother. She gave a sharp look immediately at Jeanne's waist to make sure the two pounds weren't owing to Napoleon's vitality. Jeanne, who sat near the sewing-machine, blushed under the scrutiny and protested warmly:

—Oh! No! it's not that, Madame Plouffe.

Having seen his mother's eyelids droop with disappointment, Napoleon waited until his wife had regained her natural colour and then said 'Good!'

—I wrote to Guillaume tonight, he added. We're lucky. Not wounded.

—Yes, thank God!

Eyes raised and hands folded, old Josephine seemed to grow taller. Her heart had left the kitchen, forgotten the rest of the Plouffe tribe, in order to kiss the bright face of her Guillaume, her dear, absent one. How she had prayed; how eager she was to see that wheedling, good-natured big baby appear in the doorway. Well, they weren't killing each other any more in that terrible, unknown Europe where Guillaume must be thinking so much about his mother and the dainty little meals she had prepared for him long ago.

—He wrote me yesterday, she said finally, coming out of her ecstasy. You should see how educated he is, Vide. He calls me his dear mother in three languages.

She ran to take the blue letter she had slipped under the base of the plaster Sacred Heart. The children chased each other, shouting, and Cécile, with her adopted son on her knee, pushed her chair back disdainfully to the door of her room. Josephine adjusted her spectacles, her hands trembling with pride.

'*Chère maman, loot-den*, dear mother,' she read aloud, 'You can't say I don't miss you, as I say dear mother in three languages, in French, Dutch and English. Next month, I'll add German ...'

—What do you think of that, eh? It's just like him. Not surprising, with his ability. He's found time to learn. Besides, he's been lucky. Always well fed, far from the front, a good bed; all that he's had to do is play games and study. I think I'd have died if I'd known he was near the Germans, with the bullets going right past his head, dying with hunger, his steaks badly cooked. He likes them underdone. And lying down in slimy trenches. I prayed to St. Joan enough. I think she has done pretty well for him.

—Wait a minute, Mother!

Ovide stood up and looked intently at Josephine. He pulled out several blue sheets from his pocket.

—Now that the war is over, he continued, and Guillaume is safe, I can read you certain parts of letters I received from him.

—What do you mean? What could be in them? Josephine questioned naïvely, provoked by Ovide's mysterious air.

Napoleon, who was glancing anxiously from Ovide to his mother, tried to make his children keep quiet. Ovide raised his voice solemnly:

Holland, March 1945

Hello Vide!

How's the old brother of 1914? Pretty well, I hope. (You remember when you made the kids believe you had gone to the other war, in the shed, one day?) You must have passed through here then, only you hadn't got such good transport, so that you wasted a great deal of time; we kill more quickly. That has its advantages. I must say in 1914, the picnic must

377

have been less nerve-racking. You didn't have these little birds, 45 feet long, flying around with a ton and a half of explosives in them: some damage when they fall! To say nothing of the famous German Tiger tank with its eight cannon on top, it's terrific when it fires. Be satisfied to see it in the news reels, it's safer. You're going to say I must have a lot to tell you. I have. There will be lots of things you'll have trouble digesting, but if so, take a Bromo-Seltzer, because everything I'm going to tell you is true. I wouldn't shoot you a line, you know me. When I mean to say Mount Robson is 13,750 feet high, I don't say 19,000 feet, do I? Speaking of mountains, just ask Napoleon if he ever took his bicycle to go and see if the Laurentians have snow on top in midsummer. The 'Viourge' didn't believe me when I told him that the Rockies, where I went before leaving for dear old England, were ten times higher than our Laurentians.

You ask me about food. I can't remember what steak looks like. The meat we eat here belongs to the horse family. Hardtack biscuits and corned beef, all the time. Except when you're lucky enough to steal some Dutch chickens, it's awful. I can't tell you where I am, but I've had my feet wet for two weeks and I sleep out of doors on the ground. So I'm just about frozen. Don't be surprised if my writing is all crooked. Don't ever tell Mother this, she'd probably get a boat and come and look for me. I make her think I'm in a fine hotel, first-rate food, and never hear a gun go off. A real honeymoon . . . you know all about that, Vide, ha! ha! ha!

Ovide quickly turned the page and watched his mother. Madame Plouffe's opinions on the war were by now turned completely upside down through these revelations of the real conditions of Guillaume's life. She got up, walked heavily to the stove, made sure the fire was quite out, and went back to her chair without saying a word. At one and the same time, she felt humiliated at having been thus deceived, dismayed at not having been anxious while Guillaume was enduring such a dreadful existence, and happy that he was at last safe and sound. So many plans for tasty dishes intended for the return of the absent one haunted her imagination that she lost no time in comment.

—Go on, she said simply.

You ask me to go to the opera. Frankly, I haven't a great deal of time this week. I'm pretty busy. You must have heard them say over the radio that we're in Holland to clear out a pocket of Germans. So, pray for me in Latin, it helps more, because you see we're going to make another attack tomorrow morning. For two weeks we've advanced quite rapidly, we are pretty well under fire, but we dare not advance too much, because we're not far from the sea where the great locks and the capital, Amsterdam, are situated, and if the Germans open those locks, we'll have too much water to drink. Yesterday morning, we made a small attack and my regiment had 58 dead and 25 wounded. They fell dead, right beside me as they ran. I tell you, it was a queer feeling, Vide, to see dead men your own age, dressed like you, all stiff, and you had spoken to them before the attack. I'm not using a rifle now, I'm number 2 on a mortar which is better for me, because, with a rifle, your work is to empty the houses, that means you run an 80 per cent chance of being popped off. I tell you that Germany's pretty near her own funeral as it is now. Every three days we are replaced at the front. We take back the prisoners when we go to rest in the rear.

—Well! So! Josephine exclaimed, looking quite pale.

We play softball to relax. The 22nd has offered me $25,000 for my arm for the summer season. I won't do it for less than $35,000. Just now, my case is in the hands of General Montgomery. Cécile's going to say I'm boasting. She's right! Because it's not true about the $25,000, ha! ha! ha! The Germans are wonderful athletes. I get along well with these fellows, Papa would be satisfied to hear that. Why, only the other day, I took the best òf them and made up a team and we beat the 22nd. I made 15 strike outs. My Germans carried me in triumph.

I often go out with the girls around here. I had a beautiful dame the other day, a Flemish girl. I slept at her place. I was welcomed like their own child because I gave five cigarettes to her father. At ten o'clock she came into my room to tuck me up and, over here, you know, there are lots of things that would be sinful in Quebec, but here, the war's so nerve-racking . . .

Ovide skipped several lines, because Josephine was frowning.

Anyway, the German prisoners who speak French say we're not a race of cowards. They would have liked to have us with them. Who won this war? The Russians, the Americans, the Canadians and then the '*cup-tea*'. Just talk to me about dear old England. They get all mixed up, they have so many kinds of money. While they untangle it, you wait. It's certainly tiresome. I'll tell you everything when I come back, money, difference in language, climate, the size of the cities, the kind of people. But I can tell you now that the most beautiful country I've seen is Belgium. That's where I met the best cyclists in the world.

You see, you old 1914 *machine-gunner*, I can tell you all this because I know you can tell a lake from an ocean. War, you know, is a lot harder than rings or checkers. In Canada, they called us conscripts, the *Westipouffe*, but when we come back to Canada covered with glory and parade on the Grande Allée with the 40 musicians of the 22nd you'll be seeing heroes who risked their lives for the Pope and democracy. But I didn't sign.

Yesterday I ran into Denis Boucher in a jeep. He was with some officers and he had a typewriter on his knees.

As war souvenirs I have a revolver and several German watches because when we take them prisoner, we empty out their pockets. I also have a fine little machine-gun, it only weighs 11 pounds. I should like to bring it back to Canada with some bullets. I could shoot Arrial and his charming brother, the bugler, who spent their time teasing me. Also, I'm going to try to bring back two grenades, one to let off and the other to keep as a souvenir. I'll show you the mechanism of this weapon, a grenade like that on a house can weaken the roof, all right.

—He'd better not bring that here! Josephine exclaimed.
—Here's the last letter I received, said Ovide, his eyes bulging as though he had spectacles on the end of his nose.

Excuse the writing, we've just cleared out another pocket and my friend Dinel, from Limoilou, who was shaving beside me this morning has just been blown up 40 feet by displacement of air from a bomb. Dead. You'd better not come here, you're too afraid of catching cold. What with shells weighing 50 to 60 pounds, incendiary bombs, cannon going off, bashed-in houses and broken windows, I'm just about shell-shocked, I spend my time jumping. Frankly, I'd rather listen to opera or tickle Rita, ha! ha! It's lucky the Germans haven't any more planes and very little artillery, this gives us a break. Yesterday afternoon we took a wood full of Germans. Honest to God, after our artillery fire the wood looked like toast, as the French say, who are very polite and call you 'monsieur' or 'mon petit' but don't understand words like *truck, gun* or *checker*. Well, after the artillery fire our lot went in and fought for half an hour, then the Germans surrendered because we're ferocious with the bayonet. My company had 52 dead and 10 wounded out of 125 men. The other companies didn't do so badly, either. I can tell you, you think of your mother at a time like that, when you get a torn-off arm in your face like I did yesterday. It's because I love Mother, that I think of her; it's queer how some chaps seem to think they were born grown up.

Josephine wiped her eyes.

I love Canada, too. When I get back to Halifax you can take it from me I'm going to fall flat on my face on the earth and kiss it. It's not very nice here, it's queer, and not a bit funny. You must have been praying to God an awful lot as I haven't even been wounded, because this sure is hell. You never know from one minute to the next whether your head will be hanging by itself on top of a tree.

Last night I had a little adventure, and I came near being done in. I went out on reconnaissance patrol with two Montreal soldiers. I wasn't saying a word, it was dark and I was looking to see if there were any dead lying about, because you know I never liked to pass in front of a yard entrance, back home at night, where I knew someone had died. I was holding a hand-grenade, number 36, the best grenade you can find. All at once, a short, sharp taratta, I threw myself on my stomach and my two friends fell dead, crossed like two rifles over me. I couldn't see a thing, but I knew it was a German Brada. Why? Because of the speed of the bullets. You know it right away. I prayed to God and I thought of you people. My friends' blood was running down my neck. After a while, I began to make out two Germans, pointing the Brada 50 feet in front of me. They were waiting for me to raise my head. Lucky thing, I was in a kind of a ditch. I felt just about as sick as when I was in mid-ocean. The ocean, Vide, especially in the middle after three or four days out by ship, is the place you see the most enormous waves; they're always 35–40 feet high and when they meet they rise to 50 or 60 feet. The noise they make is terrific. That's when you notice the difference between an ocean and a lake. Talking about a lake, the officers are starting to ask us about signing up for the war with Japan and I told them I was satisfied to do my little invasion by bicycle to Lake St. Joseph, ha! ha! ha! So look in our shed and see if my bicycle tyres are flat, they'll probably need some air, because you know, war-time tyres spoil. Synthetic rubber isn't worth much.

So there I was in the ditch with my dead Montreallers on my back and two Germans waiting for me to raise my head. I stayed there three hours, Vide, without stirring, thinking about God. I held on to my grenade number 36, and I waited. All at once, I noticed my Germans were getting tired. One gave a cigarette to the other who bent over to light it. I didn't lose any time, I released the pin of my grenade, then threw it with all my strength. It whizzed along. A real strike that hit one of my

Germans square in the belly. Hitler is still looking for the pieces. Then the other German, who was wounded, tried to start his machine-gun but I didn't give him the chance. I grabbed my rifle and I put two good bullets through his head. Amen.

Madame Plouffe began to run about the house, holding her head and bumping into the furniture. Then she found her way out again to the balcony; and with her arms flung open to the whole parish, she cried out:

—IT'S UNBELIEVABLE! MY GUILLAUME KILLING MEN!

THE NEW CANADIAN LIBRARY